Chapter 1

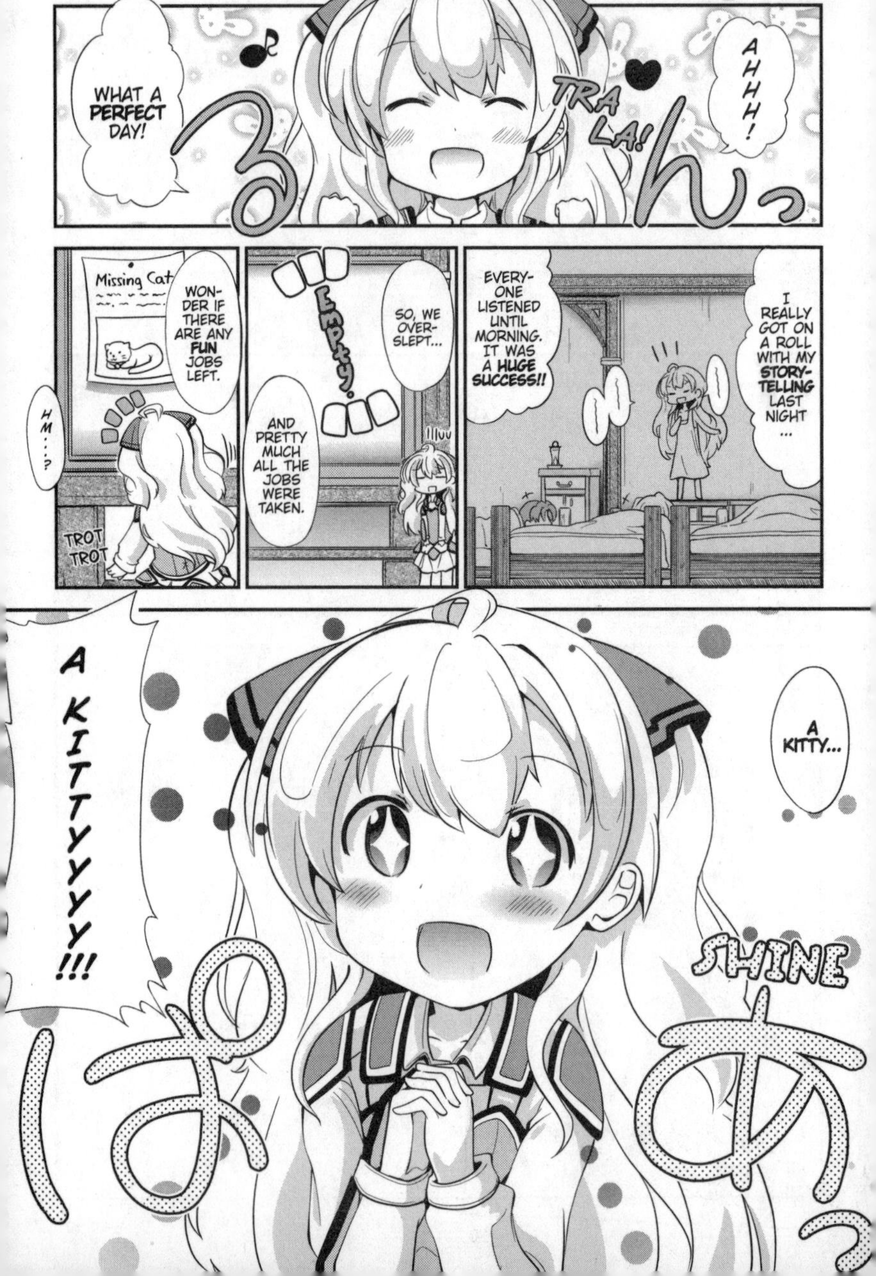
AHHHH!
TRA LA!
WHAT A PERFECT DAY!
I REALLY GOT ON A ROLL WITH MY STORY-TELLING LAST NIGHT...
EVERY-ONE LISTENED UNTIL MORNING. IT WAS A HUGE SUCCESS!!
SO, WE OVER-SLEPT...
EMPTY
AND PRETTY MUCH ALL THE JOBS WERE TAKEN.
Missing Cat
WON-DER IF THERE ARE ANY FUN JOBS LEFT.
HM...?
TROT TROT
A KITTY...
SHINE
A KITTTYYYYY!!!

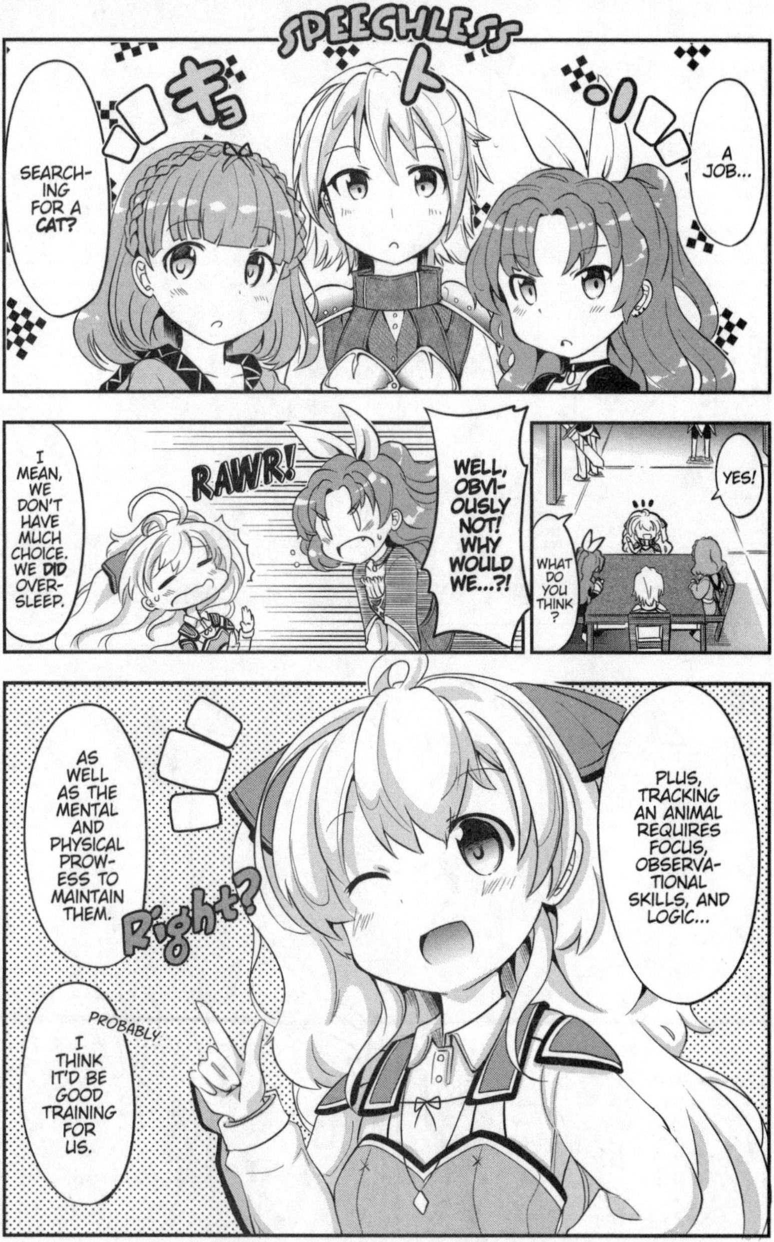
SPEECHLESS
A JOB...
SEARCHING FOR A CAT?
YES!
WHAT DO YOU THINK?
WELL, OBVIOUSLY NOT! WHY WOULD WE...?!
RAWR!
I MEAN, WE DON'T HAVE MUCH CHOICE. WE DID OVERSLEEP.
PLUS, TRACKING AN ANIMAL REQUIRES FOCUS, OBSERVATIONAL SKILLS, AND LOGIC...
AS WELL AS THE MENTAL AND PHYSICAL PROWESS TO MAINTAIN THEM.
Right?
PROBABLY
I THINK IT'D BE GOOD TRAINING FOR US.

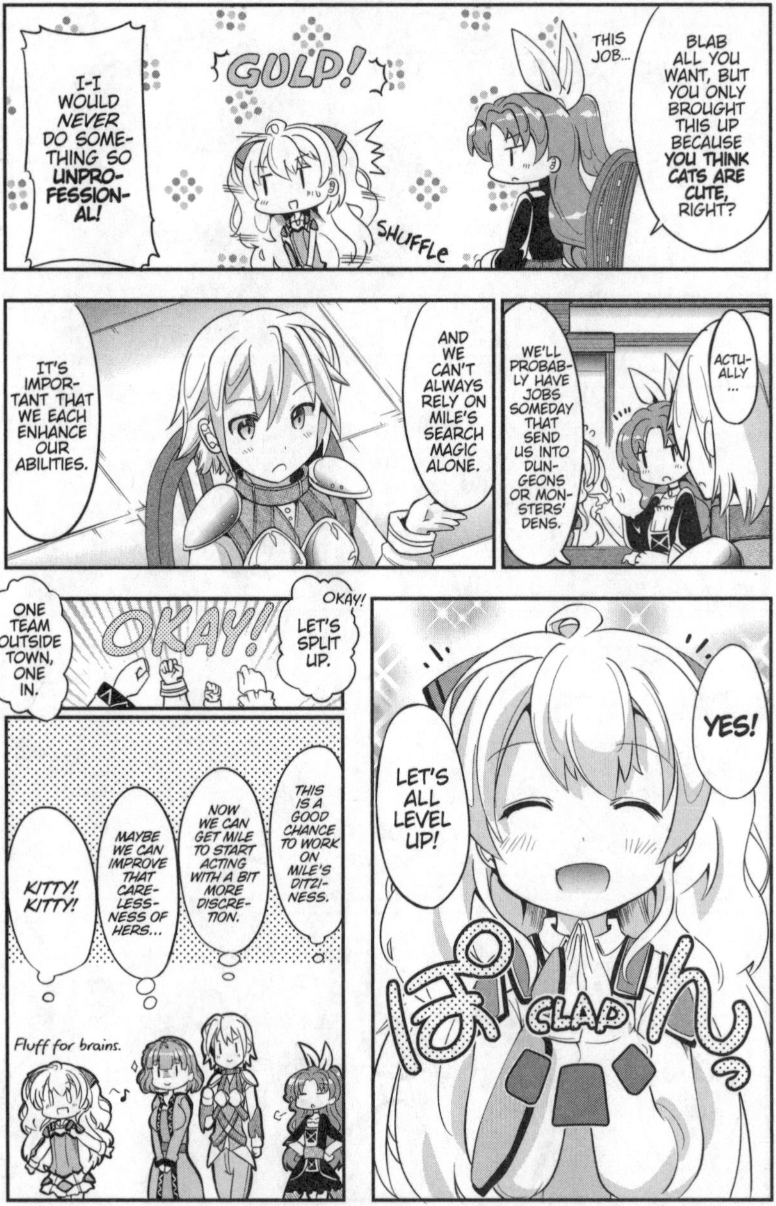
BLAB ALL YOU WANT, BUT YOU ONLY BROUGHT THIS UP BECAUSE **YOU THINK CATS ARE CUTE,** RIGHT?
THIS JOB...
GULP!
SHUFFLE
I-I WOULD *NEVER* DO SOMETHING SO **UNPROFESSIONAL!**
ACTUALLY...
WE'LL PROBABLY HAVE JOBS SOMEDAY THAT SEND US INTO DUNGEONS OR MONSTERS' DENS.
AND WE CAN'T ALWAYS RELY ON MILE'S SEARCH MAGIC ALONE.
IT'S IMPORTANT THAT WE EACH ENHANCE OUR ABILITIES.
YES!
LET'S ALL LEVEL UP!
ぽんっ
CLAP
OKAY!
LET'S SPLIT UP.
OKAY!
ONE TEAM OUTSIDE TOWN, ONE IN.
THIS IS A GOOD CHANCE TO WORK ON MILE'S DITZINESS.
NOW WE CAN GET MILE TO START ACTING WITH A BIT MORE DISCRETION.
MAYBE WE CAN IMPROVE THAT CARELESSNESS OF HERS...
KITTY! KITTY!
Fluff for brains.

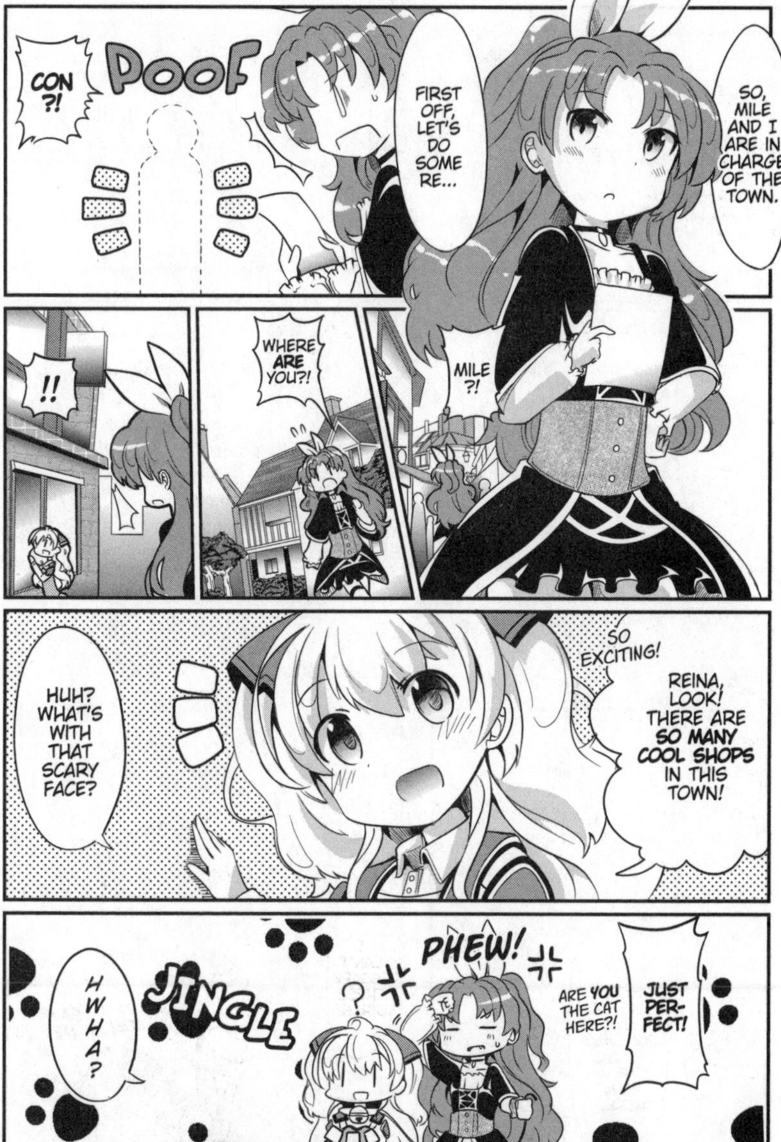
SO, MILE AND I ARE IN CHARGE OF THE TOWN.
FIRST OFF, LET'S DO SOME RE...
POOF
CON ?!
MILE ?!
WHERE ARE YOU?!
!!
SO EXCITING!
REINA, LOOK! THERE ARE SO MANY COOL SHOPS IN THIS TOWN!
HUH? WHAT'S WITH THAT SCARY FACE?
JUST PER-FECT!
ARE YOU THE CAT HERE?!
PHEW!
JINGLE
HWHA?

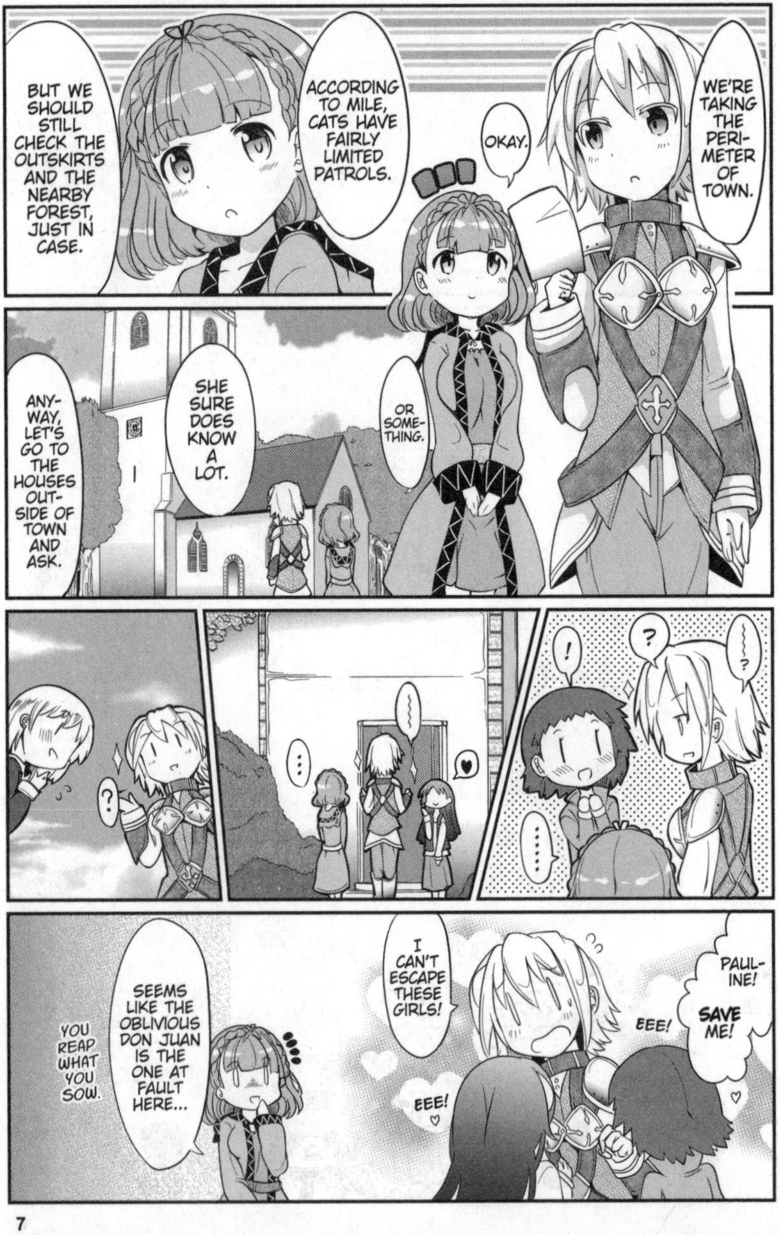

WE'RE TAKING THE PERIMETER OF TOWN.
OKAY.
ACCORDING TO MILE, CATS HAVE FAIRLY LIMITED PATROLS.
BUT WE SHOULD STILL CHECK THE OUTSKIRTS AND THE NEARBY FOREST, JUST IN CASE.
OR SOMETHING.
SHE SURE DOES KNOW A LOT.
ANYWAY, LET'S GO TO THE HOUSES OUTSIDE OF TOWN AND ASK.
PAULINE! SAVE ME!
EEE!
I CAN'T ESCAPE THESE GIRLS!
EEE!
SEEMS LIKE THE OBLIVIOUS DON JUAN IS THE ONE AT FAULT HERE...
YOU REAP WHAT YOU SOW.

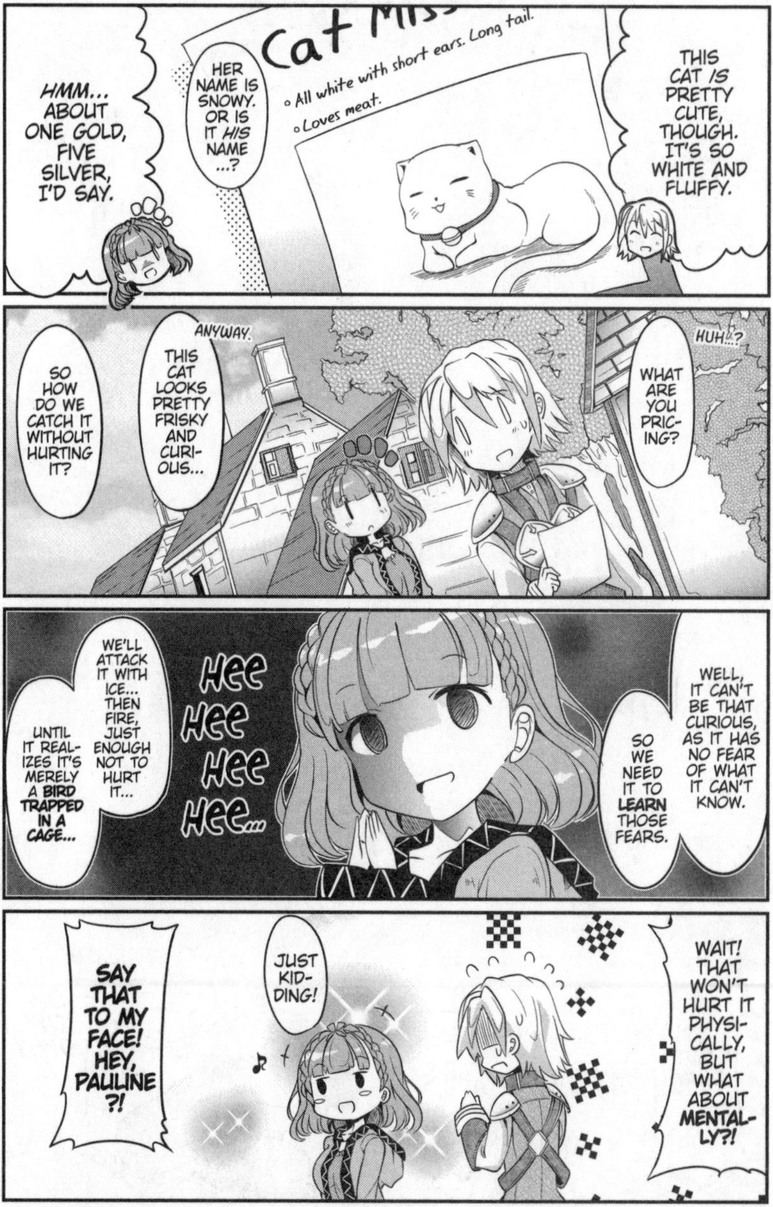
THIS CAT IS PRETTY CUTE, THOUGH. IT'S SO WHITE AND FLUFFY.
All white with short ears. Long tail.
Loves meat.
HER NAME IS SNOWY. OR IS IT HIS NAME ...?
HMM... ABOUT ONE GOLD, FIVE SILVER, I'D SAY.
HUH...?
WHAT ARE YOU PRICING?
ANYWAY.
THIS CAT LOOKS PRETTY FRISKY AND CURIOUS...
SO HOW DO WE CATCH IT WITHOUT HURTING IT?
WELL, IT CAN'T BE THAT CURIOUS, AS IT HAS NO FEAR OF WHAT IT CAN'T KNOW.
SO WE NEED IT TO LEARN THOSE FEARS.
Hee Hee Hee Hee...
WE'LL ATTACK IT WITH ICE... THEN FIRE, JUST ENOUGH NOT TO HURT IT...
UNTIL IT REALIZES IT'S MERELY A BIRD TRAPPED IN A CAGE...
WAIT! THAT WON'T HURT IT PHYSICALLY, BUT WHAT ABOUT MENTALLY?!
JUST KIDDING!
SAY THAT TO MY FACE! HEY, PAULINE?!

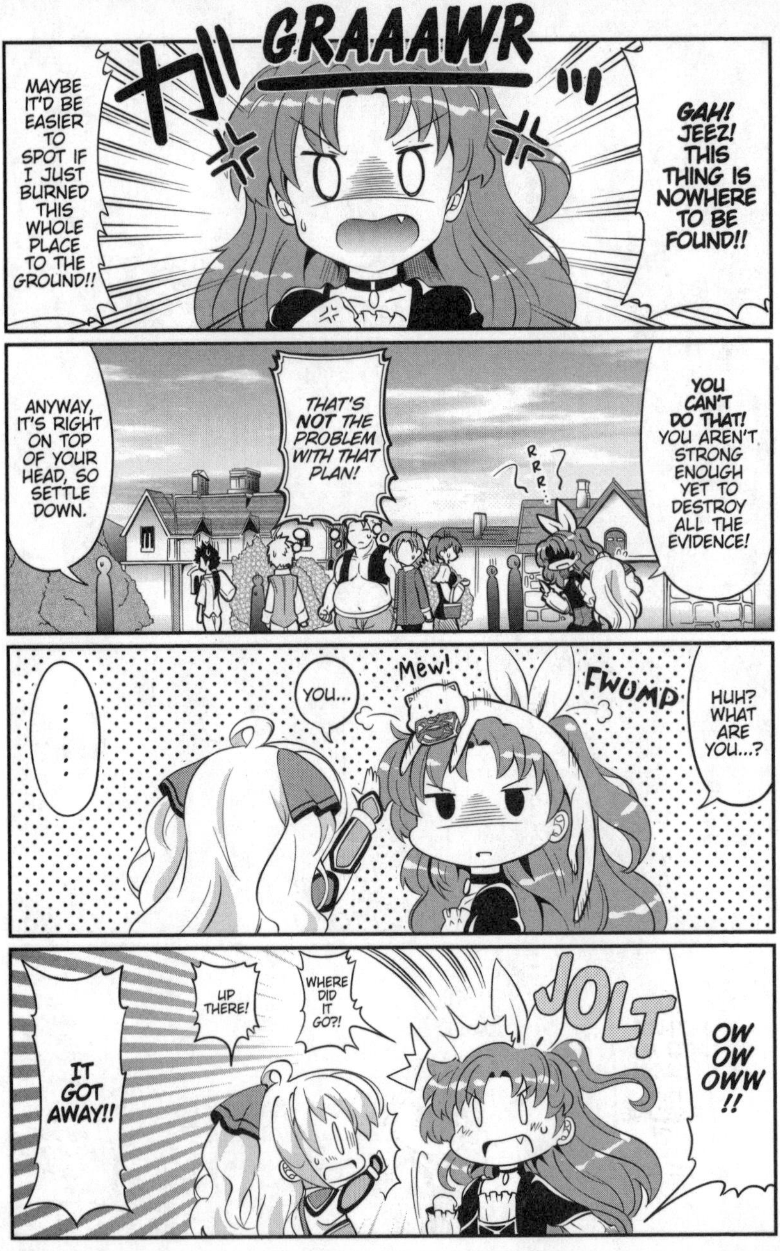
GRAAAWR
GAH! JEEZ! THIS THING IS NOWHERE TO BE FOUND!!
MAYBE IT'D BE EASIER TO SPOT IF I JUST BURNED THIS WHOLE PLACE TO THE GROUND!!
YOU CAN'T DO THAT! YOU AREN'T STRONG ENOUGH YET TO DESTROY ALL THE EVIDENCE!
RRR...
THAT'S NOT THE PROBLEM WITH THAT PLAN!
ANYWAY, IT'S RIGHT ON TOP OF YOUR HEAD, SO SETTLE DOWN.
HUH? WHAT ARE YOU...?
FWUMP
Mew!
YOU...
......
JOLT
OW OW OWW!!
WHERE DID IT GO?!
UP THERE!
IT GOT AWAY!!

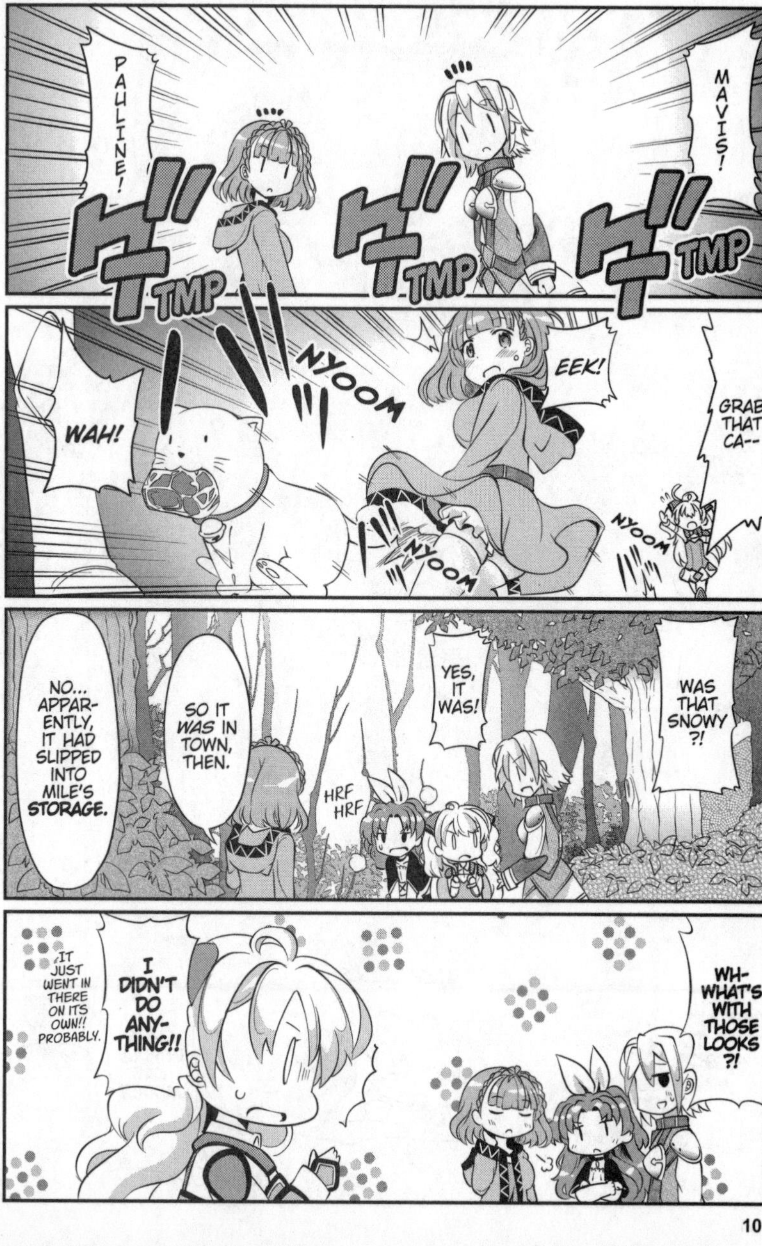
MAVIS!
TMP
TMP
TMP
PAULINE!
GRAB THAT CA--
NYOOM
EEK!
NYOOM
NYOOM
WAH!
WAS THAT SNOWY?!
YES, IT WAS!
HRF HRF
SO IT *WAS* IN TOWN, THEN.
NO... APPARENTLY, IT HAD SLIPPED INTO MILE'S **STORAGE.**
WH-WHAT'S WITH THOSE LOOKS?!
I DIDN'T DO ANYTHING!!
IT JUST WENT IN THERE ON ITS OWN!! PROBABLY.

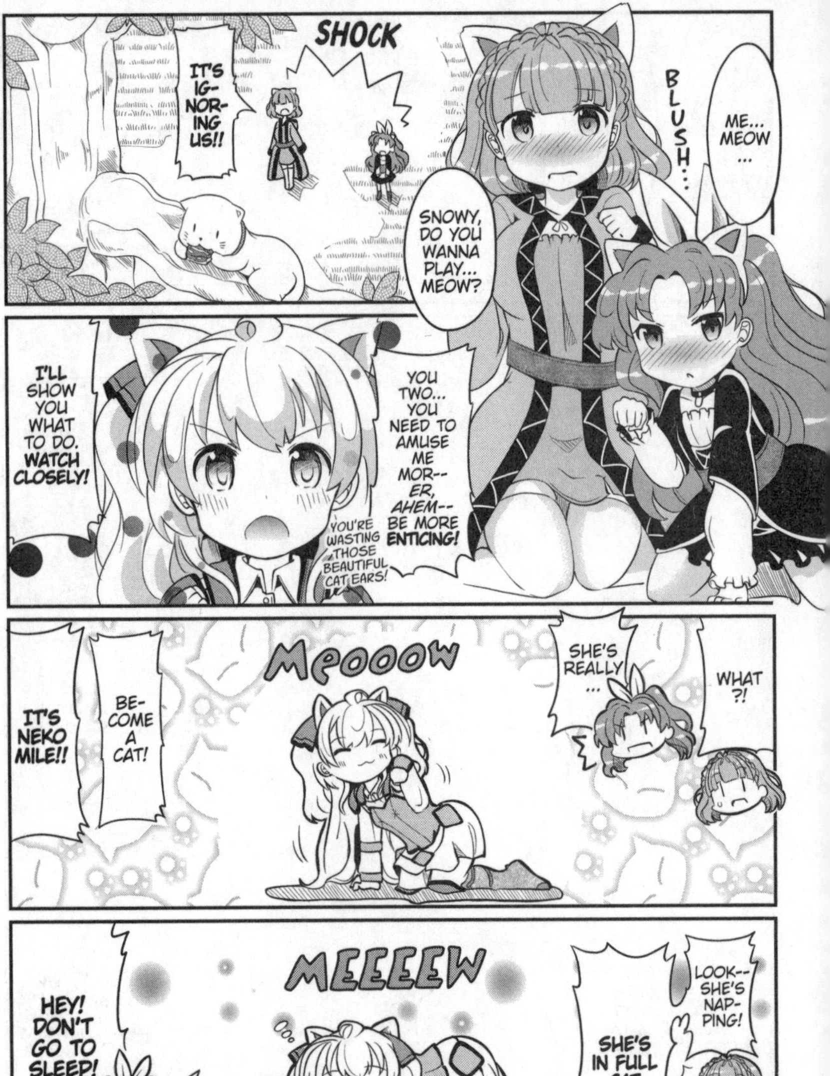
ME... MEOW ...
BLUSH...
SNOWY, DO YOU WANNA PLAY... MEOW?
SHOCK
IT'S IG-NOR-ING US!!
YOU TWO... YOU NEED TO AMUSE ME MOR-- ER, AHEM-- BE MORE ENTICING!
YOU'RE WASTING THOSE BEAUTIFUL CAT EARS!
I'LL SHOW YOU WHAT TO DO. WATCH CLOSELY!
WHAT?!
SHE'S REALLY ...
Meooow
BE-COME A CAT!
IT'S NEKO MILE!!
LOOK-- SHE'S NAP-PING!
SHE'S IN FULL CAT MODE!!
MEEEEW
HEY! DON'T GO TO SLEEP!

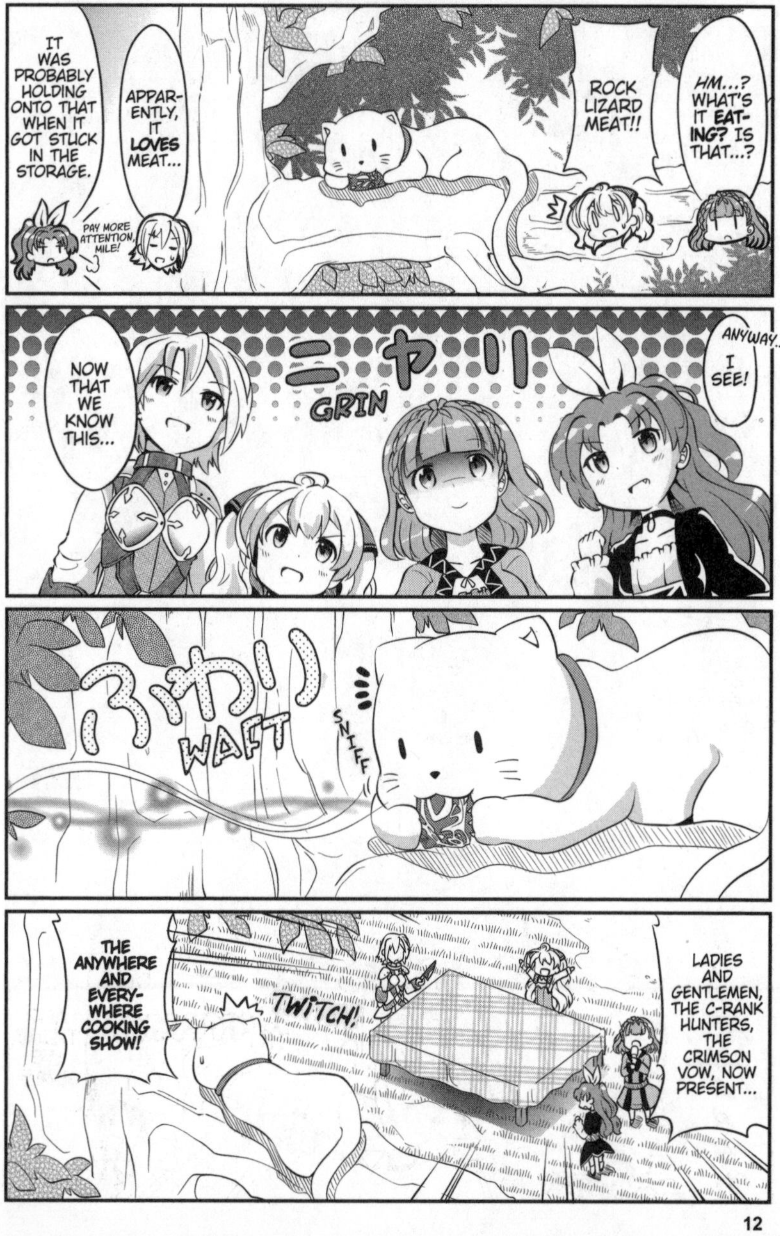
HM...? WHAT'S IT EATING? IS THAT...?
ROCK LIZARD MEAT!!
APPARENTLY, IT LOVES MEAT...
IT WAS PROBABLY HOLDING ONTO THAT WHEN IT GOT STUCK IN THE STORAGE.
PAY MORE ATTENTION, MILE!
ANYWAY... I SEE!
ニヤリ
GRIN
NOW THAT WE KNOW THIS...
ふわり
WAFT
SNIFF
LADIES AND GENTLEMEN, THE C-RANK HUNTERS, THE CRIMSON VOW, NOW PRESENT...
TWITCH!
THE ANYWHERE AND EVERYWHERE COOKING SHOW!

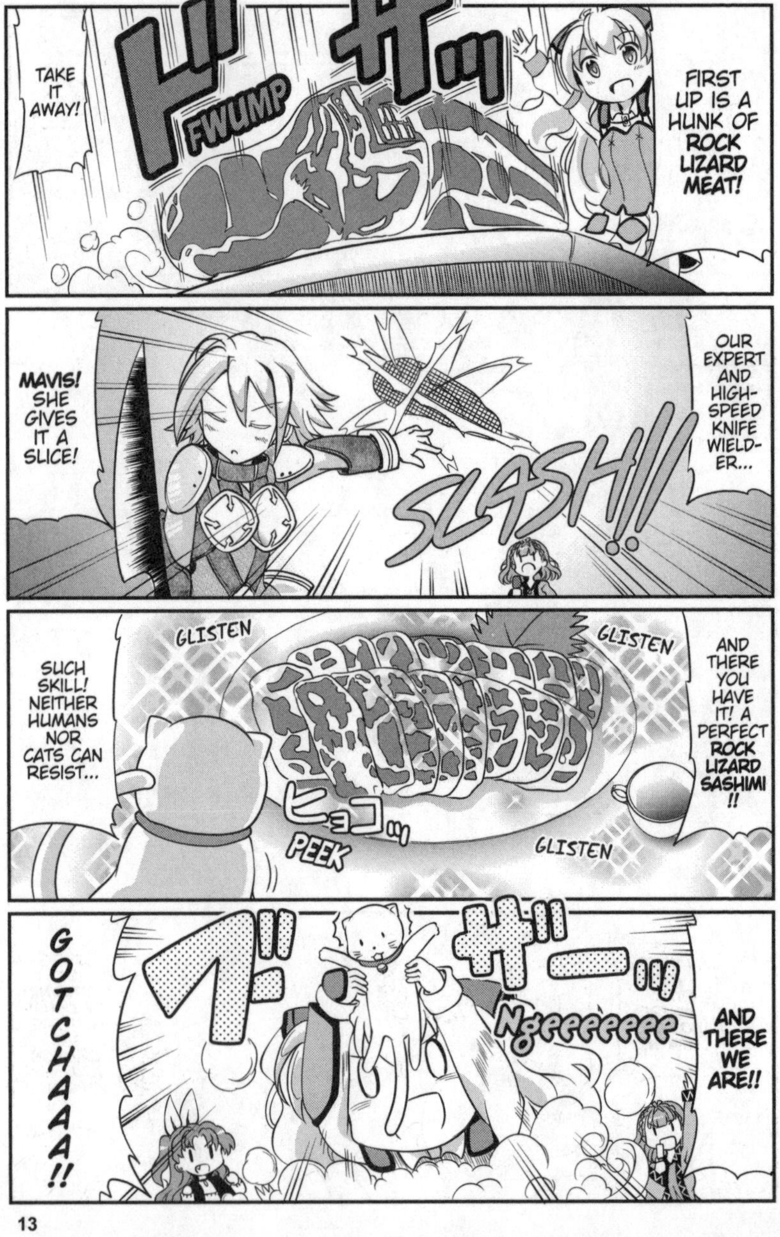
FIRST UP IS A HUNK OF ROCK LIZARD MEAT!
ドサッ
FWUMP
TAKE IT AWAY!
OUR EXPERT AND HIGH-SPEED KNIFE WIELDER...
SLASH!!
MAVIS! SHE GIVES IT A SLICE!
AND THERE YOU HAVE IT! A PERFECT ROCK LIZARD SASHIMI!!
GLISTEN
GLISTEN
GLISTEN
ヒョコッ
PEEK
SUCH SKILL! NEITHER HUMANS NOR CATS CAN RESIST...
AND THERE WE ARE!!
ブザーッ
Ngeeeeeeee
GOTCHAAAA!!

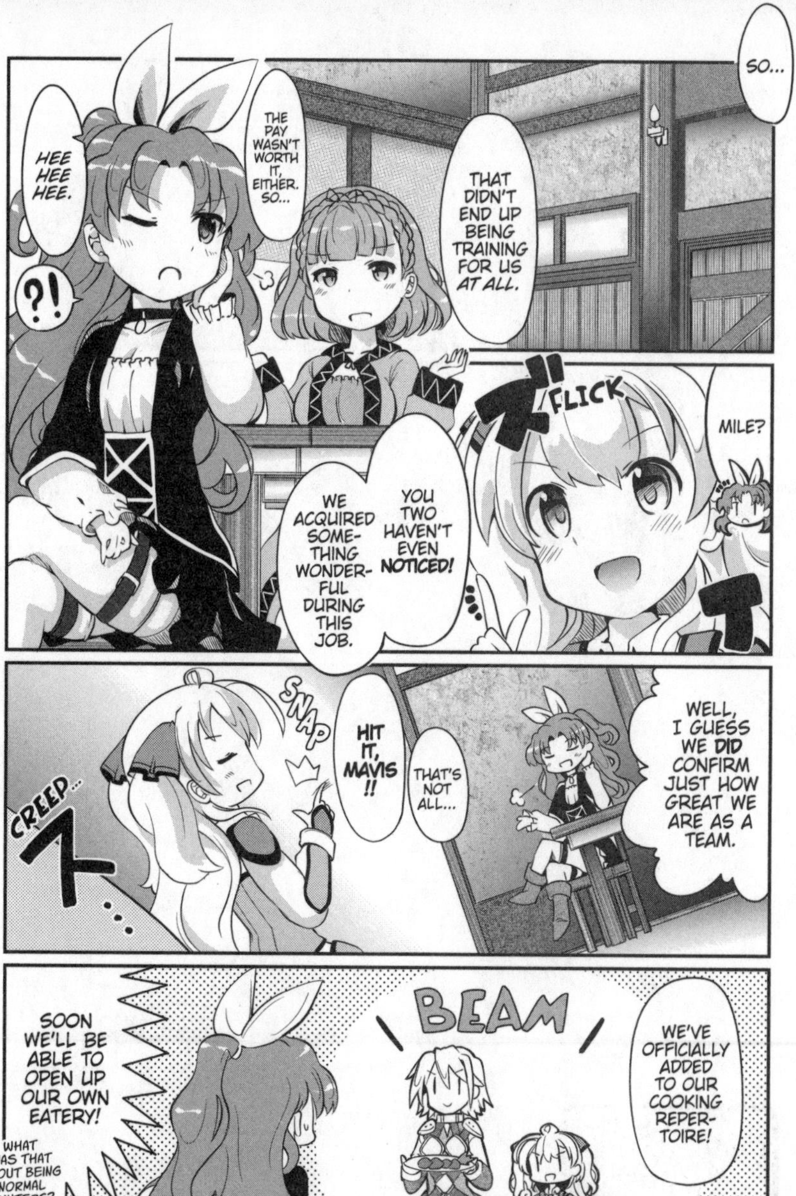
SO...
THAT DIDN'T END UP BEING TRAINING FOR US AT ALL.
THE PAY WASN'T WORTH IT, EITHER. SO...
HEE HEE HEE.
?!
FLICK
MILE?
YOU TWO HAVEN'T EVEN NOTICED!
WE ACQUIRED SOMETHING WONDERFUL DURING THIS JOB.
WELL, I GUESS WE DID CONFIRM JUST HOW GREAT WE ARE AS A TEAM.
THAT'S NOT ALL...
HIT IT, MAVIS!!
SNAP
CREEP...
WE'VE OFFICIALLY ADDED TO OUR COOKING REPERTOIRE!
BEAM
SOON WE'LL BE ABLE TO OPEN UP OUR OWN EATERY!
WHAT WAS THAT ABOUT BEING NORMAL HUNTERS?

Didn't I Say to Make My Abilities Average in the Next Life?!

EVERYDAY MISADVENTURES!

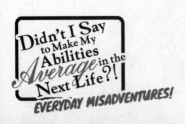

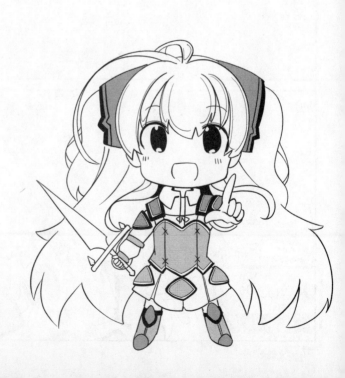

Chapter 2

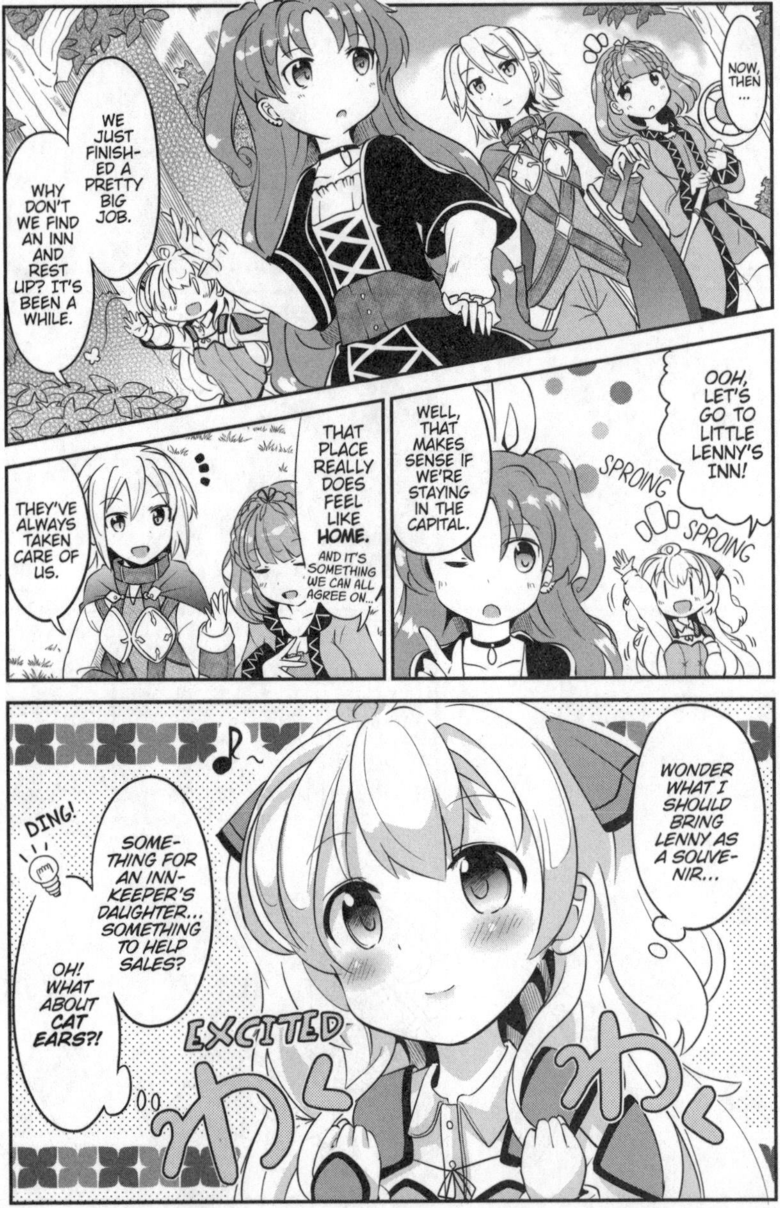
NOW, THEN...
WE JUST FINISHED A PRETTY BIG JOB.
WHY DON'T WE FIND AN INN AND REST UP? IT'S BEEN A WHILE.
OOH, LET'S GO TO LITTLE LENNY'S INN!
SPROING
SPROING
WELL, THAT MAKES SENSE IF WE'RE STAYING IN THE CAPITAL.
THAT PLACE REALLY DOES FEEL LIKE **HOME.**
AND IT'S SOMETHING WE CAN ALL AGREE ON...
THEY'VE ALWAYS TAKEN CARE OF US.
WONDER WHAT I SHOULD BRING LENNY AS A SOUVENIR...
DING!
SOMETHING FOR AN INNKEEPER'S DAUGHTER... SOMETHING TO HELP SALES?
OH! WHAT ABOUT CAT EARS?!
EXCITED
わくわく

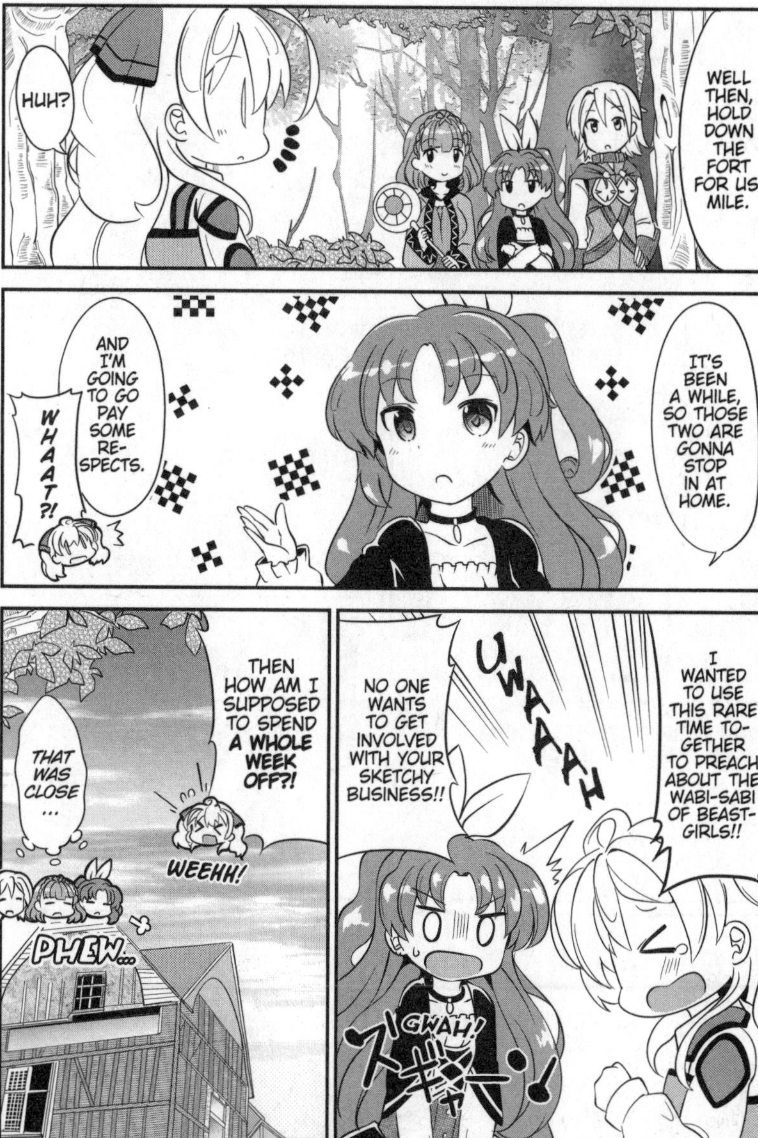
WELL THEN, HOLD DOWN THE FORT FOR US, MILE.
HUH?
IT'S BEEN A WHILE, SO THOSE TWO ARE GONNA STOP IN AT HOME.
AND I'M GOING TO GO PAY SOME RE-SPECTS.
WHAAAT?!
I WANTED TO USE THIS RARE TIME TO-GETHER TO PREACH ABOUT THE WABI-SABI OF BEAST-GIRLS!!
UWAAAAH
NO ONE WANTS TO GET INVOLVED WITH YOUR SKETCHY BUSINESS!!
GWAH!
THEN HOW AM I SUPPOSED TO SPEND A WHOLE WEEK OFF?!
WEEHH!
THAT WAS CLOSE ...
PHEW...

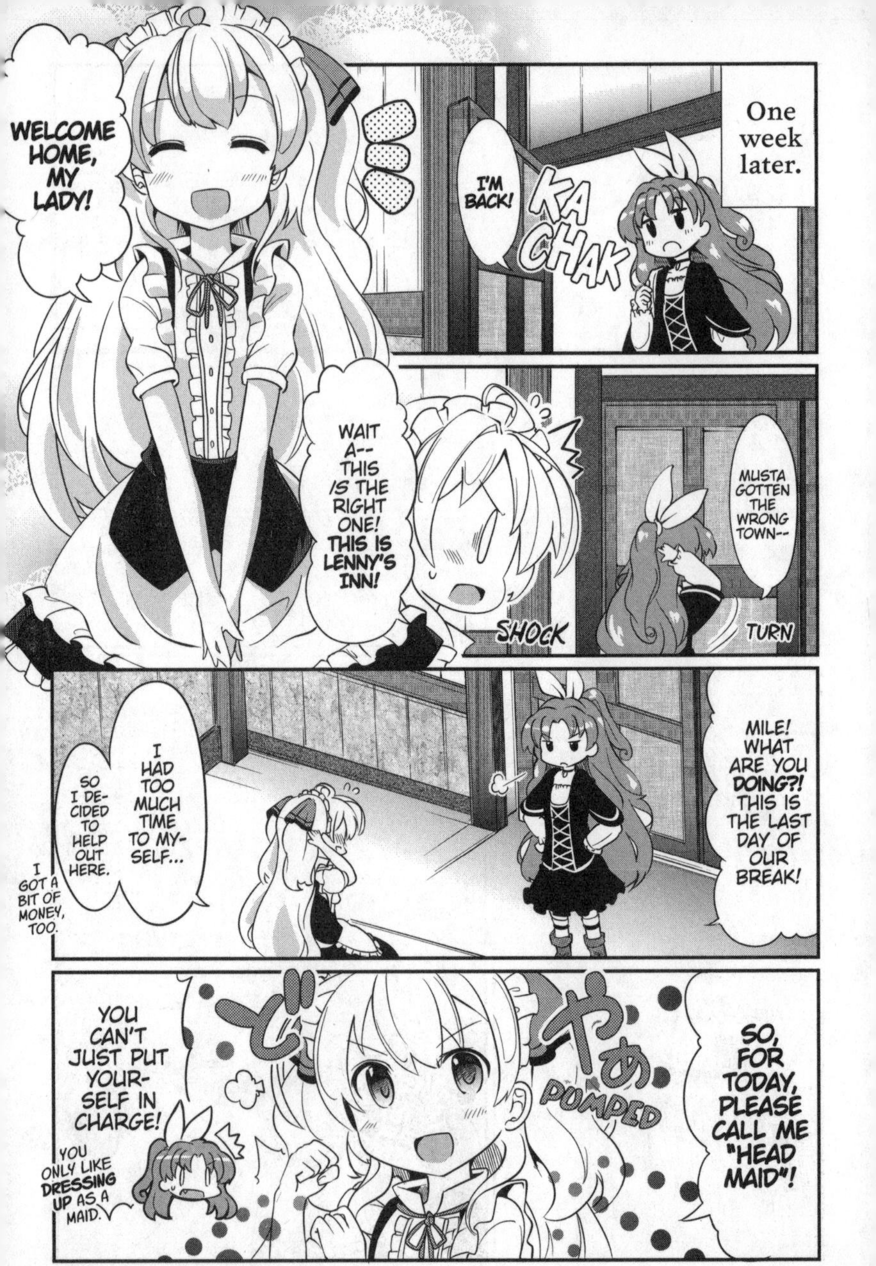

One week later.
KA CHAK
I'M BACK!
WELCOME HOME, MY LADY!
MUSTA GOTTEN THE WRONG TOWN--
TURN
WAIT A-- THIS IS THE RIGHT ONE! THIS IS LENNY'S INN!
SHOCK
MILE! WHAT ARE YOU DOING?! THIS IS THE LAST DAY OF OUR BREAK!
I HAD TOO MUCH TIME TO MY-SELF...
SO I DE-CIDED TO HELP OUT HERE.
I GOT A BIT OF MONEY, TOO.
SO, FOR TODAY, PLEASE CALL ME "HEAD MAID"!
どやあ
PUMPED
YOU CAN'T JUST PUT YOUR-SELF IN CHARGE!
YOU ONLY LIKE DRESSING UP AS A MAID.

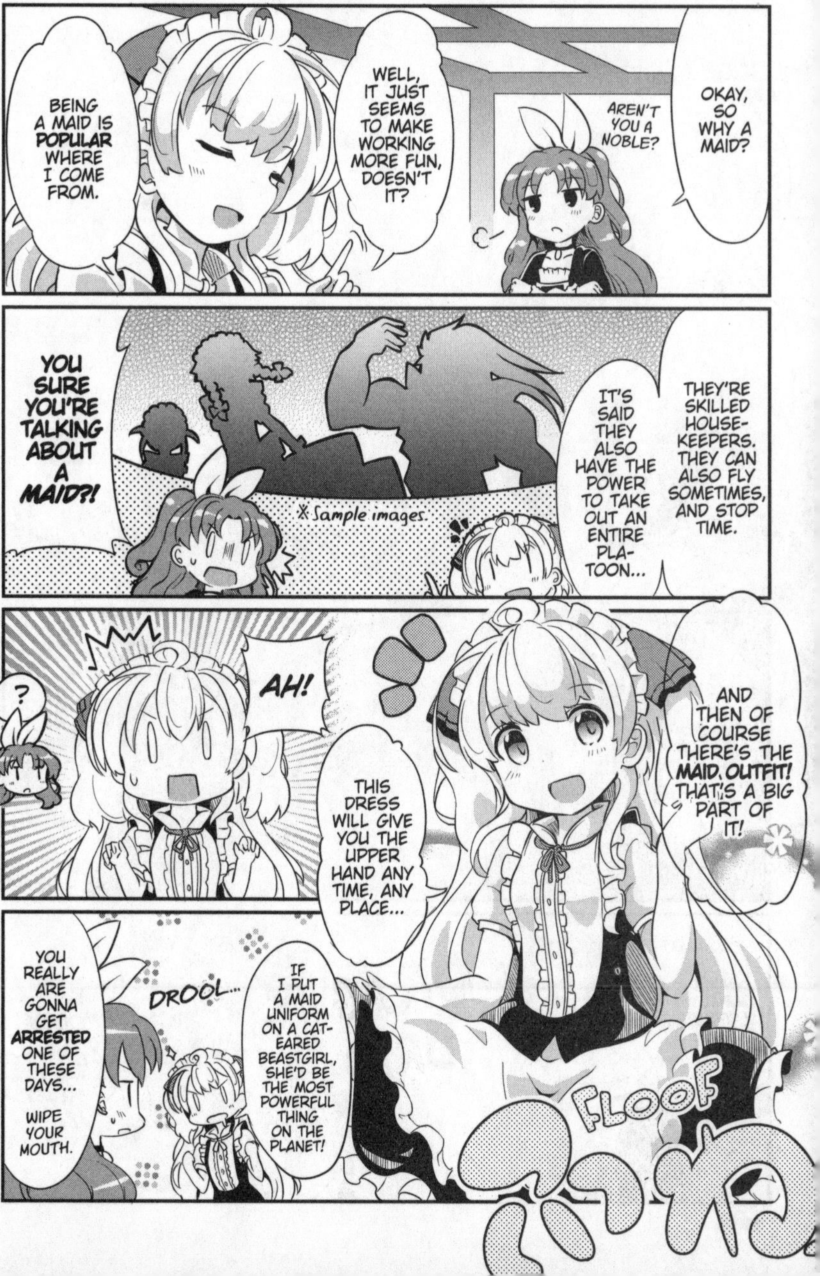
OKAY, SO WHY A MAID?
AREN'T YOU A NOBLE?
WELL, IT JUST SEEMS TO MAKE WORKING MORE FUN, DOESN'T IT?
BEING A MAID IS **POPULAR** WHERE I COME FROM.
THEY'RE SKILLED HOUSE-KEEPERS. THEY CAN ALSO FLY SOMETIMES, AND STOP TIME.
IT'S SAID THEY ALSO HAVE THE POWER TO TAKE OUT AN ENTIRE PLA-TOON...
※Sample images.
YOU SURE YOU'RE TALKING ABOUT A *MAID*?!
AND THEN OF COURSE THERE'S THE **MAID OUTFIT!** THAT'S A BIG PART OF IT!
THIS DRESS WILL GIVE YOU THE UPPER HAND ANY TIME, ANY PLACE...
FLOOF
AH!
?
IF I PUT A MAID UNIFORM ON A CAT-EARED BEASTGIRL, SHE'D BE THE MOST POWERFUL THING ON THE PLANET!
DROOL...
YOU REALLY ARE GONNA GET **ARRESTED** ONE OF THESE DAYS...
WIPE YOUR MOUTH.

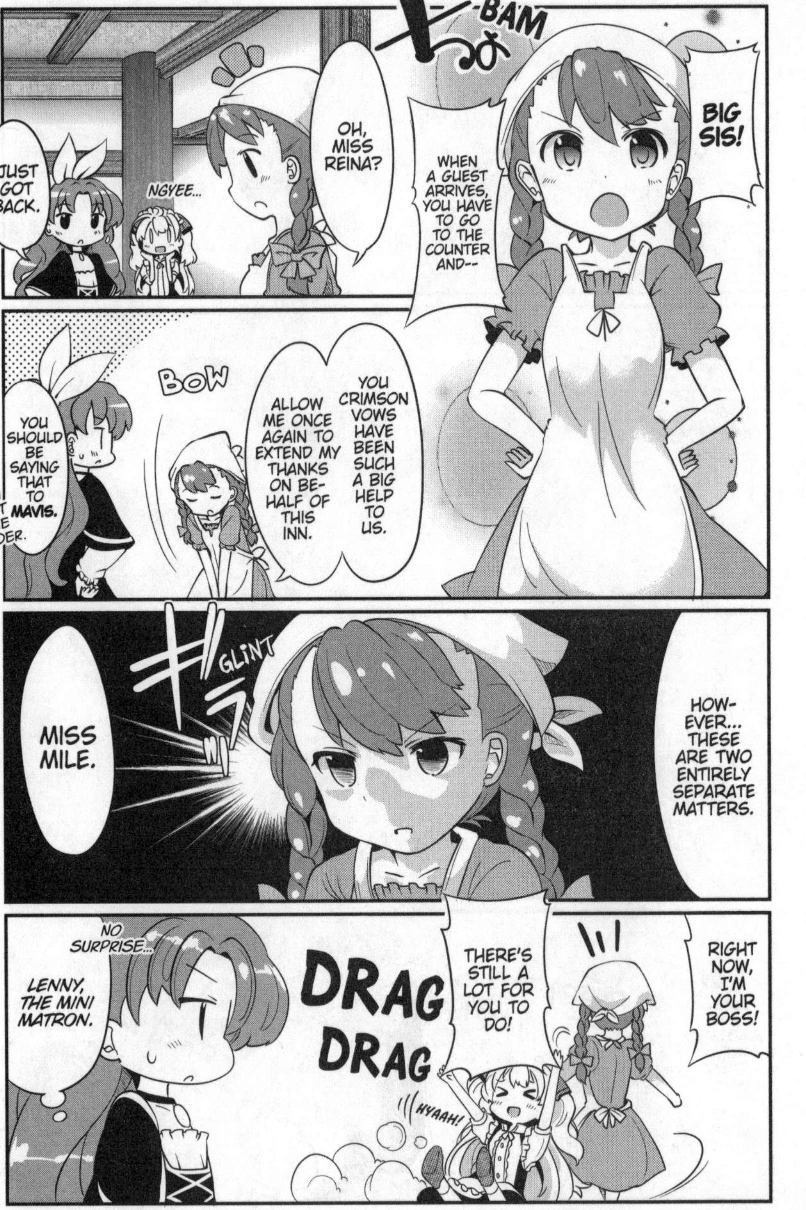
BAM
BIG SIS!
WHEN A GUEST ARRIVES, YOU HAVE TO GO TO THE COUNTER AND--
OH, MISS REINA?
NGYEE...
JUST GOT BACK.
YOU CRIMSON VOWS HAVE BEEN SUCH A BIG HELP TO US.
ALLOW ME ONCE AGAIN TO EXTEND MY THANKS ON BE-HALF OF THIS INN.
BOW
YOU SHOULD BE SAYING THAT TO MAVIS.
I'M NOT THE LEADER.
HOW-EVER... THESE ARE TWO ENTIRELY SEPARATE MATTERS.
GLINT
MISS MILE.
RIGHT NOW, I'M YOUR BOSS!
THERE'S STILL A LOT FOR YOU TO DO!
DRAG
DRAG
HYAAH!
NO SURPRISE...
LENNY, THE MINI MATRON.

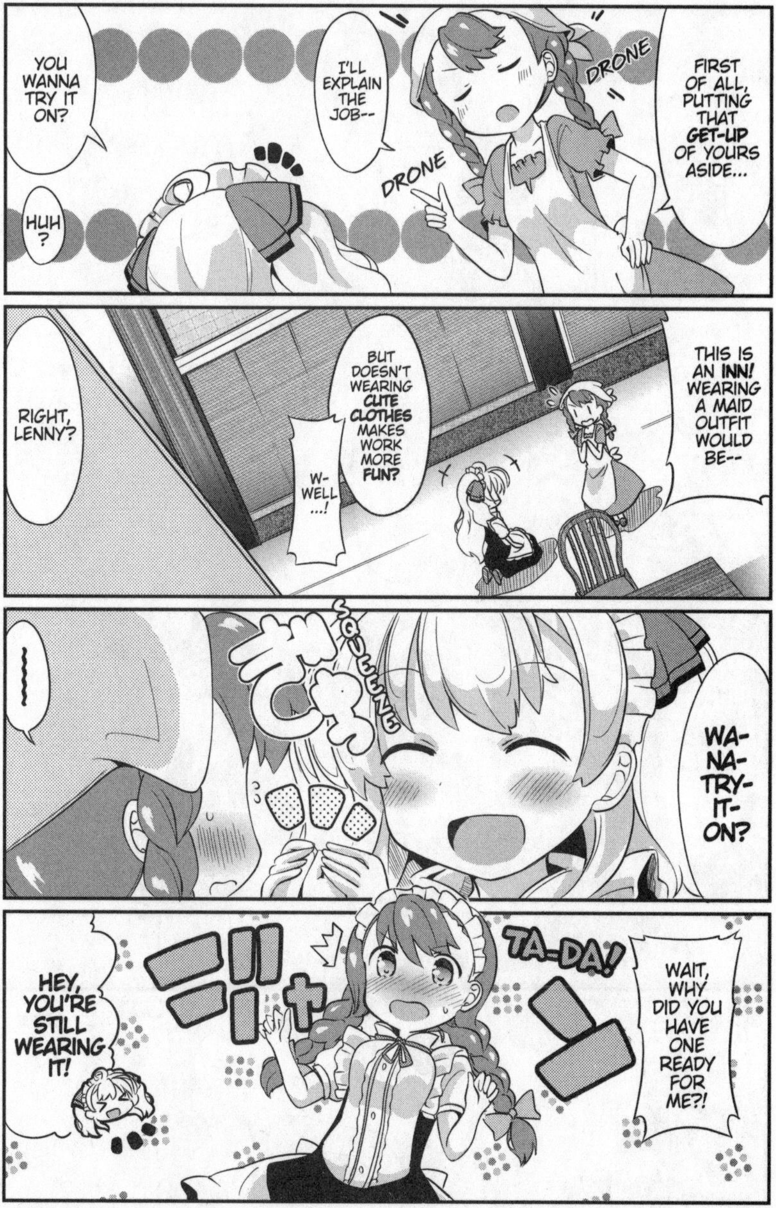
FIRST OF ALL, PUTTING THAT GET-UP OF YOURS ASIDE...
DRONE
DRONE
I'LL EXPLAIN THE JOB--
YOU WANNA TRY IT ON?
HUH?
THIS IS AN INN! WEARING A MAID OUTFIT WOULD BE--
BUT DOESN'T WEARING CUTE CLOTHES MAKES WORK MORE FUN?
W-WELL...!
RIGHT, LENNY?
WA-NA-TRY-IT-ON?
SQUEEZE
WAIT, WHY DID YOU HAVE ONE READY FOR ME?!
TA-DA!
HEY, YOU'RE STILL WEARING IT!

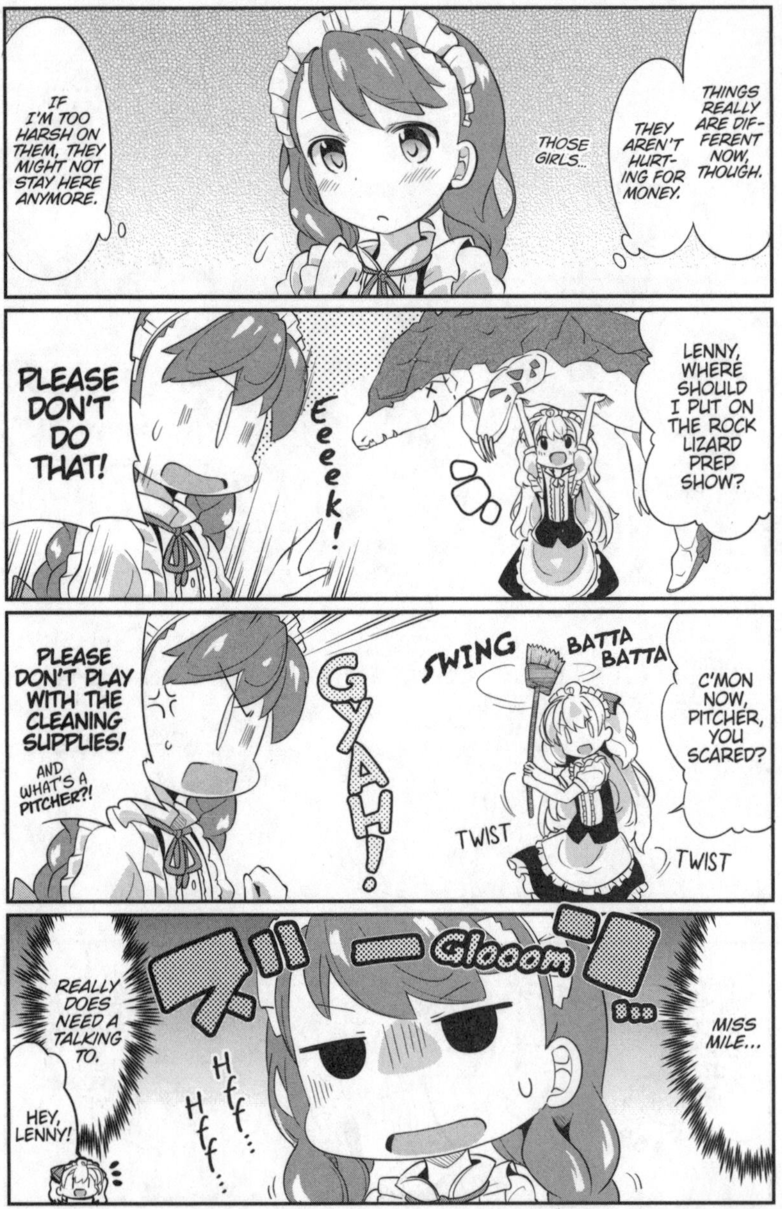
THINGS REALLY ARE DIF-FERENT NOW, THOUGH.
THEY AREN'T HURT-ING FOR MONEY.
THOSE GIRLS...
IF I'M TOO HARSH ON THEM, THEY MIGHT NOT STAY HERE ANYMORE.
LENNY, WHERE SHOULD I PUT ON THE ROCK LIZARD PREP SHOW?
Eeeek!
PLEASE DON'T DO THAT!
C'MON NOW, PITCHER, YOU SCARED?
BATTA BATTA
SWING
TWIST
TWIST
GYAH!
PLEASE DON'T PLAY WITH THE CLEANING SUPPLIES!
AND WHAT'S A PITCHER?!
MISS MILE...
Glooom...
Hff Hff...
REALLY DOES NEED A TALKING TO.
HEY, LENNY!

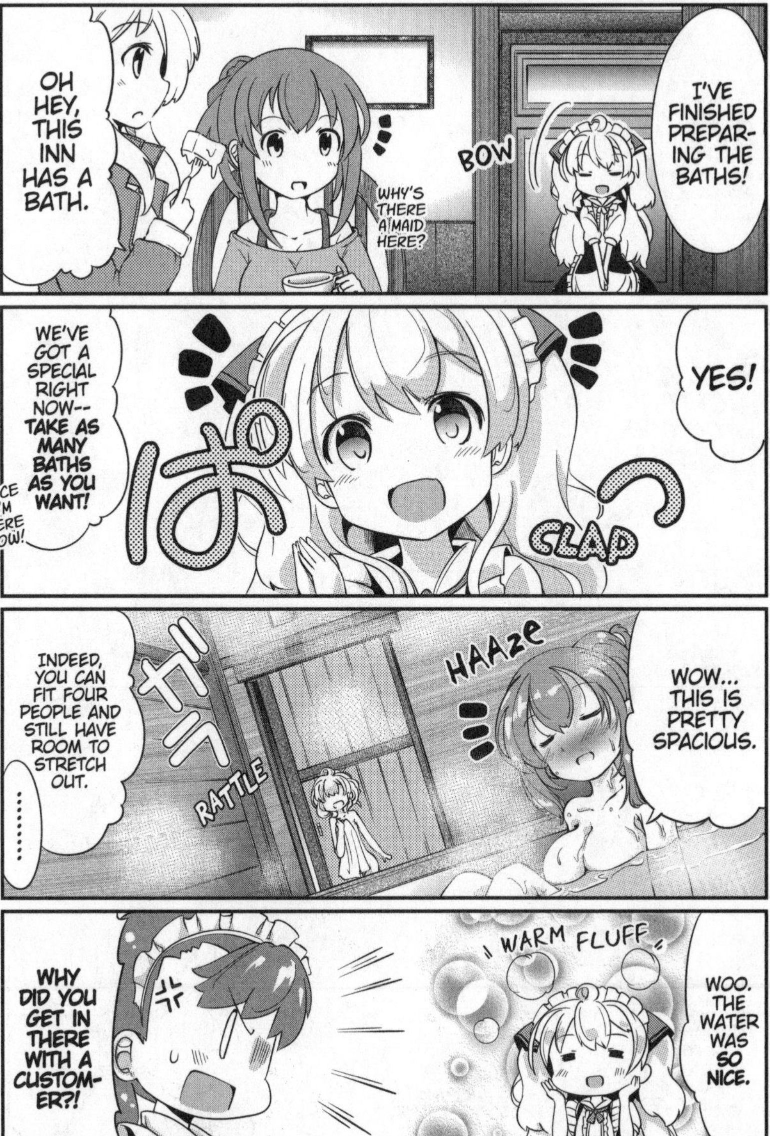
I'VE FINISHED PREPAR-ING THE BATHS!
BOW
WHY'S THERE A MAID HERE?
OH HEY, THIS INN HAS A BATH.
YES!
CLAP
WE'VE GOT A SPECIAL RIGHT NOW-- TAKE AS MANY BATHS AS YOU WANT!
SINCE I'M HERE NOW!
WOW... THIS IS PRETTY SPACIOUS.
HAAze
RATTLE
INDEED, YOU CAN FIT FOUR PEOPLE AND STILL HAVE ROOM TO STRETCH OUT.
....
WOO. THE WATER WAS SO NICE.
WARM FLUFF
WHY DID YOU GET IN THERE WITH A CUSTOM-ER?!

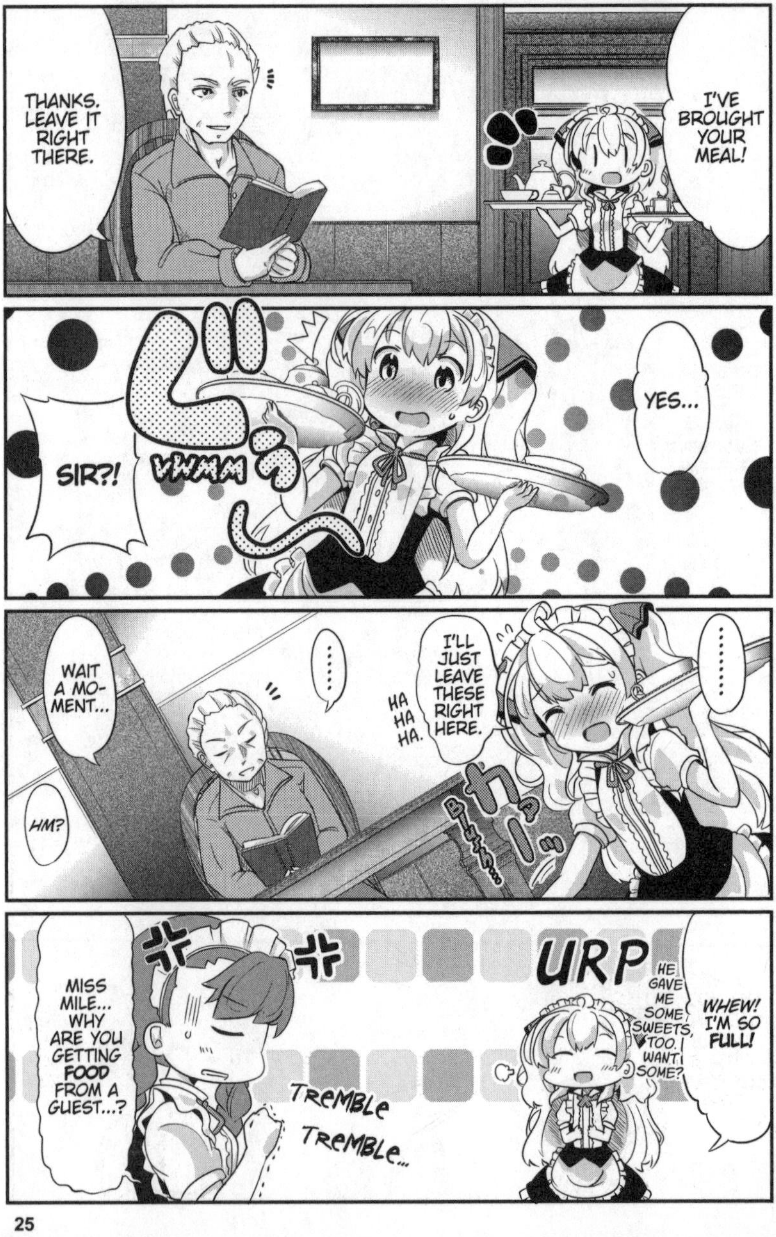
I'VE BROUGHT YOUR MEAL!
THANKS. LEAVE IT RIGHT THERE.
YES...
SIR?!
......
I'LL JUST LEAVE THESE RIGHT HERE.
HA HA HA.
......
WAIT A MO- MENT...
HM?
WHEW! I'M SO FULL!
HE GAVE ME SOME SWEETS, TOO. WANT SOME?
URP
TREMBLE TREMBLE...
MISS MILE... WHY ARE YOU GETTING FOOD FROM A GUEST...?

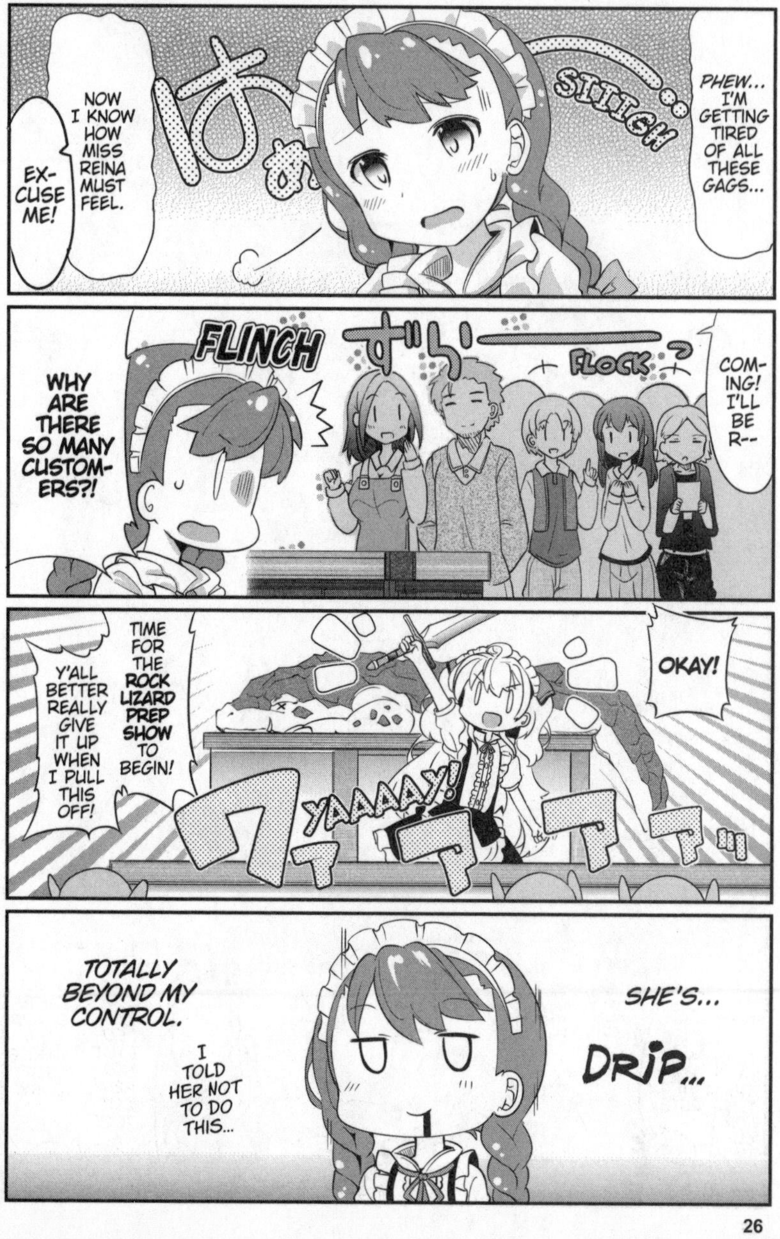
PHEW... I'M GETTING TIRED OF ALL THESE GAGS...
SIIIIGH...
NOW I KNOW HOW MISS REINA MUST FEEL.
EX-CUSE ME!
COM-ING! I'LL BE R--
FLOCK
FLINCH
WHY ARE THERE SO MANY CUSTOM-ERS?!
OKAY!
TIME FOR THE ROCK LIZARD PREP SHOW TO BEGIN!
Y'ALL BETTER REALLY GIVE IT UP WHEN I PULL THIS OFF!
YAAAAAY!
SHE'S...
DRIP...
TOTALLY BEYOND MY CONTROL.
I TOLD HER NOT TO DO THIS...

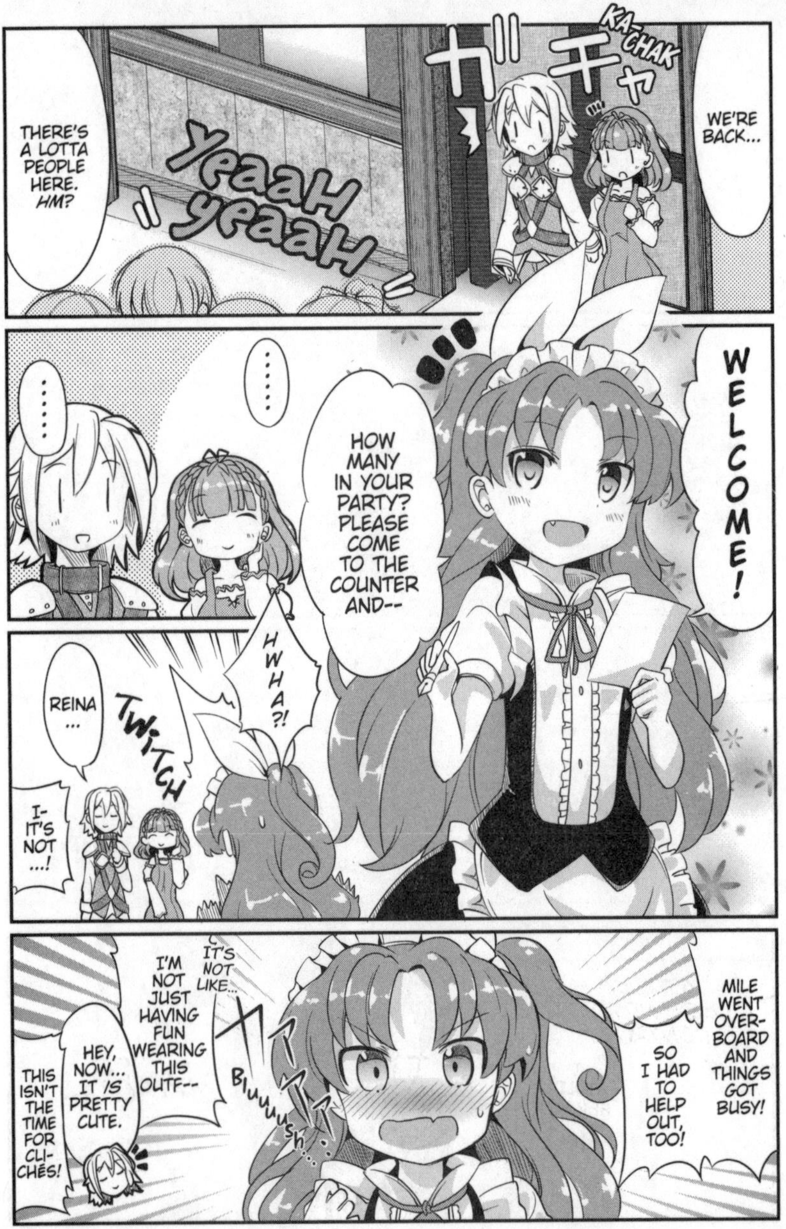
KA-CHAK
WE'RE BACK...
YEAAH YEAAH
THERE'S A LOTTA PEOPLE HERE. *HM?*
WELCOME!
HOW MANY IN YOUR PARTY? PLEASE COME TO THE COUNTER AND--
......
......
HWHA?!
TWITCH
REINA ...
I- IT'S NOT ...!
MILE WENT OVERBOARD AND THINGS GOT BUSY!
SO I HAD TO HELP OUT, TOO!
BLUUUSH...
IT'S NOT LIKE...
I'M NOT JUST HAVING FUN WEARING THIS OUTF--
HEY, NOW... IT *IS* PRETTY CUTE.
THIS ISN'T THE TIME FOR CLICHÉS!

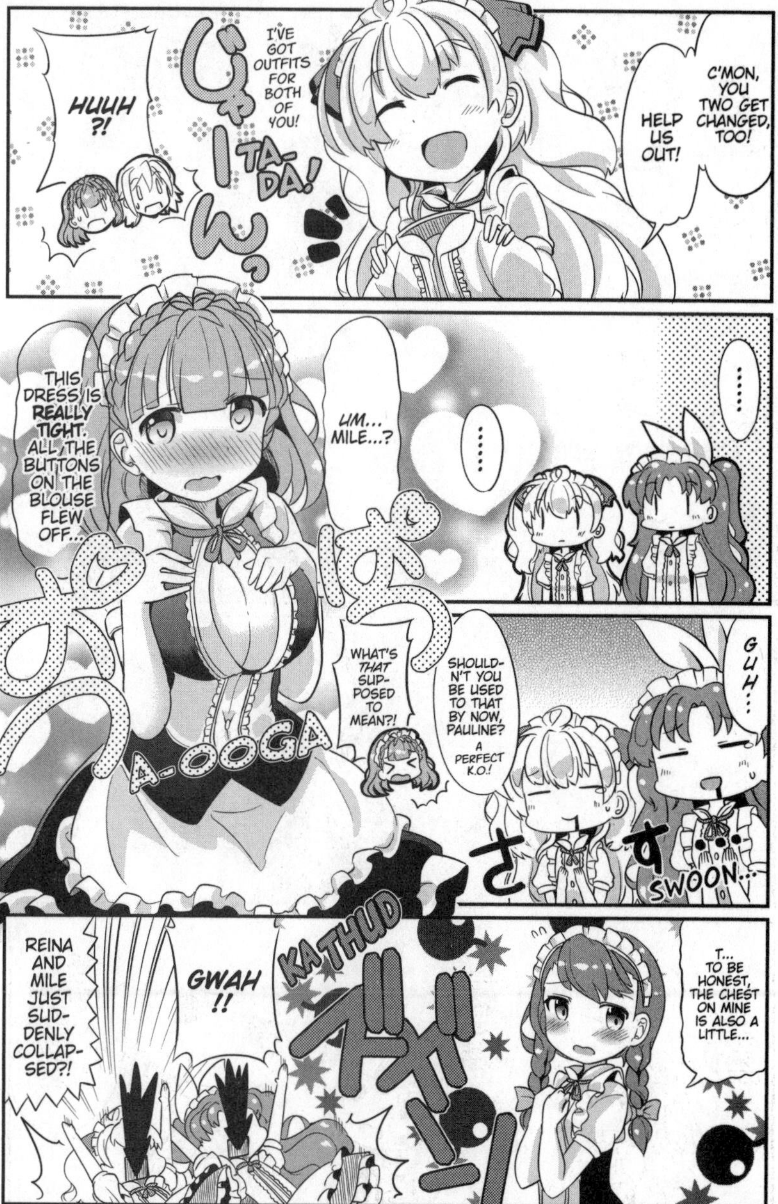
C'MON, YOU TWO GET CHANGED, TOO!
HELP US OUT!
I'VE GOT OUTFITS FOR BOTH OF YOU!
TA-DA!
HUUH?!
......
......
UM... MILE...?
GUH...
SHOULDN'T YOU BE USED TO THAT BY NOW, PAULINE?
A PERFECT K.O.!
SWOON...
WHAT'S THAT SUPPOSED TO MEAN?!
THIS DRESS IS REALLY TIGHT. ALL THE BUTTONS ON THE BLOUSE FLEW OFF...
A-OOGA
T... TO BE HONEST, THE CHEST ON MINE IS ALSO A LITTLE...
KATHUD
GWAH!!
REINA AND MILE JUST SUDDENLY COLLAPSED?!

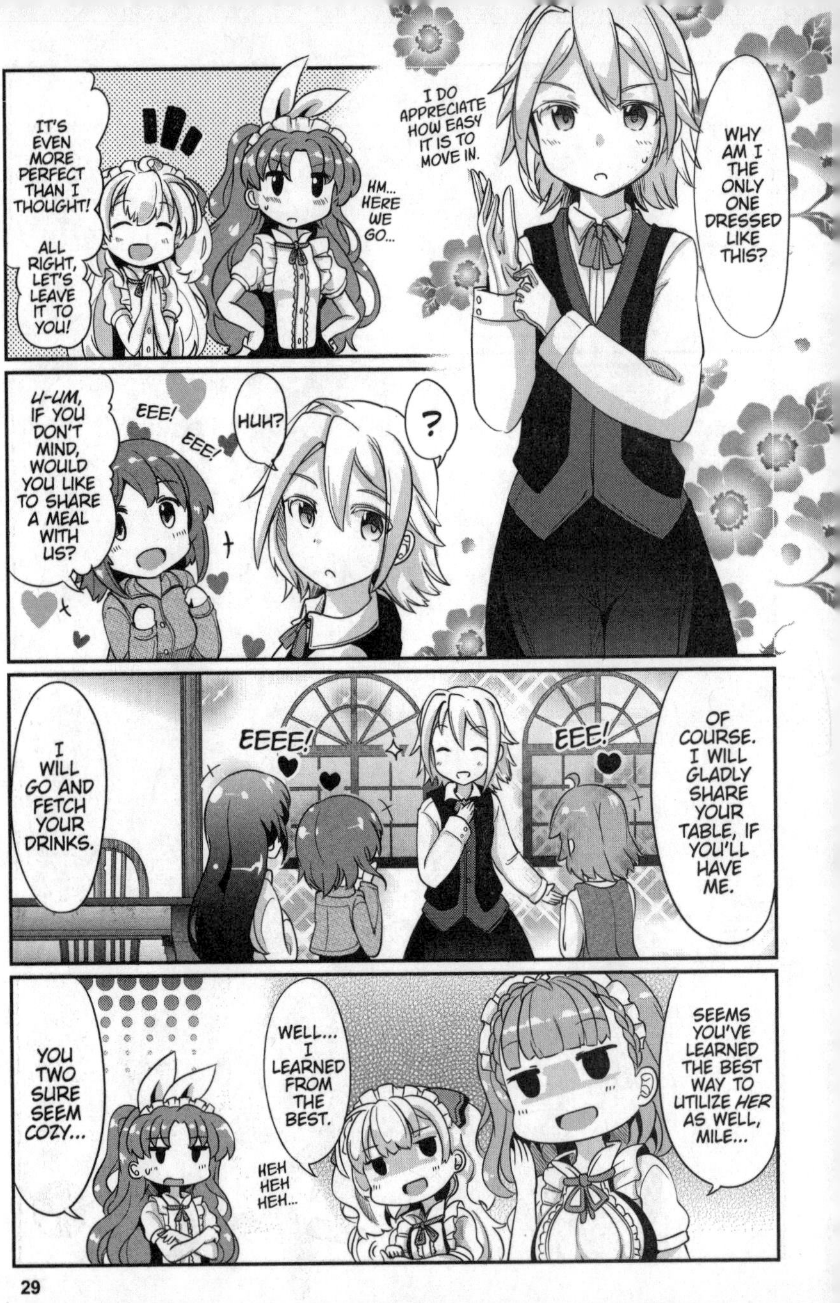
WHY AM I THE ONLY ONE DRESSED LIKE THIS?
I DO APPRECIATE HOW EASY IT IS TO MOVE IN.
IT'S EVEN MORE PERFECT THAN I THOUGHT!
ALL RIGHT, LET'S LEAVE IT TO YOU!
HM... HERE WE GO...
U-UM, IF YOU DON'T MIND, WOULD YOU LIKE TO SHARE A MEAL WITH US?
EEE!
EEE!
HUH?
?
OF COURSE. I WILL GLADLY SHARE YOUR TABLE, IF YOU'LL HAVE ME.
EEE!
EEEE!
I WILL GO AND FETCH YOUR DRINKS.
SEEMS YOU'VE LEARNED THE BEST WAY TO UTILIZE *HER* AS WELL, MILE...
WELL... I LEARNED FROM THE BEST.
HEH HEH HEH...
YOU TWO SURE SEEM COZY...

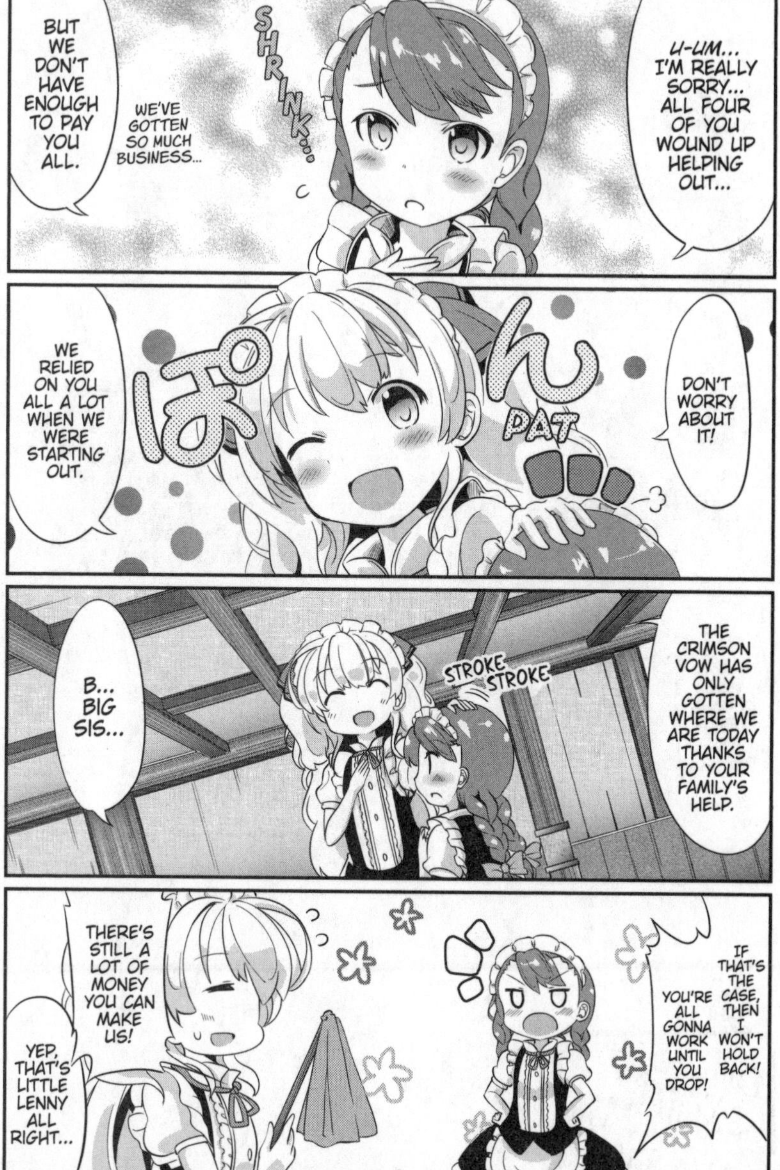
U-UM... I'M REALLY SORRY... ALL FOUR OF YOU WOUND UP HELPING OUT...
SHRINK...
WE'VE GOTTEN SO MUCH BUSINESS...
BUT WE DON'T HAVE ENOUGH TO PAY YOU ALL.
DON'T WORRY ABOUT IT!
PAT
ぽん
WE RELIED ON YOU ALL A LOT WHEN WE WERE STARTING OUT.
THE CRIMSON VOW HAS ONLY GOTTEN WHERE WE ARE TODAY THANKS TO YOUR FAMILY'S HELP.
STROKE STROKE
B... BIG SIS...
IF THAT'S THE CASE, THEN I WON'T HOLD BACK!
YOU'RE ALL GONNA WORK UNTIL YOU DROP!
THERE'S STILL A LOT OF MONEY YOU CAN MAKE US!
YEP, THAT'S LITTLE LENNY ALL RIGHT...

Didn't I Say to Make My Abilities Average in the Next Life?!

EVERYDAY MISADVENTURES!

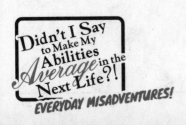

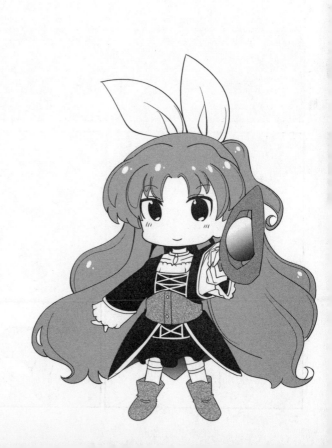

Chapter 3

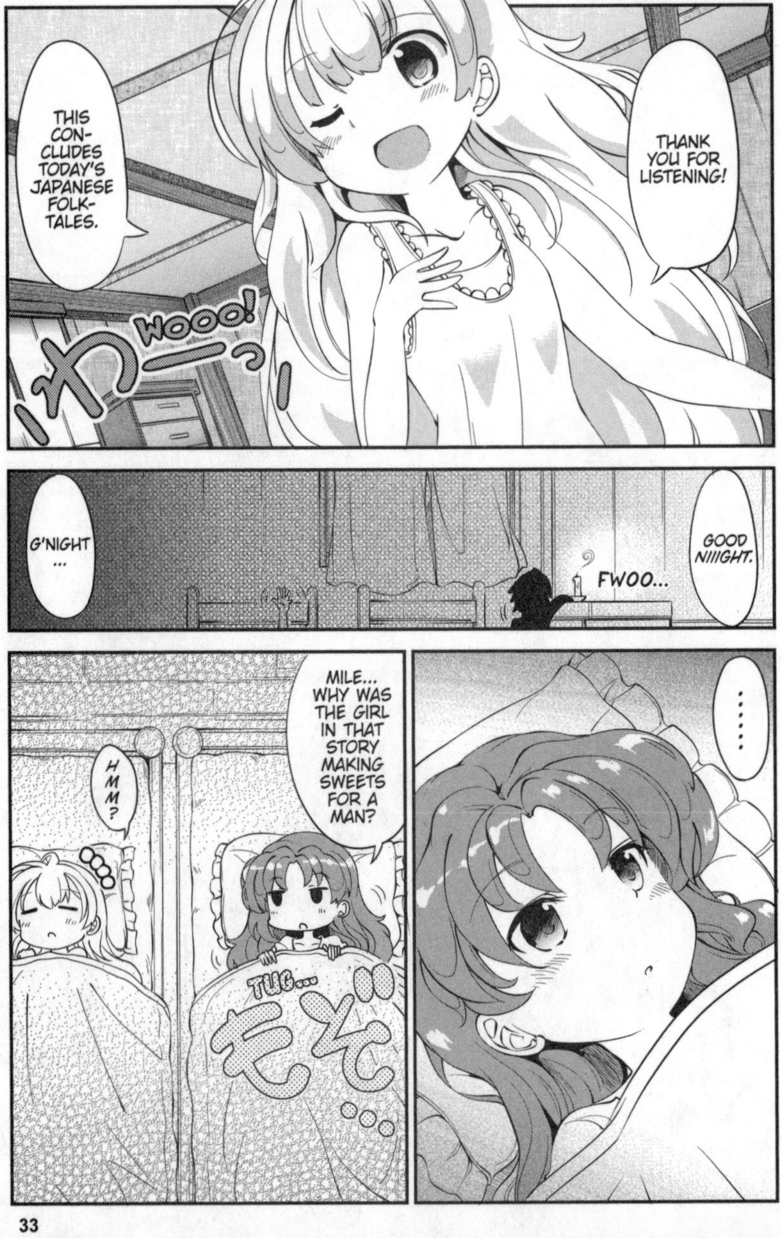
THANK YOU FOR LISTENING!
THIS CON-CLUDES TODAY'S JAPANESE FOLK-TALES.
WOOO!
GOOD NIIIGHT.
FWOO...
G'NIGHT ...
......
MILE... WHY WAS THE GIRL IN THAT STORY MAKING SWEETS FOR A MAN?
HMM?
TUG...

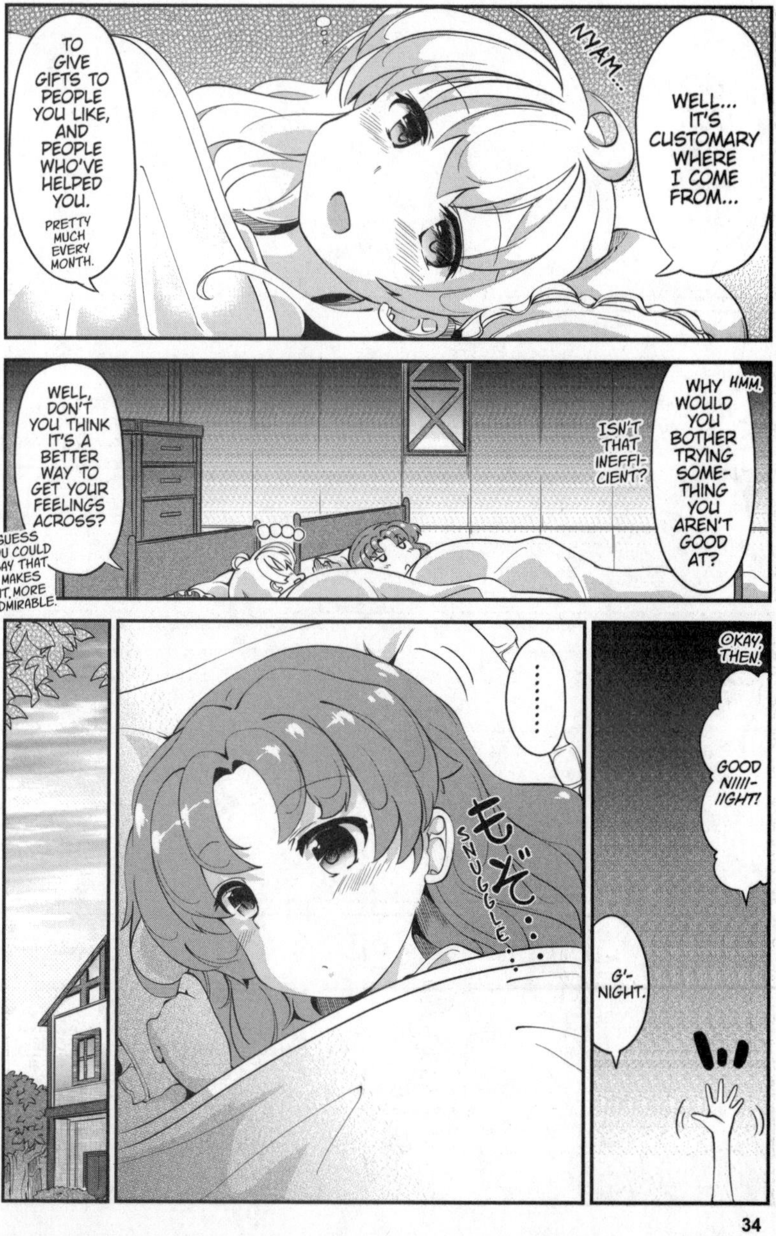
WELL... IT'S CUSTOMARY WHERE I COME FROM...
NYAM...
TO GIVE GIFTS TO PEOPLE YOU LIKE, AND PEOPLE WHO'VE HELPED YOU.
PRETTY MUCH EVERY MONTH.
HMM.
WHY WOULD YOU BOTHER TRYING SOME-THING YOU AREN'T GOOD AT?
ISN'T THAT INEFFI-CIENT?
WELL, DON'T YOU THINK IT'S A BETTER WAY TO GET YOUR FEELINGS ACROSS?
GUESS YOU COULD SAY THAT MAKES IT MORE ADMIRABLE.
OKAY, THEN.
GOOD NIIII-IIGHT!
G'-NIGHT.
......
もぞ...
SNUGGLE...

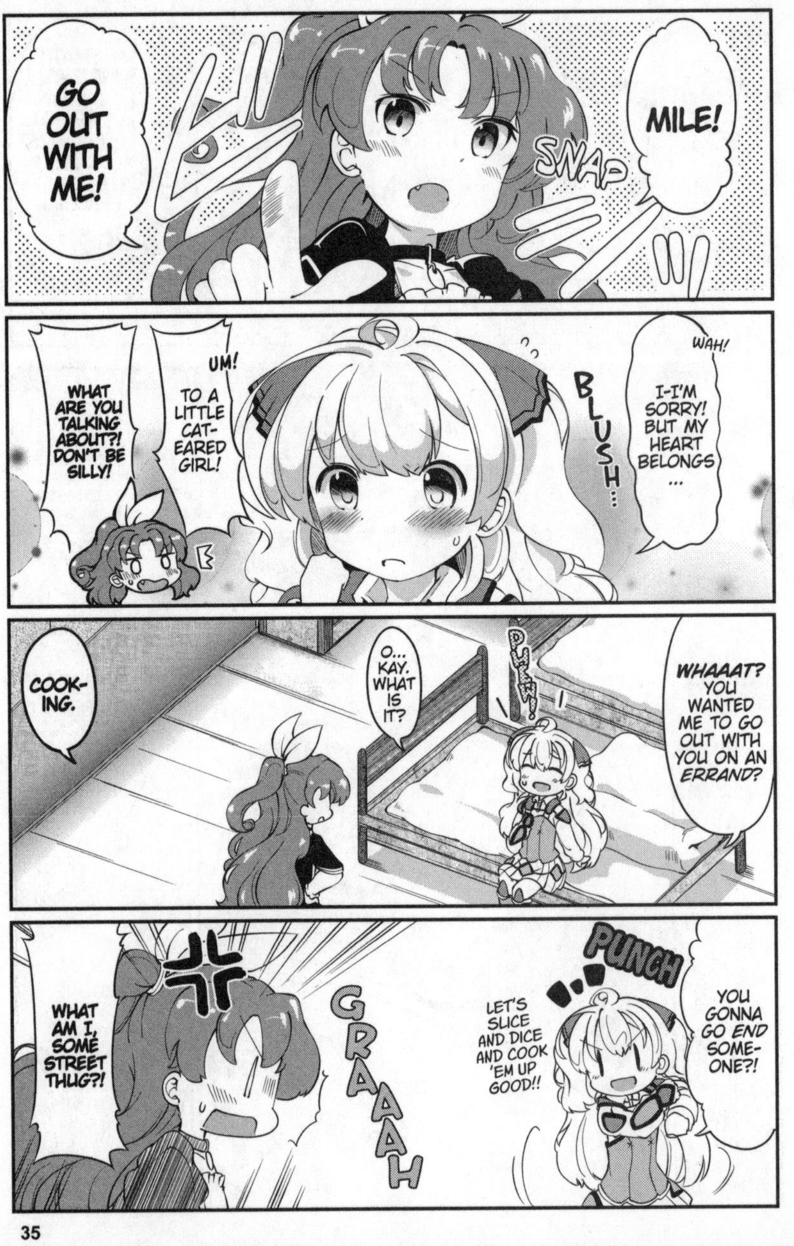
MILE!
SNAP
GO OUT WITH ME!
WAH!
I-I'M SORRY! BUT MY HEART BELONGS ...
BLUSH...
UM!
TO A LITTLE CAT-EARED GIRL!
WHAT ARE YOU TALKING ABOUT?! DON'T BE SILLY!
WHAAAT? YOU WANTED ME TO GO OUT WITH YOU ON AN *ERRAND?*
O... KAY. WHAT IS IT?
COOKING.
YOU GONNA GO *END* SOME-ONE?!
PUNCH
LET'S SLICE AND DICE AND COOK 'EM UP GOOD!!
GRAAAH
WHAT AM I, SOME STREET THUG?!

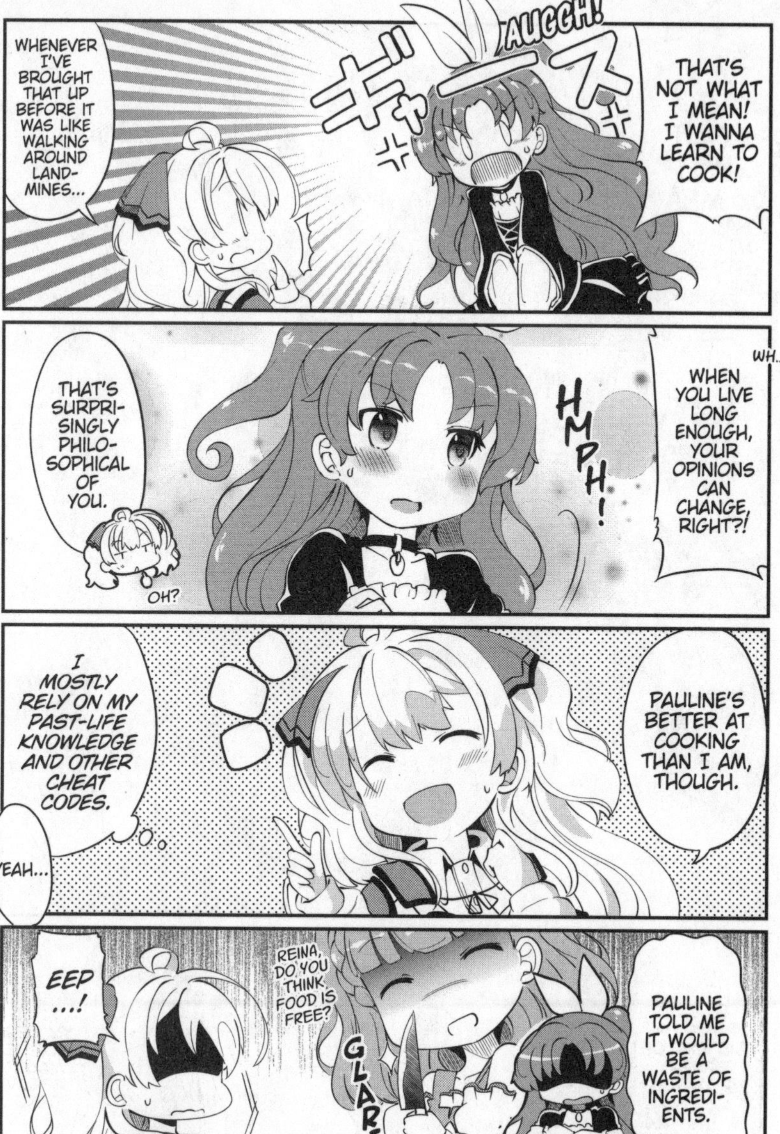
ギャース
AUGGH!
THAT'S NOT WHAT I MEAN! I WANNA LEARN TO COOK!
WHENEVER I'VE BROUGHT THAT UP BEFORE IT WAS LIKE WALKING AROUND LAND-MINES...
WH...
WHEN YOU LIVE LONG ENOUGH, YOUR OPINIONS CAN CHANGE, RIGHT?!
HMPH!
THAT'S SURPRISINGLY PHILOSOPHICAL OF YOU.
OH?
PAULINE'S BETTER AT COOKING THAN I AM, THOUGH.
I MOSTLY RELY ON MY PAST-LIFE KNOWLEDGE AND OTHER CHEAT CODES.
YEAH...
PAULINE TOLD ME IT WOULD BE A WASTE OF INGREDIENTS.
SHIVER SHIVER
REINA, DO YOU THINK FOOD IS FREE?
GLARE
FLINCH
EEP...!

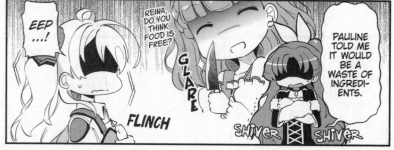

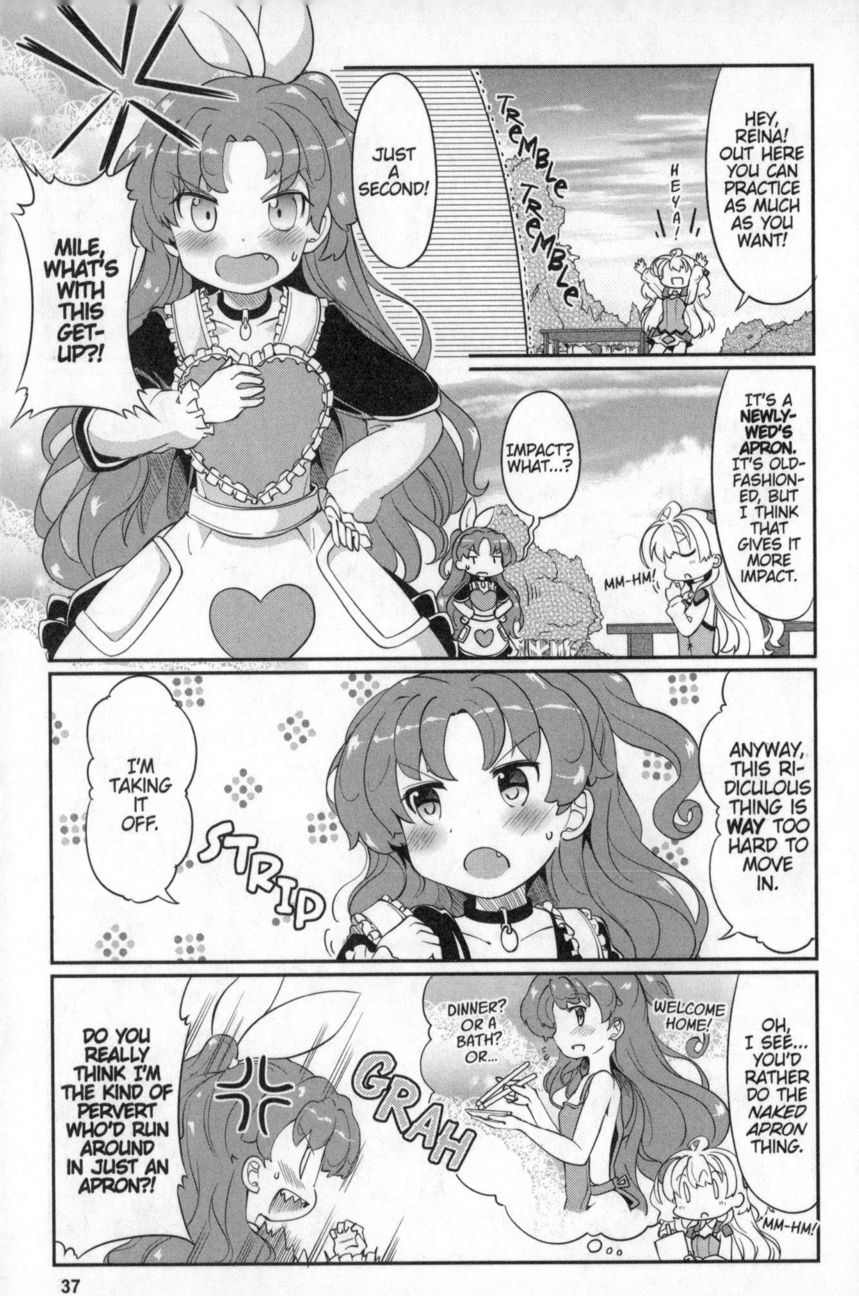
HEY, REINA! OUT HERE YOU CAN PRACTICE AS MUCH AS YOU WANT!
HEYA!
TREMBLE TREMBLE
JUST A SECOND!
IT'S A **NEWLY-WED'S APRON.** IT'S OLD-FASHIONED, BUT I THINK THAT GIVES IT MORE IMPACT.
MM-HM!
IMPACT? WHAT...?
MILE, WHAT'S WITH THIS GET-UP?!
ANYWAY, THIS RIDICULOUS THING IS **WAY** TOO HARD TO MOVE IN.
STRIP
I'M TAKING IT OFF.
OH, I SEE... YOU'D RATHER DO THE *NAKED APRON* THING.
WELCOME HOME!
DINNER? OR A BATH? OR...
MM-HM!
GRAH
DO YOU REALLY THINK I'M THE KIND OF PERVERT WHO'D RUN AROUND IN JUST AN APRON?!

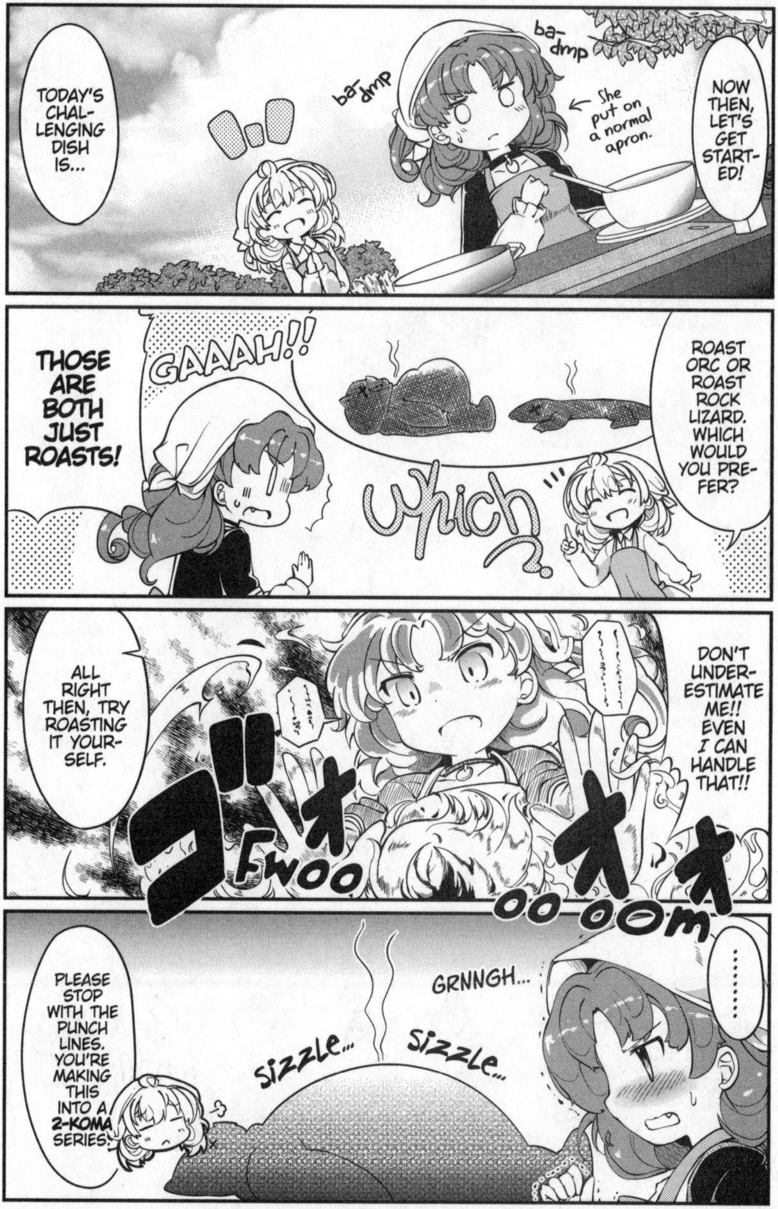
NOW THEN, LET'S GET STARTED!
ba-dmp
ba-dmp
She put on a normal apron.
TODAY'S CHALLENGING DISH IS...
ROAST ORC OR ROAST ROCK LIZARD. WHICH WOULD YOU PREFER?
which?
GAAAH!!
THOSE ARE BOTH JUST ROASTS!
DON'T UNDERESTIMATE ME!! EVEN I CAN HANDLE THAT!!
ALL RIGHT THEN, TRY ROASTING IT YOURSELF.
ゴオオオ
FWOO OO OOM
......
GRNNGH...
sizzle... sizzle...
PLEASE STOP WITH THE PUNCH LINES. YOU'RE MAKING THIS INTO A 2-KOMA SERIES!

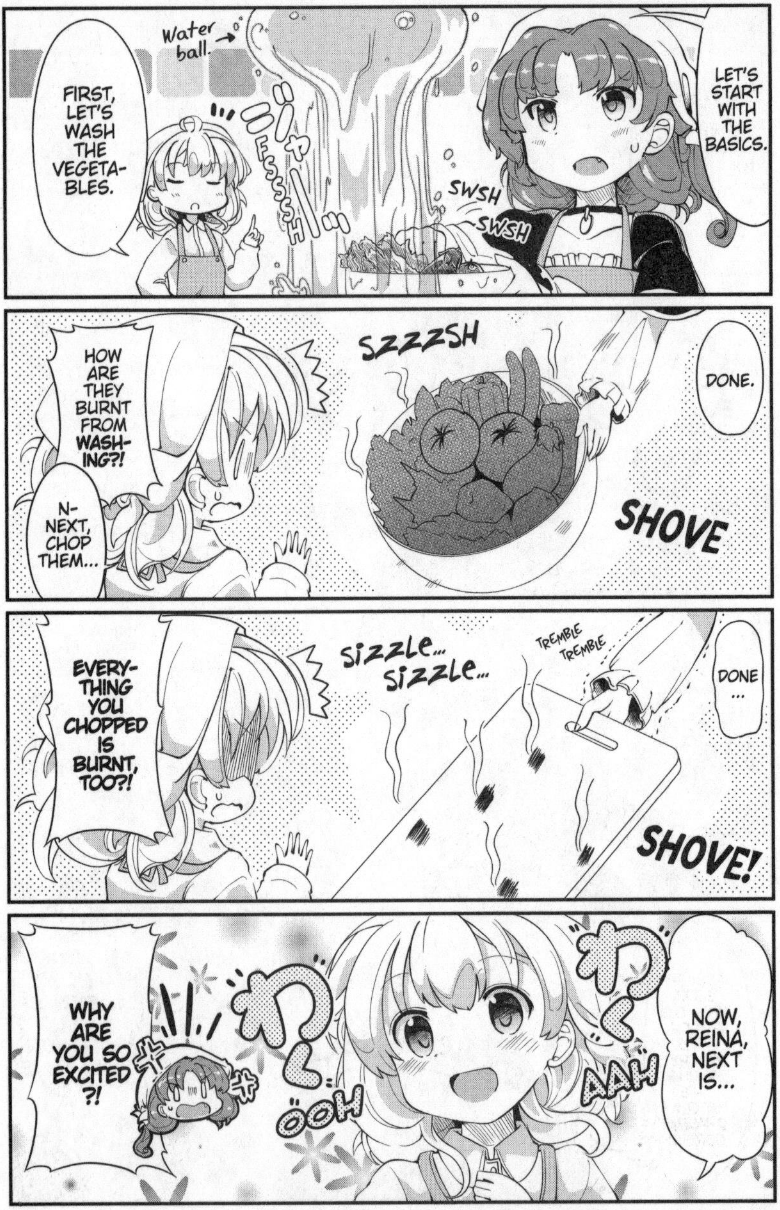
LET'S START WITH THE BASICS.
SWSH
SWSH
FSSSSH
Water ball.
FIRST, LET'S WASH THE VEGETABLES.
DONE.
SHOVE
SZZZSH
HOW ARE THEY BURNT FROM WASHING?!
N-NEXT, CHOP THEM...
DONE...
SHOVE!
TREMBLE TREMBLE
sizzle... sizzle...
EVERYTHING YOU CHOPPED IS BURNT, TOO?!
NOW, REINA, NEXT IS...
AAH
OOH
WHY ARE YOU SO EXCITED?!

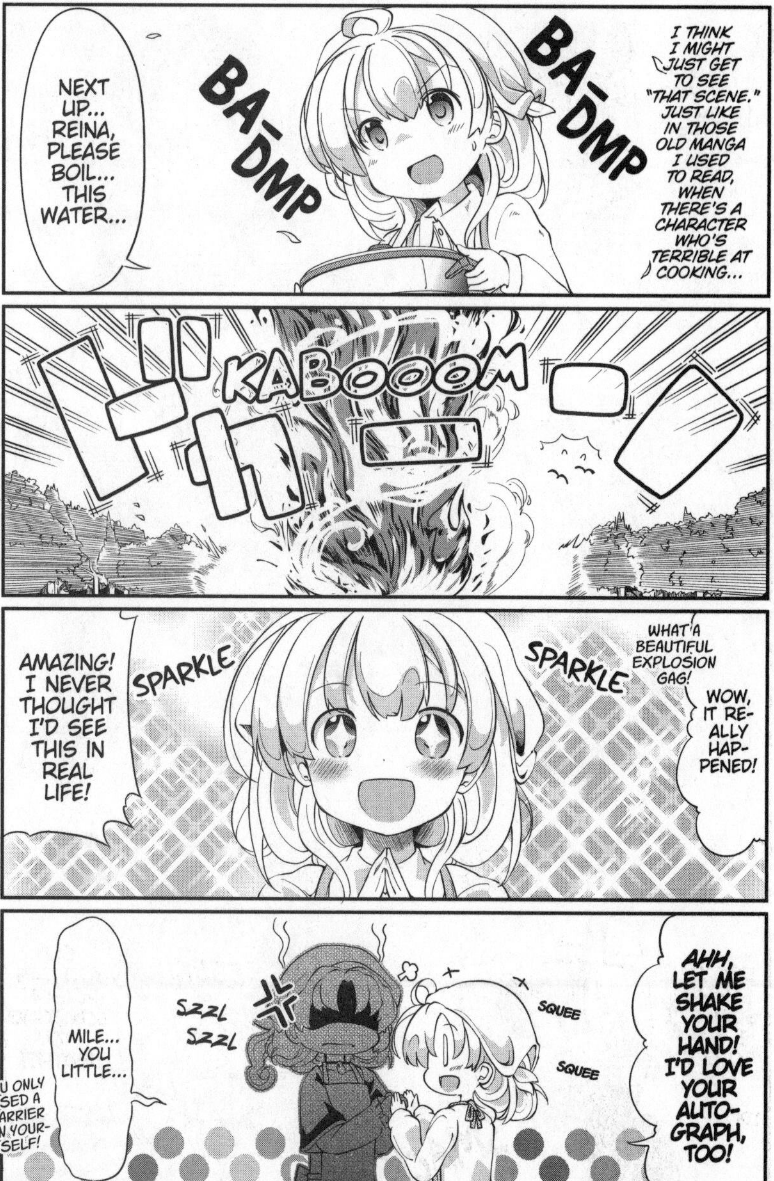
I THINK I MIGHT JUST GET TO SEE "THAT SCENE." JUST LIKE IN THOSE OLD MANGA I USED TO READ, WHEN THERE'S A CHARACTER WHO'S TERRIBLE AT COOKING...
BA-DMP
BA-DMP
NEXT UP... REINA, PLEASE BOIL... THIS WATER...
KABOOOM
WHAT A BEAUTIFUL EXPLOSION GAG!
WOW, IT REALLY HAPPENED!
SPARKLE
SPARKLE
AMAZING! I NEVER THOUGHT I'D SEE THIS IN REAL LIFE!
AHH, LET ME SHAKE YOUR HAND! I'D LOVE YOUR AUTOGRAPH, TOO!
SQUEE
SQUEE
SZZL
SZZL
MILE... YOU LITTLE...
YOU ONLY USED A BARRIER ON YOURSELF!

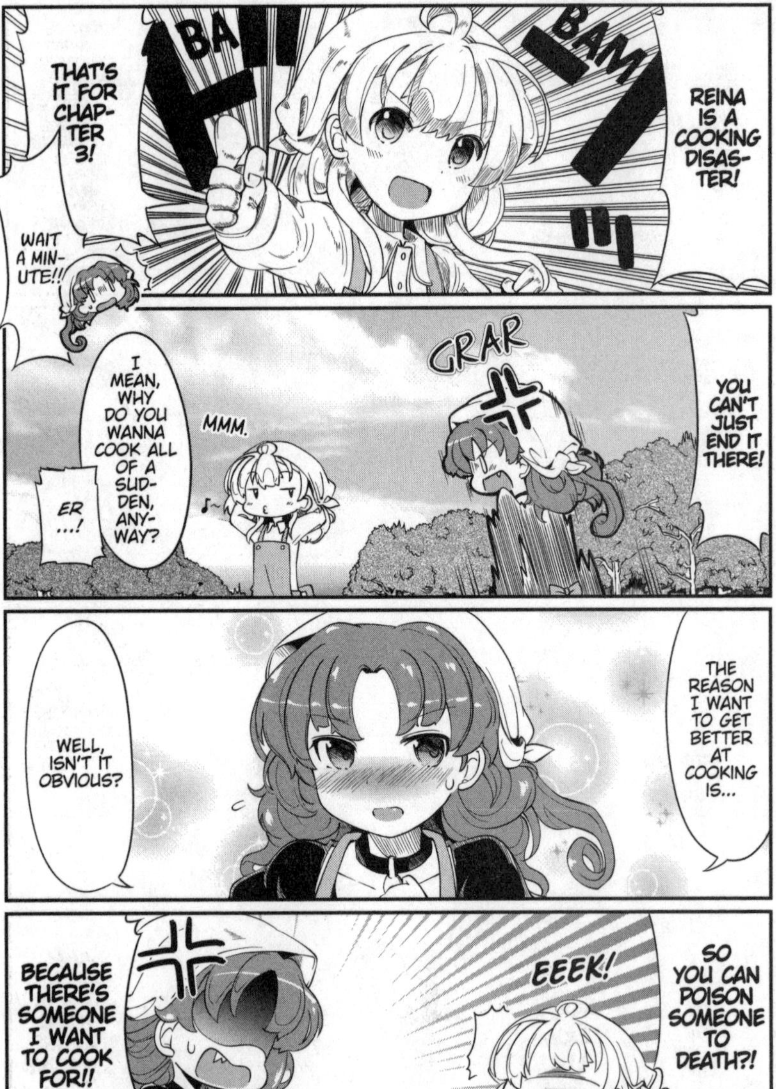
REINA IS A COOKING DISASTER!
BAM
BA
THAT'S IT FOR CHAPTER 3!
WAIT A MINUTE!!
YOU CAN'T JUST END IT THERE!
GRAR
MMM.
I MEAN, WHY DO YOU WANNA COOK ALL OF A SUDDEN, ANYWAY?
ER ...!
THE REASON I WANT TO GET BETTER AT COOKING IS...
WELL, ISN'T IT OBVIOUS?
SO YOU CAN POISON SOMEONE TO DEATH?!
EEEK!
BECAUSE THERE'S SOMEONE I WANT TO COOK FOR!!
IDIOT!!
SMACK

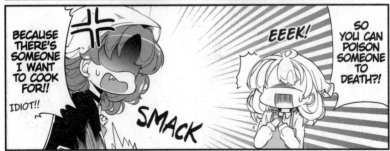

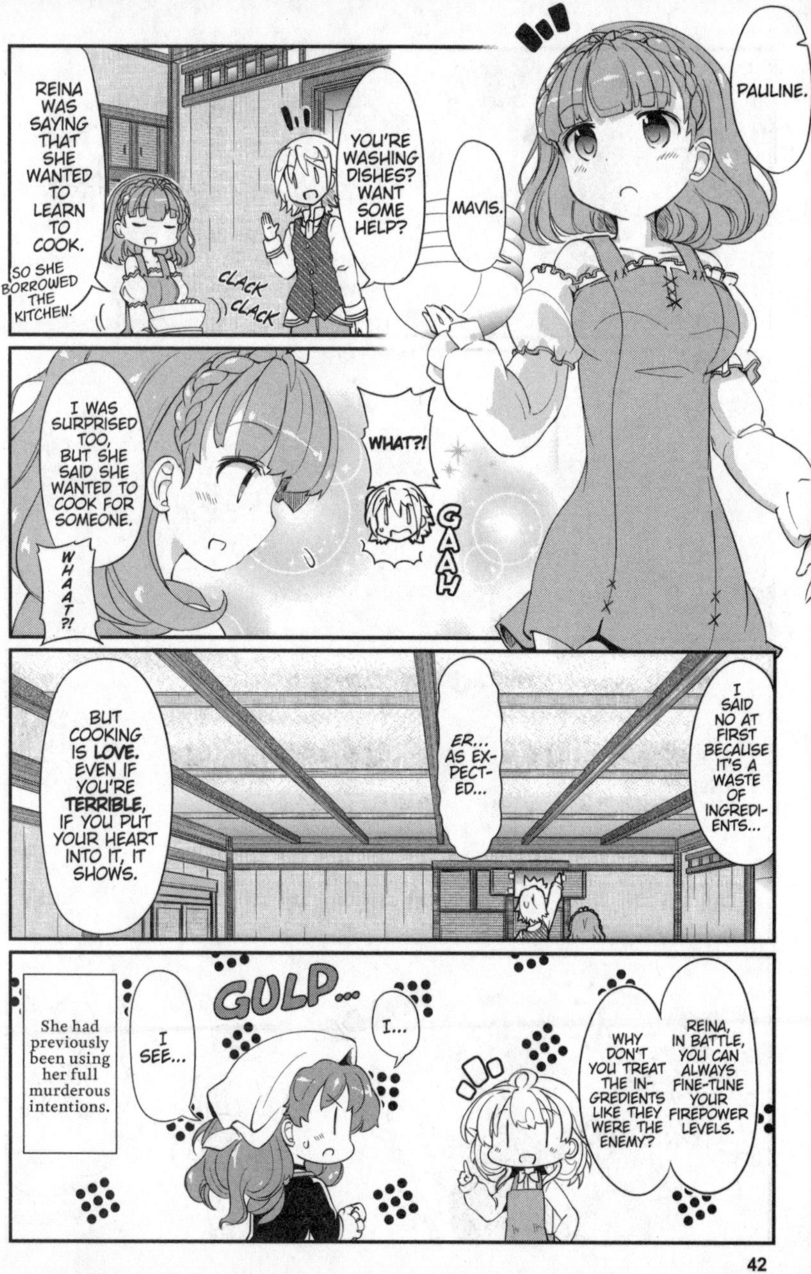

PAULINE.
MAVIS.
YOU'RE WASHING DISHES? WANT SOME HELP?
REINA WAS SAYING THAT SHE WANTED TO LEARN TO COOK.
SO SHE BORROWED THE KITCHEN.
CLACK
CLACK
I WAS SURPRISED TOO, BUT SHE SAID SHE WANTED TO COOK FOR SOMEONE.
WHAT?!
GAAH
WHAAAT?!
I SAID NO AT FIRST BECAUSE IT'S A WASTE OF INGREDI-ENTS...
ER... AS EX-PECT-ED...
BUT COOKING IS LOVE. EVEN IF YOU'RE TERRIBLE, IF YOU PUT YOUR HEART INTO IT, IT SHOWS.
REINA, IN BATTLE, YOU CAN ALWAYS FINE-TUNE YOUR FIREPOWER LEVELS.
WHY DON'T YOU TREAT THE IN-GREDIENTS LIKE THEY WERE THE ENEMY?
GULP...
I...
I SEE...
She had previously been using her full murderous intentions.

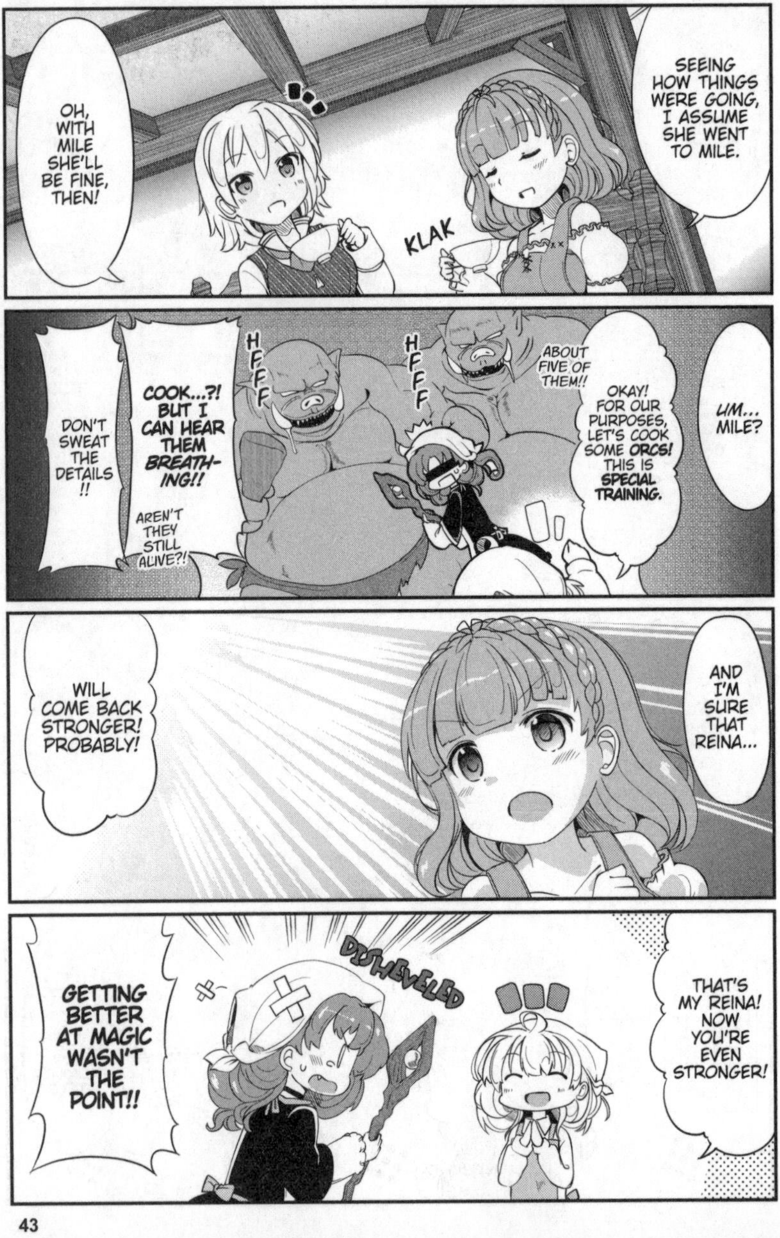
SEEING HOW THINGS WERE GOING, I ASSUME SHE WENT TO MILE.
OH, WITH MILE SHE'LL BE FINE, THEN!
KLAK
UM... MILE?
OKAY! FOR OUR PURPOSES, LET'S COOK SOME ORCS! THIS IS SPECIAL TRAINING.
ABOUT FIVE OF THEM!!
HFFF
HFFF
COOK...?! BUT I CAN HEAR THEM BREATHING!!
AREN'T THEY STILL ALIVE?!
DON'T SWEAT THE DETAILS!!
AND I'M SURE THAT REINA...
WILL COME BACK STRONGER! PROBABLY!
THAT'S MY REINA! NOW YOU'RE EVEN STRONGER!
DISHEVELED
GETTING BETTER AT MAGIC WASN'T THE POINT!!

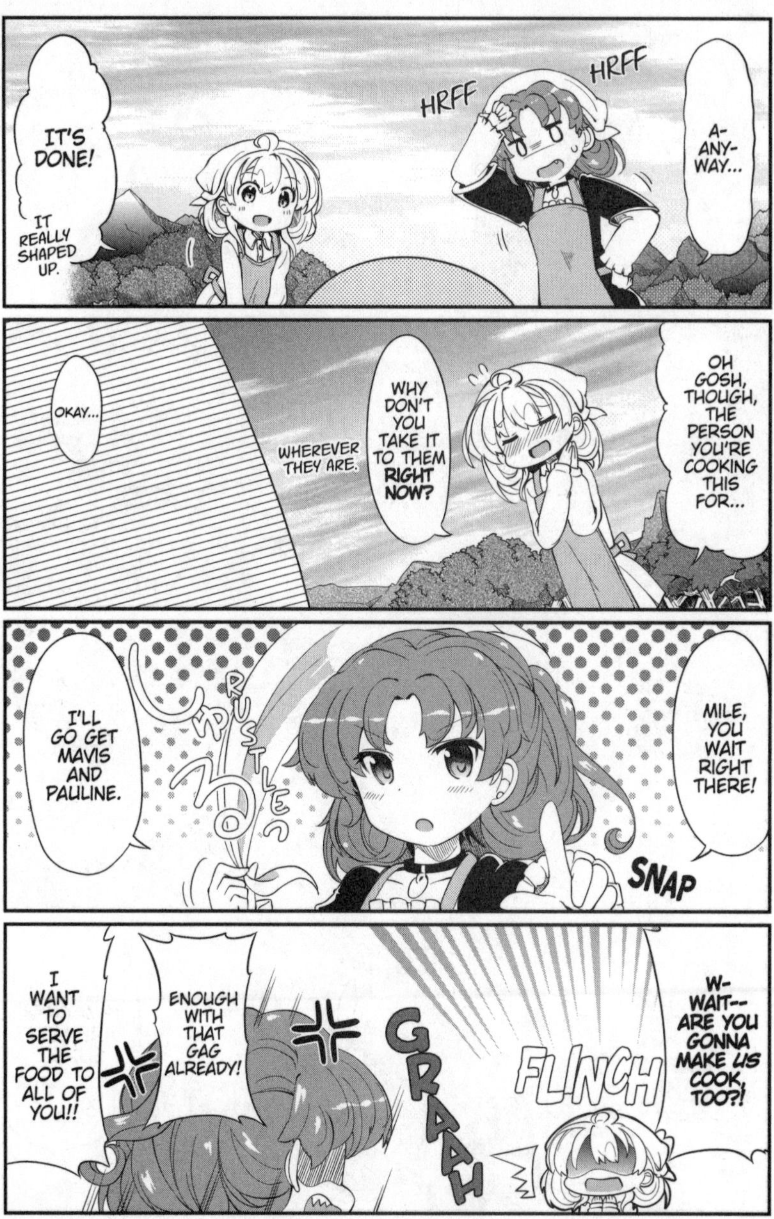
A-ANYWAY...
HRFF
HRFF
IT'S DONE!
IT REALLY SHAPED UP.
OH GOSH, THOUGH, THE PERSON YOU'RE COOKING THIS FOR...
WHY DON'T YOU TAKE IT TO THEM RIGHT NOW?
WHEREVER THEY ARE.
OKAY...
MILE, YOU WAIT RIGHT THERE!
SNAP
I'LL GO GET MAVIS AND PAULINE.
RUSTLE
W-WAIT-- ARE YOU GONNA MAKE US COOK, TOO?!
FLINCH
GRAAH
ENOUGH WITH THAT GAG ALREADY!
I WANT TO SERVE THE FOOD TO ALL OF YOU!!

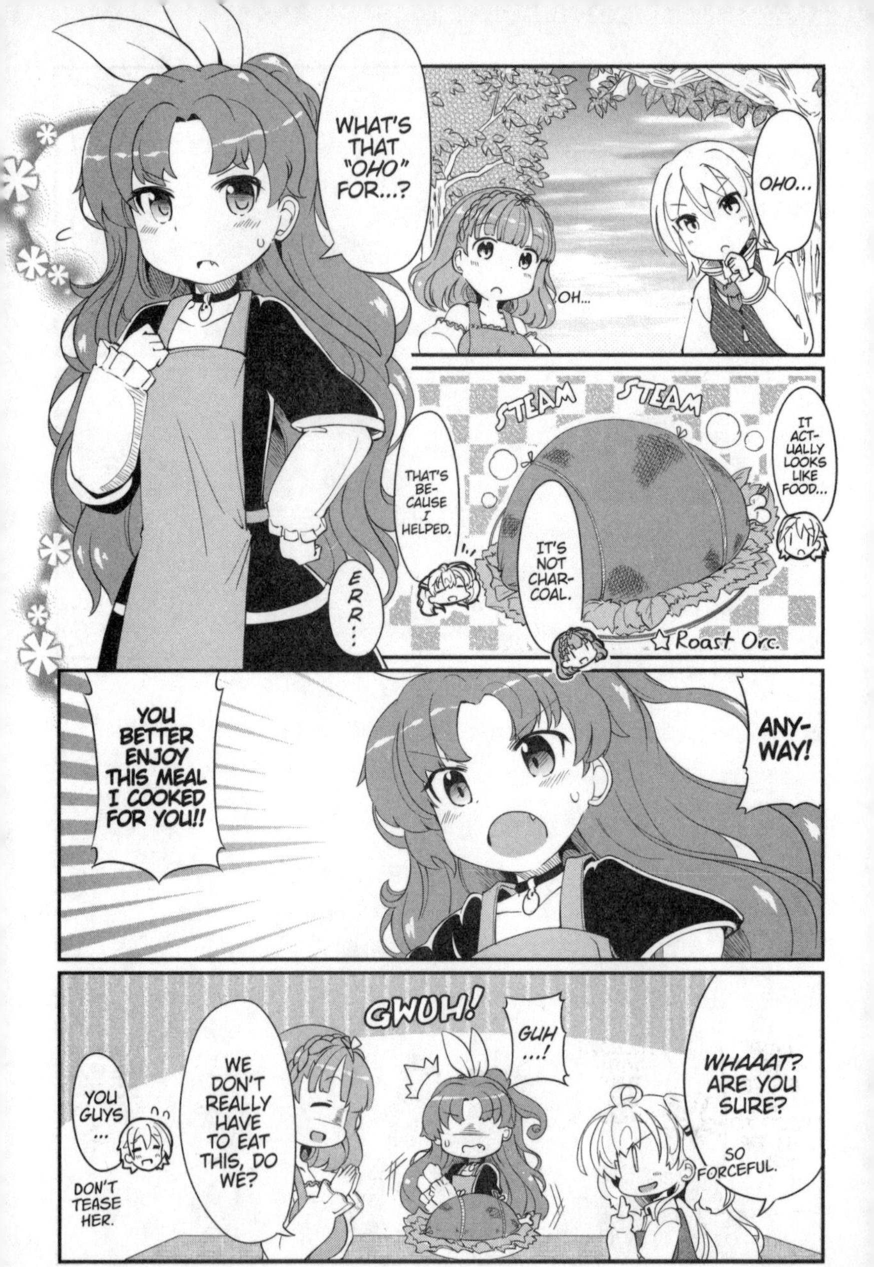
OHO...
OH...
STEAM STEAM
IT ACT-UALLY LOOKS LIKE FOOD...
IT'S NOT CHAR-COAL.
THAT'S BE-CAUSE I HELPED.
☆Roast Orc.
WHAT'S THAT "OHO" FOR...?
ERR...
ANY-WAY!
YOU BETTER ENJOY THIS MEAL I COOKED FOR YOU!!
WHAAAT? ARE YOU SURE?
SO FORCEFUL.
GWUH!
GUH ...!
WE DON'T REALLY HAVE TO EAT THIS, DO WE?
YOU GUYS ...
DON'T TEASE HER.

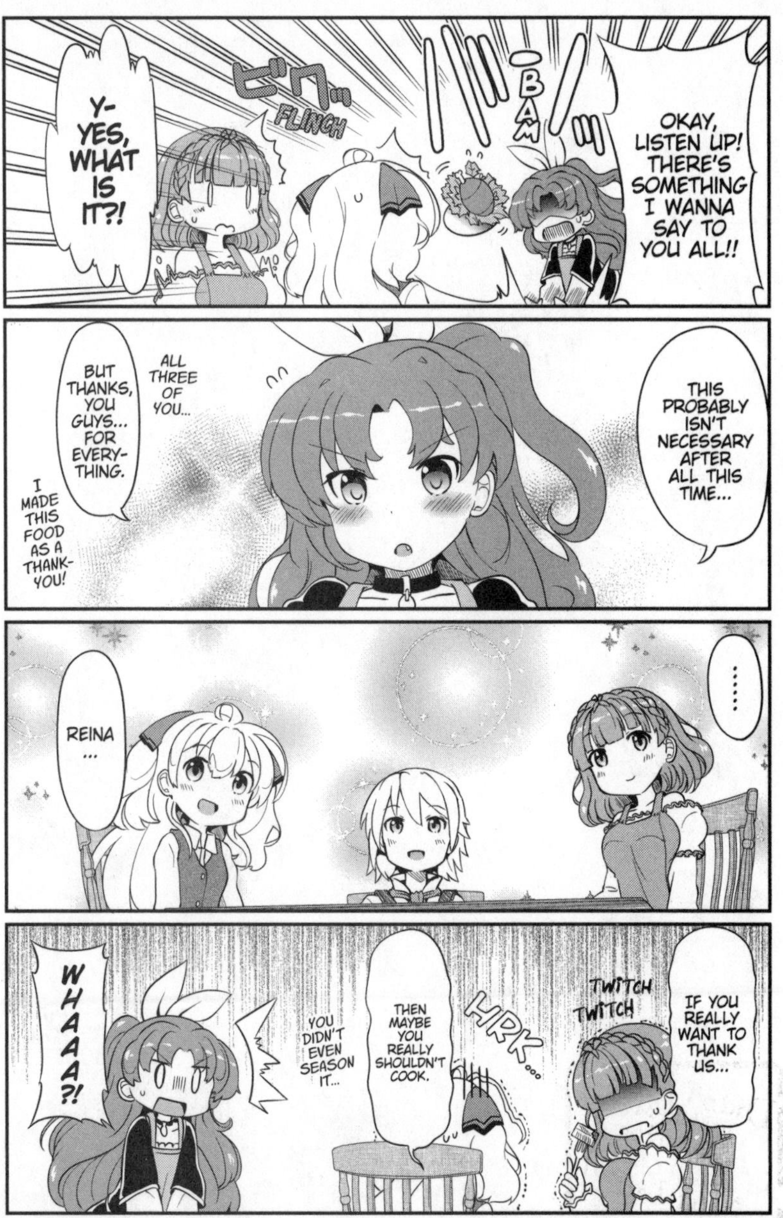
OKAY, LISTEN UP! THERE'S SOMETHING I WANNA SAY TO YOU ALL!!
BAM
FLINCH
Y-YES, WHAT IS IT?!
THIS PROBABLY ISN'T NECESSARY AFTER ALL THIS TIME...
BUT THANKS, YOU GUYS... FOR EVERYTHING.
ALL THREE OF YOU...
I MADE THIS FOOD AS A THANK-YOU!
......
REINA...
IF YOU REALLY WANT TO THANK US...
TWITCH TWITCH
HRK...
THEN MAYBE YOU REALLY SHOULDN'T COOK.
YOU DIDN'T EVEN SEASON IT...
WHAAAA?!

Didn't I Say to Make My Abilities Average in the Next Life?!
EVERYDAY MISADVENTURES!

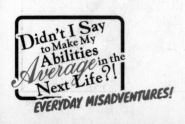

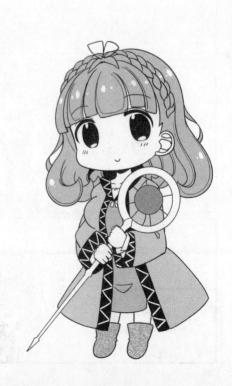

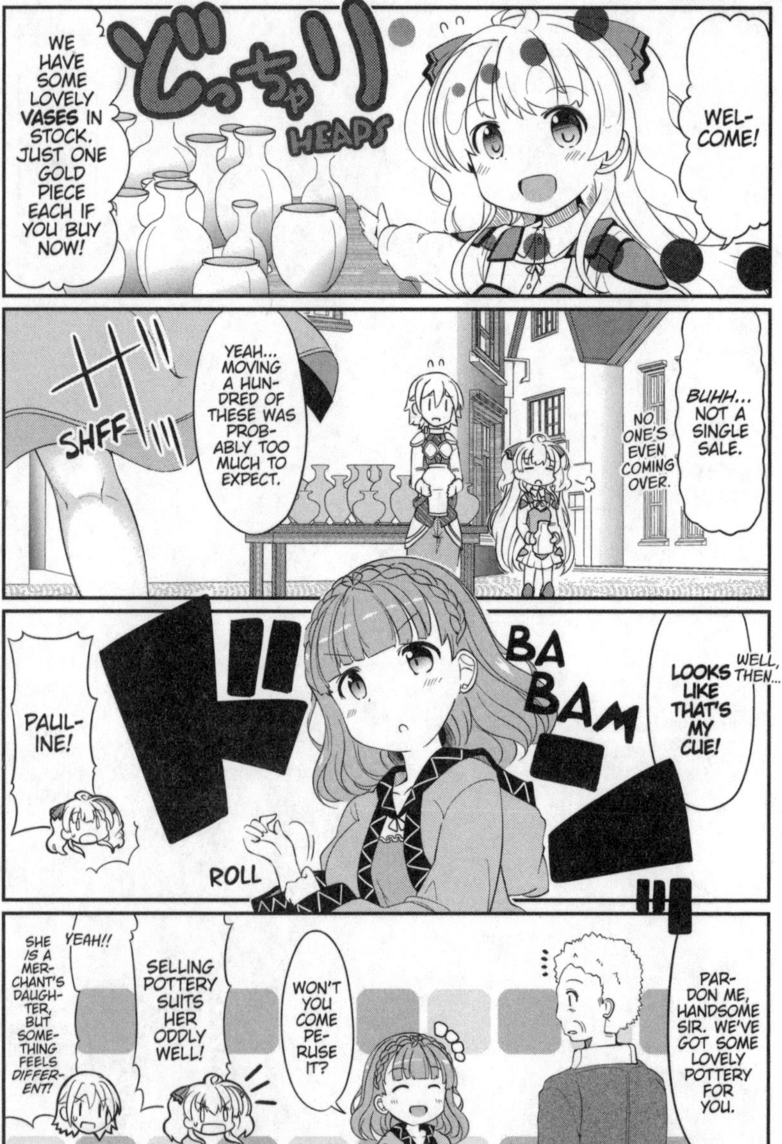
WEL-COME!
どっちゃり
HEAPS
WE HAVE SOME LOVELY VASES IN STOCK. JUST ONE GOLD PIECE EACH IF YOU BUY NOW!
BUHH... NOT A SINGLE SALE.
NO ONE'S EVEN COMING OVER.
YEAH... MOVING A HUNDRED OF THESE WAS PROBABLY TOO MUCH TO EXPECT.
SHFF
WELL, THEN...
LOOKS LIKE THAT'S MY CUE!
BA BAM
ROLL
PAULINE!
PARDON ME, HANDSOME SIR. WE'VE GOT SOME LOVELY POTTERY FOR YOU.
WON'T YOU COME PERUSE IT?
SELLING POTTERY SUITS HER ODDLY WELL!
YEAH!!
SHE IS A MERCHANT'S DAUGHTER, BUT SOMETHING FEELS DIFFERENT!

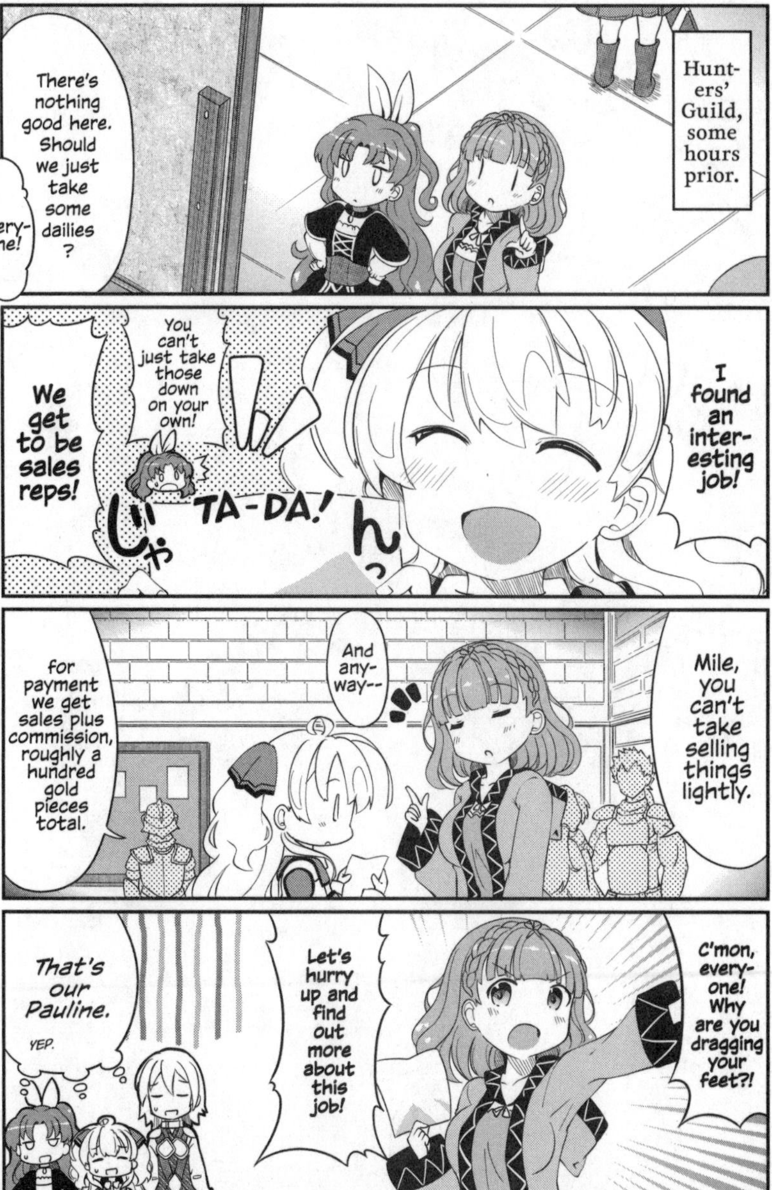
Hunters' Guild, some hours prior.
There's nothing good here. Should we just take some dailies?
Everyone!
I found an interesting job!
TA-DA!
You can't just take those down on your own!
We get to be sales reps!
Mile, you can't take selling things lightly.
And anyway--
for payment we get sales plus commission, roughly a hundred gold pieces total.
C'mon, everyone! Why are you dragging your feet?!
Let's hurry up and find out more about this job!
That's our Pauline.
YEP.

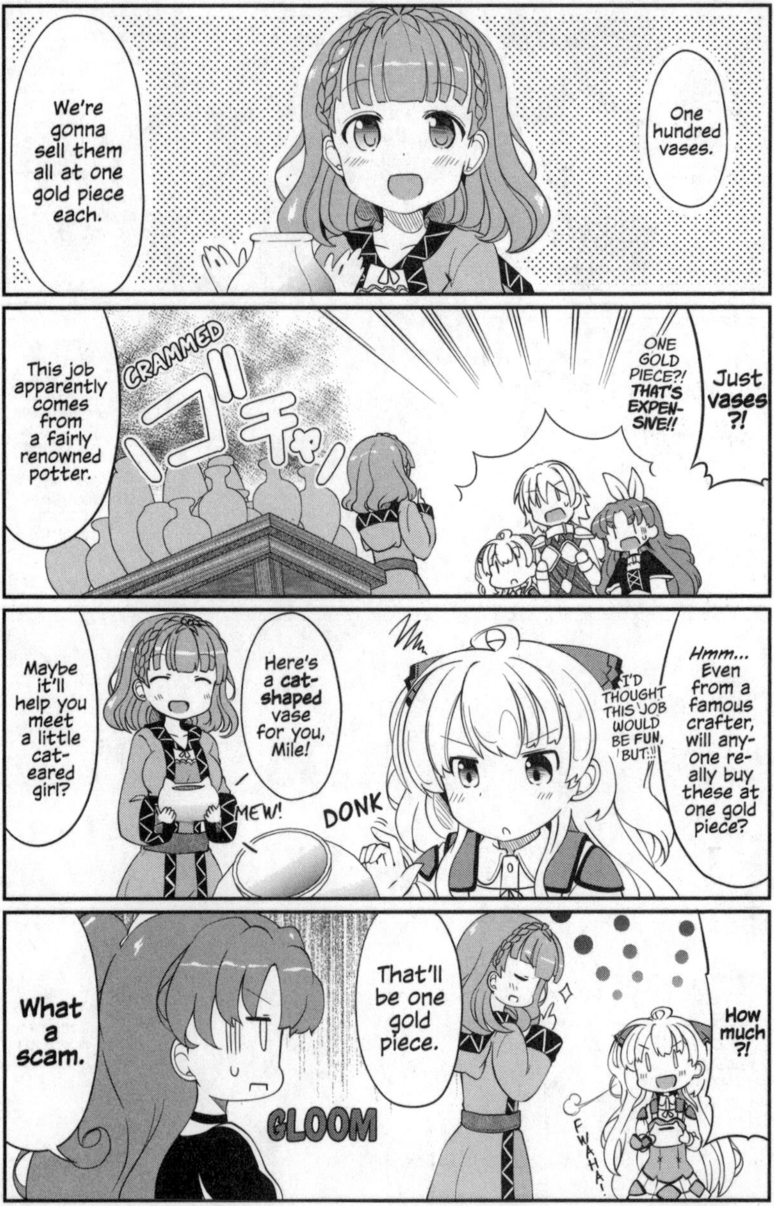

One hundred vases.
We're gonna sell them all at one gold piece each.
Just vases?!
ONE GOLD PIECE?! THAT'S EXPENSIVE!!
CRAMMED
This job apparently comes from a fairly renowned potter.
Hmm... Even from a famous crafter, will anyone really buy these at one gold piece?
I'D THOUGHT THIS JOB WOULD BE FUN, BUT...
DONK
MEW!
Here's a cat-shaped vase for you, Mile!
Maybe it'll help you meet a little cat-eared girl?
How much?!
FWAHA!
That'll be one gold piece.
GLOOM
What a scam.

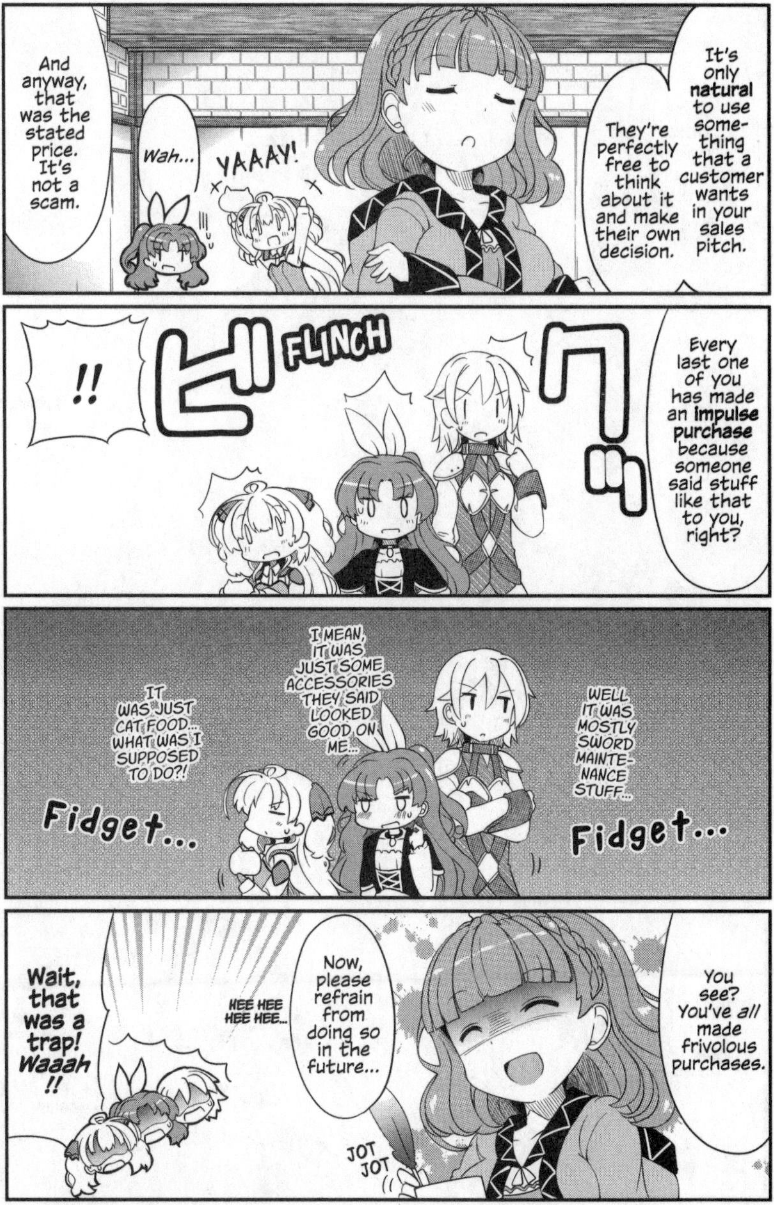

It's only natural to use something that a customer wants in your sales pitch.
They're perfectly free to think about it and make their own decision.
YAAAY!
Wah...
And anyway, that was the stated price. It's not a scam.
Every last one of you has made an impulse purchase because someone said stuff like that to you, right?
FLINCH
!!
WELL IT WAS MOSTLY SWORD MAINTENANCE STUFF...
I MEAN, IT WAS JUST SOME ACCESSORIES THEY SAID LOOKED GOOD ON ME...
IT WAS JUST CAT FOOD... WHAT WAS I SUPPOSED TO DO?!
Fidget...
Fidget...
You see? You've all made frivolous purchases.
Now, please refrain from doing so in the future...
HEE HEE HEE HEE...
JOT JOT
Wait, that was a trap! Waaah!!

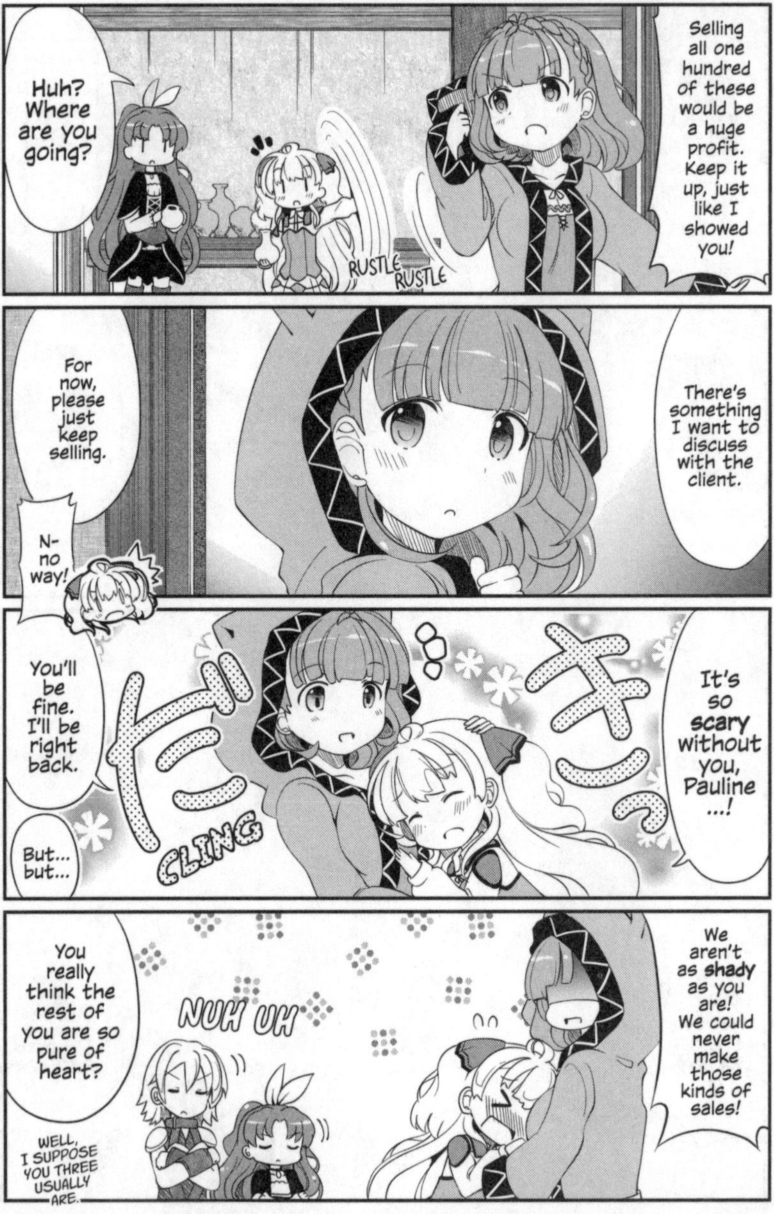
Selling all one hundred of these would be a huge profit. Keep it up, just like I showed you!
RUSTLE RUSTLE
Huh? Where are you going?
There's something I want to discuss with the client.
For now, please just keep selling.
N- no way!
It's so **scary** without you, Pauline ...!
CLING
You'll be fine. I'll be right back.
But... but...
We aren't as **shady** as you are! We could never make those kinds of sales!
NUH UH
You really think the rest of you are so pure of heart?
WELL, I SUPPOSE YOU THREE USUALLY ARE.

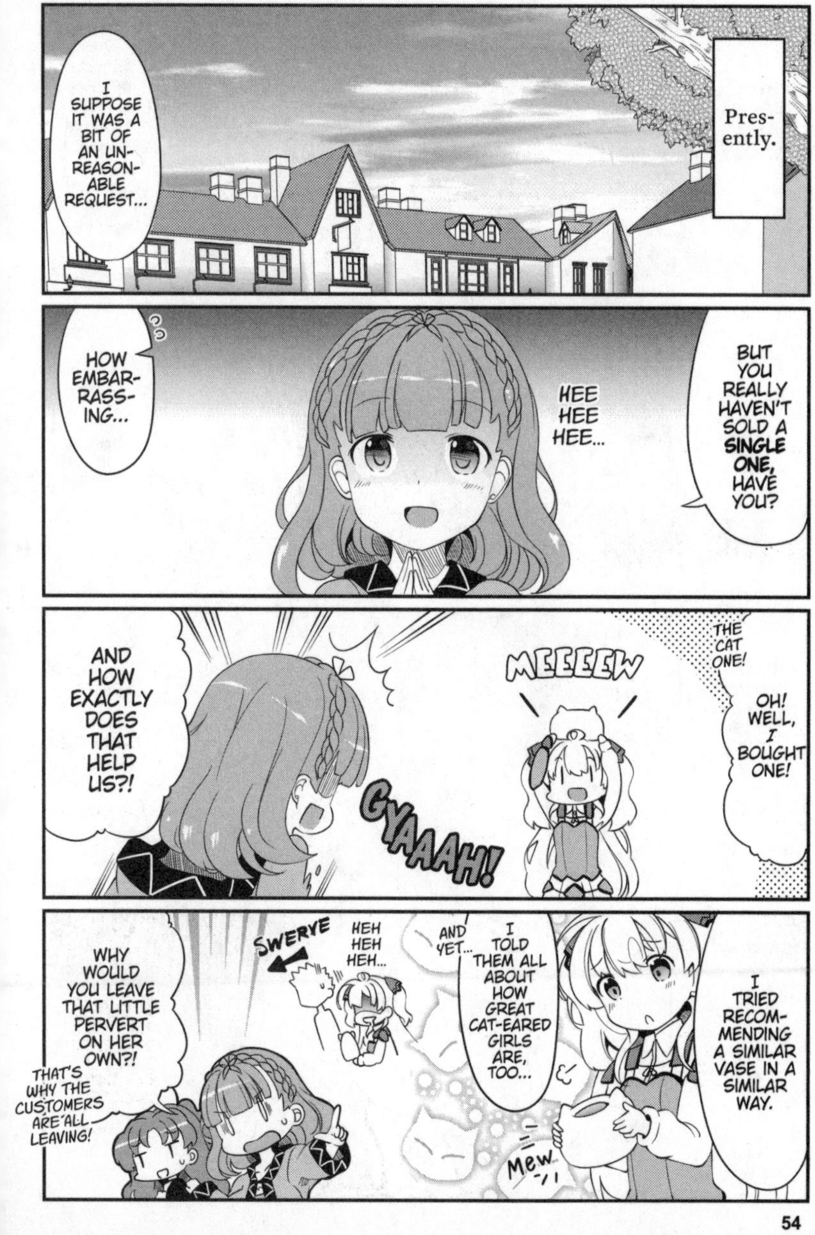
Presently.
I SUPPOSE IT WAS A BIT OF AN UNREASONABLE REQUEST...
BUT YOU REALLY HAVEN'T SOLD A SINGLE ONE, HAVE YOU?
HEE HEE HEE...
HOW EMBARRASSING...
THE CAT ONE!
OH! WELL, I BOUGHT ONE!
MEEEEW
GYAAAH!
AND HOW EXACTLY DOES THAT HELP US?!
I TRIED RECOMMENDING A SIMILAR VASE IN A SIMILAR WAY.
Mew
I TOLD THEM ALL ABOUT HOW GREAT CAT-EARED GIRLS ARE, TOO...
AND YET...
HEH HEH HEH...
SWERVE
WHY WOULD YOU LEAVE THAT LITTLE PERVERT ON HER OWN?!
THAT'S WHY THE CUSTOMERS ARE ALL LEAVING!

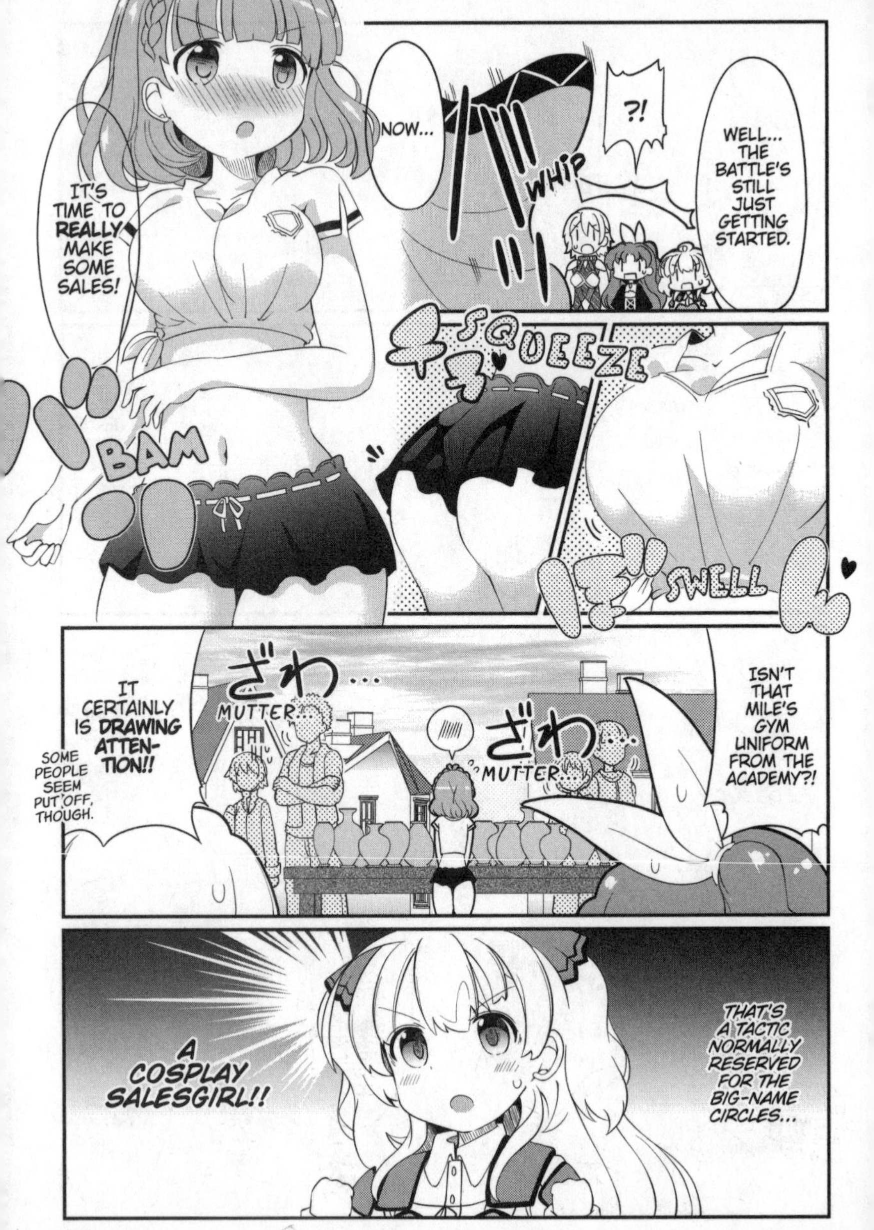
WELL... THE BATTLE'S STILL JUST GETTING STARTED.
?!
WHIP
NOW...
SWELL
SQUEEZE
IT'S TIME TO REALLY MAKE SOME SALES!
BAM
ISN'T THAT MILE'S GYM UNIFORM FROM THE ACADEMY?!
ざわ
MUTTER
ざわ...
MUTTER
IT CERTAINLY IS DRAWING ATTENTION!!
SOME PEOPLE SEEM PUT OFF, THOUGH.
THAT'S A TACTIC NORMALLY RESERVED FOR THE BIG-NAME CIRCLES...
A COSPLAY SALESGIRL!!

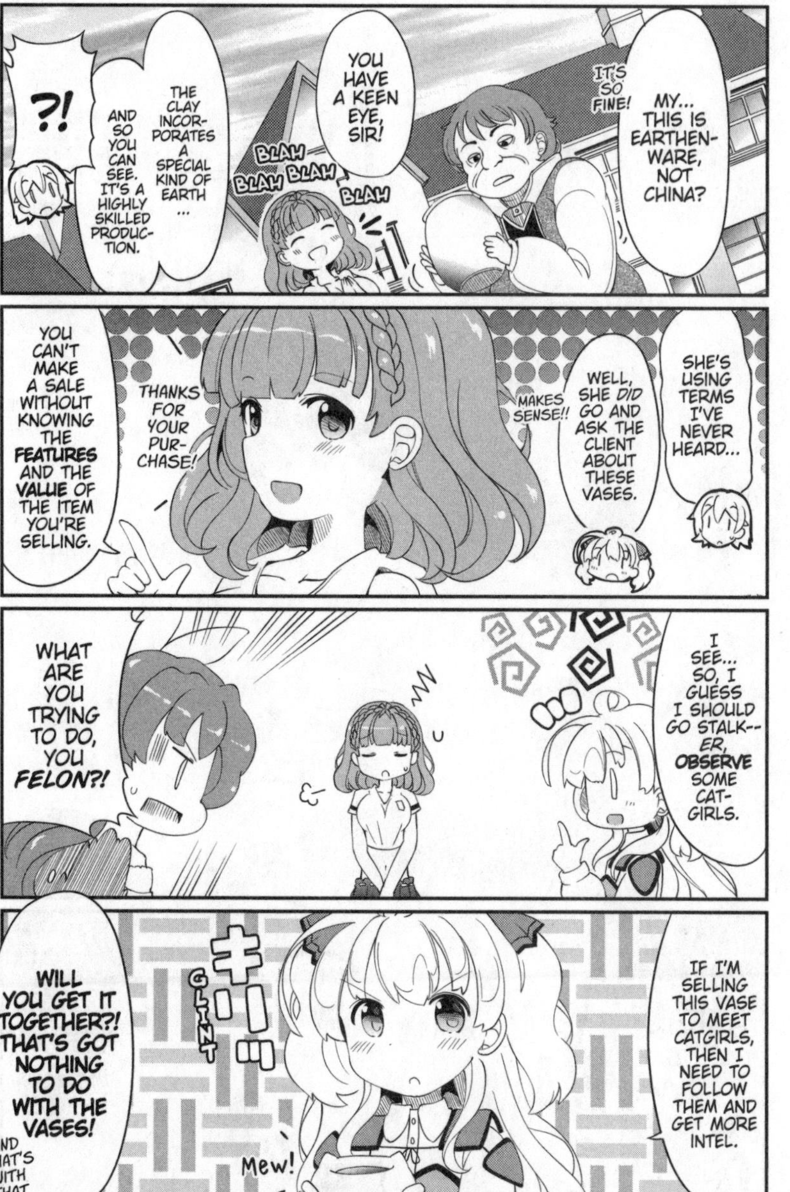
MY... THIS IS EARTHENWARE, NOT CHINA?
IT'S SO FINE!
YOU HAVE A KEEN EYE, SIR!
BLAH BLAH BLAH BLAH BLAH
THE CLAY INCORPORATES A SPECIAL KIND OF EARTH...
AND SO YOU CAN SEE. IT'S A HIGHLY SKILLED PRODUCTION.
?!
SHE'S USING TERMS I'VE NEVER HEARD...
WELL, SHE *DID* GO AND ASK THE CLIENT ABOUT THESE VASES.
MAKES SENSE!!
THANKS FOR YOUR PURCHASE!
YOU CAN'T MAKE A SALE WITHOUT KNOWING THE **FEATURES** AND THE **VALUE** OF THE ITEM YOU'RE SELLING.
I SEE... SO, I GUESS I SHOULD GO STALK-- *ER,* **OBSERVE** SOME CATGIRLS.
...
WHAT ARE YOU TRYING TO DO, YOU *FELON?!*
IF I'M SELLING THIS VASE TO MEET CATGIRLS, THEN I NEED TO FOLLOW THEM AND GET MORE INTEL.
GLINT
Mew!
WILL YOU GET IT TOGETHER?! THAT'S GOT NOTHING TO DO WITH THE VASES!
AND WHAT'S WITH THAT SERIOUS FACE?

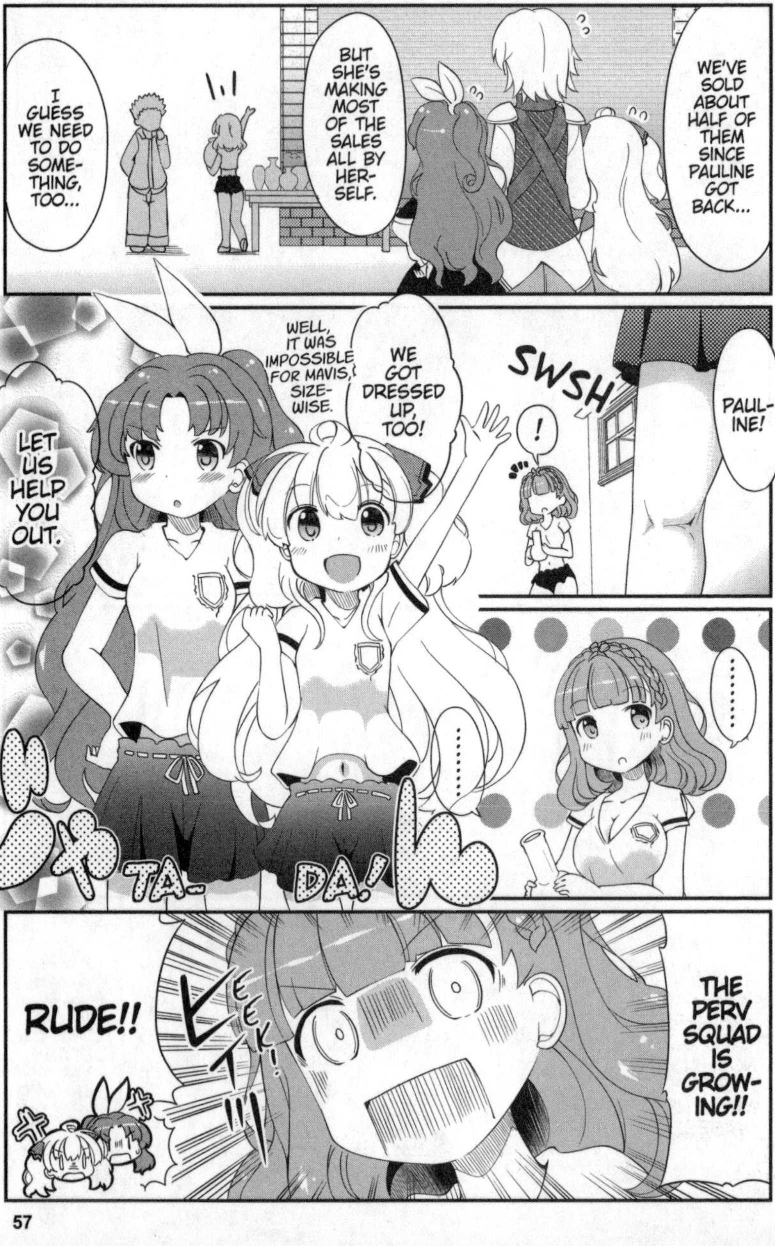
WE'VE SOLD ABOUT HALF OF THEM SINCE PAULINE GOT BACK...
BUT SHE'S MAKING MOST OF THE SALES ALL BY HER-SELF.
I GUESS WE NEED TO DO SOME-THING, TOO...
PAUL-INE!
SWSH
!
......
......
WE GOT DRESSED UP, TOO!
WELL, IT WAS IMPOSSIBLE FOR MAVIS, SIZE-WISE.
LET US HELP YOU OUT.
TA-DA!
THE PERV SQUAD IS GROW-ING!!
EEEK!!!
RUDE!!

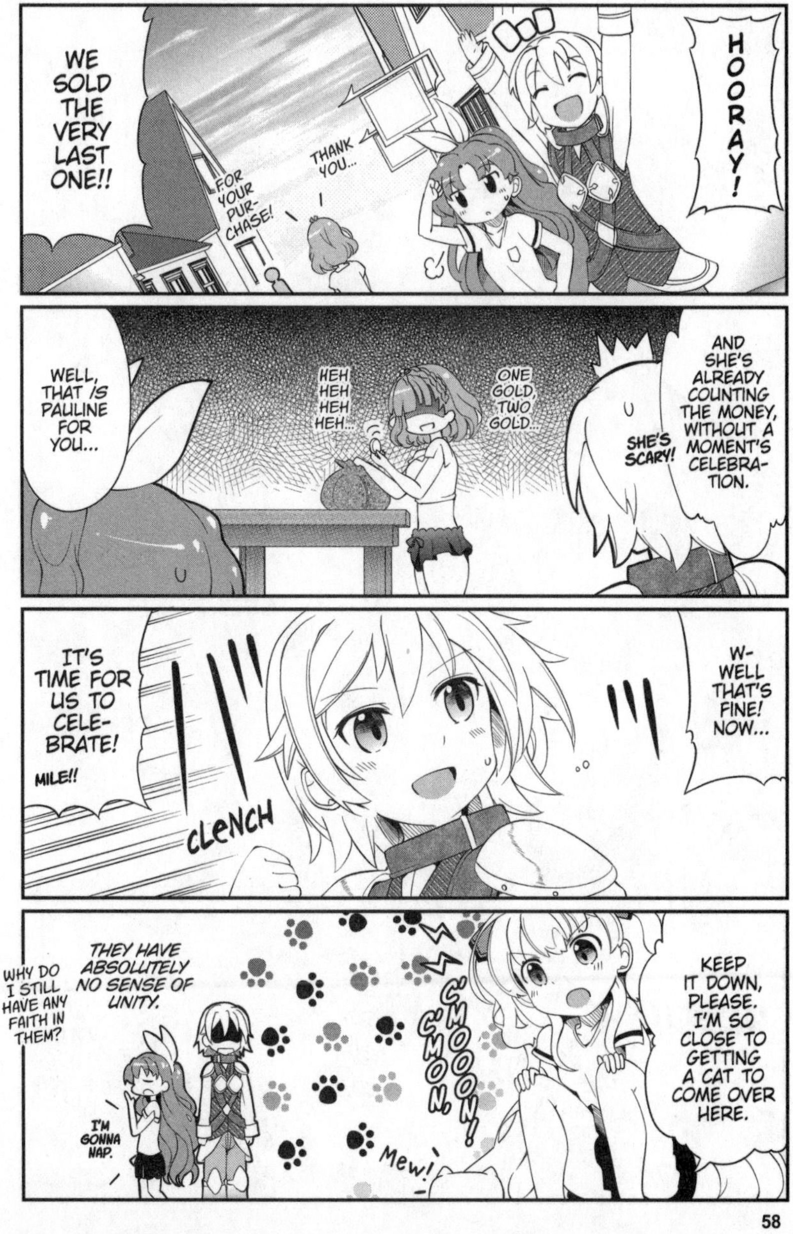
HOORAY!
WE SOLD THE VERY LAST ONE!!
THANK YOU...
FOR YOUR PURCHASE!
AND SHE'S ALREADY COUNTING THE MONEY, WITHOUT A MOMENT'S CELEBRATION.
SHE'S SCARY!
ONE GOLD, TWO GOLD...
HEH HEH HEH HEH...
WELL, THAT IS PAULINE FOR YOU...
W-WELL THAT'S FINE! NOW...
CLENCH
IT'S TIME FOR US TO CELEBRATE!
MILE!!
KEEP IT DOWN, PLEASE. I'M SO CLOSE TO GETTING A CAT TO COME OVER HERE.
C'MOOOON! C'MON,
Mew!
THEY HAVE ABSOLUTELY NO SENSE OF UNITY.
WHY DO I STILL HAVE ANY FAITH IN THEM?
I'M GONNA NAP.

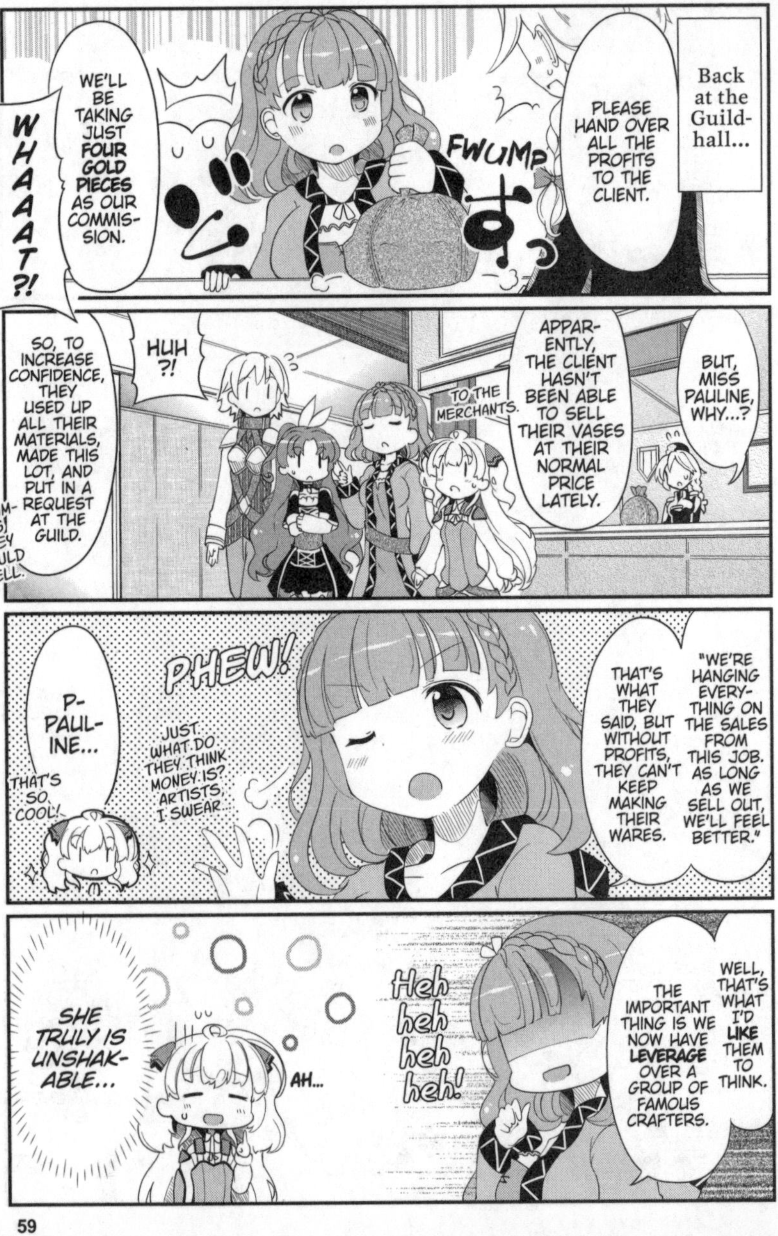
Back at the Guild-hall...
PLEASE HAND OVER ALL THE PROFITS TO THE CLIENT.
FWUMP
WE'LL BE TAKING JUST **FOUR GOLD PIECES** AS OUR COMMISSION.
WHAAAAT?!
BUT, MISS PAULINE, WHY...?
APPARENTLY, THE CLIENT HASN'T BEEN ABLE TO SELL THEIR VASES AT THEIR NORMAL PRICE LATELY.
TO THE MERCHANTS.
HUH?!
SO, TO INCREASE CONFIDENCE, THEY USED UP ALL THEIR MATERIALS, MADE THIS LOT, AND PUT IN A REQUEST AT THE GUILD.
ASSUMING THEY WOULD SELL.
"WE'RE HANGING EVERYTHING ON THE SALES FROM THIS JOB. AS LONG AS WE SELL OUT, WE'LL FEEL BETTER."
THAT'S WHAT THEY SAID, BUT WITHOUT PROFITS, THEY CAN'T KEEP MAKING THEIR WARES.
PHEW!
JUST WHAT DO THEY THINK MONEY IS? ARTISTS, I SWEAR...
P-PAULINE...
THAT'S SO COOL!
WELL, THAT'S WHAT I'D **LIKE** THEM TO THINK.
THE IMPORTANT THING IS WE NOW HAVE **LEVERAGE** OVER A GROUP OF FAMOUS CRAFTERS.
Heh heh heh heh!
AH...
SHE TRULY IS UNSHAKABLE...

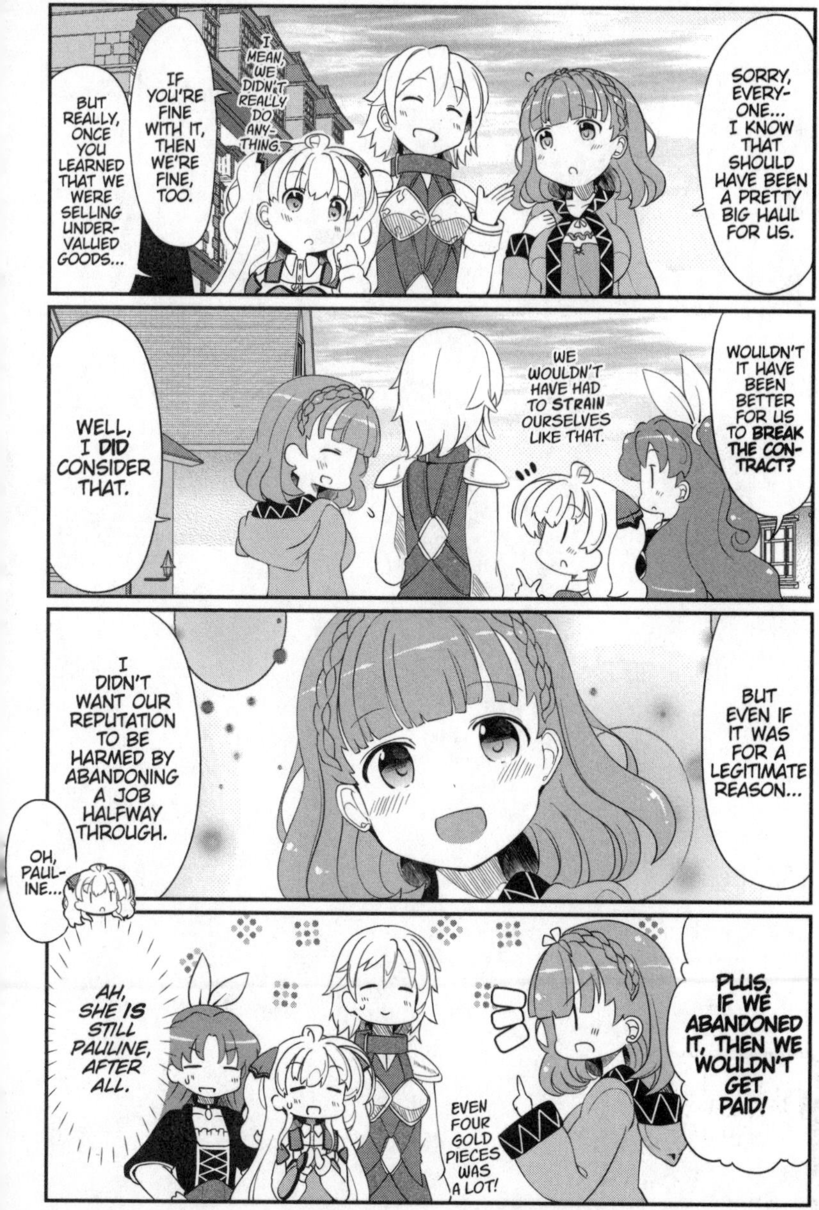
SORRY, EVERYONE... I KNOW THAT SHOULD HAVE BEEN A PRETTY BIG HAUL FOR US.
I MEAN, WE DIDN'T REALLY DO ANYTHING.
IF YOU'RE FINE WITH IT, THEN WE'RE FINE, TOO.
BUT REALLY, ONCE YOU LEARNED THAT WE WERE SELLING UNDERVALUED GOODS...
WOULDN'T IT HAVE BEEN BETTER FOR US TO BREAK THE CONTRACT?
WE WOULDN'T HAVE HAD TO STRAIN OURSELVES LIKE THAT.
WELL, I DID CONSIDER THAT.
BUT EVEN IF IT WAS FOR A LEGITIMATE REASON...
I DIDN'T WANT OUR REPUTATION TO BE HARMED BY ABANDONING A JOB HALFWAY THROUGH.
OH, PAULINE...
PLUS, IF WE ABANDONED IT, THEN WE WOULDN'T GET PAID!
EVEN FOUR GOLD PIECES WAS A LOT!
AH, SHE IS STILL PAULINE, AFTER ALL.

Didn't I Say to Make My Abilities Average in the Next Life?!
EVERYDAY MISADVENTURES!

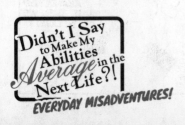

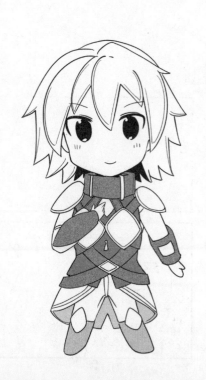

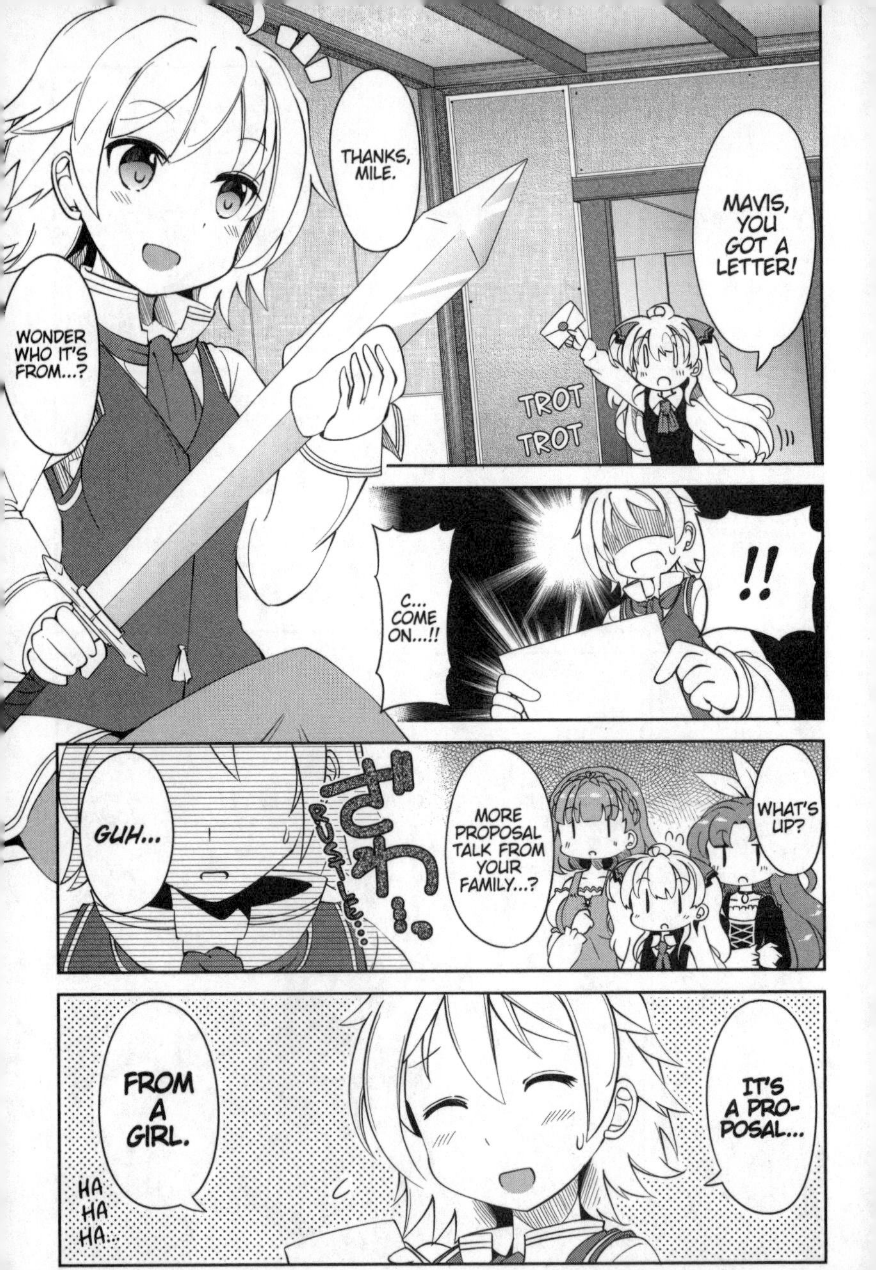
MAVIS, YOU GOT A LETTER!
TROT TROT
!!
C... COME ON...!!
THANKS, MILE.
WONDER WHO IT'S FROM...?
WHAT'S UP?
MORE PROPOSAL TALK FROM YOUR FAMILY...?
ざわ...
RUSTLE...
GUH...
IT'S A PRO-POSAL...
FROM A GIRL.
HA HA HA...

Chapter 5

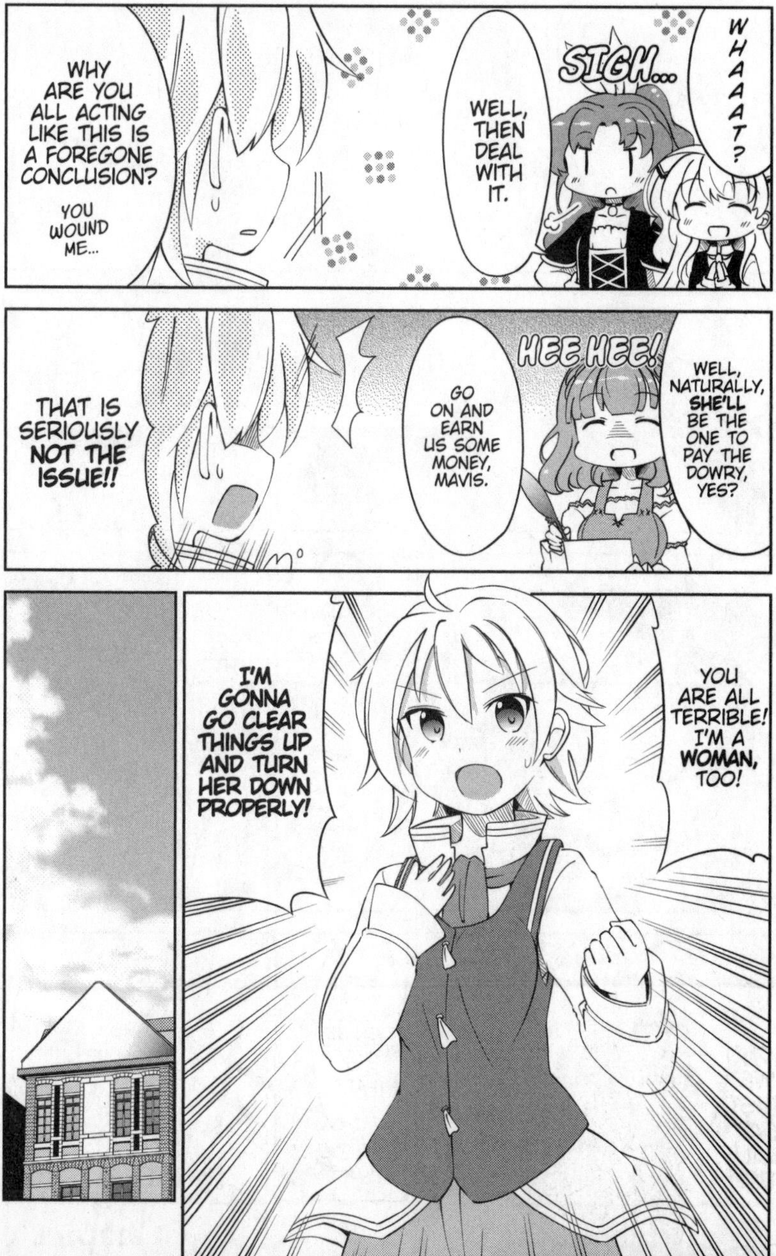
WHAAAT?
SIGH...
WELL, THEN DEAL WITH IT.
WHY ARE YOU ALL ACTING LIKE THIS IS A FOREGONE CONCLUSION?
YOU WOUND ME...
WELL, NATURALLY, SHE'LL BE THE ONE TO PAY THE DOWRY, YES?
HEE HEE!
GO ON AND EARN US SOME MONEY, MAVIS.
THAT IS SERIOUSLY NOT THE ISSUE!!
YOU ARE ALL TERRIBLE! I'M A WOMAN, TOO!
I'M GONNA GO CLEAR THINGS UP AND TURN HER DOWN PROPERLY!

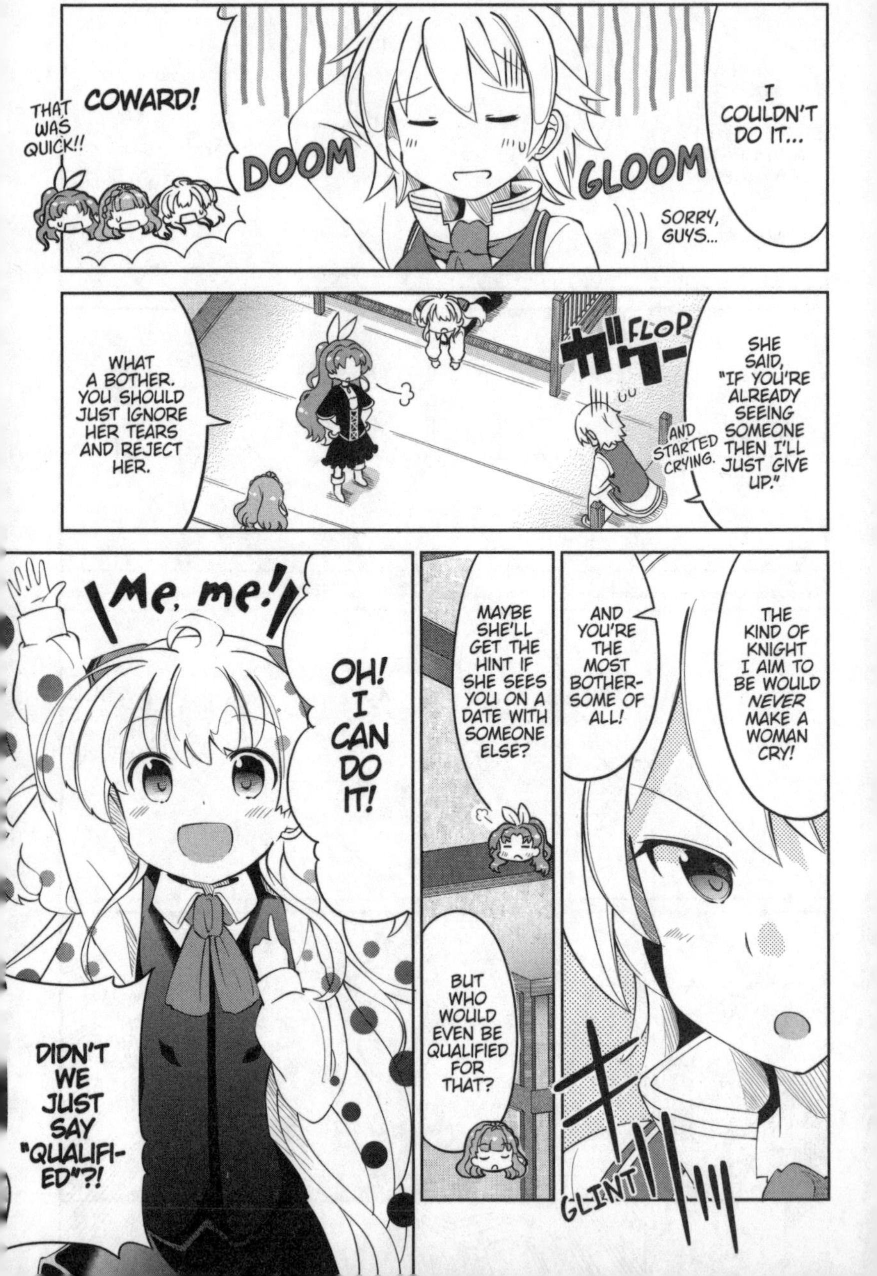
I COULDN'T DO IT...
GLOOM
SORRY, GUYS...
DOOM
COWARD!
THAT WAS QUICK!!
SHE SAID, "IF YOU'RE ALREADY SEEING SOMEONE THEN I'LL JUST GIVE UP."
FLOP
AND STARTED CRYING.
WHAT A BOTHER. YOU SHOULD JUST IGNORE HER TEARS AND REJECT HER.
THE KIND OF KNIGHT I AIM TO BE WOULD *NEVER* MAKE A WOMAN CRY!
GLINT
AND YOU'RE THE MOST BOTHER-SOME OF ALL!
MAYBE SHE'LL GET THE HINT IF SHE SEES YOU ON A DATE WITH SOMEONE ELSE?
BUT WHO WOULD EVEN BE QUALIFIED FOR THAT?
Me, me!
OH! I CAN DO IT!
DIDN'T WE JUST SAY "QUALIFI-ED"?!

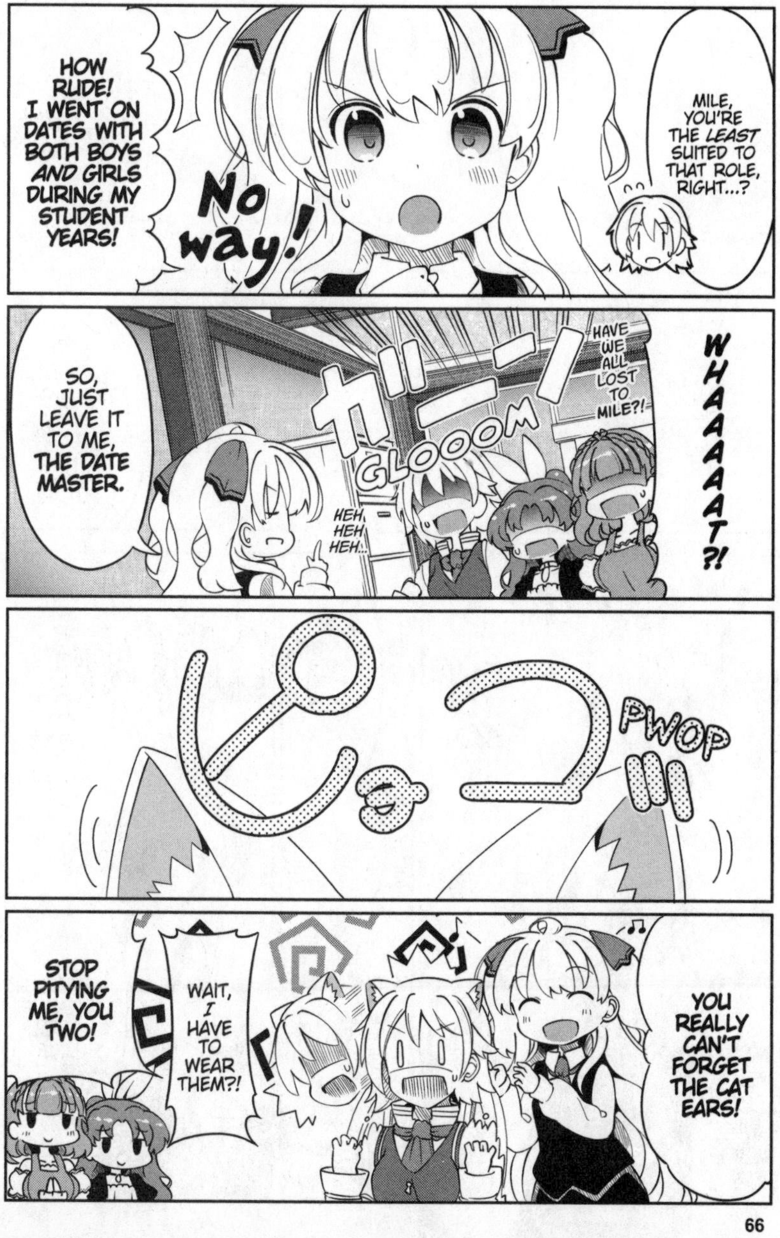
MILE, YOU'RE THE *LEAST* SUITED TO THAT ROLE, RIGHT...?
No way!
HOW RUDE! I WENT ON DATES WITH BOTH BOYS *AND* GIRLS DURING MY STUDENT YEARS!
WHAAAAAAT?!
HAVE WE ALL LOST TO MILE?!
GLOOOM
HEH HEH HEH...
SO, JUST LEAVE IT TO ME, THE DATE MASTER.
PWOP
YOU REALLY CAN'T FORGET THE CAT EARS!
WAIT, I HAVE TO WEAR THEM?!
STOP PITYING ME, YOU TWO!

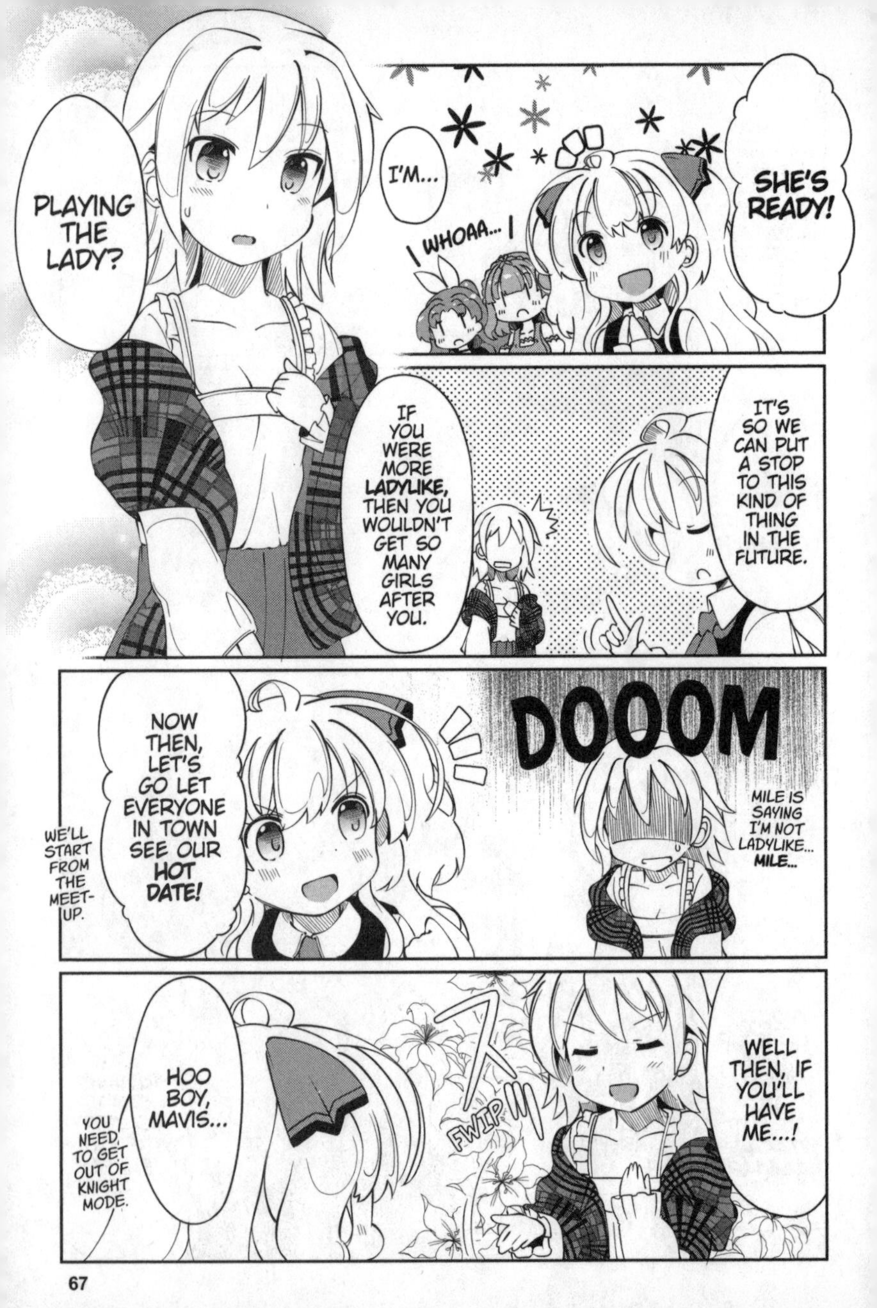
SHE'S READY!
WHOAA...
I'M...
IT'S SO WE CAN PUT A STOP TO THIS KIND OF THING IN THE FUTURE.
IF YOU WERE MORE LADYLIKE, THEN YOU WOULDN'T GET SO MANY GIRLS AFTER YOU.
PLAYING THE LADY?
DOOOM
MILE IS SAYING I'M NOT LADYLIKE... MILE...
NOW THEN, LET'S GO LET EVERYONE IN TOWN SEE OUR HOT DATE!
WE'LL START FROM THE MEET-UP.
WELL THEN, IF YOU'LL HAVE ME...!
FWIP
HOO BOY, MAVIS...
YOU NEED TO GET OUT OF KNIGHT MODE.

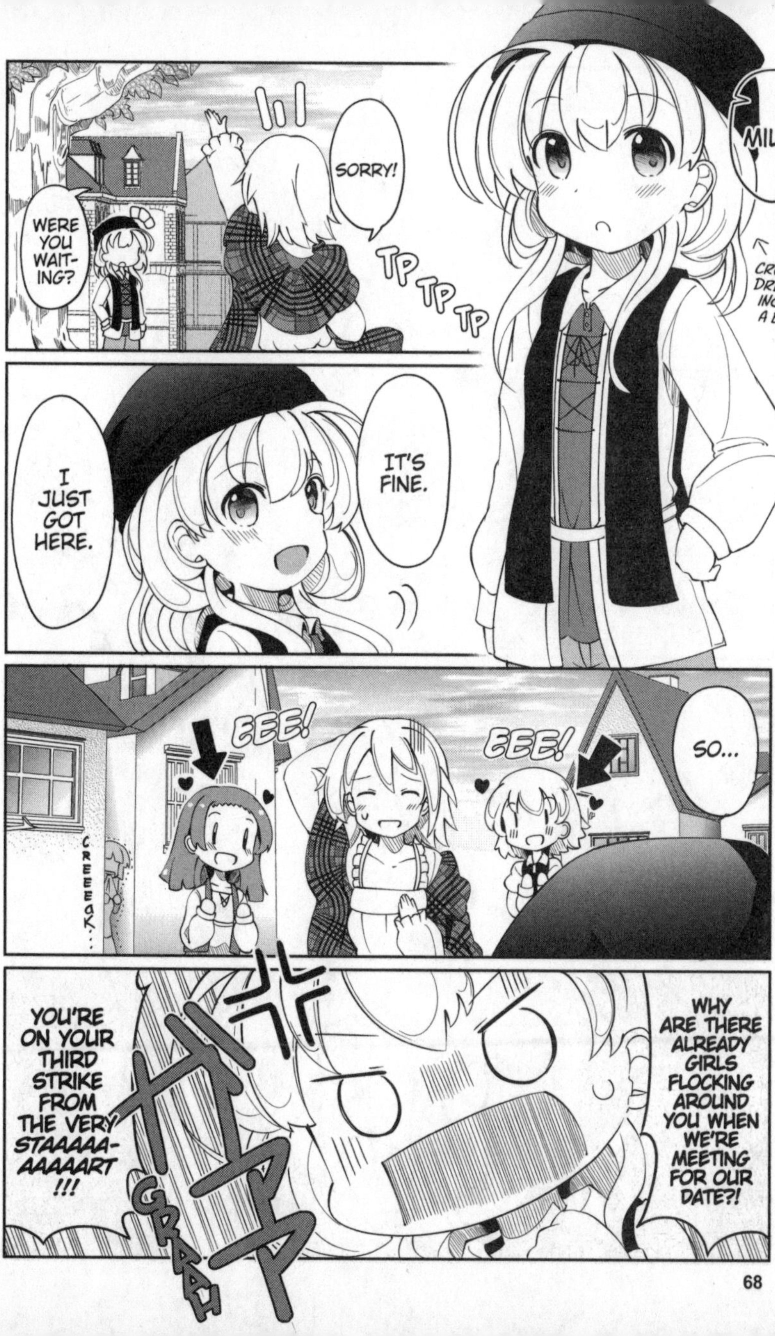
MILE!
CROSS-DRESSING AS A BOY.
SORRY!
TP TP TP
WERE YOU WAITING?
IT'S FINE.
I JUST GOT HERE.
SO...
EEE!
EEE!
CREEEAK...
WHY ARE THERE ALREADY GIRLS FLOCKING AROUND YOU WHEN WE'RE MEETING FOR OUR DATE?!
YOU'RE ON YOUR THIRD STRIKE FROM THE VERY STAAAAAA-AAAAART!!!
GRAAH

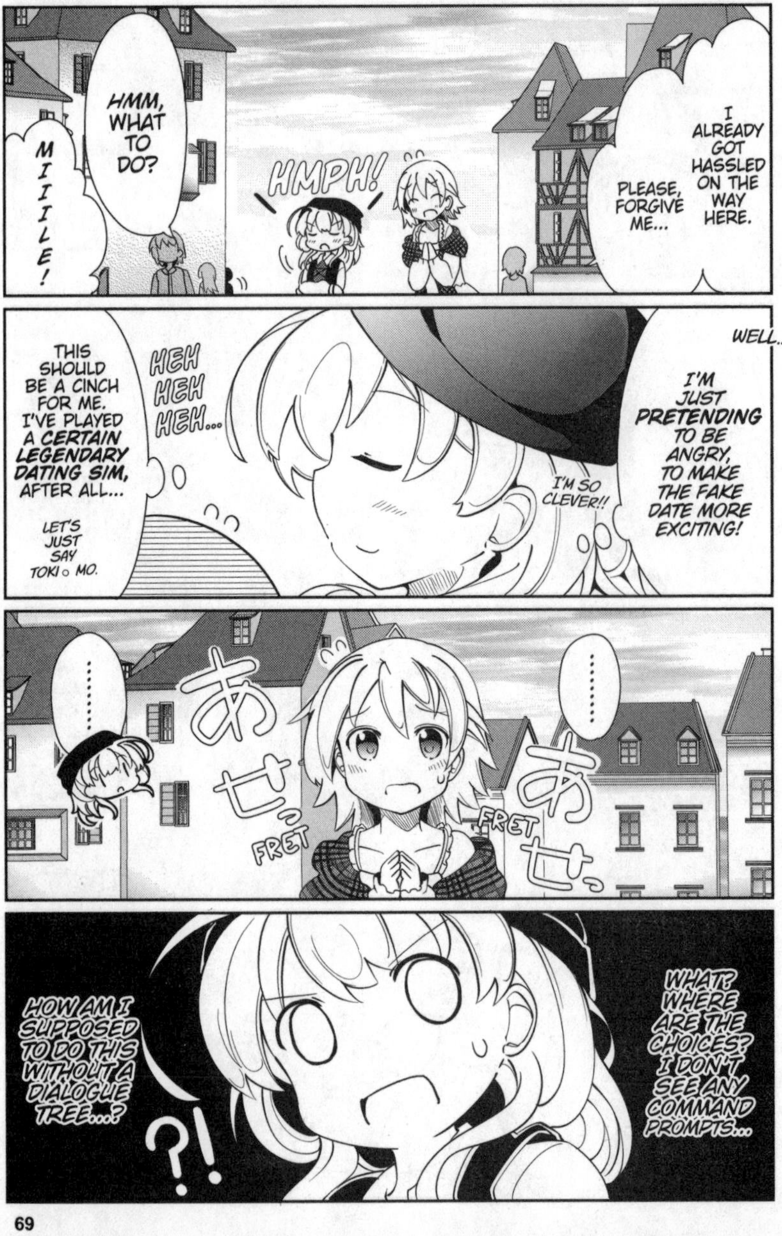
I ALREADY GOT HASSLED ON THE WAY HERE.
PLEASE, FORGIVE ME...
HMPH!
HMM, WHAT TO DO?
MIIILE!
WELL...
I'M JUST PRETENDING TO BE ANGRY, TO MAKE THE FAKE DATE MORE EXCITING!
I'M SO CLEVER!!
HEH HEH HEH...
THIS SHOULD BE A CINCH FOR ME. I'VE PLAYED A CERTAIN LEGENDARY DATING SIM, AFTER ALL...
LET'S JUST SAY TOKI○MO.
......
あせっ
FRET
あせっ
FRET
......
WHAT? WHERE ARE THE CHOICES? I DON'T SEE ANY COMMAND PROMPTS...
HOW AM I SUPPOSED TO DO THIS WITHOUT A DIALOGUE TREE...?
?!

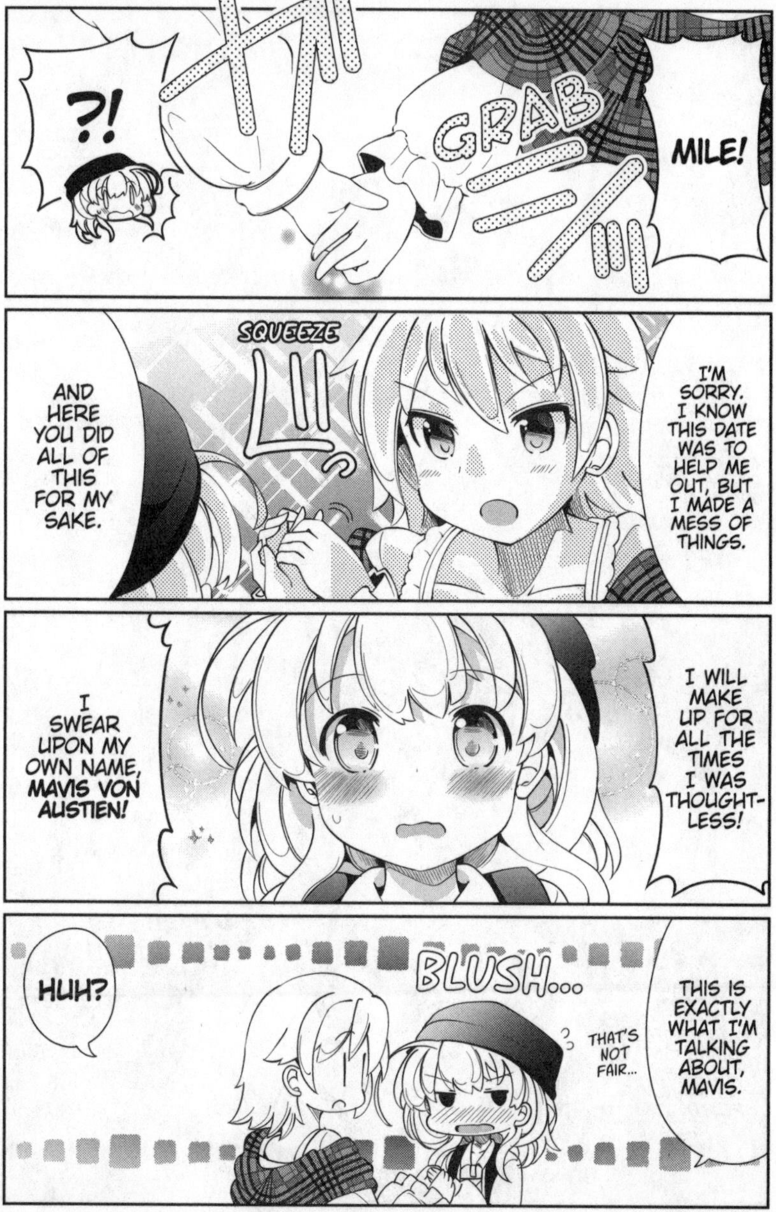
MILE!
GRAB
?!
I'M SORRY. I KNOW THIS DATE WAS TO HELP ME OUT, BUT I MADE A MESS OF THINGS.
SQUEEZE
AND HERE YOU DID ALL OF THIS FOR MY SAKE.
I WILL MAKE UP FOR ALL THE TIMES I WAS THOUGHT-LESS!
I SWEAR UPON MY OWN NAME, MAVIS VON AUSTIEN!
THIS IS EXACTLY WHAT I'M TALKING ABOUT, MAVIS.
THAT'S NOT FAIR...
BLUSH...
HUH?

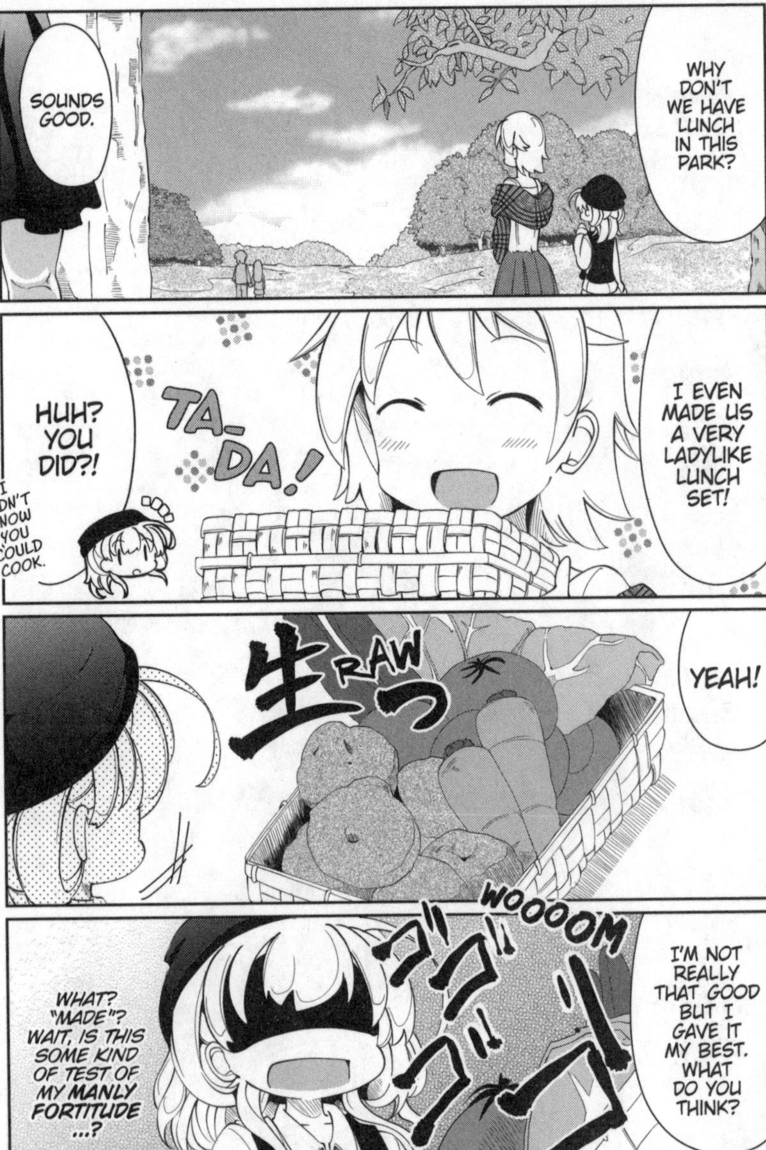

WHY DON'T WE HAVE LUNCH IN THIS PARK?
SOUNDS GOOD.
I EVEN MADE US A VERY LADYLIKE LUNCH SET!
TA-DA!
HUH? YOU DID?!
I DIDN'T KNOW YOU COULD COOK.
YEAH!
生つ
RAW
I'M NOT REALLY THAT GOOD BUT I GAVE IT MY BEST. WHAT DO YOU THINK?
WOOOOM
WHAT? "MADE"? WAIT, IS THIS SOME KIND OF TEST OF MY MANLY FORTITUDE ...?

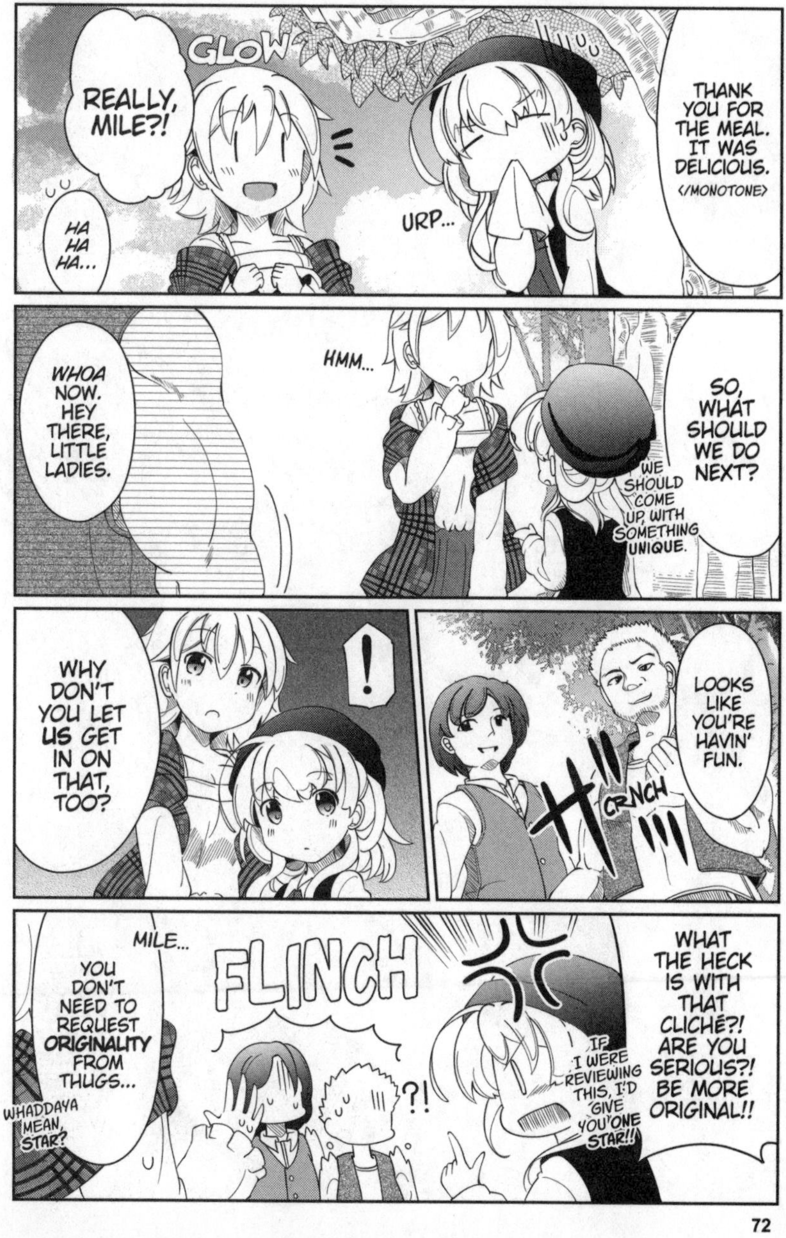
THANK YOU FOR THE MEAL. IT WAS DELICIOUS.
</MONOTONE>
URP...
GLOW
REALLY, MILE?!
HA HA HA...
SO, WHAT SHOULD WE DO NEXT?
WE SHOULD COME UP, WITH SOMETHING UNIQUE.
HMM...
WHOA NOW. HEY THERE, LITTLE LADIES.
LOOKS LIKE YOU'RE HAVIN' FUN.
CRNCH
!
WHY DON'T YOU LET US GET IN ON THAT, TOO?
WHAT THE HECK IS WITH THAT CLICHÉ?! ARE YOU SERIOUS?! BE MORE ORIGINAL!!
IF I WERE REVIEWING THIS, I'D GIVE YOU ONE STAR!!
?!
FLINCH
MILE...
YOU DON'T NEED TO REQUEST ORIGINALITY FROM THUGS...
WHADDAYA MEAN, STAR?

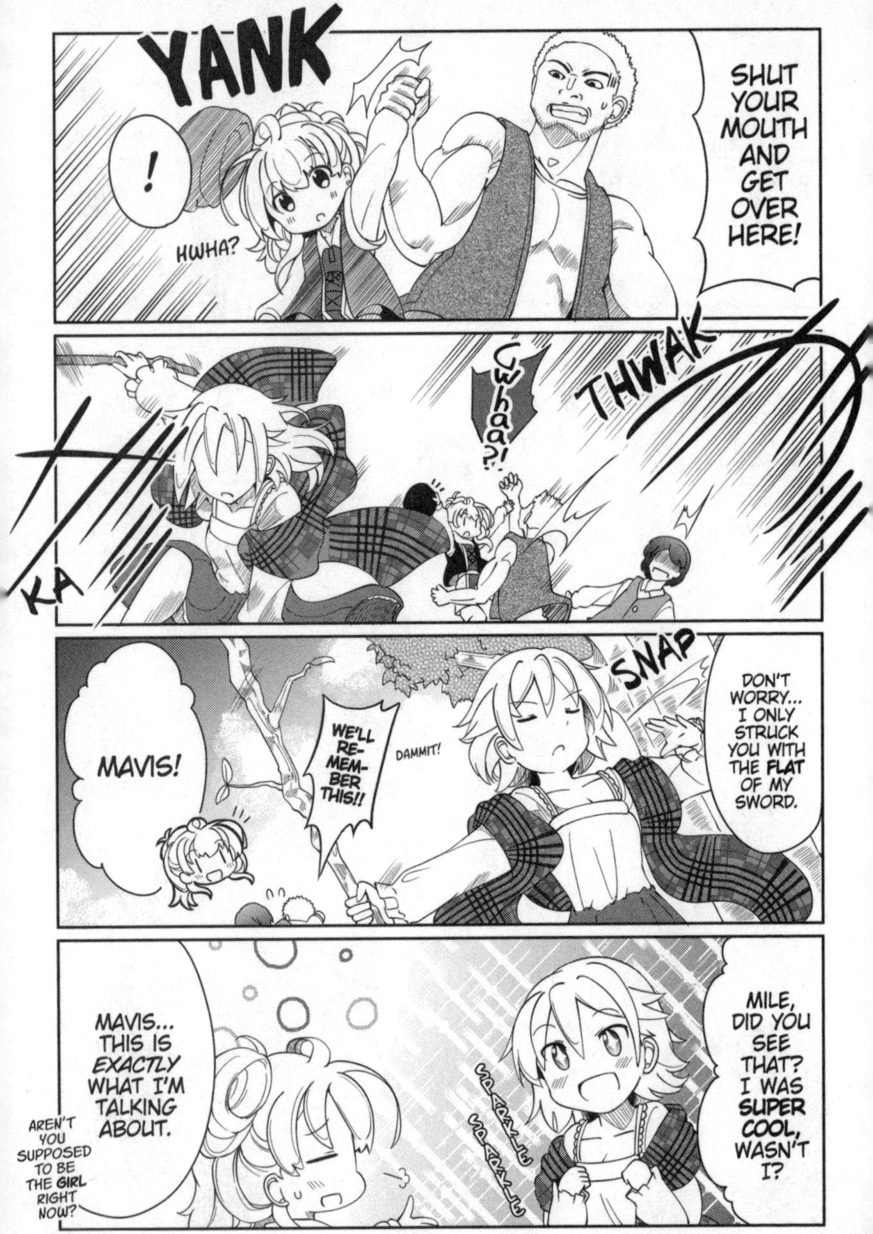
SHUT YOUR MOUTH AND GET OVER HERE!
YANK
!
HWHA?
THWAK
Gwhaa?!
KA
SNAP
DON'T WORRY... I ONLY STRUCK YOU WITH THE FLAT OF MY SWORD.
DAMMIT!
WE'LL RE-MEM-BER THIS!!
MAVIS!
MILE, DID YOU SEE THAT? I WAS SUPER COOL, WASN'T I?
MAVIS... THIS IS EXACTLY WHAT I'M TALKING ABOUT.
AREN'T YOU SUPPOSED TO BE THE GIRL RIGHT NOW?

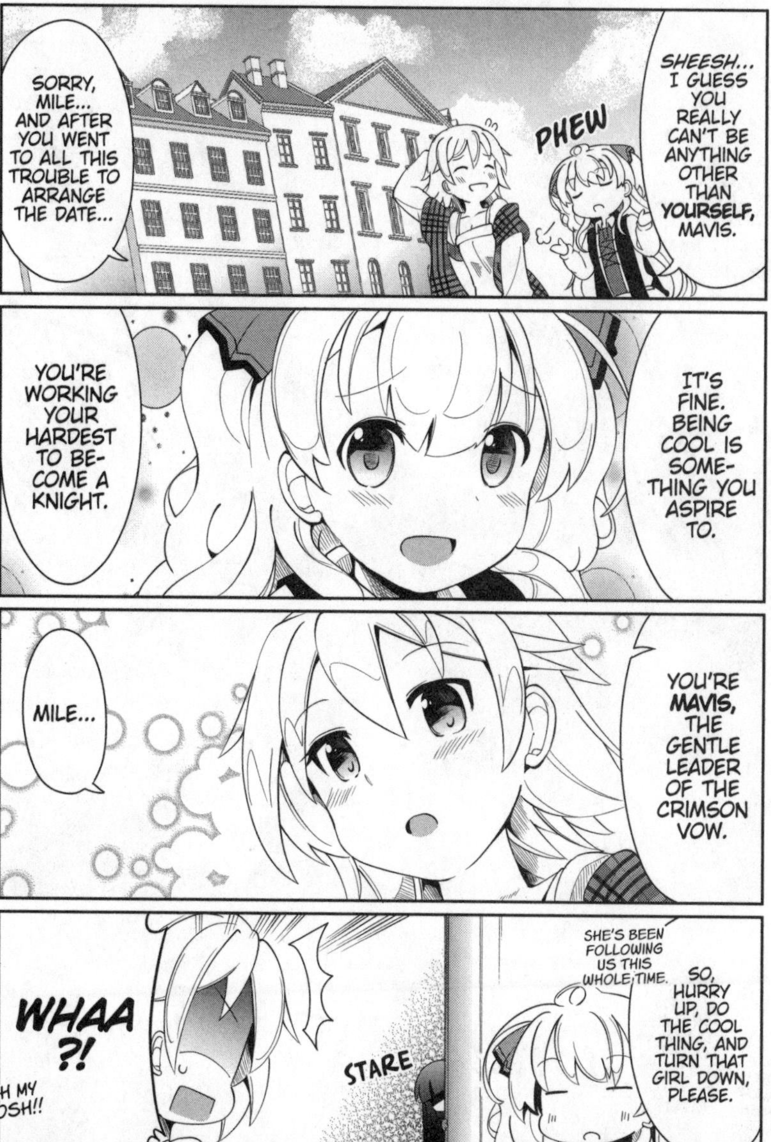
SHEESH... I GUESS YOU REALLY CAN'T BE ANYTHING OTHER THAN **YOURSELF,** MAVIS.
PHEW
SORRY, MILE... AND AFTER YOU WENT TO ALL THIS TROUBLE TO ARRANGE THE DATE...
IT'S FINE. BEING COOL IS SOME-THING YOU ASPIRE TO.
YOU'RE WORKING YOUR HARDEST TO BE-COME A KNIGHT.
YOU'RE **MAVIS,** THE GENTLE LEADER OF THE CRIMSON VOW.
MILE...
SHE'S BEEN FOLLOWING US THIS WHOLE TIME.
SO, HURRY UP, DO THE COOL THING, AND TURN THAT GIRL DOWN, PLEASE.
STARE
WHAA ?!
OH MY GOSH!!

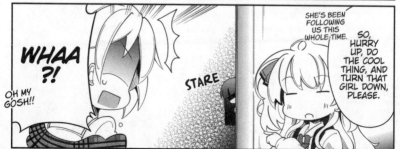

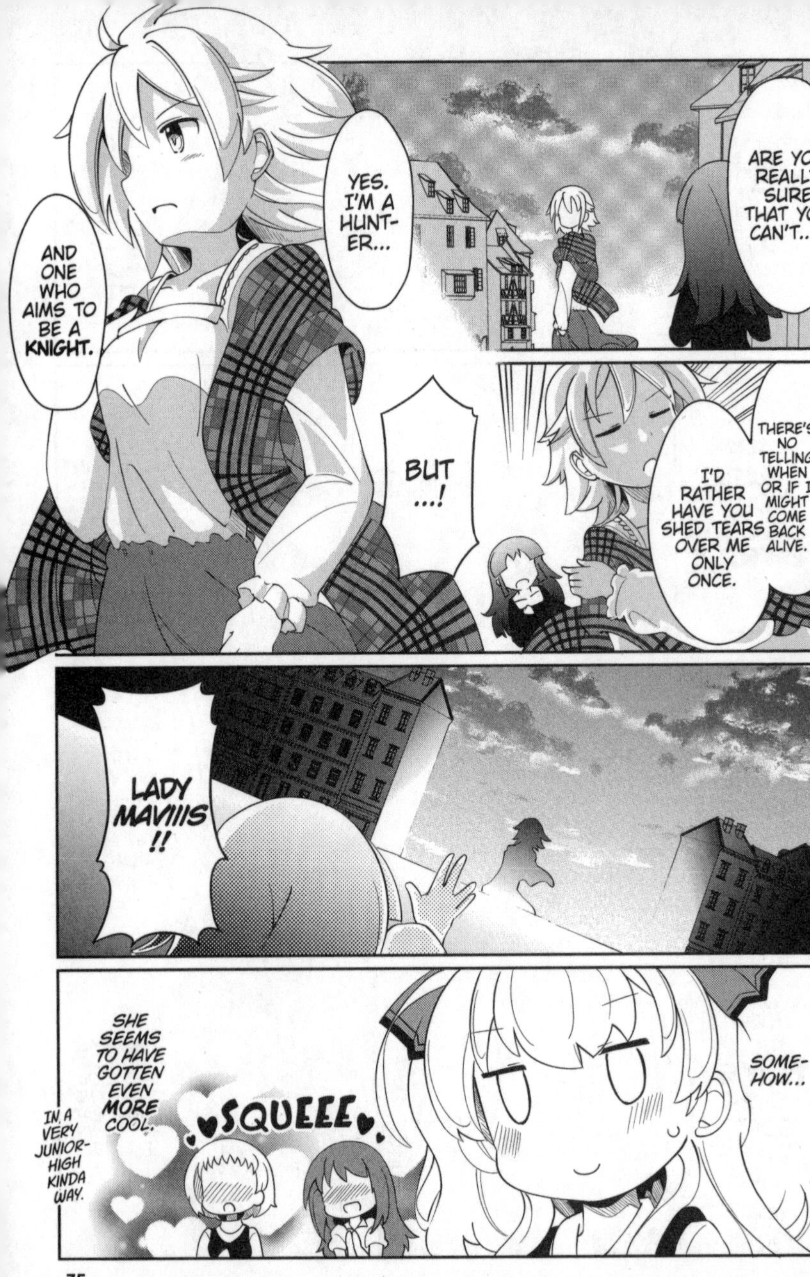
ARE YOU REALLY SURE THAT YOU CAN'T...?
YES. I'M A HUNTER...
THERE'S NO TELLING WHEN OR IF I MIGHT COME BACK ALIVE.
I'D RATHER HAVE YOU SHED TEARS OVER ME ONLY ONCE.
BUT...!
AND ONE WHO AIMS TO BE A KNIGHT.
LADY MAVIIIS!!
SOME-HOW...
SHE SEEMS TO HAVE GOTTEN EVEN MORE COOL.
SQUEEE
IN A VERY JUNIOR-HIGH KINDA WAY.

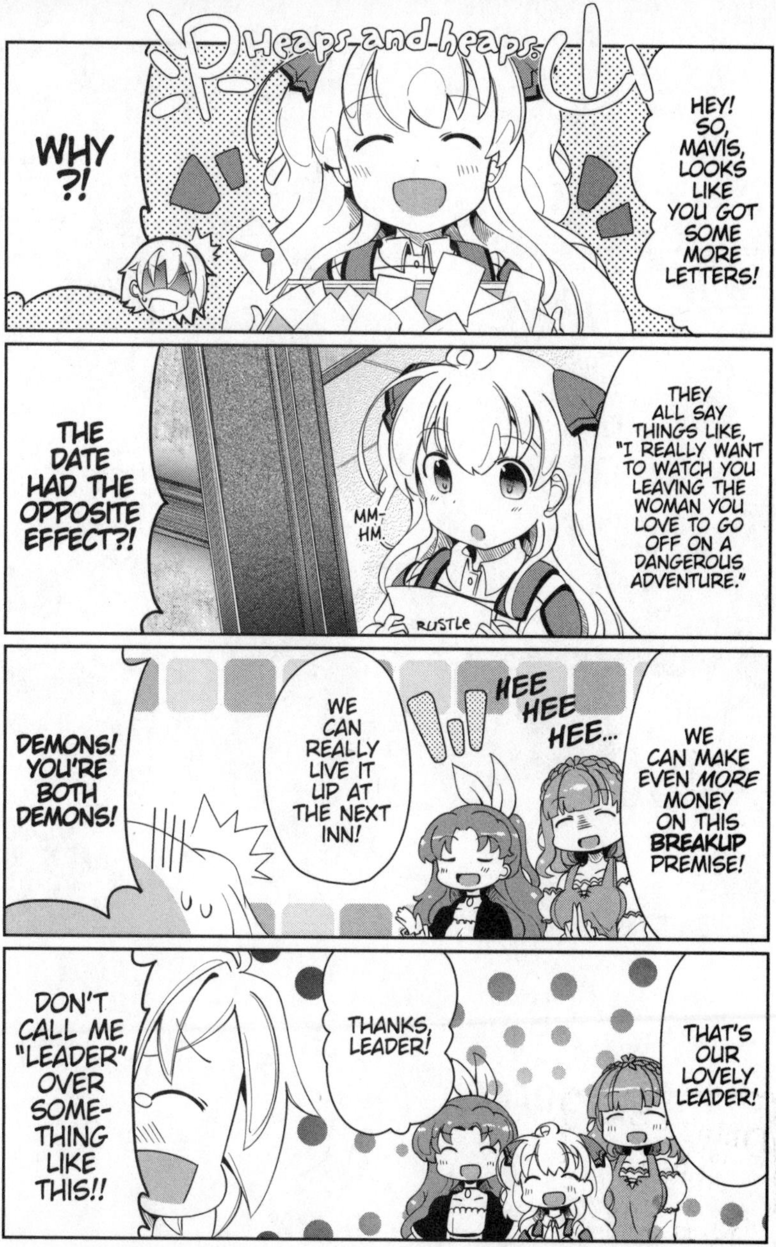
Heaps and heaps.
HEY! SO, MAVIS, LOOKS LIKE YOU GOT SOME MORE LETTERS!
WHY?!
THEY ALL SAY THINGS LIKE, "I REALLY WANT TO WATCH YOU LEAVING THE WOMAN YOU LOVE TO GO OFF ON A DANGEROUS ADVENTURE."
MM-HM.
RUSTLE
THE DATE HAD THE OPPOSITE EFFECT?!
WE CAN MAKE EVEN MORE MONEY ON THIS BREAKUP PREMISE!
HEE HEE HEE...
WE CAN REALLY LIVE IT UP AT THE NEXT INN!
DEMONS! YOU'RE BOTH DEMONS!
THAT'S OUR LOVELY LEADER!
THANKS, LEADER!
DON'T CALL ME "LEADER" OVER SOME-THING LIKE THIS!!

Didn't I Say to Make My Abilities Average in the Next Life?!
EVERYDAY MISADVENTURES!

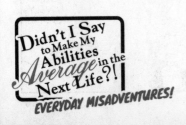

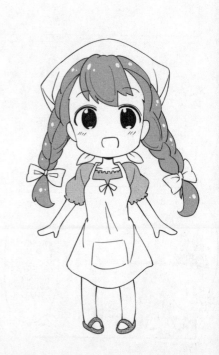

Chapter 6

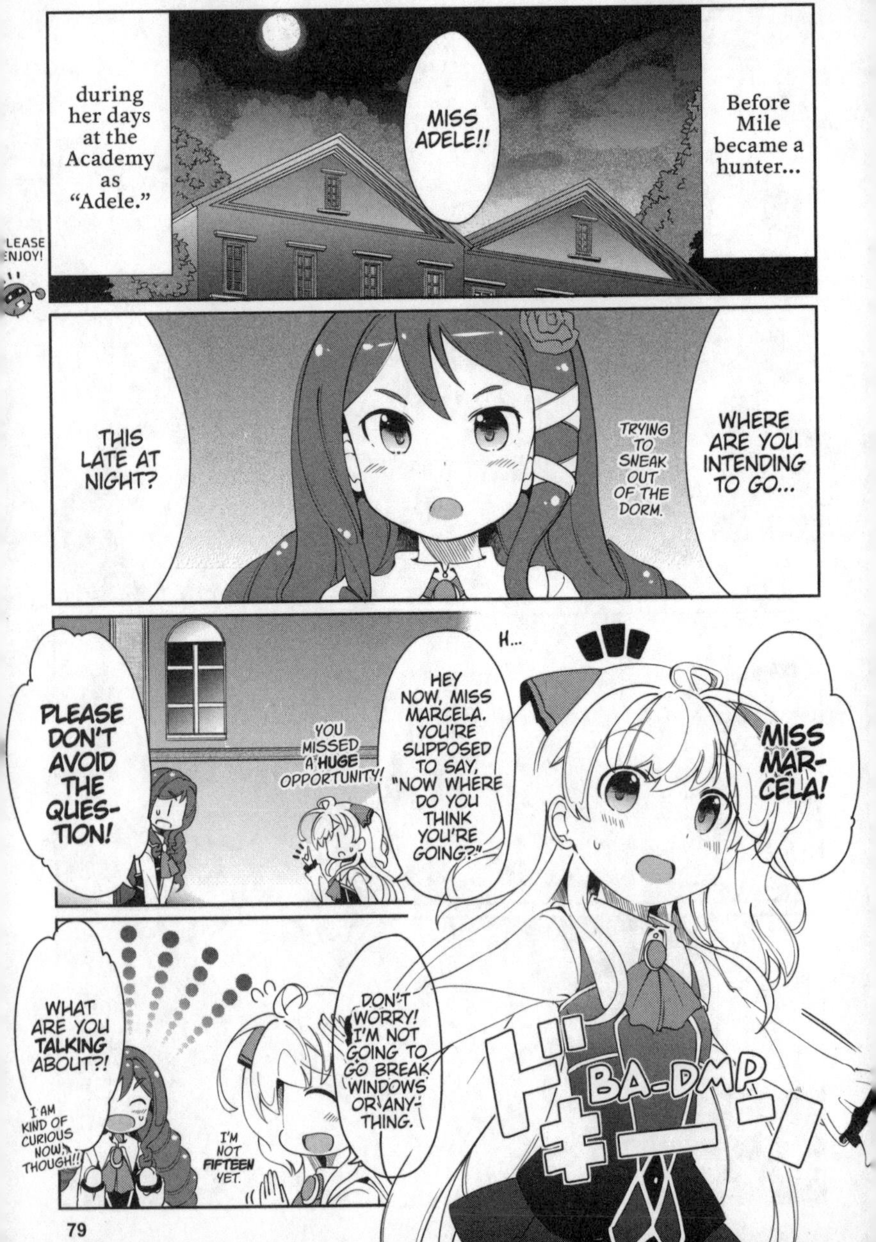

Before Mile became a hunter...
MISS ADELE!!
during her days at the Academy as "Adele."
LEASE ENJOY!
WHERE ARE YOU INTENDING TO GO...
TRYING TO SNEAK OUT OF THE DORM.
THIS LATE AT NIGHT?
MISS MARCELA!
H...
HEY NOW, MISS MARCELA. YOU'RE SUPPOSED TO SAY, "NOW WHERE DO YOU THINK YOU'RE GOING?"
YOU MISSED A HUGE OPPORTUNITY!
PLEASE DON'T AVOID THE QUESTION!
BA-DMP
DON'T WORRY! I'M NOT GOING TO GO BREAK WINDOWS OR ANYTHING.
I'M NOT FIFTEEN YET.
WHAT ARE YOU TALKING ABOUT?!
I AM KIND OF CURIOUS NOW, THOUGH!!

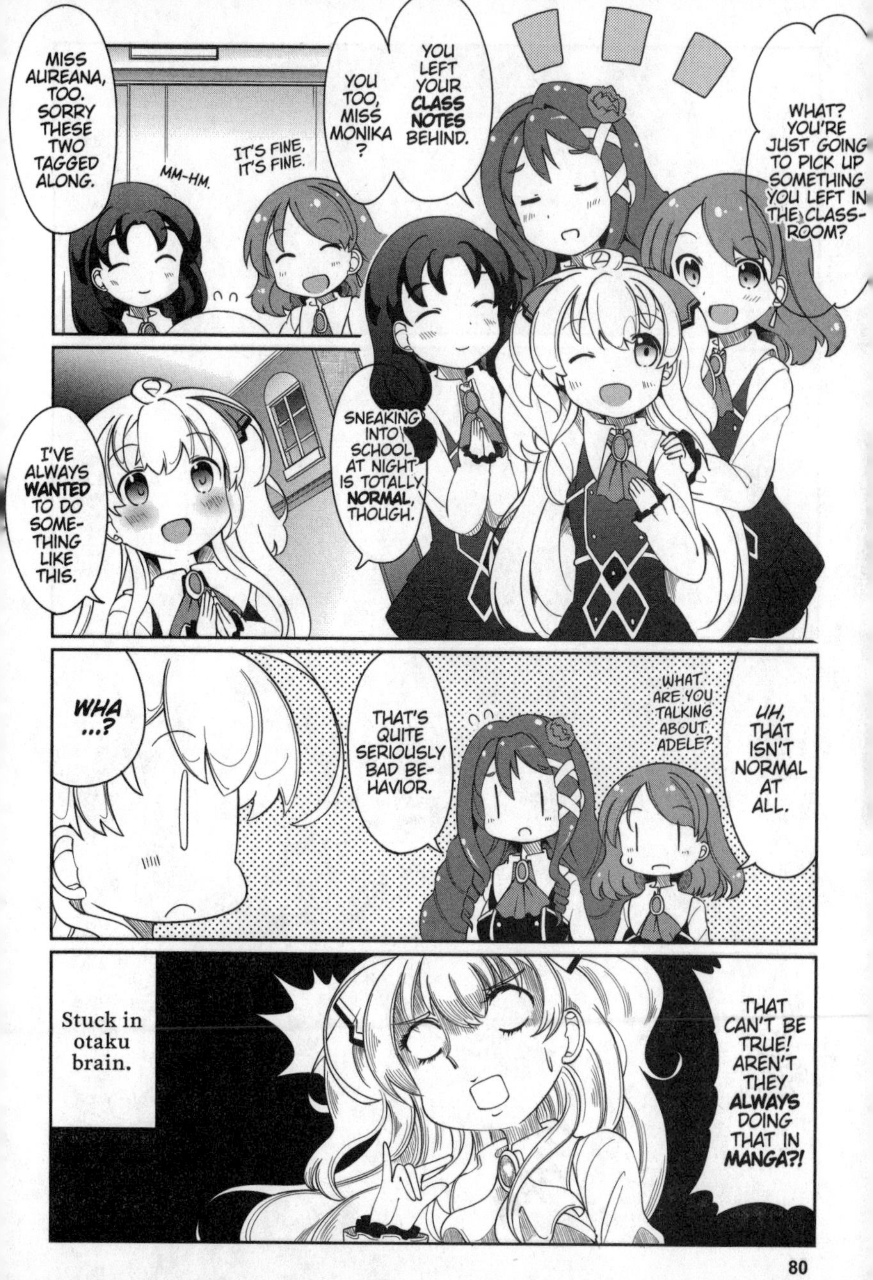
WHAT? YOU'RE JUST GOING TO PICK UP SOMETHING YOU LEFT IN THE CLASS-ROOM?
YOU LEFT YOUR **CLASS NOTES** BEHIND.
YOU TOO, MISS MONIKA?
SNEAKING INTO SCHOOL AT NIGHT IS TOTALLY **NORMAL**, THOUGH.
MISS AUREANA, TOO. SORRY THESE TWO TAGGED ALONG.
IT'S FINE, IT'S FINE.
MM-HM.
I'VE ALWAYS **WANTED** TO DO SOME-THING LIKE THIS.
UH, THAT ISN'T NORMAL AT ALL.
WHAT ARE YOU TALKING ABOUT, ADELE?
THAT'S QUITE SERIOUSLY BAD BE-HAVIOR.
WHA...?
THAT CAN'T BE TRUE! AREN'T THEY **ALWAYS** DOING THAT IN **MANGA?!**
Stuck in otaku brain.

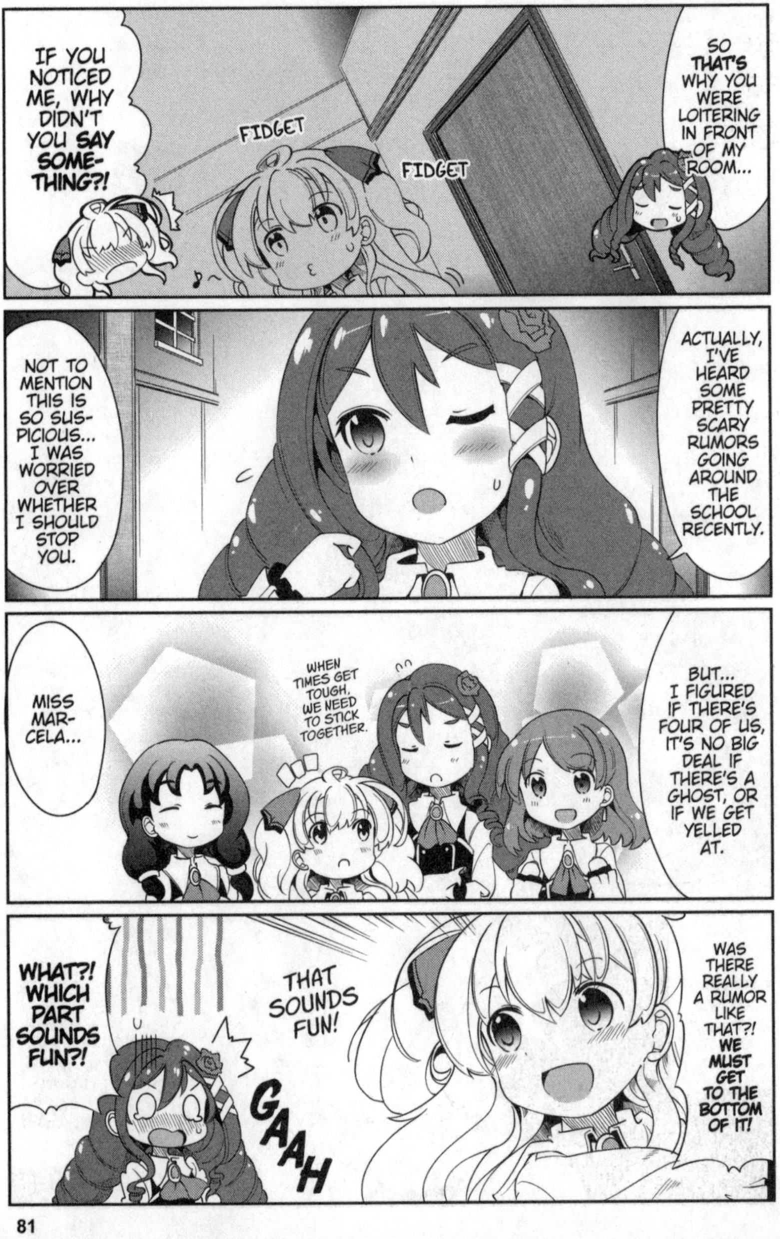
SO THAT'S WHY YOU WERE LOITERING IN FRONT OF MY ROOM...
FIDGET
FIDGET
IF YOU NOTICED ME, WHY DIDN'T YOU SAY SOME-THING?!
ACTUALLY, I'VE HEARD SOME PRETTY SCARY RUMORS GOING AROUND THE SCHOOL RECENTLY.
NOT TO MENTION THIS IS SO SUS-PICIOUS... I WAS WORRIED OVER WHETHER I SHOULD STOP YOU.
BUT... I FIGURED IF THERE'S FOUR OF US, IT'S NO BIG DEAL IF THERE'S A GHOST, OR IF WE GET YELLED AT.
WHEN TIMES GET TOUGH, WE NEED TO STICK TOGETHER.
MISS MAR-CELA...
WAS THERE REALLY A RUMOR LIKE THAT?! WE MUST GET TO THE BOTTOM OF IT!
THAT SOUNDS FUN!
WHAT?! WHICH PART SOUNDS FUN?!
GAAH

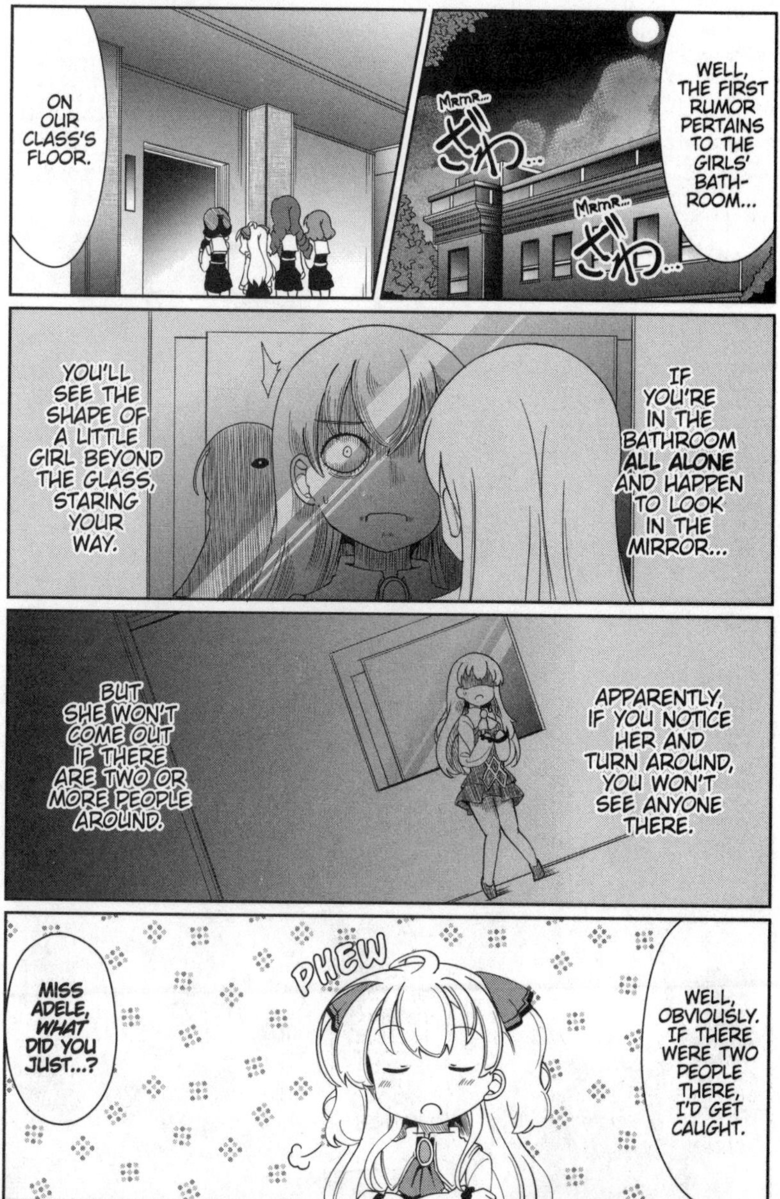
WELL, THE FIRST RUMOR PERTAINS TO THE GIRLS' BATHROOM...
Mrmr... ざわ...
Mrmr... ざわ...
ON OUR CLASS'S FLOOR.
IF YOU'RE IN THE BATHROOM ALL ALONE AND HAPPEN TO LOOK IN THE MIRROR...
YOU'LL SEE THE SHAPE OF A LITTLE GIRL BEYOND THE GLASS, STARING YOUR WAY.
APPARENTLY, IF YOU NOTICE HER AND TURN AROUND, YOU WON'T SEE ANYONE THERE.
BUT SHE WON'T COME OUT IF THERE ARE TWO OR MORE PEOPLE AROUND.
WELL, OBVIOUSLY. IF THERE WERE TWO PEOPLE THERE, I'D GET CAUGHT.
PHEW
MISS ADELE, WHAT DID YOU JUST...?

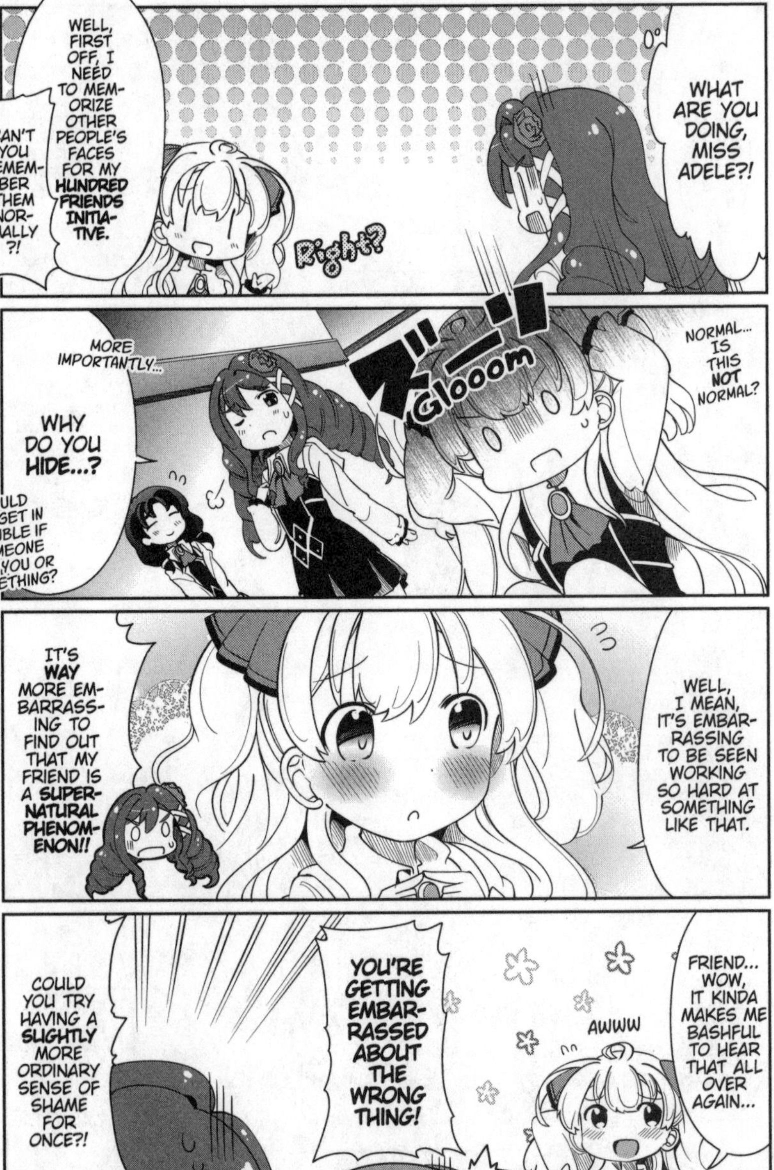
WHAT ARE YOU DOING, MISS ADELE?!
WELL, FIRST OFF, I NEED TO MEMORIZE OTHER PEOPLE'S FACES FOR MY HUNDRED FRIENDS INITIATIVE.
Right?
CAN'T YOU REMEMBER THEM NORMALLY?!
Glooom
NORMAL... IS THIS NOT NORMAL?
MORE IMPORTANTLY...
WHY DO YOU HIDE...?
WOULD YOU GET IN TROUBLE IF SOMEONE SAW YOU OR SOMETHING?
WELL, I MEAN, IT'S EMBARRASSING TO BE SEEN WORKING SO HARD AT SOMETHING LIKE THAT.
IT'S WAY MORE EMBARRASSING TO FIND OUT THAT MY FRIEND IS A SUPERNATURAL PHENOMENON!!
FRIEND... WOW, IT KINDA MAKES ME BASHFUL TO HEAR THAT ALL OVER AGAIN...
AWWW
YOU'RE GETTING EMBARRASSED ABOUT THE WRONG THING!
COULD YOU TRY HAVING A SLIGHTLY MORE ORDINARY SENSE OF SHAME FOR ONCE?!

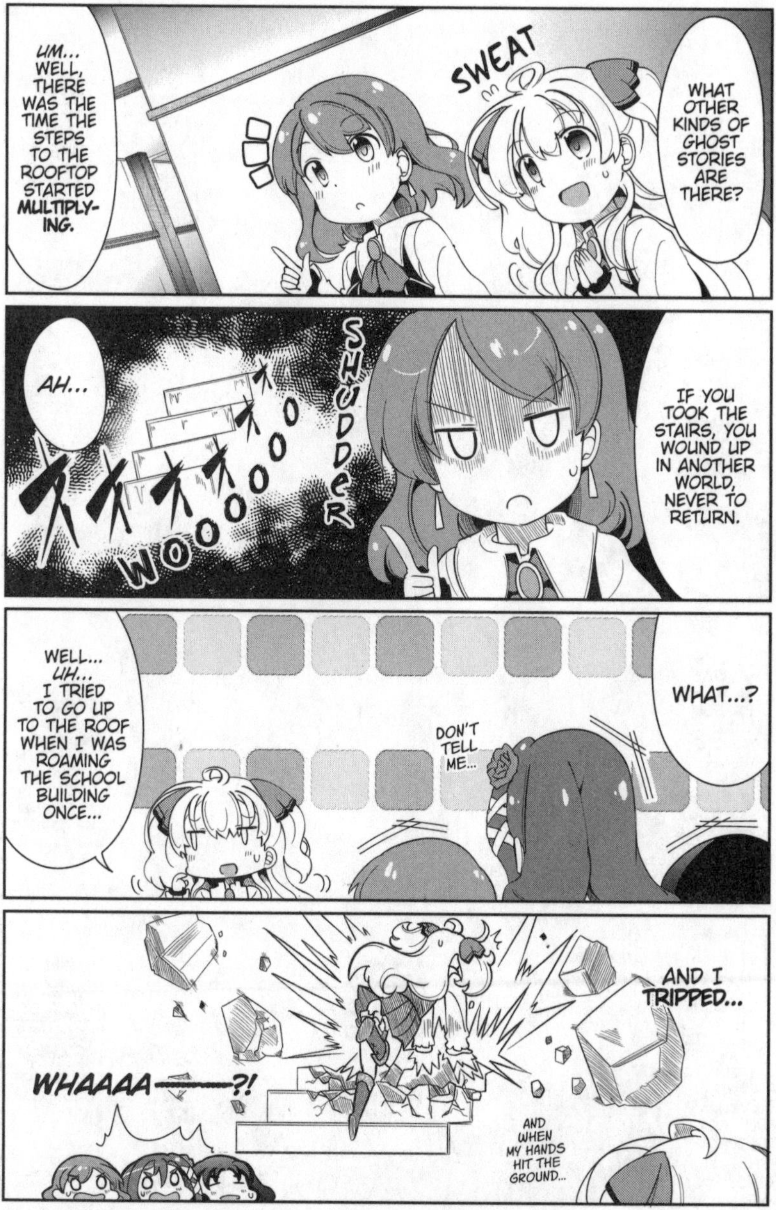
WHAT OTHER KINDS OF GHOST STORIES ARE THERE?
SWEAT
UM... WELL, THERE WAS THE TIME THE STEPS TO THE ROOFTOP STARTED MULTIPLYING.
IF YOU TOOK THE STAIRS, YOU WOUND UP IN ANOTHER WORLD, NEVER TO RETURN.
SHUDDER
WOOOOOO
AH...
WHAT...?
DON'T TELL ME...
WELL... UH... I TRIED TO GO UP TO THE ROOF WHEN I WAS ROAMING THE SCHOOL BUILDING ONCE...
AND I TRIPPED...
AND WHEN MY HANDS HIT THE GROUND...
WHAAAA――?!

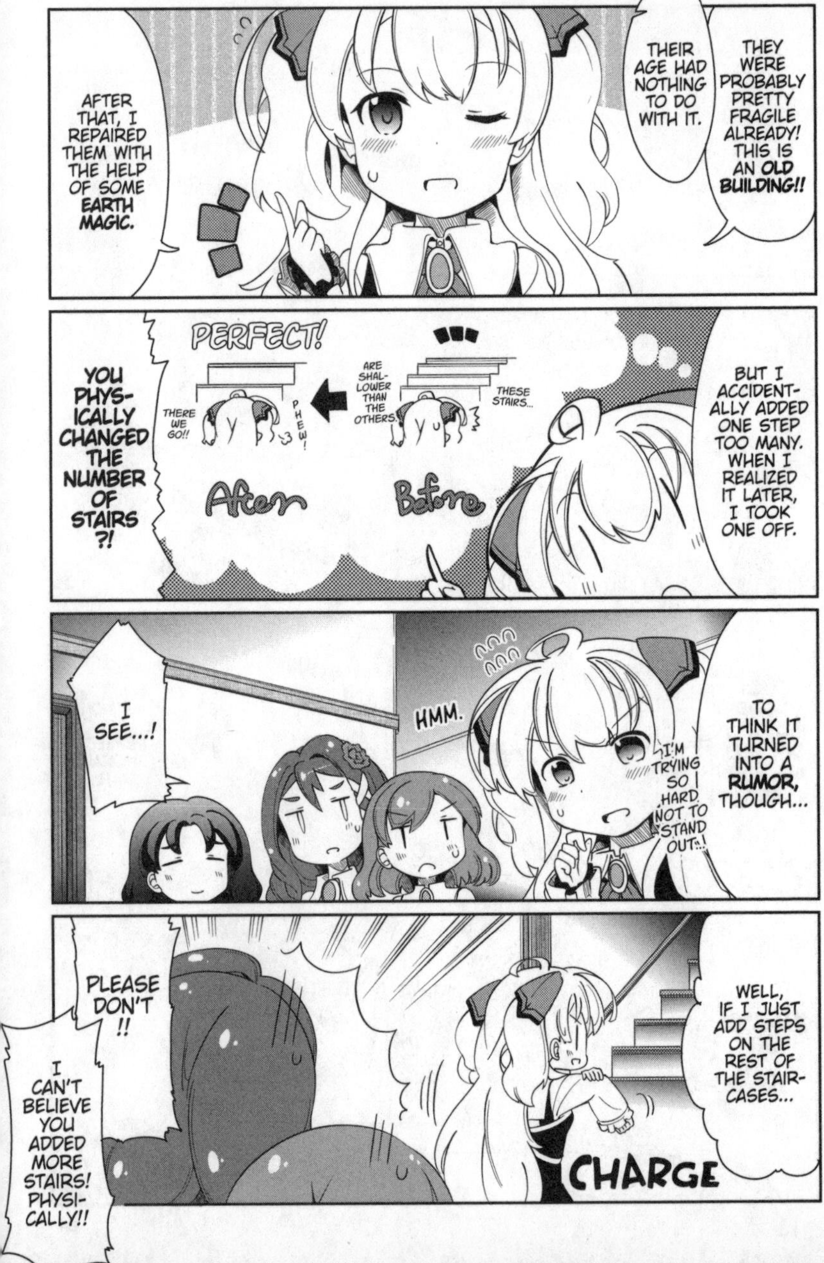
THEY WERE PROBABLY PRETTY FRAGILE ALREADY! THIS IS AN OLD BUILDING!!
THEIR AGE HAD NOTHING TO DO WITH IT.
AFTER THAT, I REPAIRED THEM WITH THE HELP OF SOME EARTH MAGIC.
BUT I ACCIDENTALLY ADDED ONE STEP TOO MANY. WHEN I REALIZED IT LATER, I TOOK ONE OFF.
THESE STAIRS...
ARE SHALLOWER THAN THE OTHERS.
Before
PHEW!
THERE WE GO!!
PERFECT!
After
YOU PHYSICALLY CHANGED THE NUMBER OF STAIRS?!
TO THINK IT TURNED INTO A RUMOR, THOUGH...
I'M TRYING SO HARD NOT TO STAND OUT...!
HMM.
I SEE...!
WELL, IF I JUST ADD STEPS ON THE REST OF THE STAIRCASES...
CHARGE
PLEASE DON'T!!
I CAN'T BELIEVE YOU ADDED MORE STAIRS! PHYSICALLY!!

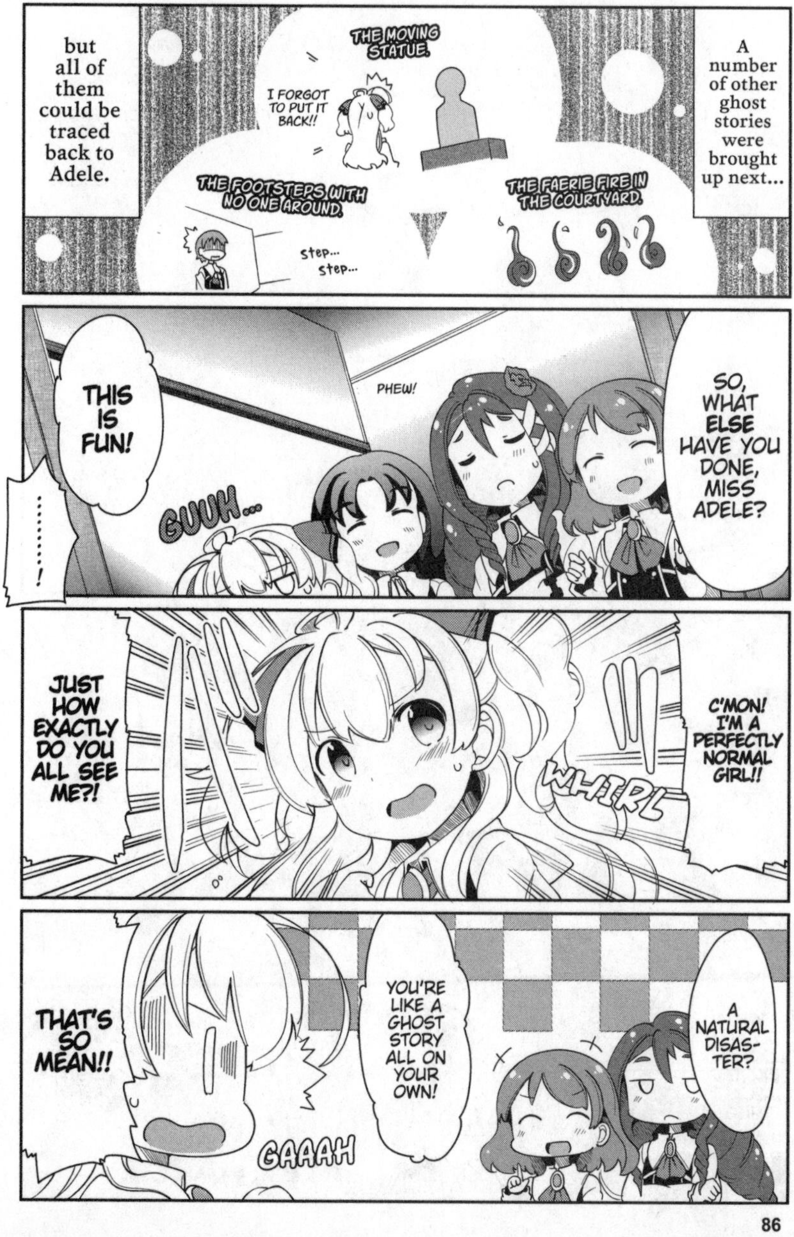
A number of other ghost stories were brought up next...
THE MOVING STATUE.
I FORGOT TO PUT IT BACK!!
THE FAERIE FIRE IN THE COURTYARD.
THE FOOTSTEPS WITH NO ONE AROUND.
step... step...
but all of them could be traced back to Adele.
SO, WHAT ELSE HAVE YOU DONE, MISS ADELE?
PHEW!
GUUH...
THIS IS FUN!
......!
C'MON! I'M A PERFECTLY NORMAL GIRL!!
WHIRL
JUST HOW EXACTLY DO YOU ALL SEE ME?!
A NATURAL DISASTER?
YOU'RE LIKE A GHOST STORY ALL ON YOUR OWN!
GAAAH
THAT'S SO MEAN!!

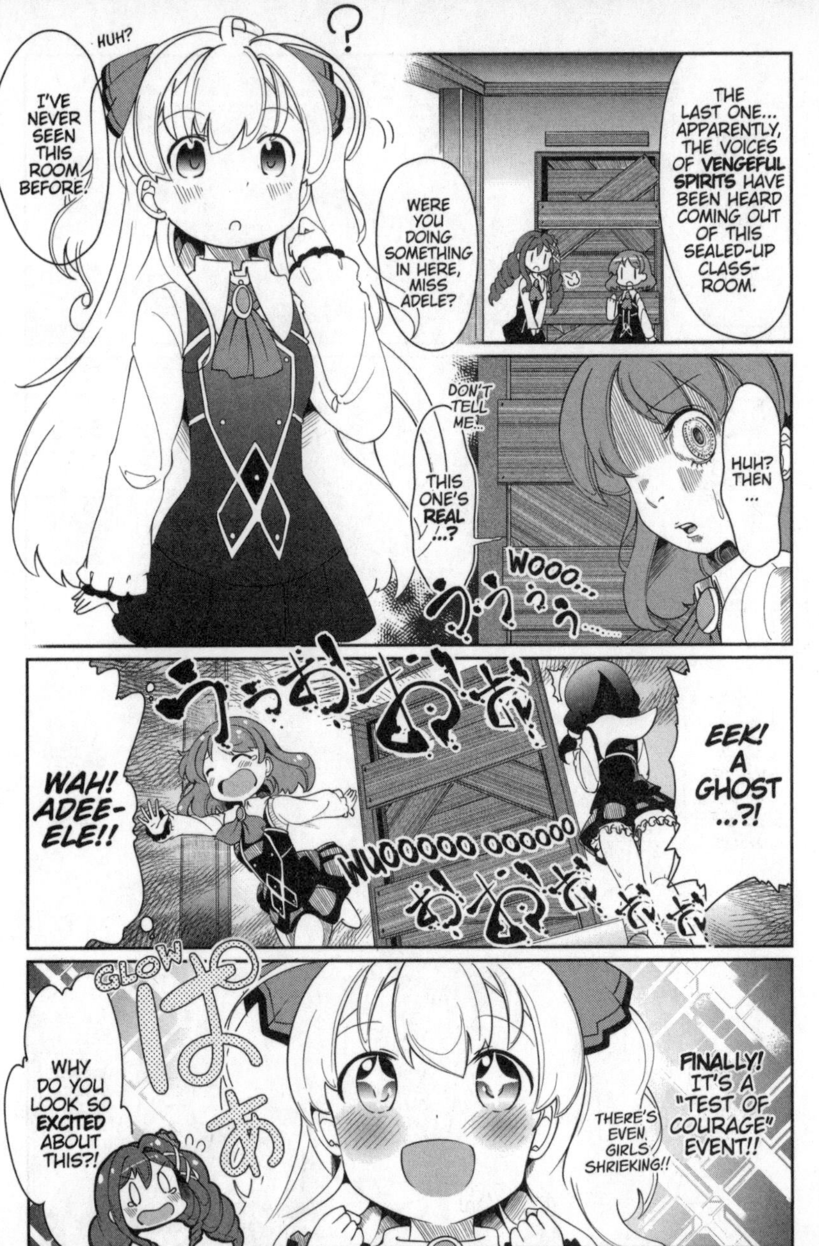
THE LAST ONE... APPARENTLY, THE VOICES OF VENGEFUL SPIRITS HAVE BEEN HEARD COMING OUT OF THIS SEALED-UP CLASS-ROOM.
WERE YOU DOING SOMETHING IN HERE, MISS ADELE?
HUH? THEN ...
DON'T TELL ME... THIS ONE'S REAL ...?
WOOO...
HUH?
I'VE NEVER SEEN THIS ROOM BEFORE.
EEK! A GHOST ...?!
WUOOOOO OOOOOO
WAH! ADEEE-ELE!!
FINALLY! IT'S A "TEST OF COURAGE" EVENT!!
THERE'S EVEN GIRLS SHRIEKING!!
GLOW
WHY DO YOU LOOK SO EXCITED ABOUT THIS?!

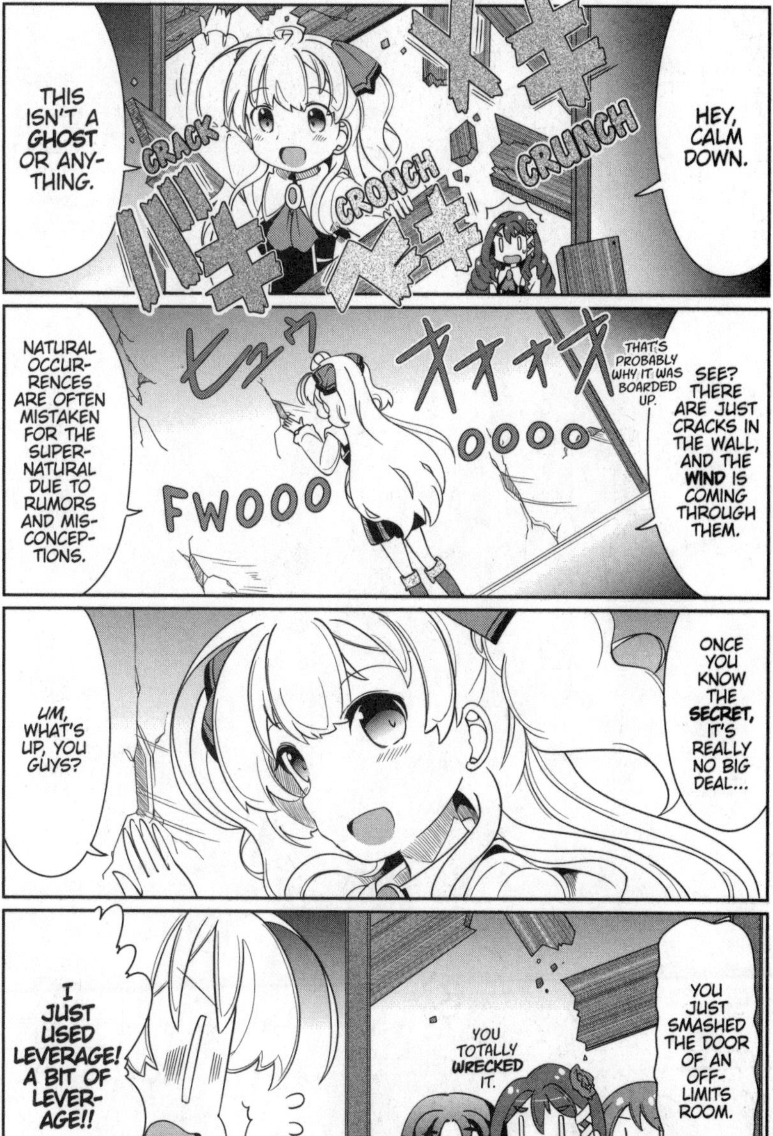
HEY, CALM DOWN.
メキ
CRUNCH
CRONCH
CRACK
バキ
メキ
THIS ISN'T A **GHOST** OR ANYTHING.
SEE? THERE ARE JUST CRACKS IN THE WALL, AND THE **WIND** IS COMING THROUGH THEM.
THAT'S PROBABLY WHY IT WAS BOARDED UP.
オォォォ
OOOO
ヒュウ
FWOOO
NATURAL OCCURRENCES ARE OFTEN MISTAKEN FOR THE SUPERNATURAL DUE TO RUMORS AND MISCONCEPTIONS.
ONCE YOU KNOW THE **SECRET**, IT'S REALLY NO BIG DEAL...
UM, WHAT'S UP, YOU GUYS?
YOU JUST SMASHED THE DOOR OF AN OFF-LIMITS ROOM.
YOU TOTALLY **WRECKED** IT.
I JUST USED LEVERAGE! A BIT OF LEVERAGE!!

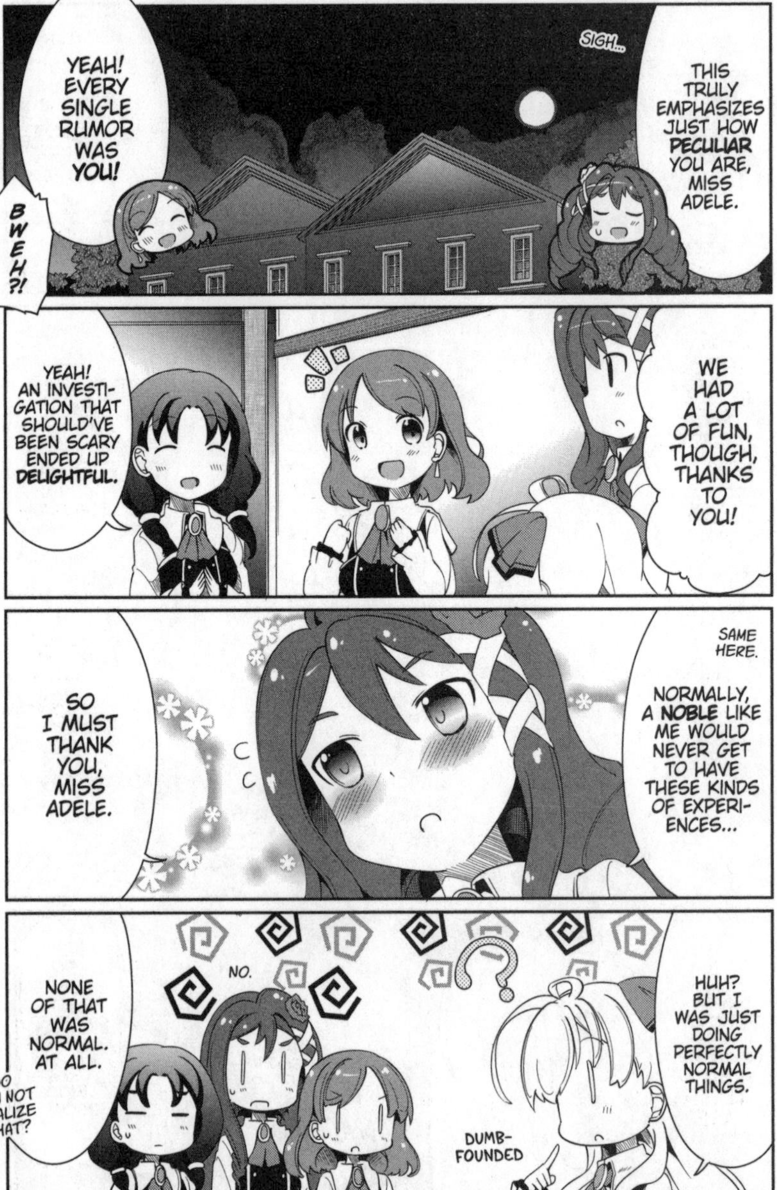
SIGH...
THIS TRULY EMPHASIZES JUST HOW PECULIAR YOU ARE, MISS ADELE.
YEAH! EVERY SINGLE RUMOR WAS YOU!
BWEH?!
WE HAD A LOT OF FUN, THOUGH, THANKS TO YOU!
YEAH! AN INVESTIGATION THAT SHOULD'VE BEEN SCARY ENDED UP DELIGHTFUL.
SAME HERE.
NORMALLY, A NOBLE LIKE ME WOULD NEVER GET TO HAVE THESE KINDS OF EXPERIENCES...
SO I MUST THANK YOU, MISS ADELE.
HUH? BUT I WAS JUST DOING PERFECTLY NORMAL THINGS.
DUMB-FOUNDED
NO.
NONE OF THAT WAS NORMAL. AT ALL.
DO YOU NOT REALIZE THAT?

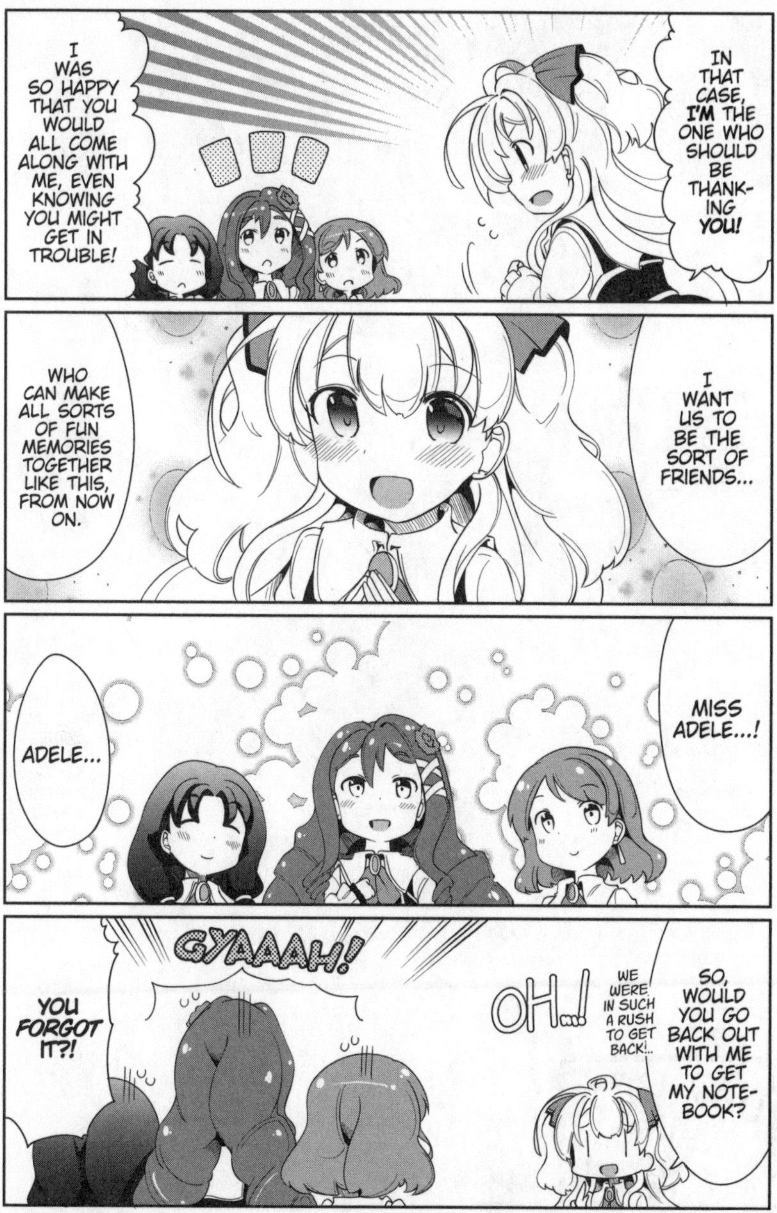
IN THAT CASE, I'M THE ONE WHO SHOULD BE THANKING YOU!
I WAS SO HAPPY THAT YOU WOULD ALL COME ALONG WITH ME, EVEN KNOWING YOU MIGHT GET IN TROUBLE!
I WANT US TO BE THE SORT OF FRIENDS...
WHO CAN MAKE ALL SORTS OF FUN MEMORIES TOGETHER LIKE THIS, FROM NOW ON.
MISS ADELE...!
ADELE...
SO, WOULD YOU GO BACK OUT WITH ME TO GET MY NOTE-BOOK?
WE WERE IN SUCH A RUSH TO GET BACK!...
OH...!
GYAAAH!
YOU FORGOT IT?!

Didn't I Say to Make My Abilities Average in the Next Life?!

EVERYDAY MISADVENTURES!

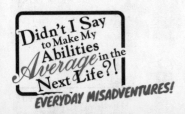

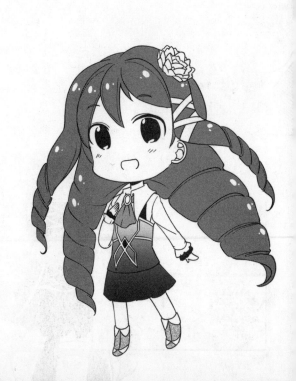

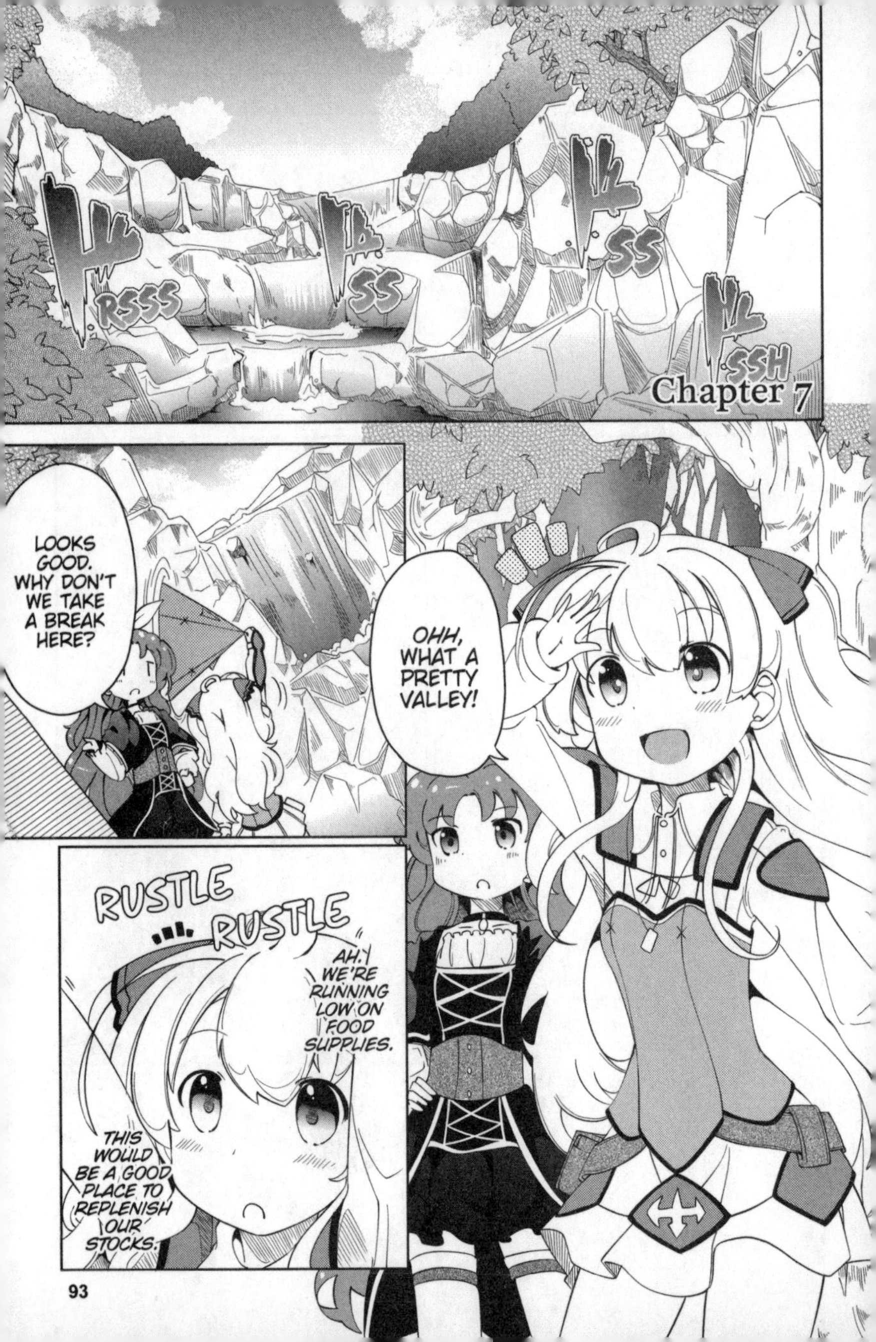
SSH
SS
SS
RSSS
Chapter 7
OHH, WHAT A PRETTY VALLEY!
LOOKS GOOD. WHY DON'T WE TAKE A BREAK HERE?
RUSTLE RUSTLE
AH. WE'RE RUNNING LOW ON FOOD SUPPLIES.
THIS WOULD BE A GOOD PLACE TO REPLENISH OUR STOCKS.

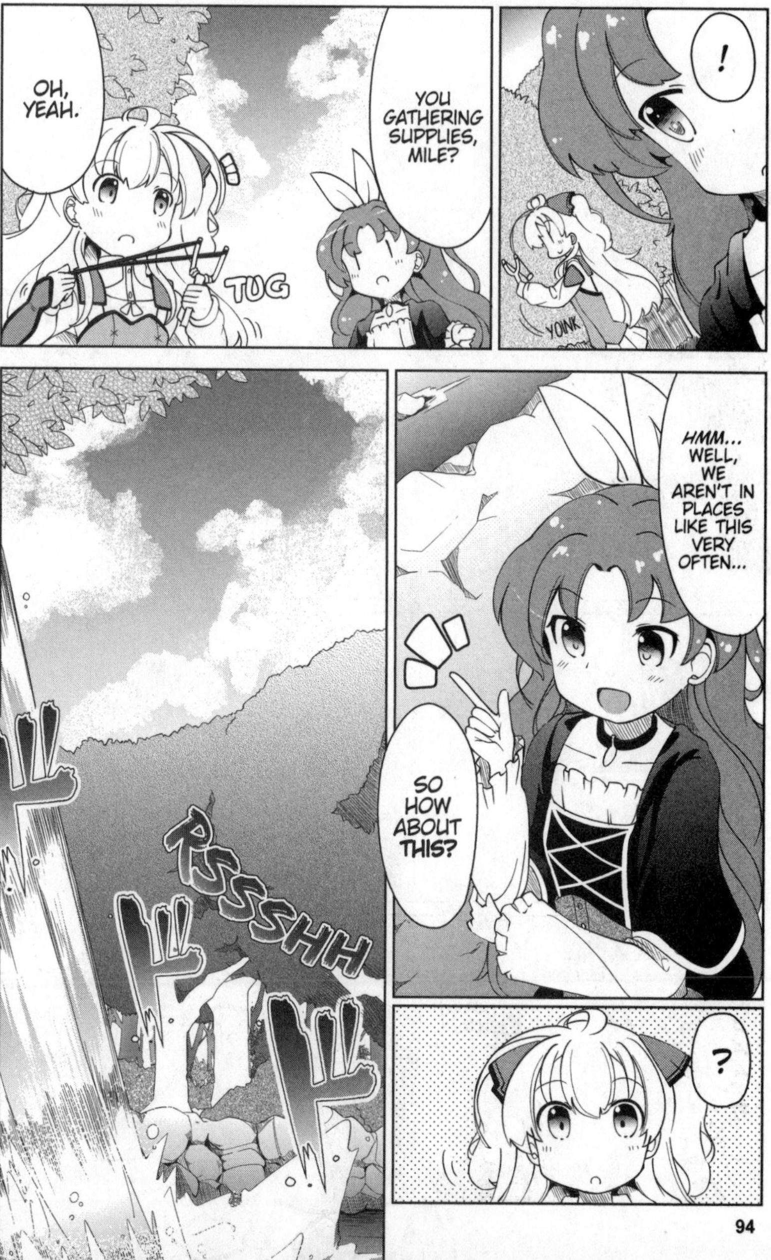
!
YOINK
YOU GATHERING SUPPLIES, MILE?
OH, YEAH.
TUG
HMM... WELL, WE AREN'T IN PLACES LIKE THIS VERY OFTEN...
SO HOW ABOUT THIS?
?
RSSSHH
ドドドド

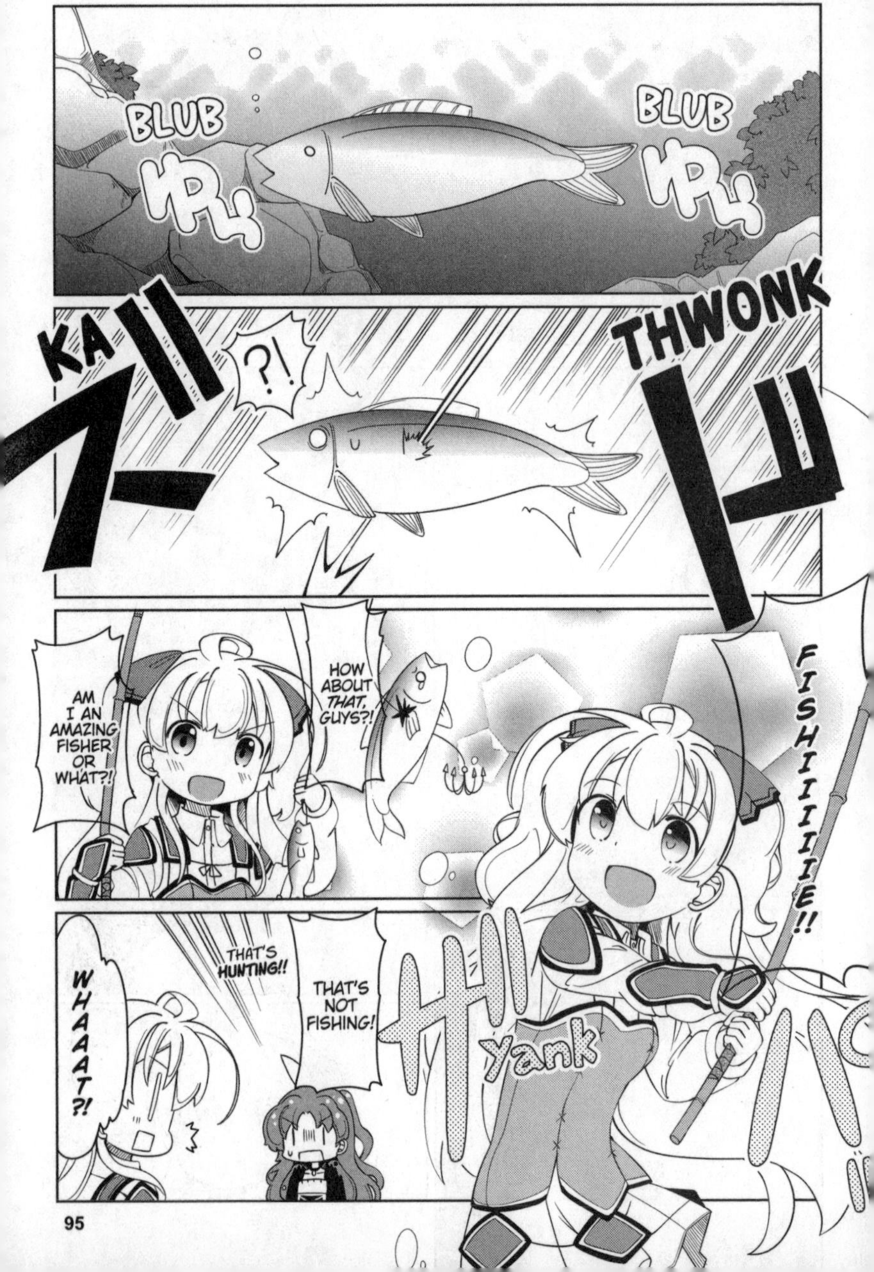
BLUB
BLUB
THWONK
KA
?!
FISHIIIIIIE!!
yank
HOW ABOUT *THAT*, GUYS?!
AM I AN AMAZING FISHER OR WHAT?!
THAT'S NOT FISHING!
THAT'S **HUNTING!!**
WHAAAAT?!

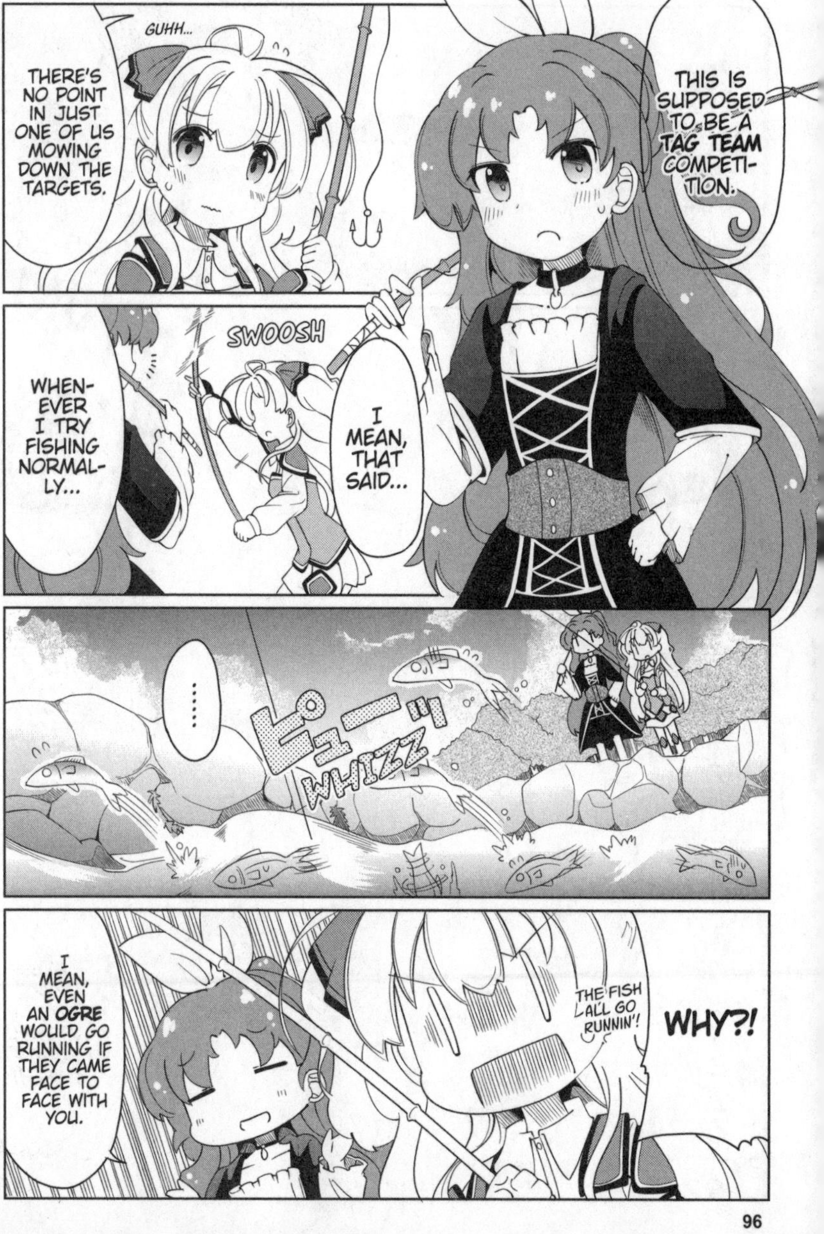
THIS IS SUPPOSED TO BE A TAG TEAM COMPETITION.
GUHH...
THERE'S NO POINT IN JUST ONE OF US MOWING DOWN THE TARGETS.
I MEAN, THAT SAID...
SWOOSH
WHENEVER I TRY FISHING NORMALLY...
......
ピューーッ
WHIZZ
WHY?!
THE FISH ALL'LL GO RUNNIN'!
I MEAN, EVEN AN OGRE WOULD GO RUNNING IF THEY CAME FACE TO FACE WITH YOU.

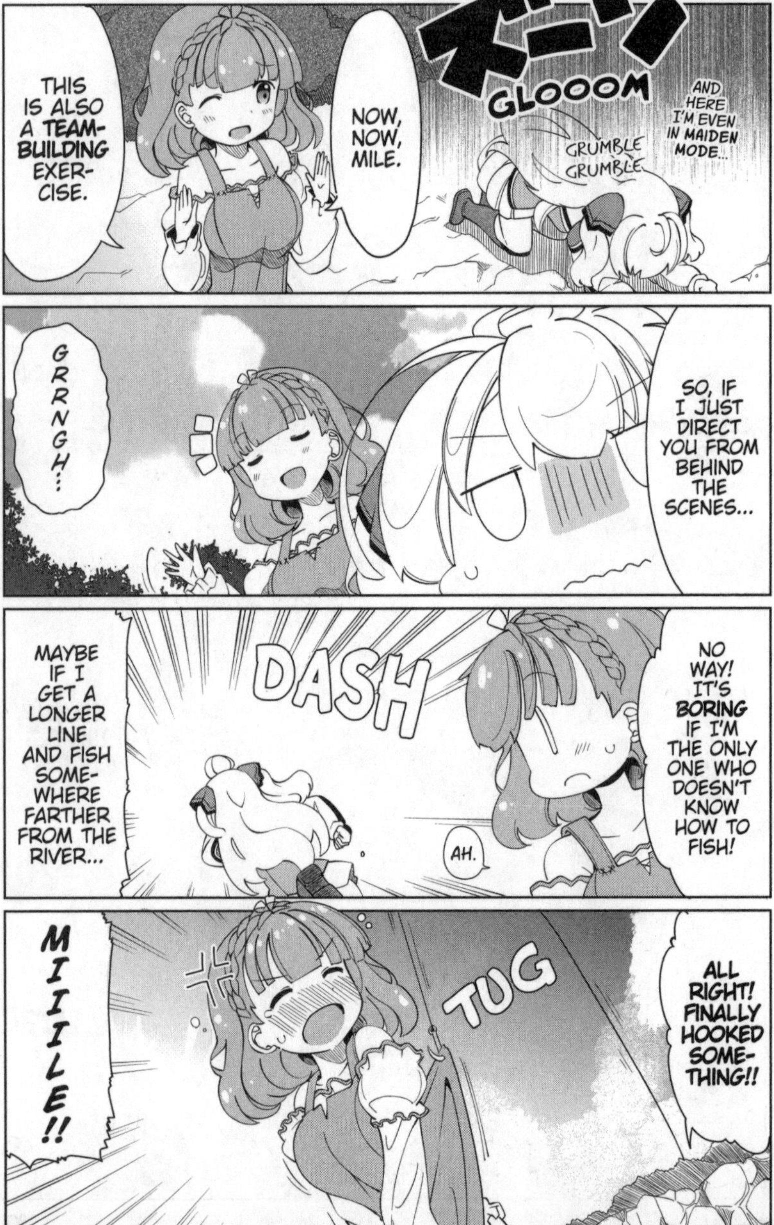

ズーン
GLOOOM
AND HERE I'M EVEN IN MAIDEN MODE...
GRUMBLE GRUMBLE
NOW, NOW, MILE.
THIS IS ALSO A **TEAM-BUILDING** EXERCISE.
SO, IF I JUST DIRECT YOU FROM BEHIND THE SCENES...
GRRNGH...
NO WAY! IT'S **BORING** IF I'M THE ONLY ONE WHO DOESN'T KNOW HOW TO FISH!
DASH
AH.
MAYBE IF I GET A LONGER LINE AND FISH SOMEWHERE FARTHER FROM THE RIVER...
ALL RIGHT! FINALLY HOOKED SOMETHING!!
TUG
MIIILE!!

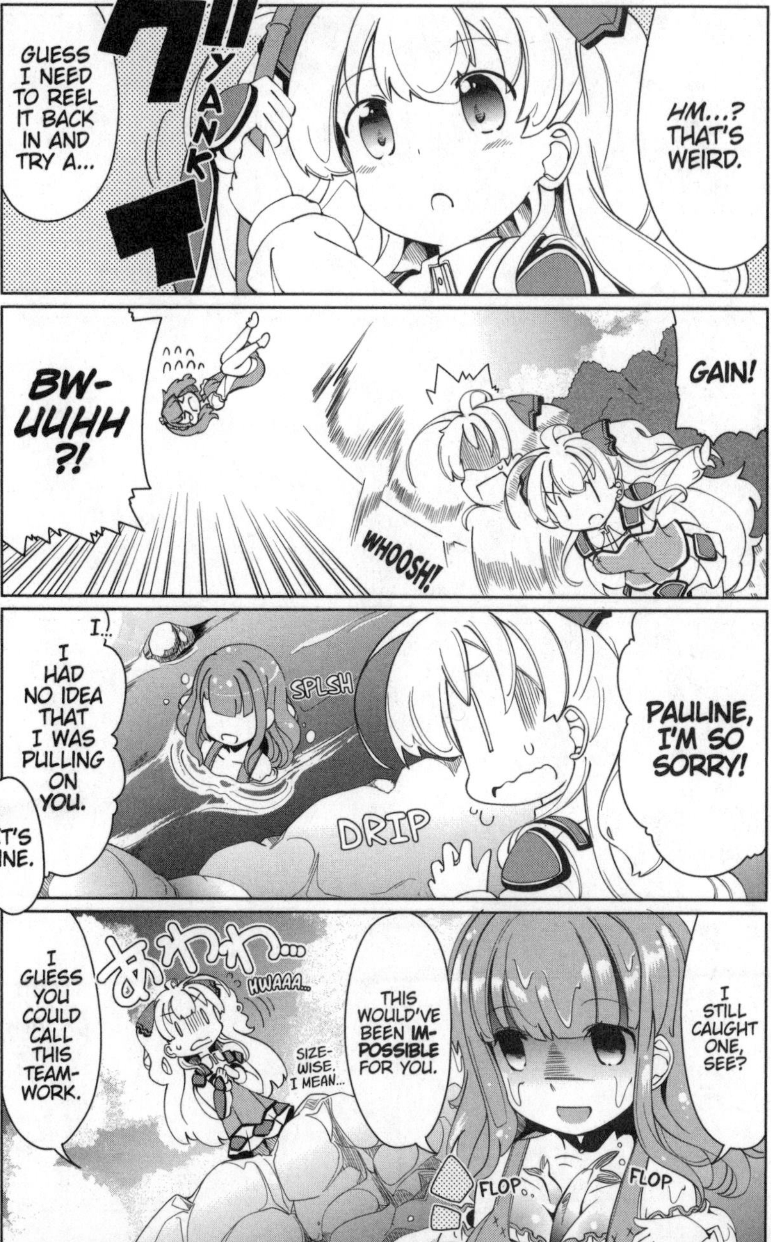
HM...? THAT'S WEIRD.
GUESS I NEED TO REEL IT BACK IN AND TRY A...
グイ
YANK
GAIN!
WHOOSH!
BW-UUHH?!
PAULINE, I'M SO SORRY!
DRIP
SPLSH
I...
I HAD NO IDEA THAT I WAS PULLING ON YOU.
IT'S FINE.
I STILL CAUGHT ONE, SEE?
FLOP
FLOP
THIS WOULD'VE BEEN IMPOSSIBLE FOR YOU.
SIZE-WISE, I MEAN...
あわわ...
HWAAA...
I GUESS YOU COULD CALL THIS TEAMWORK.

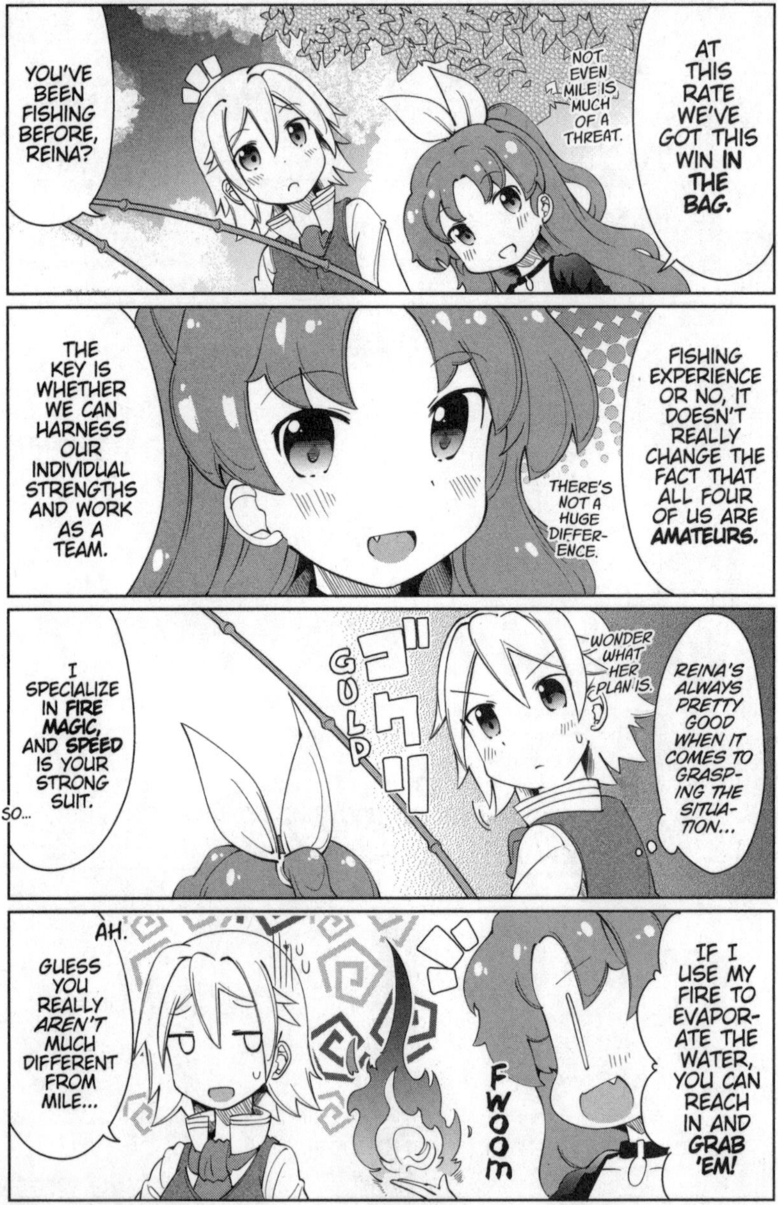
AT THIS RATE WE'VE GOT THIS WIN IN THE BAG.
NOT EVEN MILE IS MUCH OF A THREAT.
YOU'VE BEEN FISHING BEFORE, REINA?
FISHING EXPERIENCE OR NO, IT DOESN'T REALLY CHANGE THE FACT THAT ALL FOUR OF US ARE AMATEURS.
THERE'S NOT A HUGE DIFFER-ENCE.
THE KEY IS WHETHER WE CAN HARNESS OUR INDIVIDUAL STRENGTHS AND WORK AS A TEAM.
REINA'S ALWAYS PRETTY GOOD WHEN IT COMES TO GRASP-ING THE SITUA-TION...
WONDER WHAT HER PLAN IS.
GULP
I SPECIALIZE IN FIRE MAGIC, AND SPEED IS YOUR STRONG SUIT.
SO...
IF I USE MY FIRE TO EVAPOR-ATE THE WATER, YOU CAN REACH IN AND GRAB 'EM!
FWOOM
AH.
GUESS YOU REALLY AREN'T MUCH DIFFERENT FROM MILE...

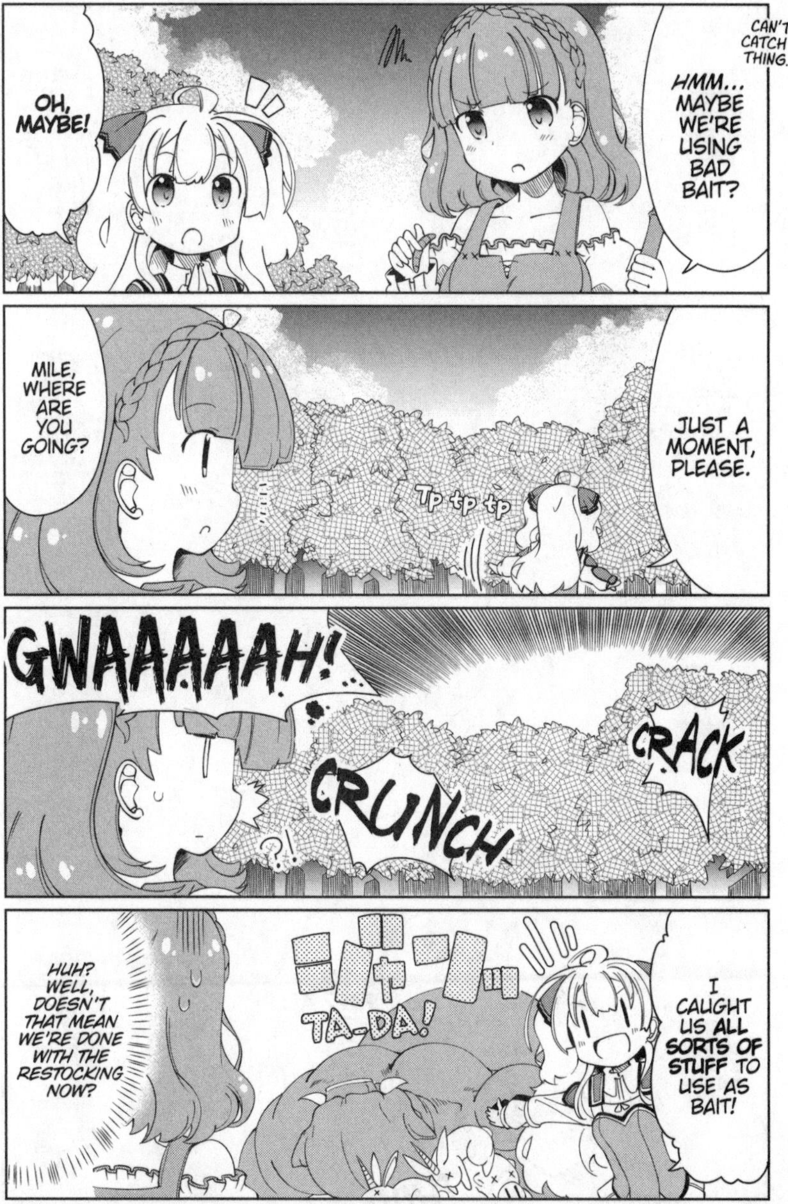

CAN'T CATCH A THING...
HMM... MAYBE WE'RE USING BAD BAIT?
OH, MAYBE!
JUST A MOMENT, PLEASE.
Tp tp tp
MILE, WHERE ARE YOU GOING?
GWAAAAAAH!
CRACK
CRUNCH
?!
I CAUGHT US ALL SORTS OF STUFF TO USE AS BAIT!
TA-DA!
HUH? WELL, DOESN'T THAT MEAN WE'RE DONE WITH THE RESTOCKING NOW?

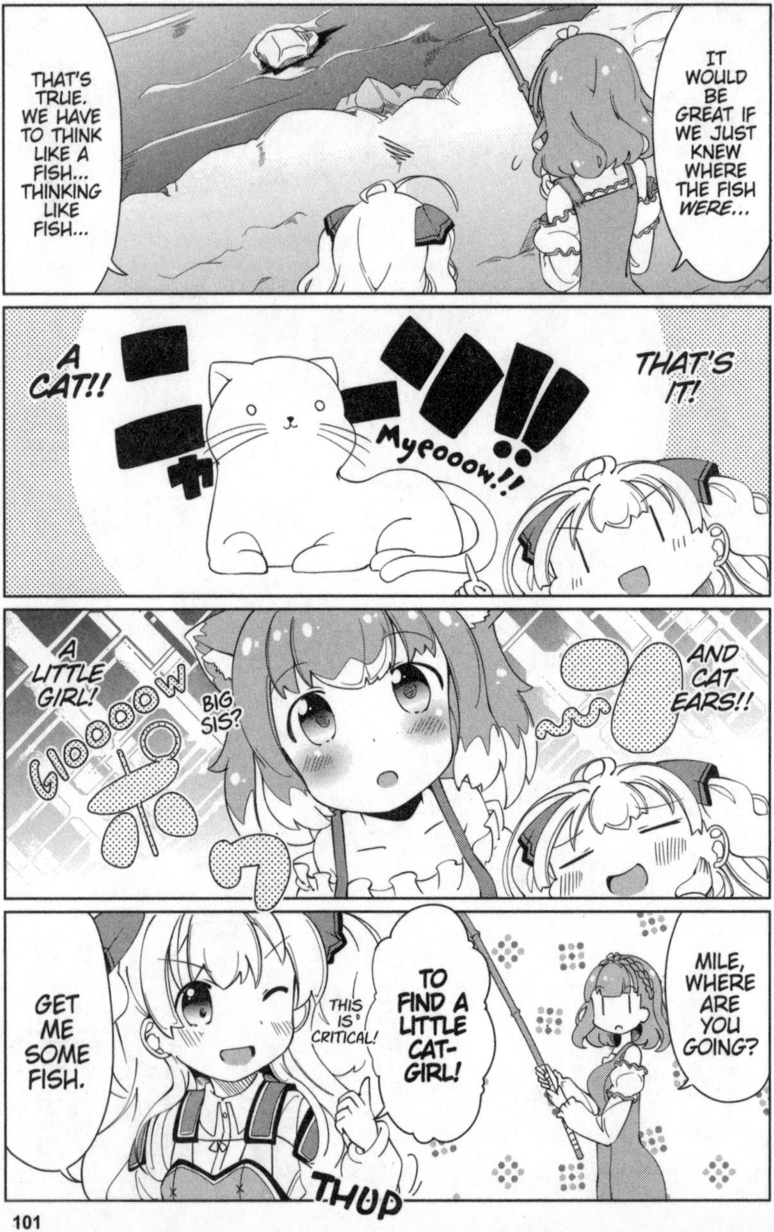

IT WOULD BE GREAT IF WE JUST KNEW WHERE THE FISH WERE...
THAT'S TRUE. WE HAVE TO THINK LIKE A FISH... THINKING LIKE FISH...
THAT'S IT!
A CAT!!
Myeooow!!
AND CAT EARS!!
A LITTLE GIRL!
BIG SIS?
Gloooow
MILE, WHERE ARE YOU GOING?
TO FIND A LITTLE CAT-GIRL!
THIS IS CRITICAL!
GET ME SOME FISH.
THUP

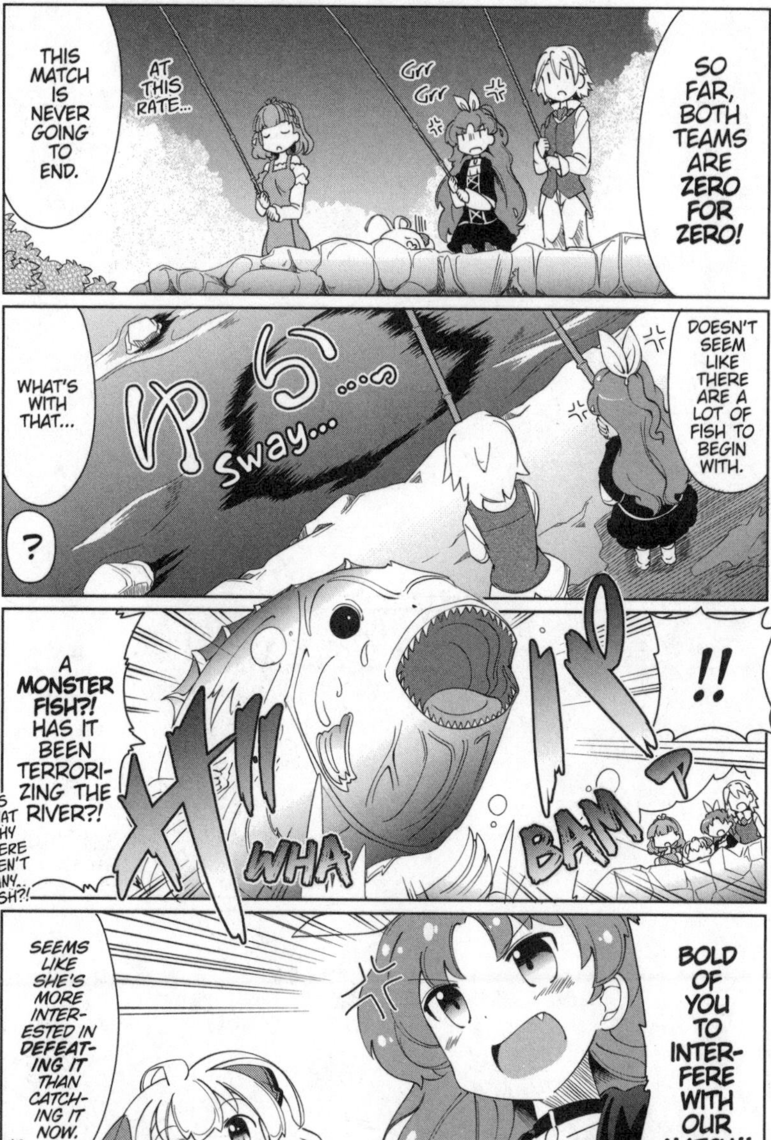
SO FAR, BOTH TEAMS ARE ZERO FOR ZERO!
Grr Grr
AT THIS RATE...
THIS MATCH IS NEVER GOING TO END.
DOESN'T SEEM LIKE THERE ARE A LOT OF FISH TO BEGIN WITH.
ゆら…
sway...
WHAT'S WITH THAT...
?
!!
BAM
WHA
A MONSTER FISH?! HAS IT BEEN TERRORIZING THE RIVER?!
IS THAT WHY THERE AREN'T ANY FISH?!
BOLD OF YOU TO INTERFERE WITH OUR MATCH!!
SEEMS LIKE SHE'S MORE INTERESTED IN DEFEATING IT THAN CATCHING IT NOW.
THAT'S OUR REINA.

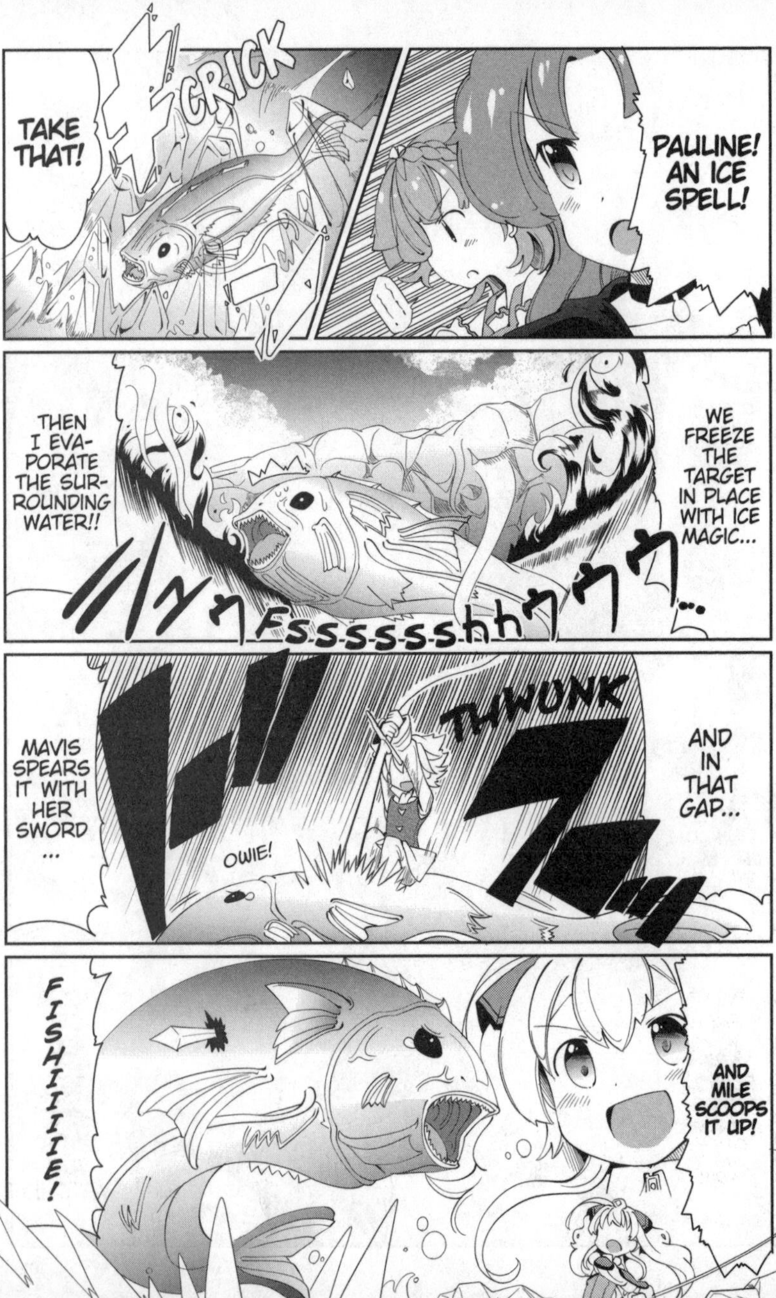
PAULINE! AN ICE SPELL!
CRICK
TAKE THAT!
WE FREEZE THE TARGET IN PLACE WITH ICE MAGIC...
THEN I EVA-PORATE THE SUR-ROUNDING WATER!!
FSSSSSSSHHH...
AND IN THAT GAP...
THWUNK
MAVIS SPEARS IT WITH HER SWORD...
OWIE!
AND MILE SCOOPS IT UP!
FISHIIIIIE!

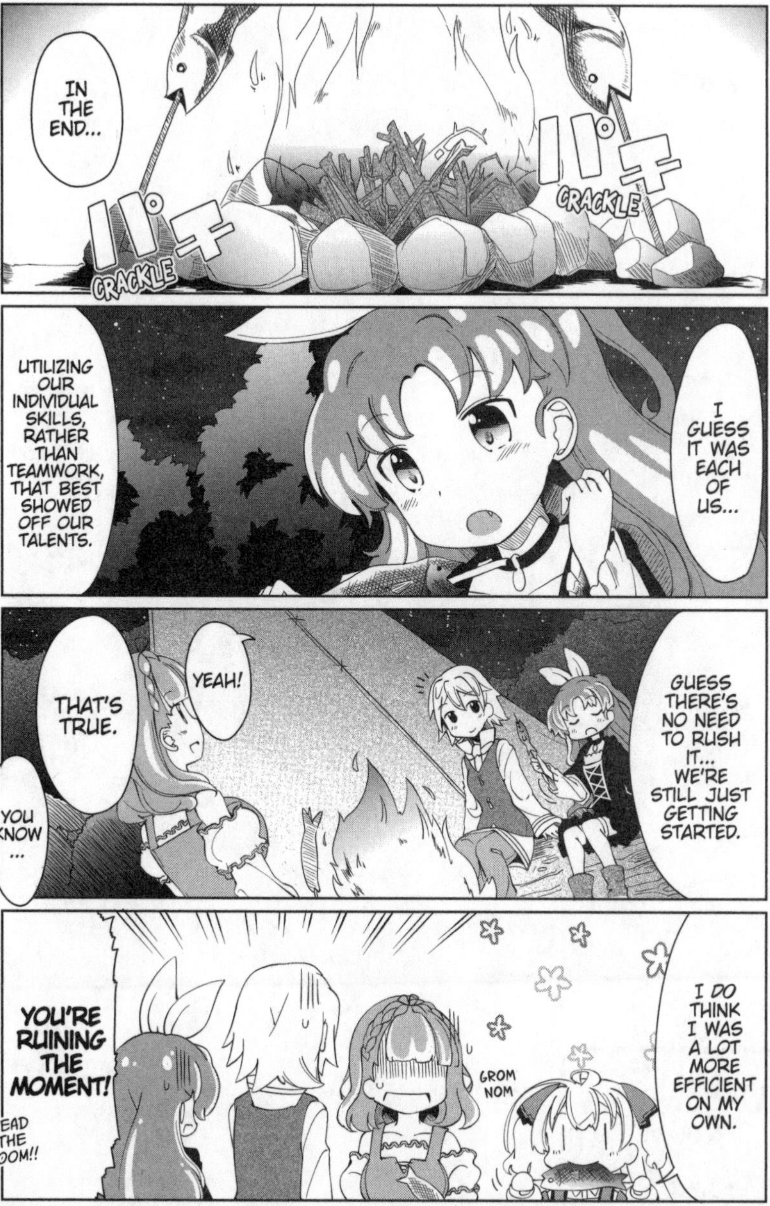
IN THE END...
パチ CRACKLE
パチ CRACKLE
I GUESS IT WAS EACH OF US...
UTILIZING OUR INDIVIDUAL SKILLS, RATHER THAN TEAMWORK, THAT BEST SHOWED OFF OUR TALENTS.
GUESS THERE'S NO NEED TO RUSH IT... WE'RE STILL JUST GETTING STARTED.
YEAH!
THAT'S TRUE.
YOU KNOW...
I *DO* THINK I WAS A LOT MORE EFFICIENT ON MY OWN.
GROM NOM
YOU'RE RUINING THE MOMENT!
READ THE ROOM!!

Didn't I Say to Make My Abilities Average in the Next Life?!

EVERYDAY MISADVENTURES!

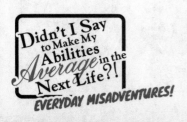

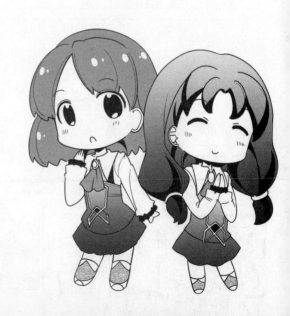

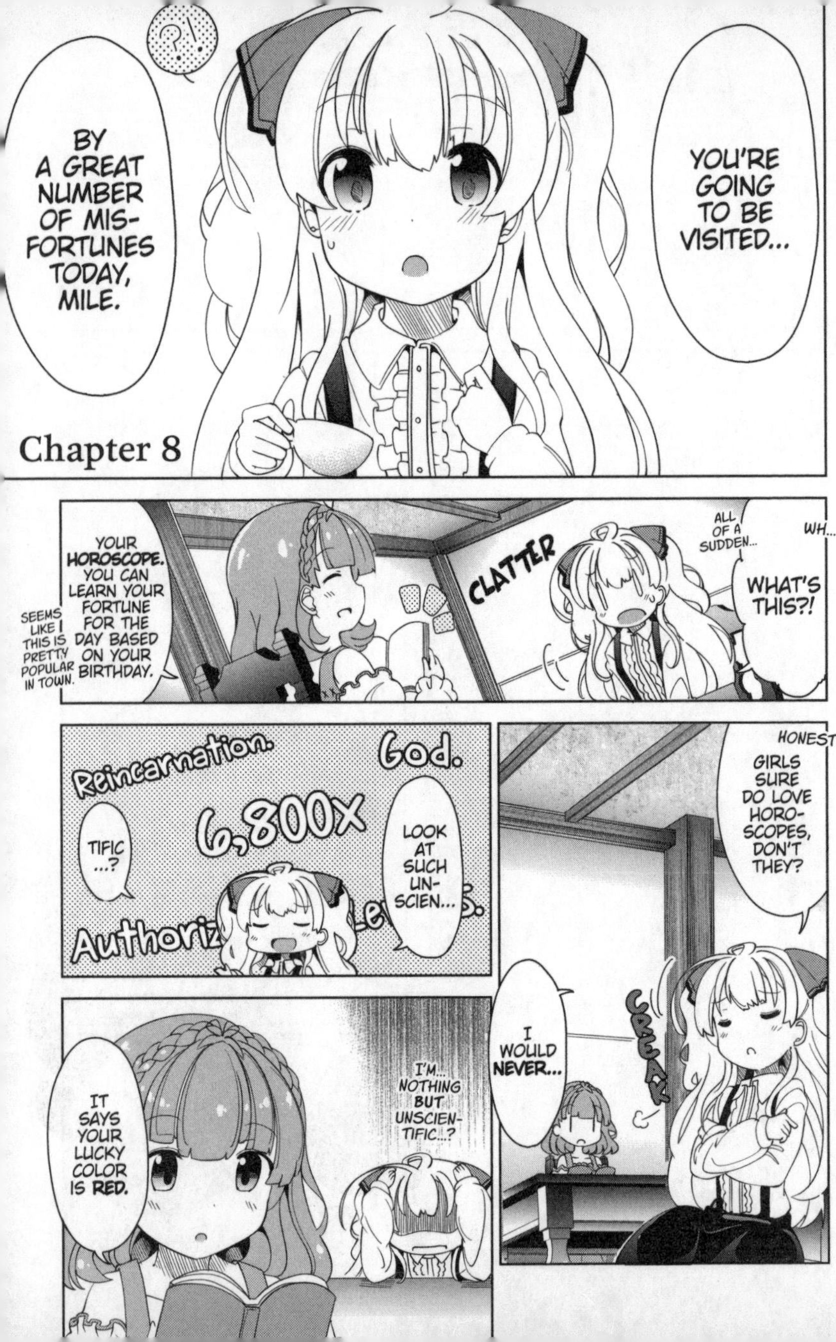
YOU'RE GOING TO BE VISITED...
?!
BY A GREAT NUMBER OF MIS-FORTUNES TODAY, MILE.
Chapter 8
WH...
WHAT'S THIS?!
ALL OF A SUDDEN...
CLATTER
YOUR HOROSCOPE. YOU CAN LEARN YOUR FORTUNE FOR THE DAY BASED ON YOUR BIRTHDAY.
SEEMS LIKE THIS IS PRETTY POPULAR IN TOWN.
HONESTLY. GIRLS SURE DO LOVE HORO-SCOPES, DON'T THEY?
CREAK
I WOULD NEVER...
God.
Reincarnation.
6,800x
LOOK AT SUCH UN-SCIEN...
TIFIC ...?
Authoriz
I'M... NOTHING BUT UNSCIEN-TIFIC...?
IT SAYS YOUR LUCKY COLOR IS RED.

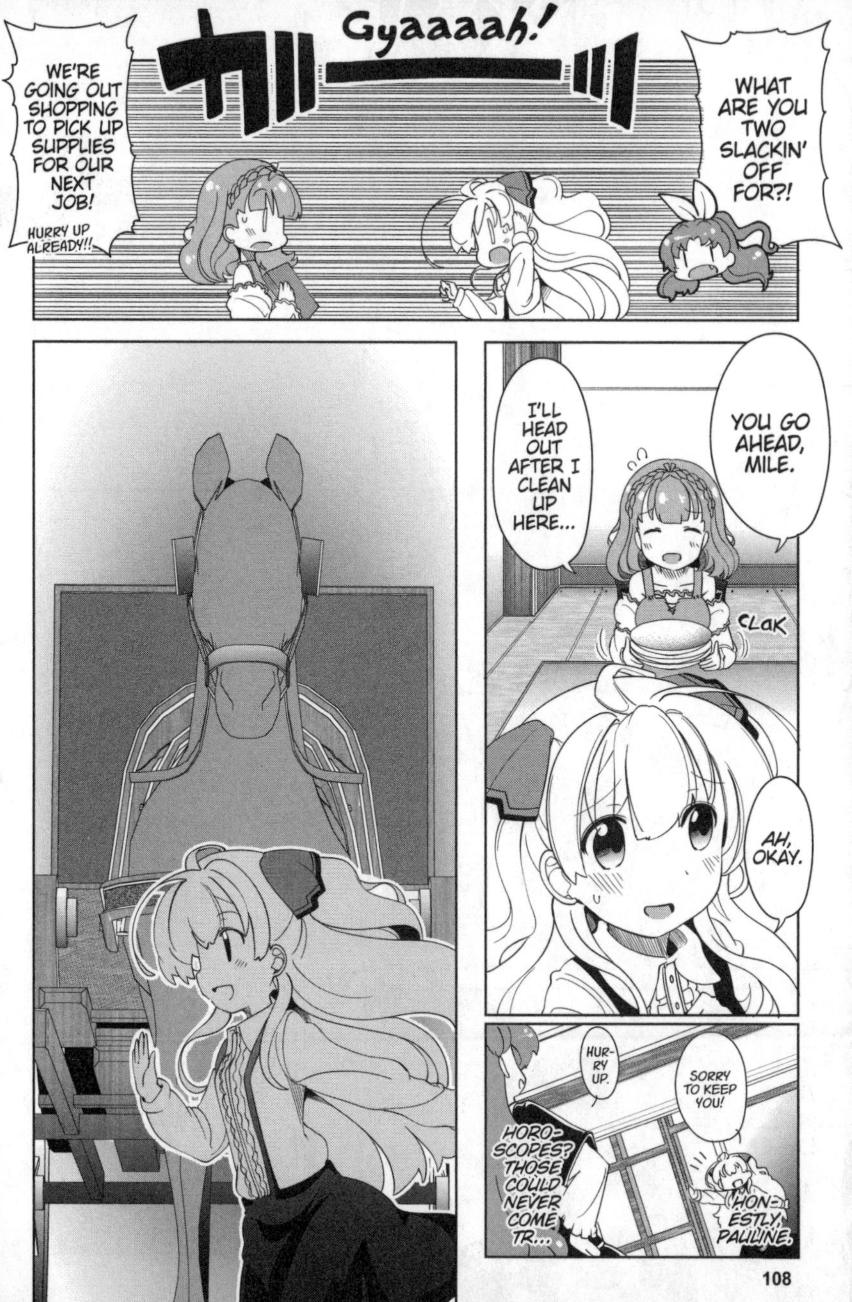

WHAT ARE YOU TWO SLACKIN' OFF FOR?!
Gyaaaah!
WE'RE GOING OUT SHOPPING TO PICK UP SUPPLIES FOR OUR NEXT JOB!
HURRY UP ALREADY!!
YOU GO AHEAD, MILE.
I'LL HEAD OUT AFTER I CLEAN UP HERE...
CLAK
AH, OKAY.
SORRY TO KEEP YOU!
HUR-RY UP.
HON-ESTLY, PAULINE.
HORO-SCOPES? THOSE COULD NEVER COME TR...

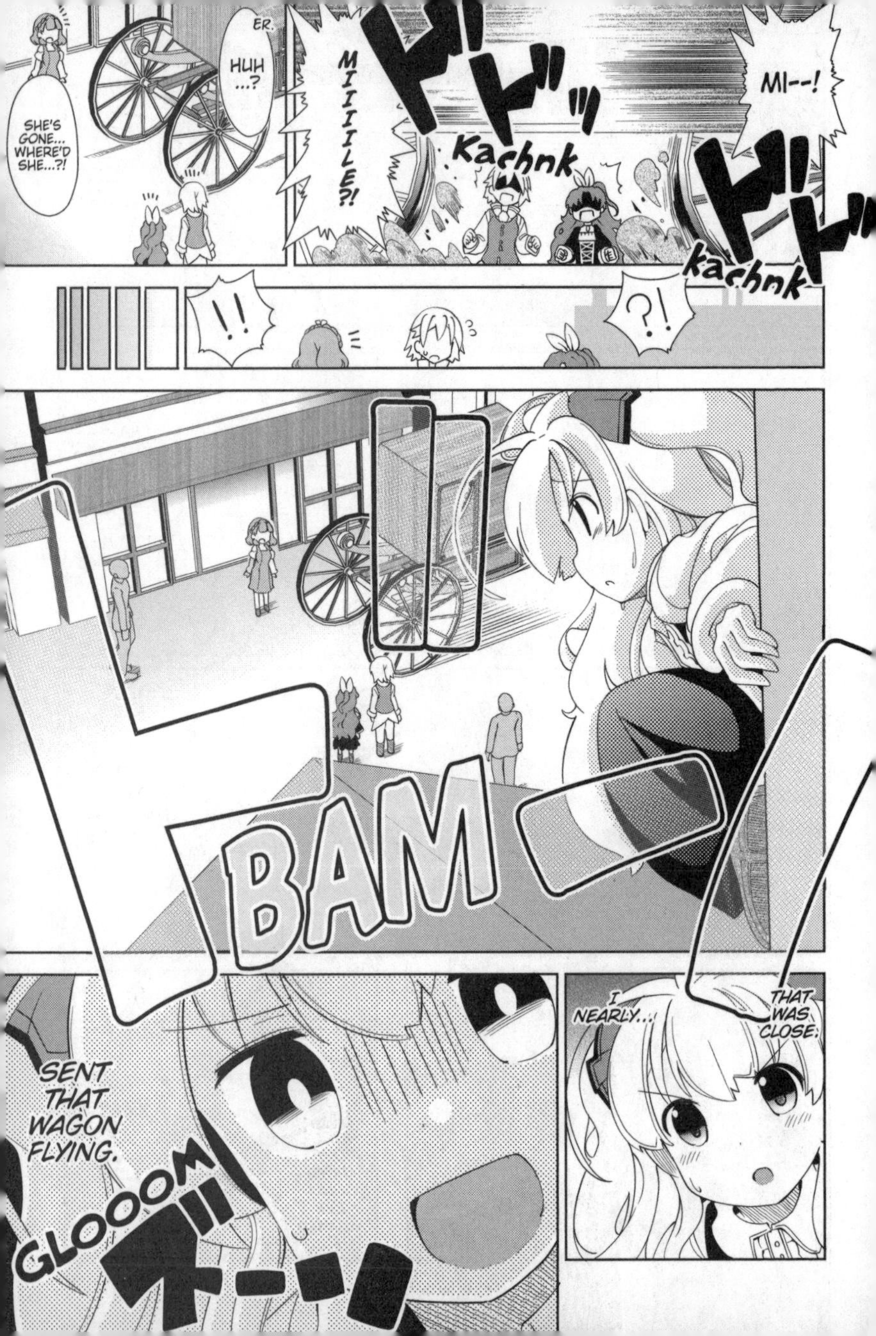

MI--!
MIIIILE?!
Kachnk
kachnk
ER.
HUH ...?
SHE'S GONE... WHERE'D SHE...?!
?!
!!
BAM
THAT WAS CLOSE.
I NEARLY...
SENT THAT WAGON FLYING.
GLOOOM

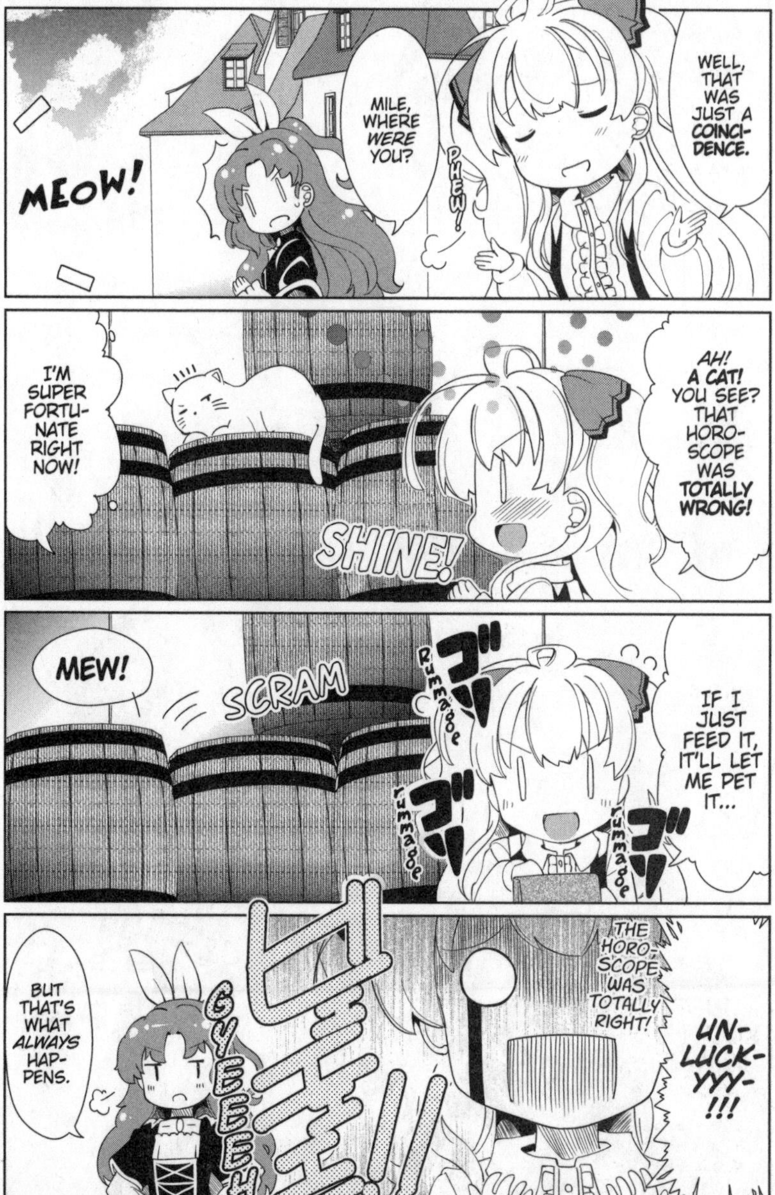

WELL, THAT WAS JUST A COINCIDENCE.
PHEW!
MILE, WHERE WERE YOU?
MEOW!
AH! A CAT! YOU SEE? THAT HOROSCOPE WAS TOTALLY WRONG!
SHINE!
I'M SUPER FORTUNATE RIGHT NOW!
IF I JUST FEED IT, IT'LL LET ME PET IT...
rummage
rummage
rummage
SCRAM
MEW!
UN-LUCK-YYY-!!!
THE HOROSCOPE WAS TOTALLY RIGHT!
GYEEEH!!
BUT THAT'S WHAT ALWAYS HAPPENS.

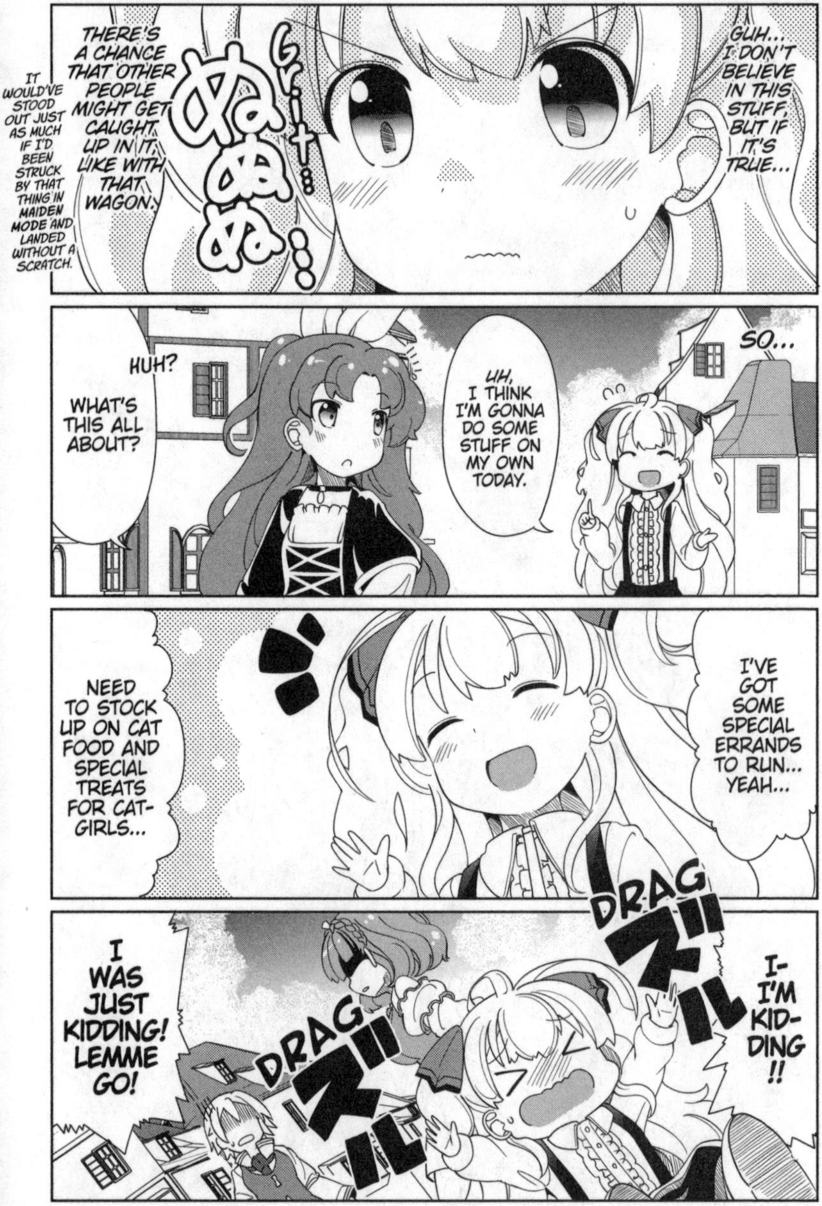
GUH... I DON'T BELIEVE IN THIS STUFF, BUT IF IT'S TRUE...
Grit
ぬぬぬ..
THERE'S A CHANCE THAT OTHER PEOPLE MIGHT GET CAUGHT UP IN IT, LIKE WITH THAT WAGON.
IT WOULD'VE STOOD OUT JUST AS MUCH IF I'D BEEN STRUCK BY THAT THING IN MAIDEN MODE AND LANDED WITHOUT A SCRATCH.
SO...
UH, I THINK I'M GONNA DO SOME STUFF ON MY OWN TODAY.
HUH?
WHAT'S THIS ALL ABOUT?
I'VE GOT SOME SPECIAL ERRANDS TO RUN... YEAH...
NEED TO STOCK UP ON CAT FOOD AND SPECIAL TREATS FOR CAT-GIRLS...
DRAG ズリ
I- I'M KID-DING!!
DRAG ズリ
I WAS JUST KIDDING! LEMME GO!

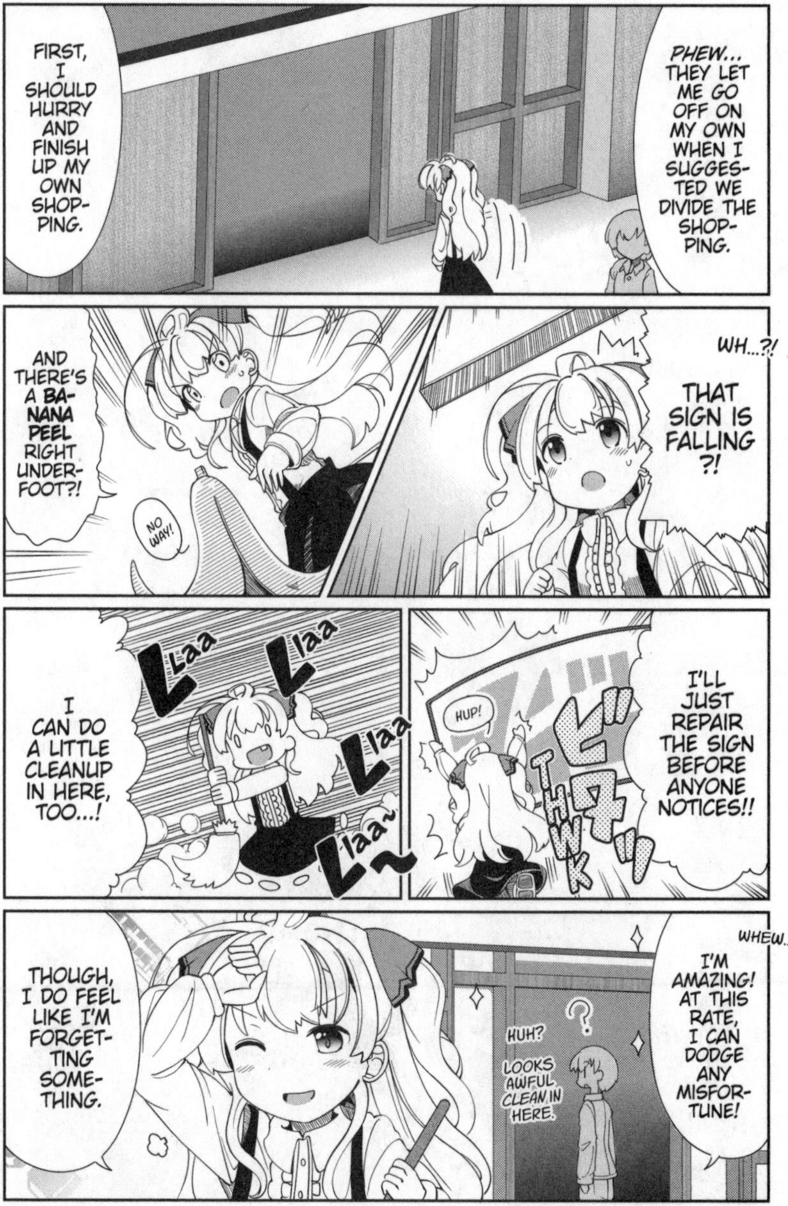
PHEW... THEY LET ME GO OFF ON MY OWN WHEN I SUGGESTED WE DIVIDE THE SHOPPING.
FIRST, I SHOULD HURRY AND FINISH UP MY OWN SHOPPING.
WH...?!
THAT SIGN IS FALLING?!
AND THERE'S A BANANA PEEL RIGHT UNDERFOOT?!
NO WAY!
I'LL JUST REPAIR THE SIGN BEFORE ANYONE NOTICES!!
HUP!
THWK
I CAN DO A LITTLE CLEANUP IN HERE, TOO...!
Laa laa Laa laa~
WHEW...
I'M AMAZING! AT THIS RATE, I CAN DODGE ANY MISFORTUNE!
HUH? LOOKS AWFUL CLEAN IN HERE.
THOUGH, I DO FEEL LIKE I'M FORGETTING SOMETHING.

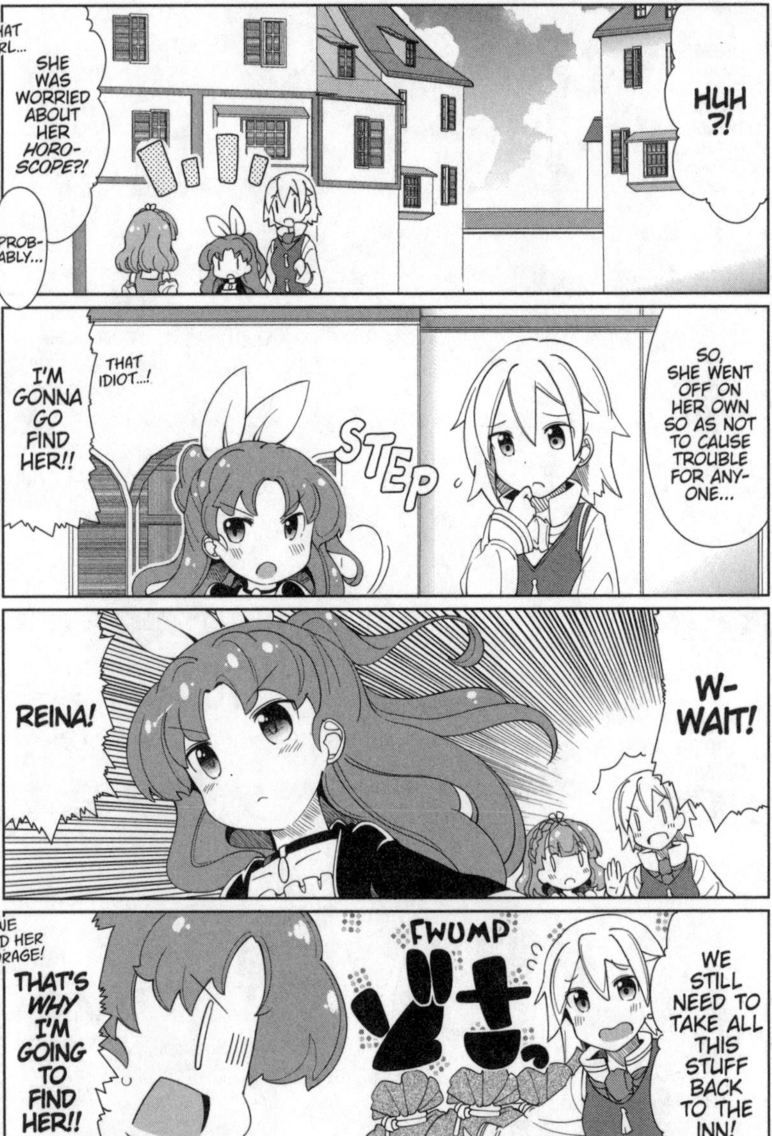
HUH?!
THAT GIRL...
SHE WAS WORRIED ABOUT HER HOROSCOPE?!
PROBABLY...
SO, SHE WENT OFF ON HER OWN SO AS NOT TO CAUSE TROUBLE FOR ANYONE...
STEP
THAT IDIOT...!
I'M GONNA GO FIND HER!!
W-WAIT!
REINA!
WE STILL NEED TO TAKE ALL THIS STUFF BACK TO THE INN!
FWUMP
WE NEED HER STORAGE!
THAT'S WHY I'M GOING TO FIND HER!!

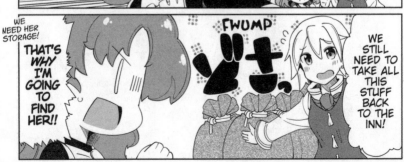

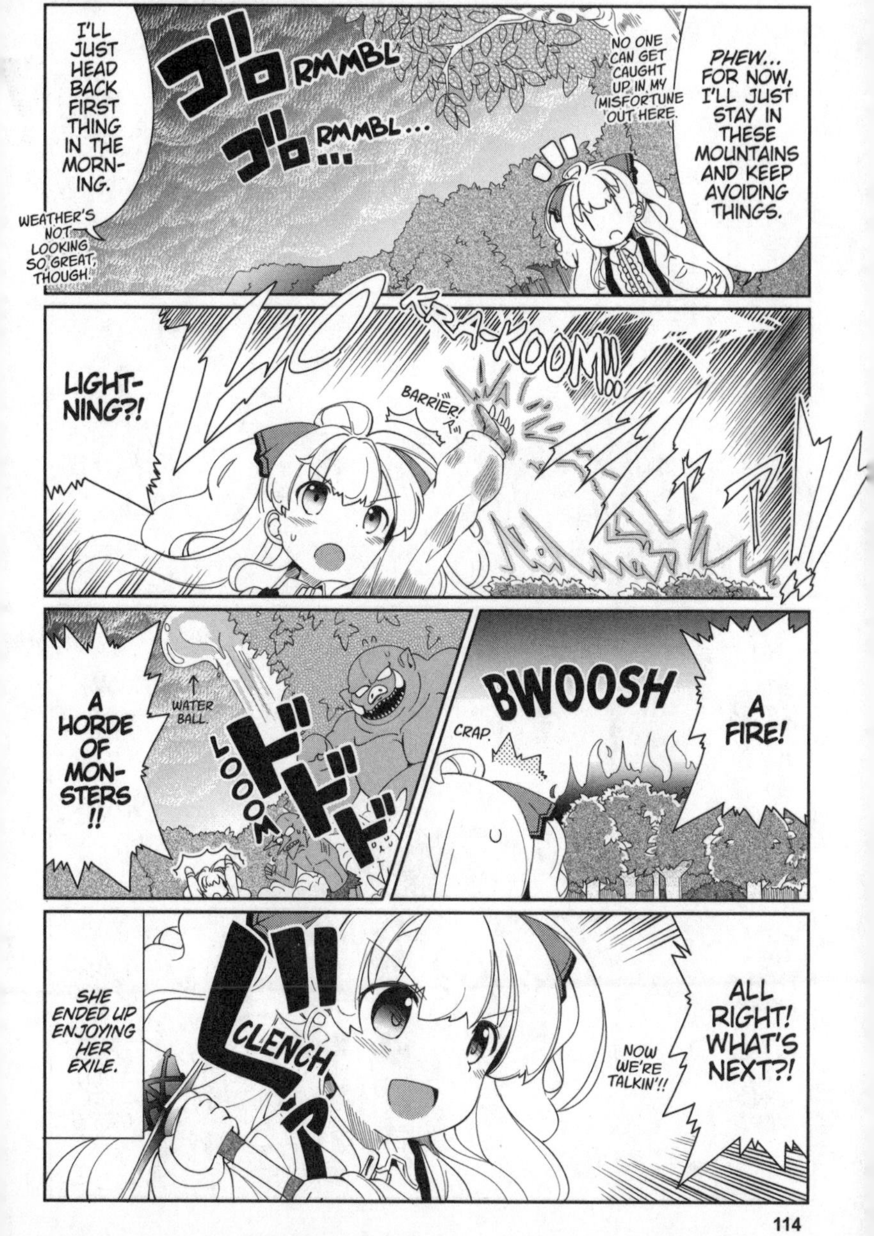
PHEW... FOR NOW, I'LL JUST STAY IN THESE MOUNTAINS AND KEEP AVOIDING THINGS.
NO ONE CAN GET CAUGHT UP IN MY MISFORTUNE OUT HERE.
ゴロ RMMBL
ゴロ... RMMBL...
I'LL JUST HEAD BACK FIRST THING IN THE MORN-ING.
WEATHER'S NOT LOOKING SO GREAT, THOUGH.
KRA-KOOM!!
BARRIER!
LIGHT-NING?!
A FIRE!
BWOOSH
CRAP.
WATER BALL.
A HORDE OF MON-STERS!!
ドドド
LOOOOM
ALL RIGHT! WHAT'S NEXT?!
NOW WE'RE TALKIN'!!
CLENCH
SHE ENDED UP ENJOYING HER EXILE.

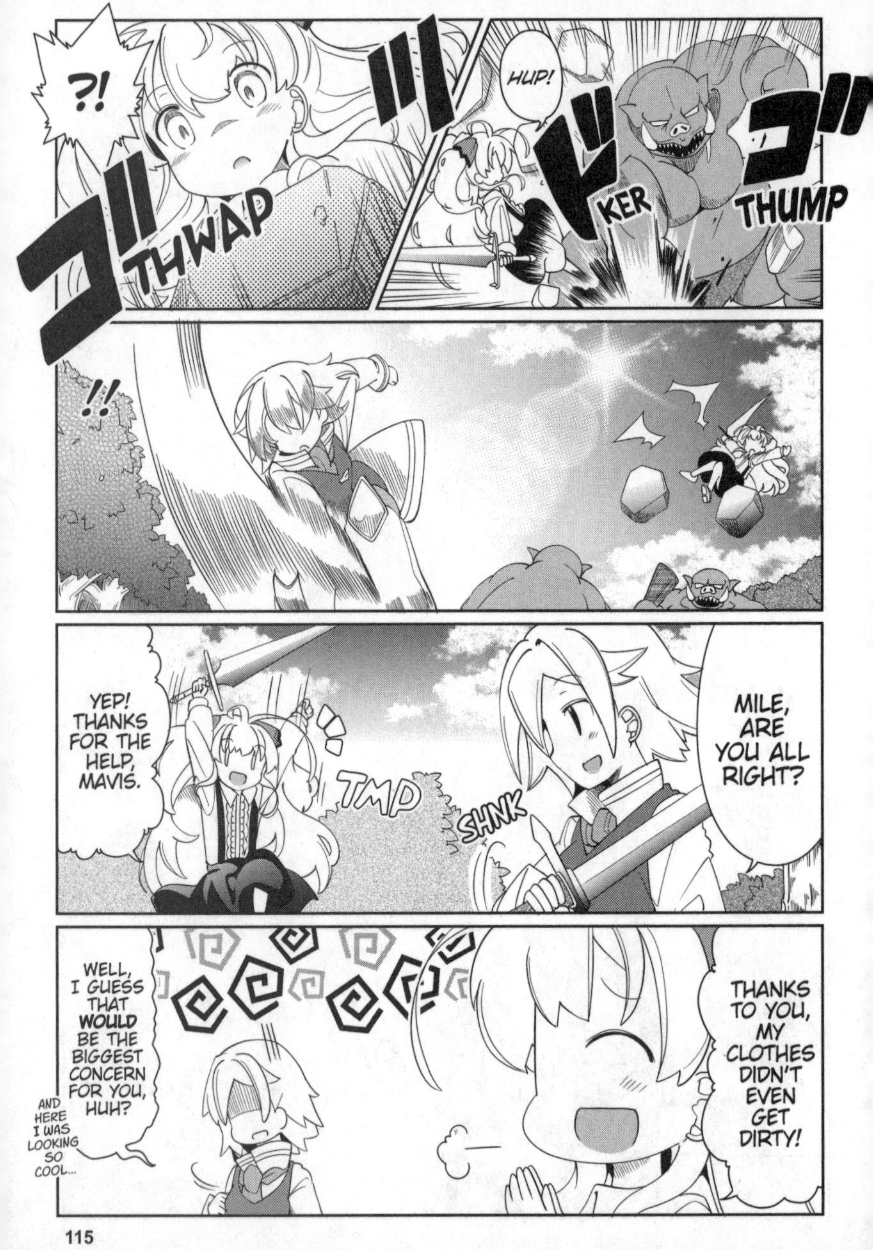

HUP!
ド
KER
ゴ
THUMP
?!
ゴ
THWAP
!!
MILE, ARE YOU ALL RIGHT?
SHNK
TMD
YEP! THANKS FOR THE HELP, MAVIS.
THANKS TO YOU, MY CLOTHES DIDN'T EVEN GET DIRTY!
WELL, I GUESS THAT **WOULD** BE THE BIGGEST CONCERN FOR YOU, HUH?
AND HERE I WAS LOOKING SO COOL...

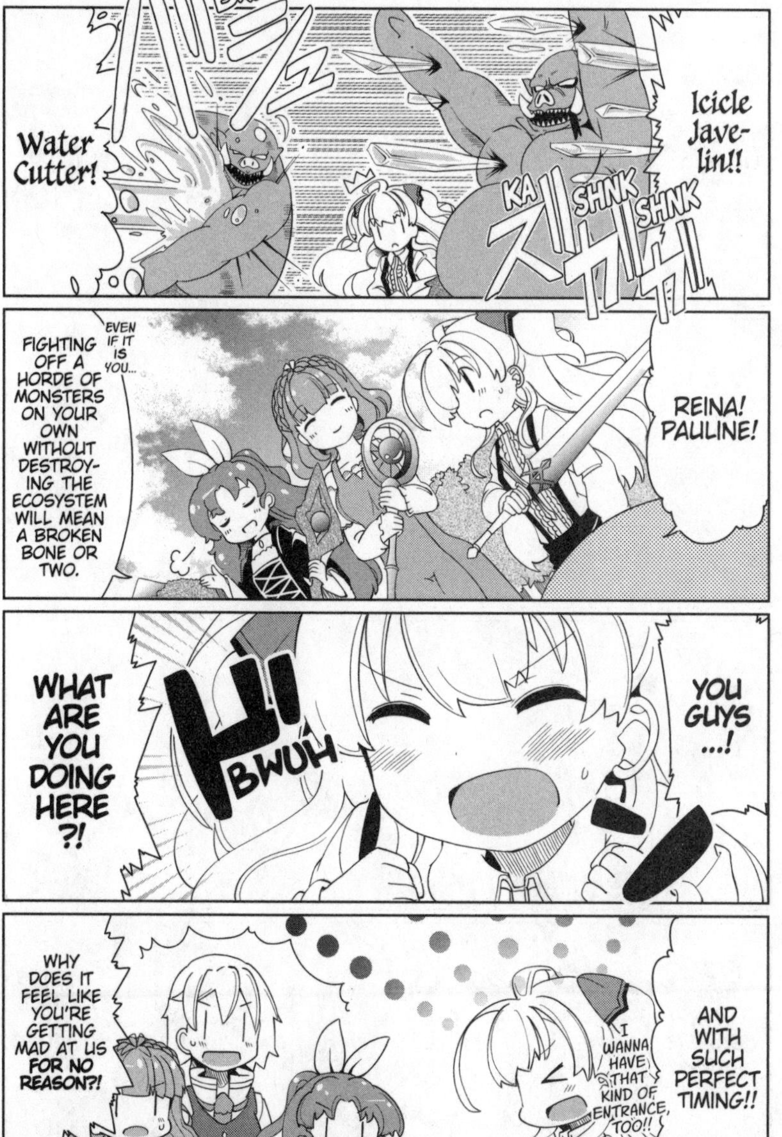

Icicle Jave-lin!!
KA SHNK SHNK
Bwsssh
Water Cutter!
REINA! PAULINE!
EVEN IF IT IS YOU...
FIGHTING OFF A HORDE OF MONSTERS ON YOUR OWN WITHOUT DESTROY-ING THE ECOSYSTEM WILL MEAN A BROKEN BONE OR TWO.
YOU GUYS ...!
BWUH
WHAT ARE YOU DOING HERE ?!
AND WITH SUCH PERFECT TIMING!!
I WANNA HAVE THAT KIND OF ENTRANCE, TOO!!
WHY DOES IT FEEL LIKE YOU'RE GETTING MAD AT US FOR NO REASON?!

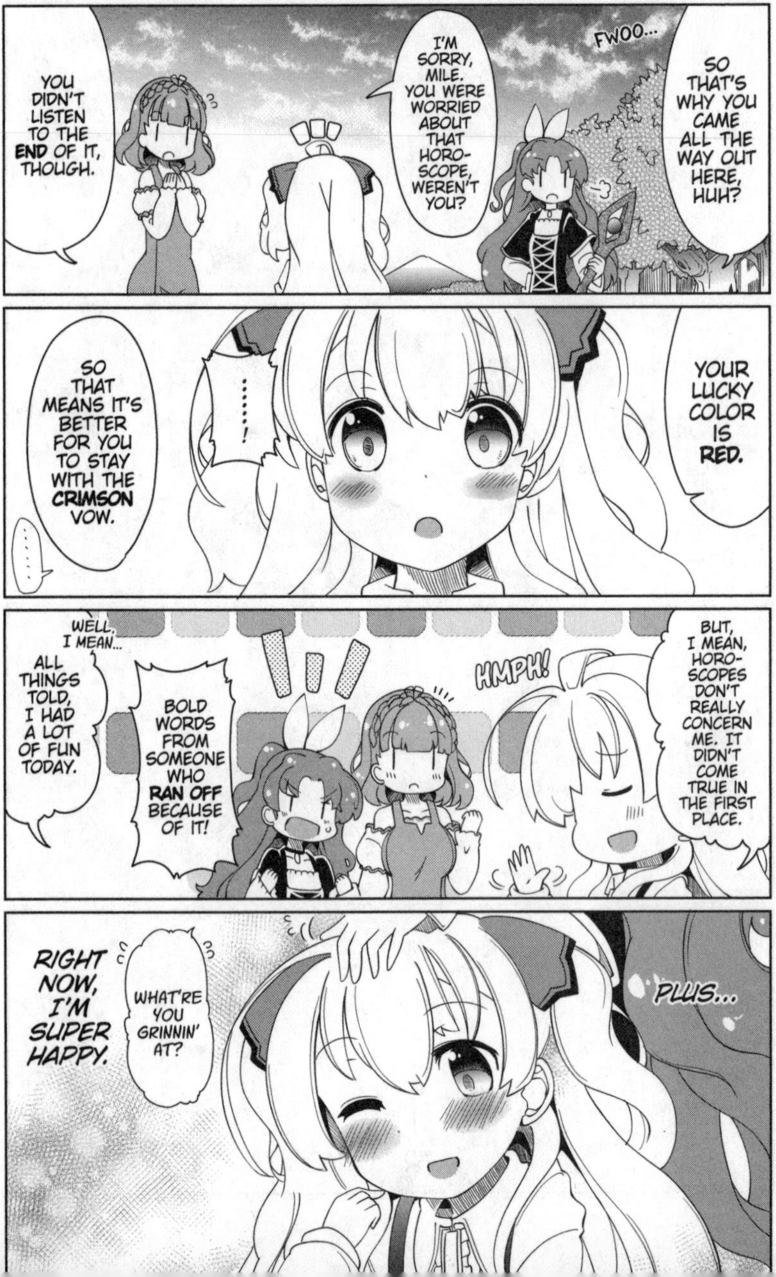
FWOO...
SO THAT'S WHY YOU CAME ALL THE WAY OUT HERE, HUH?
I'M SORRY, MILE. YOU WERE WORRIED ABOUT THAT HORO-SCOPE, WEREN'T YOU?
YOU DIDN'T LISTEN TO THE END OF IT, THOUGH.
YOUR LUCKY COLOR IS RED.
......!
SO THAT MEANS IT'S BETTER FOR YOU TO STAY WITH THE CRIMSON VOW.
......
BUT, I MEAN, HORO-SCOPES DON'T REALLY CONCERN ME. IT DIDN'T COME TRUE IN THE FIRST PLACE.
HMPH!
BOLD WORDS FROM SOMEONE WHO RAN OFF BECAUSE OF IT!
WELL, I MEAN...
ALL THINGS TOLD, I HAD A LOT OF FUN TODAY.
PLUS...
WHAT'RE YOU GRINNIN' AT?
RIGHT NOW, I'M SUPER HAPPY.

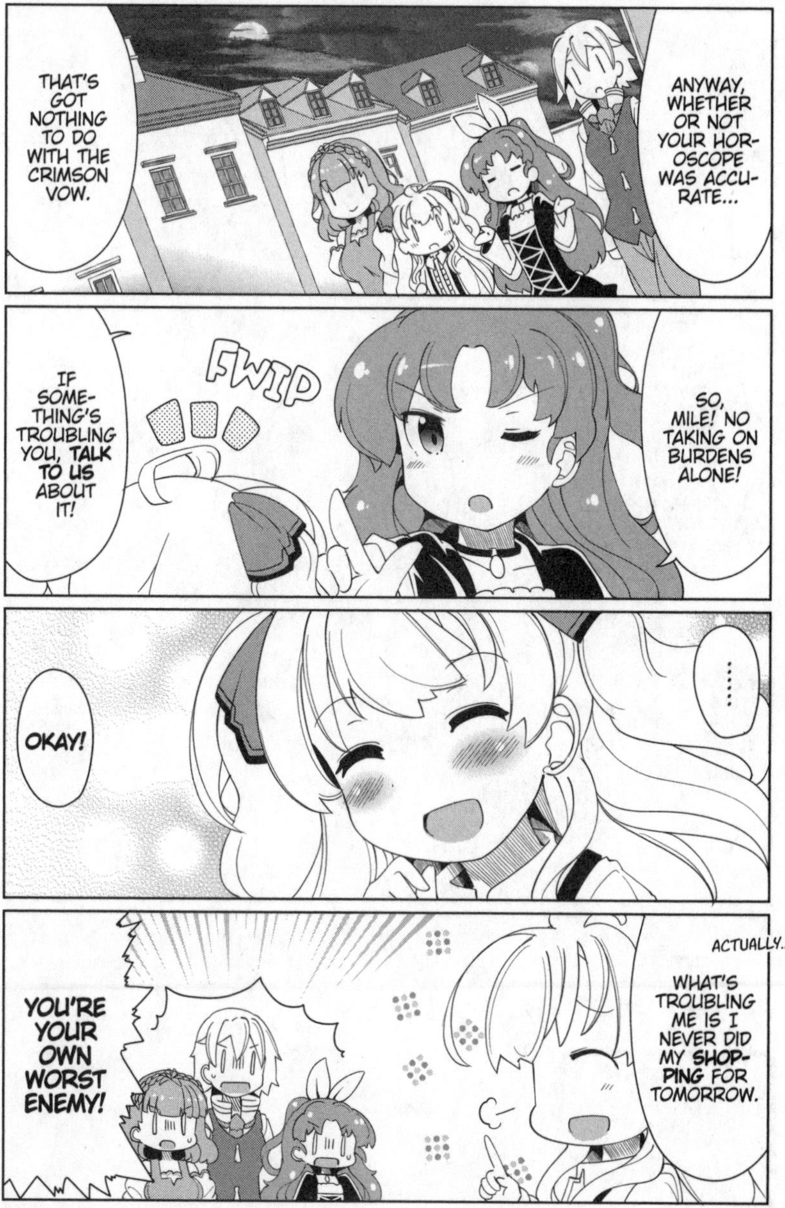
ANYWAY, WHETHER OR NOT YOUR HOROSCOPE WAS ACCURATE...
THAT'S GOT NOTHING TO DO WITH THE CRIMSON VOW.
SO, MILE! NO TAKING ON BURDENS ALONE!
FWIP
IF SOMETHING'S TROUBLING YOU, TALK TO US ABOUT IT!
......
OKAY!
ACTUALLY...
WHAT'S TROUBLING ME IS I NEVER DID MY SHOPPING FOR TOMORROW.
YOU'RE YOUR OWN WORST ENEMY!

Didn't I Say to Make My Abilities Average in the Next Life?!
EVERYDAY MISADVENTURES!

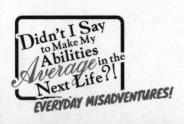

I LOVE KITTIES...

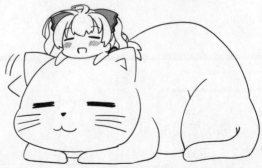

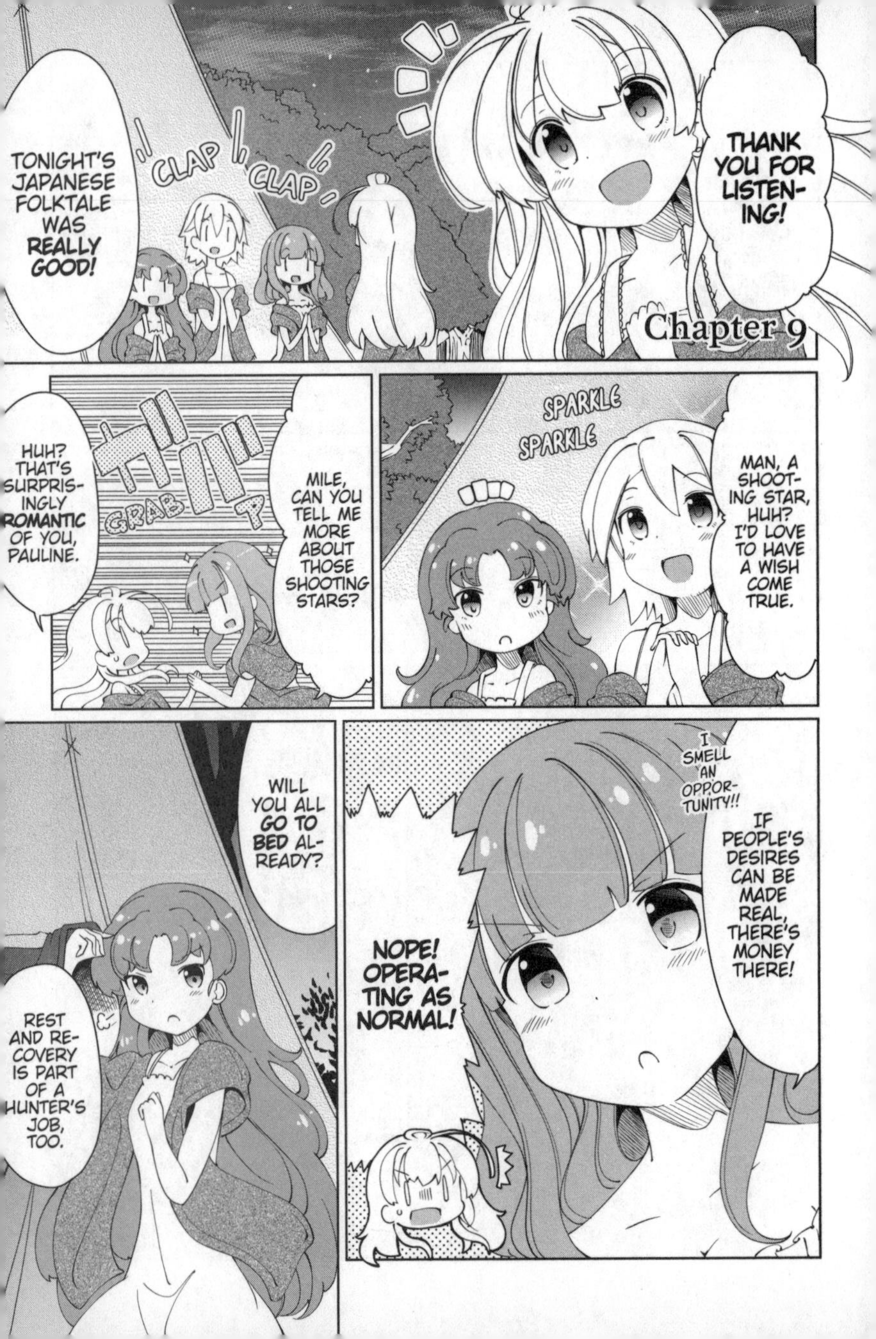
THANK YOU FOR LISTENING!
Chapter 9
CLAP CLAP
TONIGHT'S JAPANESE FOLKTALE WAS REALLY GOOD!
SPARKLE SPARKLE
MAN, A SHOOTING STAR, HUH? I'D LOVE TO HAVE A WISH COME TRUE.
MILE, CAN YOU TELL ME MORE ABOUT THOSE SHOOTING STARS?
GRAB
HUH? THAT'S SURPRISINGLY ROMANTIC OF YOU, PAULINE.
I SMELL AN OPPORTUNITY!!
IF PEOPLE'S DESIRES CAN BE MADE REAL, THERE'S MONEY THERE!
NOPE! OPERATING AS NORMAL!
WILL YOU ALL GO TO BED ALREADY?
REST AND RECOVERY IS PART OF A HUNTER'S JOB, TOO.

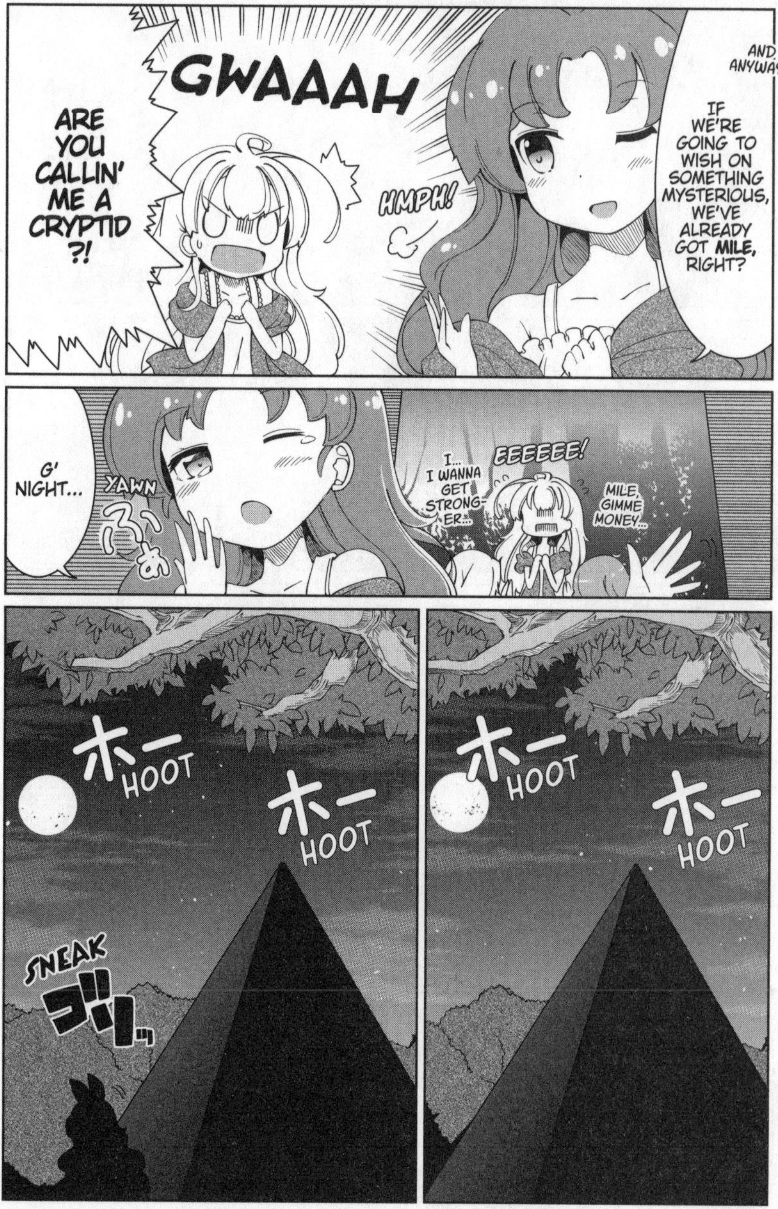
AND ANYWAY...
IF WE'RE GOING TO WISH ON SOMETHING MYSTERIOUS, WE'VE ALREADY GOT MILE, RIGHT?
HMPH!
GWAAAH
ARE YOU CALLIN' ME A CRYPTID?!
MILE, GIMME MONEY...
EEEEEE!
I... I WANNA GET STRONG-ER...
YAWN
ふあ
G' NIGHT...
ホー
HOOT
ホー
HOOT
ホー
HOOT
ホー
HOOT
SNEAK

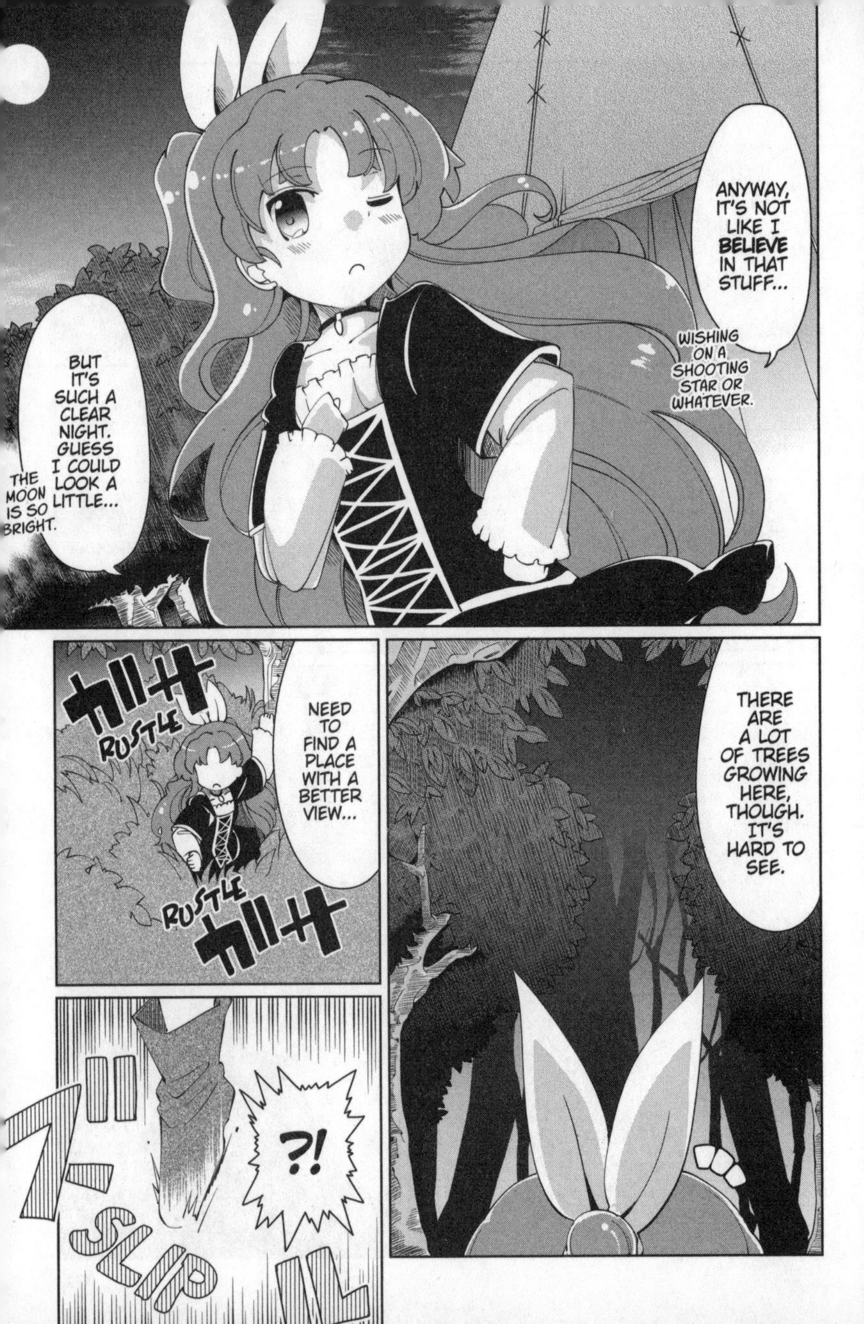
ANYWAY, IT'S NOT LIKE I **BELIEVE** IN THAT STUFF...
WISHING ON A SHOOTING STAR OR WHATEVER.
BUT IT'S SUCH A CLEAR NIGHT. GUESS I COULD LOOK A LITTLE...
THE MOON IS SO BRIGHT.
THERE ARE A LOT OF TREES GROWING HERE, THOUGH. IT'S HARD TO SEE.
RUSTLE
NEED TO FIND A PLACE WITH A BETTER VIEW...
RUSTLE
?!
SLIP

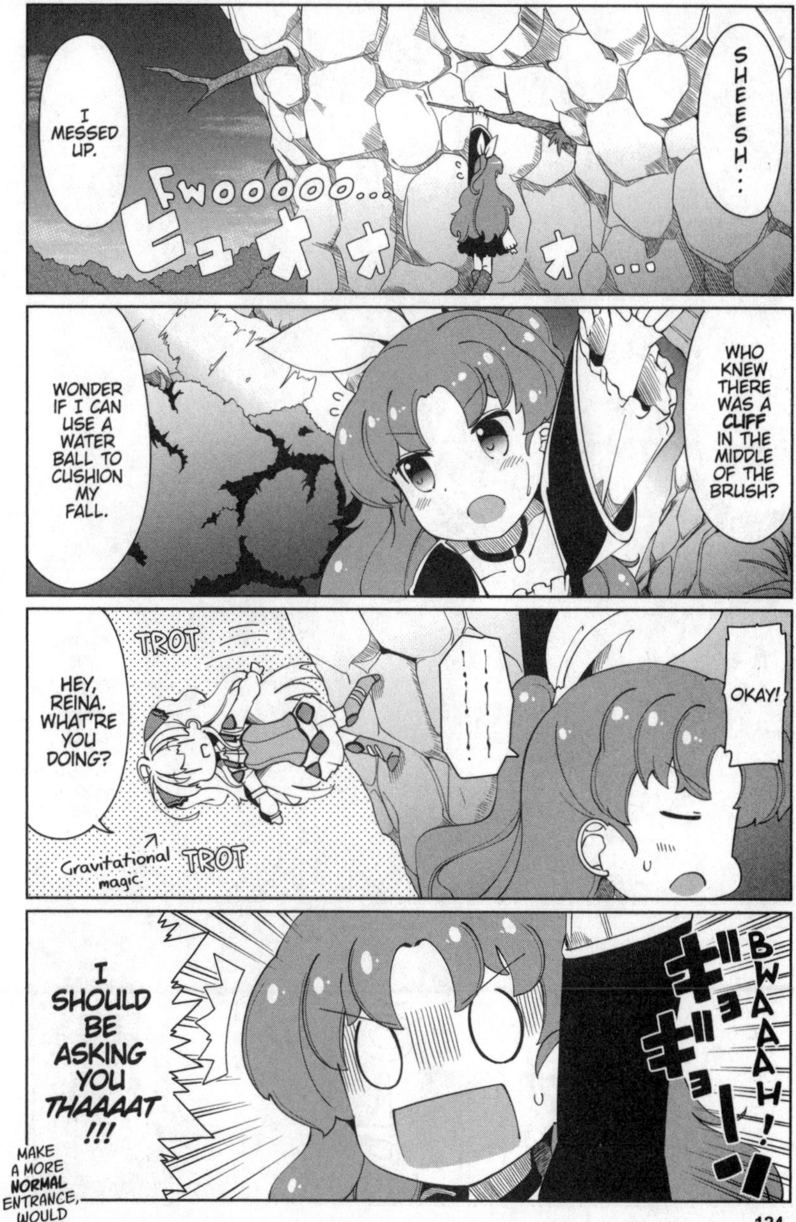
SHEESH...
FWOOOOOO...
ヒュオォォォ...
I MESSED UP.
WHO KNEW THERE WAS A **CLIFF** IN THE MIDDLE OF THE BRUSH?
WONDER IF I CAN USE A WATER BALL TO CUSHION MY FALL.
OKAY!
!!
TROT
HEY, REINA. WHAT'RE YOU DOING?
Gravitational magic.
TROT
BWAAAH!!
ギョギョーッ
I SHOULD BE ASKING YOU *THAAAAT*!!!
MAKE A MORE **NORMAL** ENTRANCE, WOULD YOU?!

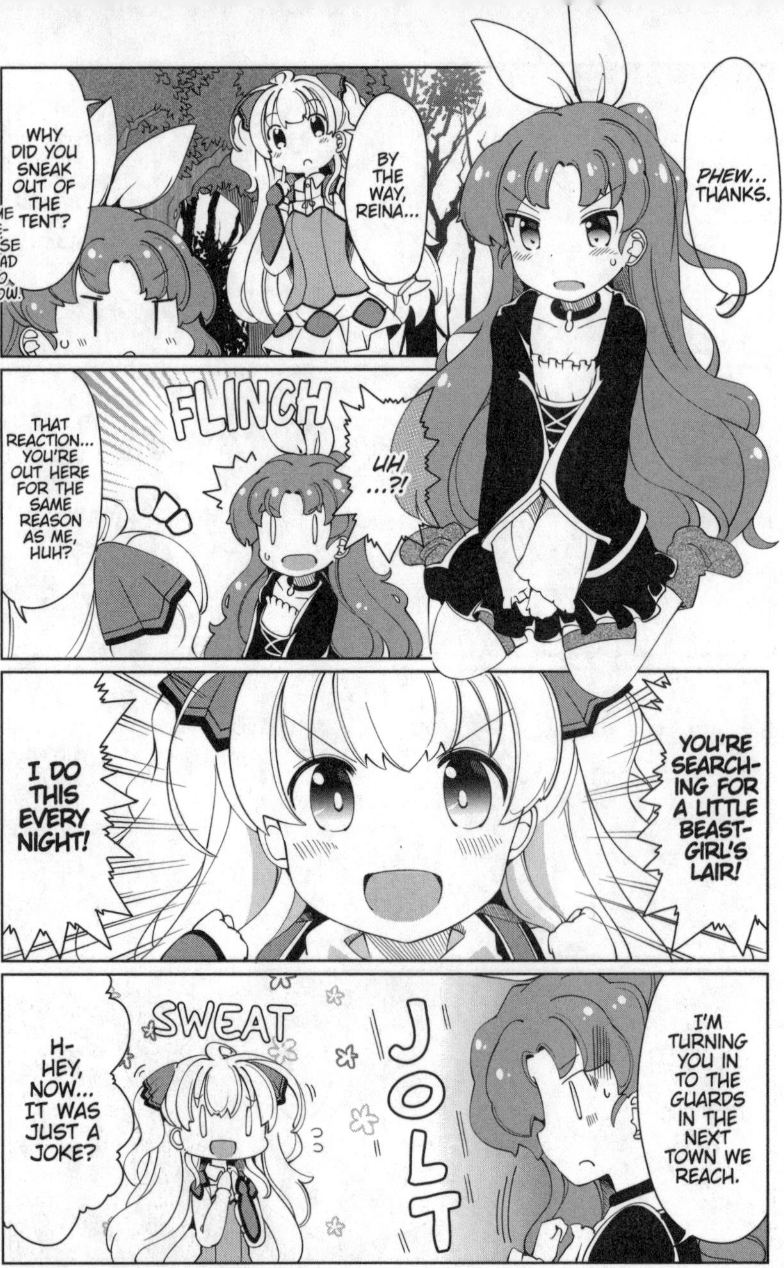
PHEW... THANKS.
BY THE WAY, REINA...
WHY DID YOU SNEAK OUT OF THE TENT?
I CAME BE-CAUSE I HAD TO KNOW.
UH ...?!
FLINCH
THAT REACTION... YOU'RE OUT HERE FOR THE SAME REASON AS ME, HUH?
YOU'RE SEARCH-ING FOR A LITTLE BEAST-GIRL'S LAIR!
I DO THIS EVERY NIGHT!
I'M TURNING YOU IN TO THE GUARDS IN THE NEXT TOWN WE REACH.
JOLT
SWEAT
H-HEY, NOW... IT WAS JUST A JOKE?

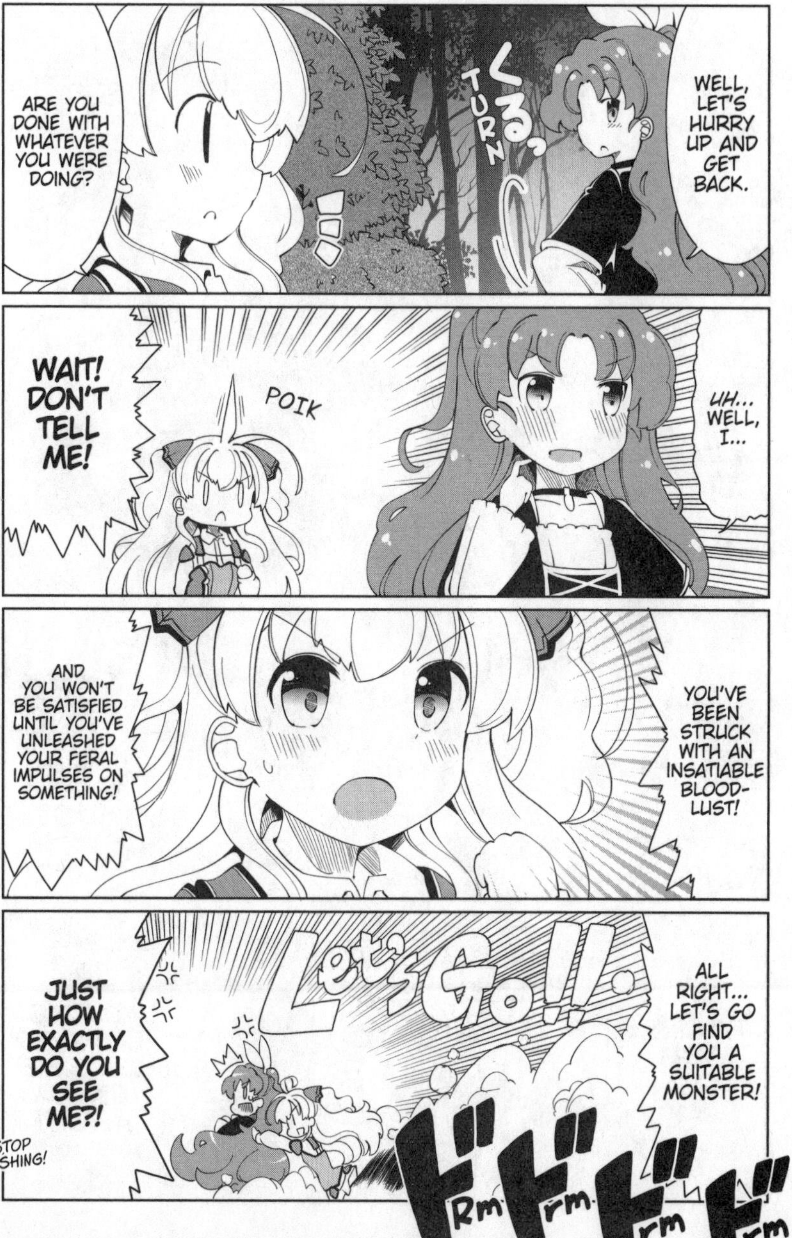
WELL, LET'S HURRY UP AND GET BACK.
くるっ
TURN
ARE YOU DONE WITH WHATEVER YOU WERE DOING?
UH... WELL, I...
POIK
WAIT! DON'T TELL ME!
YOU'VE BEEN STRUCK WITH AN INSATIABLE BLOOD-LUST!
AND YOU WON'T BE SATISFIED UNTIL YOU'VE UNLEASHED YOUR FERAL IMPULSES ON SOMETHING!
ALL RIGHT... LET'S GO FIND YOU A SUITABLE MONSTER!
Let's Go!!
JUST HOW EXACTLY DO YOU SEE ME?!
STOP PUSHING!
ドドドド
Rm rm rm rm

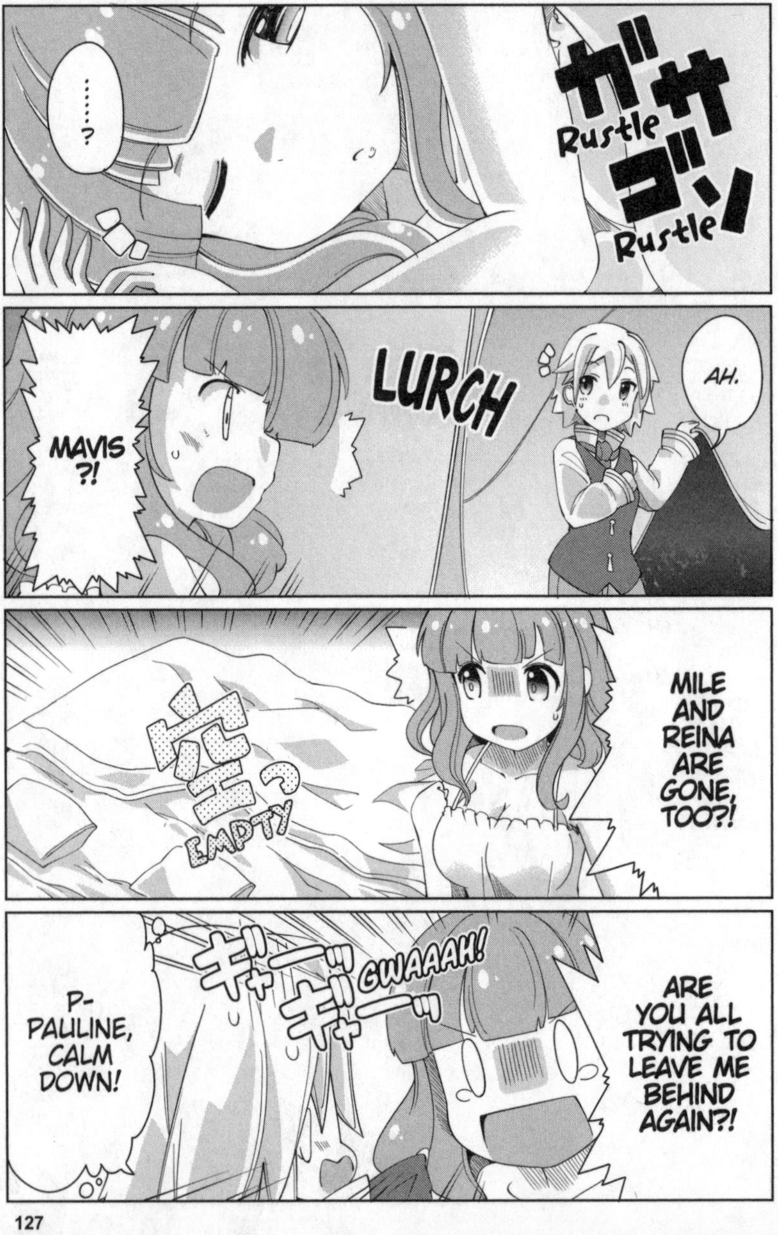
ガサ
Rustle
ゴソ
Rustle
……?
AH.
LURCH
MAVIS?!
MILE AND REINA ARE GONE, TOO?!
空っ
EMPTY
ARE YOU ALL TRYING TO LEAVE ME BEHIND AGAIN?!
ギャーッ ギャーッ
GWAAAH!
P-PAULINE, CALM DOWN!

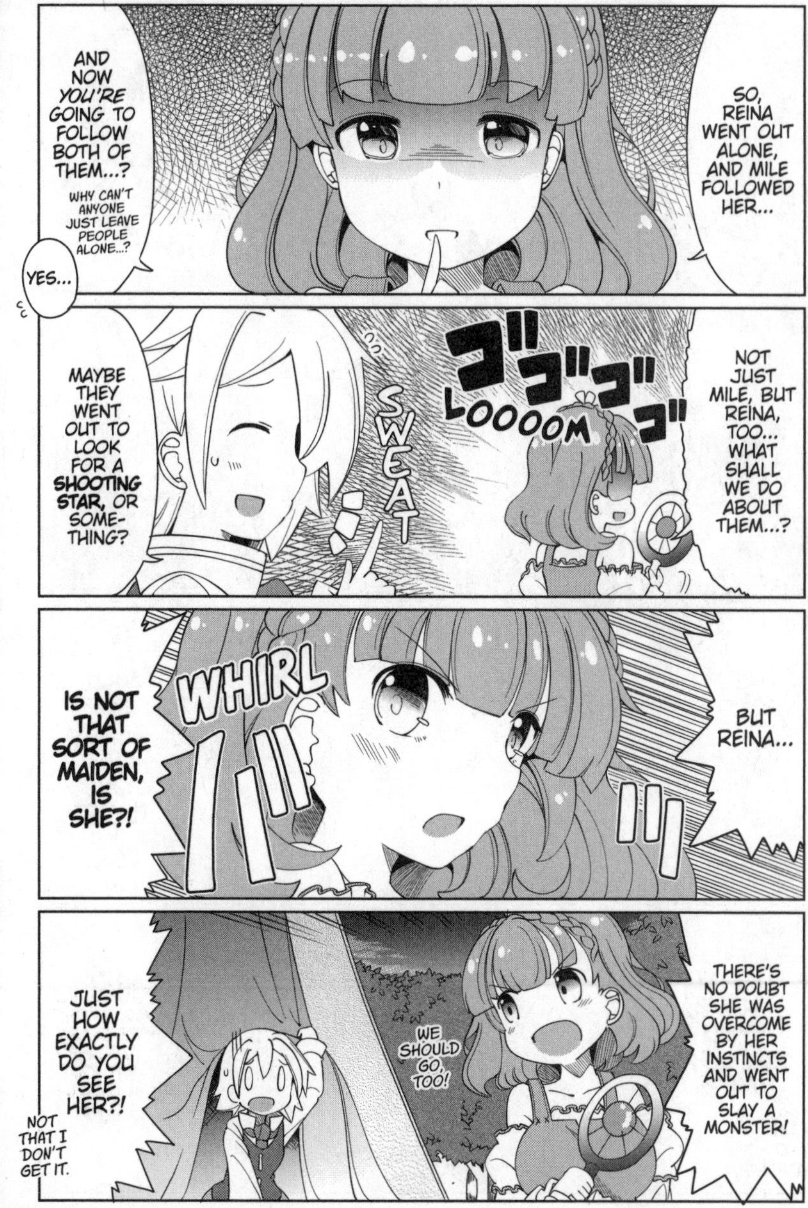
SO, REINA WENT OUT ALONE, AND MILE FOLLOWED HER...
AND NOW YOU'RE GOING TO FOLLOW BOTH OF THEM...?
WHY CAN'T ANYONE JUST LEAVE PEOPLE ALONE...?
YES...
NOT JUST MILE, BUT REINA, TOO... WHAT SHALL WE DO ABOUT THEM...?
ゴゴゴゴ
LOOOOM
SWEAT
MAYBE THEY WENT OUT TO LOOK FOR A SHOOTING STAR, OR SOME-THING?
BUT REINA...
WHIRL
IS NOT THAT SORT OF MAIDEN, IS SHE?!
THERE'S NO DOUBT SHE WAS OVERCOME BY HER INSTINCTS AND WENT OUT TO SLAY A MONSTER!
WE SHOULD GO, TOO!
JUST HOW EXACTLY DO YOU SEE HER?!
NOT THAT I DON'T GET IT.

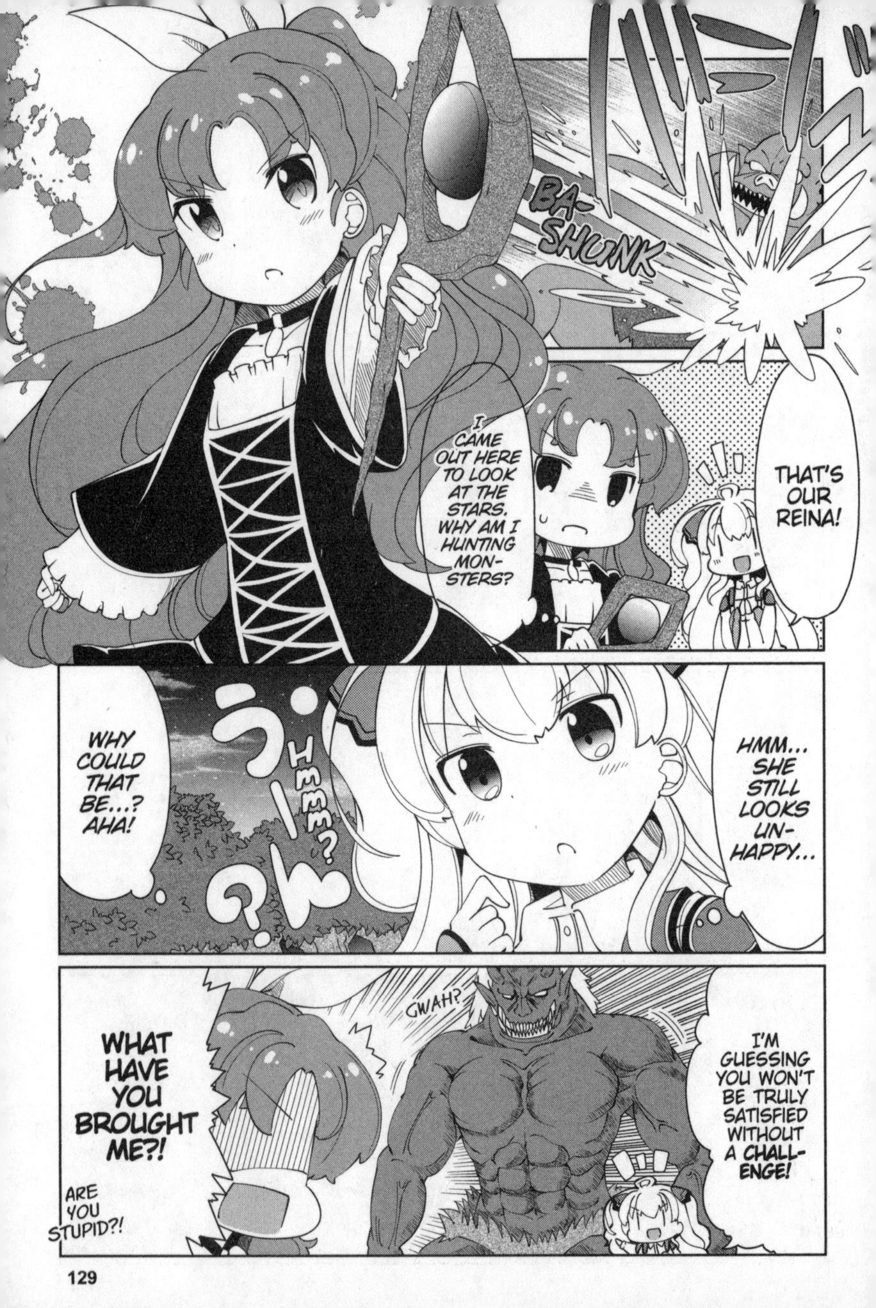
BA-SHUNK
THAT'S OUR REINA!
I CAME OUT HERE TO LOOK AT THE STARS. WHY AM I HUNTING MON-STERS?
HMM... SHE STILL LOOKS UN-HAPPY...
HMMM?
WHY COULD THAT BE...? AHA!
I'M GUESSING YOU WON'T BE TRULY SATISFIED WITHOUT A CHALL-ENGE!
GWAH?
WHAT HAVE YOU BROUGHT ME?!
ARE YOU STUPID?!

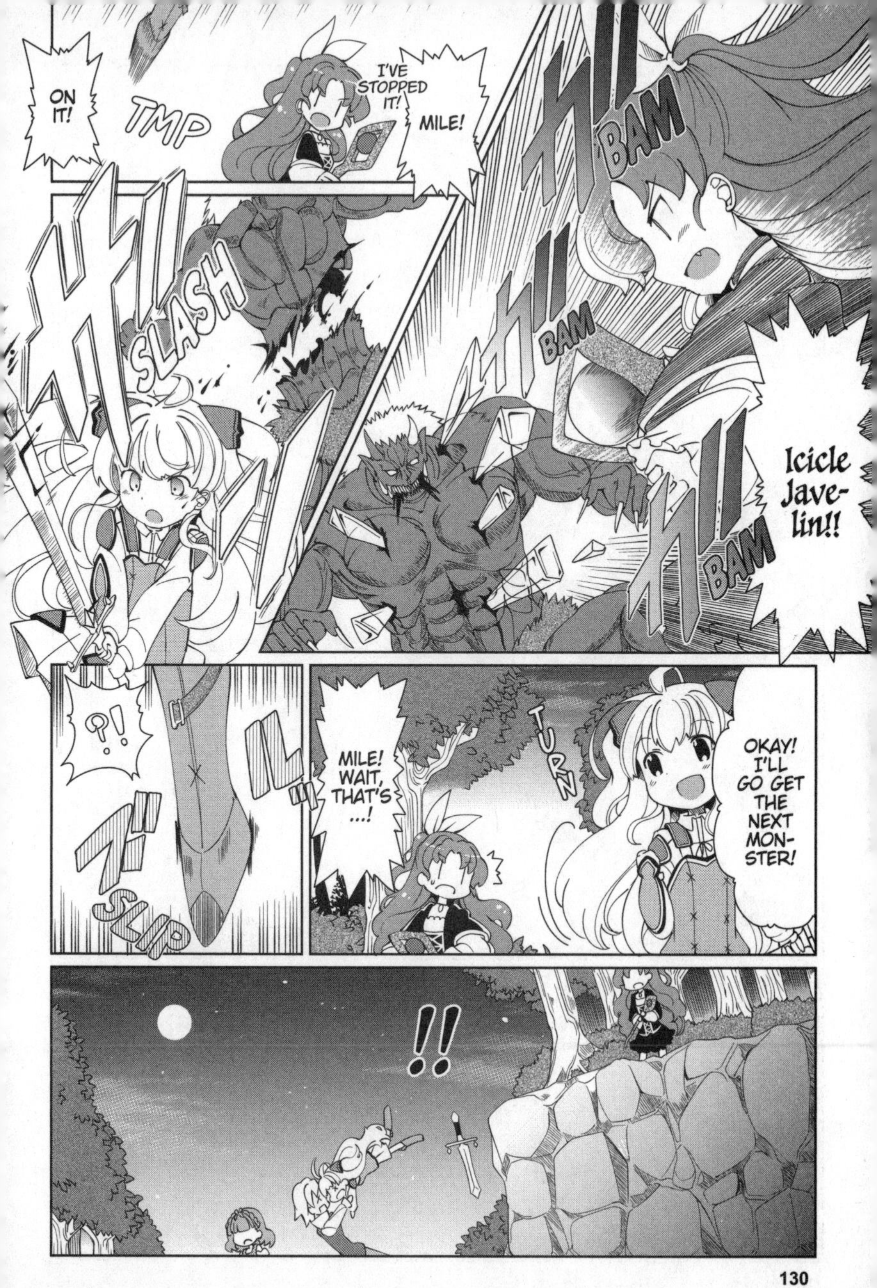
BAM
BAM
BAM
Icicle Javelin!!
I'VE STOPPED IT!
MILE!
ON IT!
TMP
SLASH
OKAY! I'LL GO GET THE NEXT MONSTER!
TURN
MILE! WAIT, THAT'S ...!
?!
SLIP
!!

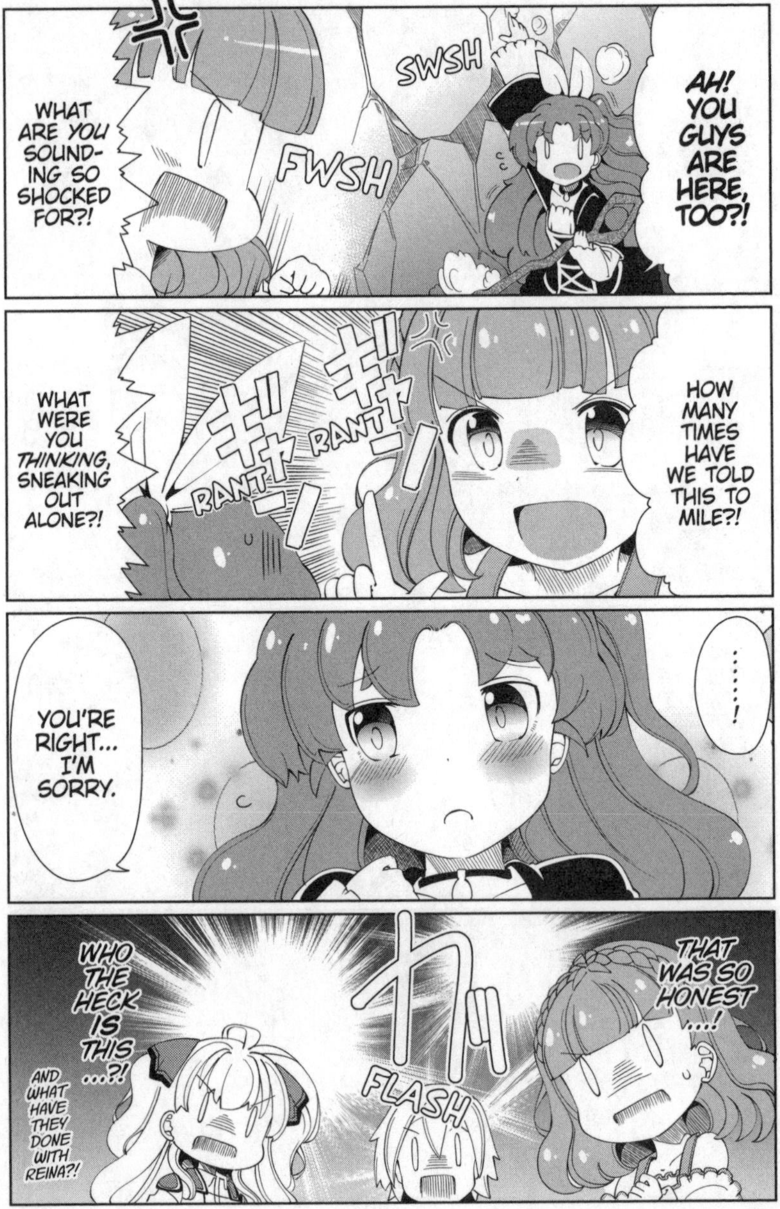

AH! YOU GUYS ARE HERE, TOO?!
SWSH
FWSH
WHAT ARE YOU SOUNDING SO SHOCKED FOR?!
HOW MANY TIMES HAVE WE TOLD THIS TO MILE?!
RANT
RANT
WHAT WERE YOU THINKING, SNEAKING OUT ALONE?!
......!
YOU'RE RIGHT... I'M SORRY.
THAT WAS SO HONEST ...!
FLASH
WHO THE HECK IS THIS ...?!
AND WHAT HAVE THEY DONE WITH REINA?!

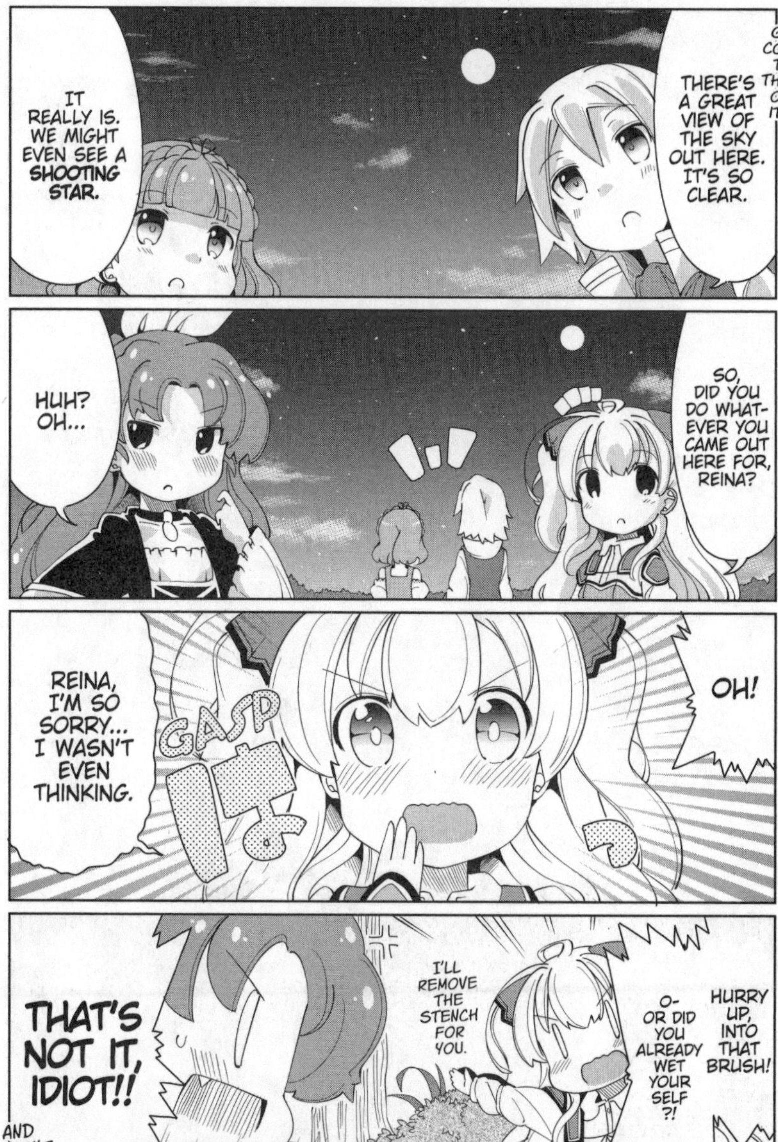

THERE'S A GREAT VIEW OF THE SKY OUT HERE. IT'S SO CLEAR.
OH, COME TO THINK OF IT...
IT REALLY IS. WE MIGHT EVEN SEE A SHOOTING STAR.
SO, DID YOU DO WHAT-EVER YOU CAME OUT HERE FOR, REINA?
HUH? OH...
OH!
GASP
REINA, I'M SO SORRY... I WASN'T EVEN THINKING.
HURRY UP, INTO THAT BRUSH!
O- OR DID YOU ALREADY WET YOUR SELF?!
I'LL REMOVE THE STENCH FOR YOU.
THAT'S NOT IT, IDIOT!!
AND I DON'T STINK!

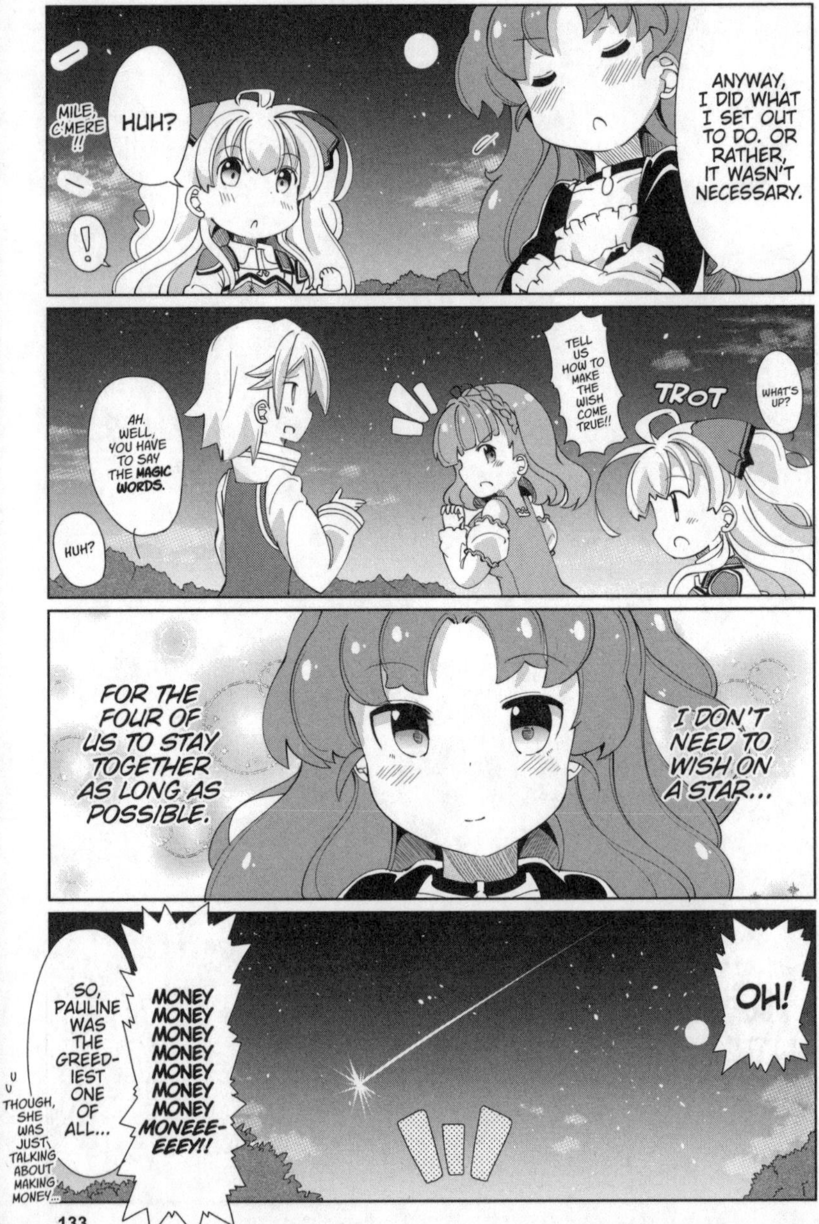
ANYWAY, I DID WHAT I SET OUT TO DO. OR RATHER, IT WASN'T NECESSARY.
HUH?
MILE, C'MERE!!
WHAT'S UP?
TROT
TELL US HOW TO MAKE THE WISH COME TRUE!!
AH. WELL, YOU HAVE TO SAY THE MAGIC WORDS.
HUH?
I DON'T NEED TO WISH ON A STAR...
FOR THE FOUR OF US TO STAY TOGETHER AS LONG AS POSSIBLE.
OH!
MONEY MONEY MONEY MONEY MONEY MONEY MONEY MONEEE-EEEY!!
SO, PAULINE WAS THE GREEDIEST ONE OF ALL...
THOUGH, SHE WAS JUST TALKING ABOUT MAKING MONEY...

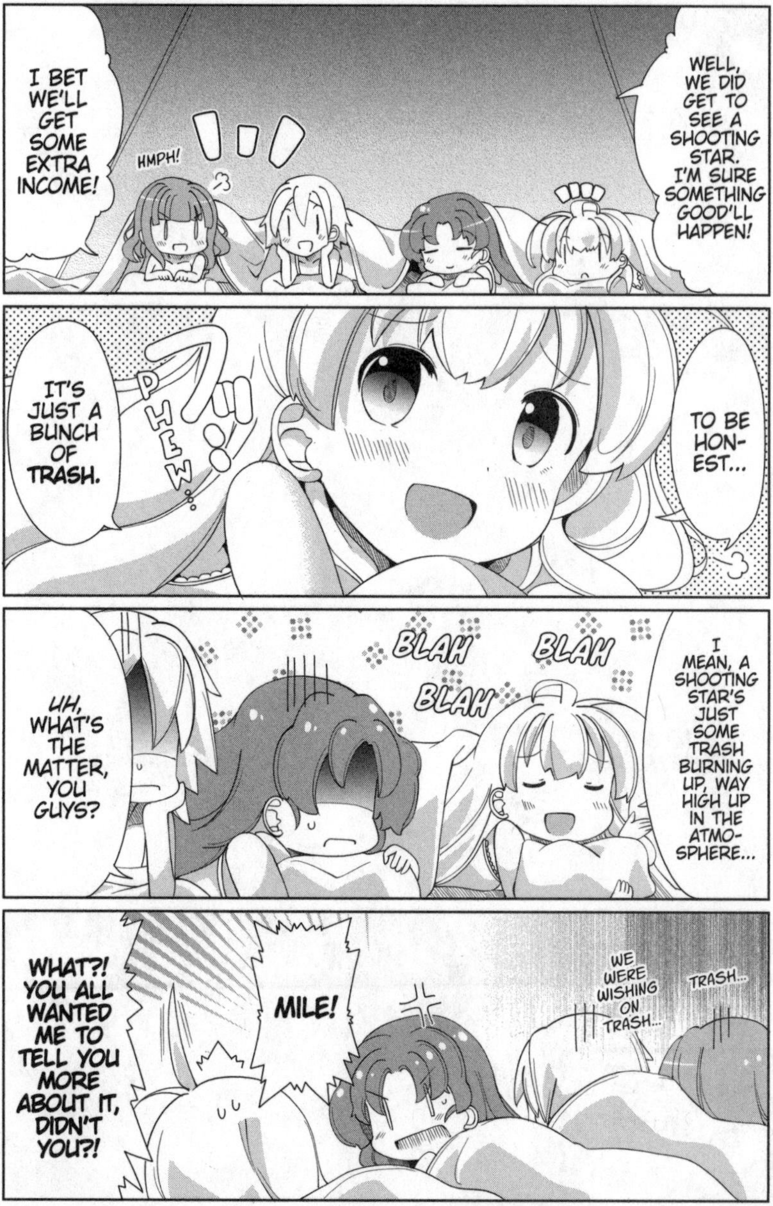
WELL, WE DID GET TO SEE A SHOOTING STAR. I'M SURE SOMETHING GOOD'LL HAPPEN!
HMPH!
I BET WE'LL GET SOME EXTRA INCOME!
TO BE HON-EST...
PHEW...
IT'S JUST A BUNCH OF TRASH.
I MEAN, A SHOOTING STAR'S JUST SOME TRASH BURNING UP, WAY HIGH UP IN THE ATMOS-PHERE...
BLAH BLAH
BLAH
UH, WHAT'S THE MATTER, YOU GUYS?
TRASH...
WE WERE WISHING ON TRASH...
MILE!
WHAT?! YOU ALL WANTED ME TO TELL YOU MORE ABOUT IT, DIDN'T YOU?!

Didn't I Say to Make My Abilities Average in the Next Life?!

EVERYDAY MISADVENTURES!

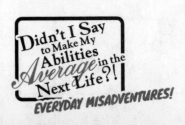

Didn't I Say to Make My Abilities Average in the Next Life?!

EVERYDAY MISADVENTURES!

BONUS STORY
Didn't I Say to Make My Abilities Average in the Next Life?!

A Kidnapping

"*Ohh noo...*"

With a halfhearted scream, she was swept away.

Pauline, that is.

The other three Vows watched, waving.

"See you later!!" they called.

Pauline had been spirited away boldly, in broad daylight, right in front of her allies' noses. Furthermore, no one seemed worried about this in the least—including Pauline, the abductee.

After all, this did happen quite often...

"*Umm...* So, where are we and why have you brought me here...?*" asked Pauline, not seeming at all concerned for her safety.

The man who seemed to be the leader of the kidnappers replied, "You're in a certain mansion—"

"Huh? A serpent mansion?"

"No! It's a *certain noble's* mansion!"

Apparently, this was *not* a mansion belonging to a snake charmer.

"We need you to cure a certain noble's illness."

"What? A serpent noble?"

"Will you lay off the snake thing?!"

The kidnapper, understandably, was getting irritated. However, upon hearing them mention an illness, Pauline understood that this was just par for the course. Healing magic was typically highly effective for managing injuries, but if someone recklessly tried to use healing magic on a disease without the requisite knowledge of said disease, the magic could actually make things worse—even bringing about the worst-case scenario. Healing an illness with magic thus required an intense amount of concentration. Typically, only those who had exhausted all other options would pay the exorbitant fees to hire world-class healing mages, especially as the customers were required to sign contracts absolving the healers of any responsibility should anything go wrong.

The mages, for their part, certainly didn't want to cause anyone's death, so they generally did not accept a job unless they were receiving quite a large amount of money for it. Indeed, many mages would not accept such jobs at all, no matter how much they were offered. That said, few people were willing to gamble such a large amount of money in the first place—particularly given the chances that they could die if things went wrong.

Though the dwelling to which Pauline had been brought *could* technically be called a mansion, it was quite small, and while it was nicely cleaned and maintained, it seemed somewhat run-down and a bit shabby. In other words, it reeked of poverty.

I'm guessing they're willing to put in all on the line by using magic to cure an illness, but they don't have the money to hire a renowned mage, Pauline thought. Furthermore, while abducting a renowned healing mage would cause a huge commotion, Pauline, despite her reputation as a skilled healer,

was only a C-rank hunter. Abducting *her* would not prompt retaliation by a noble family or the Crown. As long as they returned her safely when the job was done, the kidnappers would be in the clear.

And so, this was the way these things usually transpired. When Pauline succeeded, she would be heralded as the master's savior, and should anyone else in their family fall ill, they would be sure to seek out her services again. So, they would thank her profusely, hand over a few gold coins, and bring her safely home.

Even if things did not follow the typical pattern, Pauline just had to get serious and release the full force of her spice-induced "hot" magic, and that would be that. Unless they came at her with lethal force from the start, most foes found it difficult to defeat Pauline in close range combat...no matter how many goons they had assembled.

So, for Pauline, these kidnappings had become her bread and butter—a relatively decent side-hustle, an easy way to earn a little extra gold.

Of course, this sort of work was limited to mages who were highly confident in their healing-magic skill. If a healer were to cause their employer's death, they would likely be repaid not with gold but the business end of a blade. As a result, most mage-type hunters tended to make a break for it on the spot.

Certainly, mages who worked as hunters were not limited to healing magic alone. They might also be asked for attack spells, defense spells, or support spells; to conjure up fire or water; whether they had any magic that could repel insects, or cool everyone down when it was hot outside, et cetera, et cetera... Even if a mage were to insist that they specialized in healing magic, no one was likely to listen to them. Mages were

a one-stop shop. A jack-of-all-trades. Being at the beck and call of their allies' every whim was the lot of the mage hunter.

As a result, hardly any mage hunters could be expected to have the luxury of throwing themselves into the research and study necessary to grasp the basic understanding of healing magic, let alone that required for the highly difficult magic of curing disease, which would never be requested of them on the battlefield.

Healing illnesses was a service that not even high-ranking temple priests could provide. The danger and the risk of killing the patient was too great, so no matter what ridiculous amounts of money they were offered, priests refused the requests as "contrary to the Goddess's will"—with the exception, that is, of particularly corrupt priests. That said, those who sought the priesthood would never have been wielders of powerful healing magic in the first place.

Thus, it was only natural that the kidnappers would set their sights on Pauline; and given how many people followed the same line of thinking and came to the same conclusions, this had become a common occurrence for Pauline. Given the knowledge of illnesses and the workings of the human body that she picked up from Mile, and the fact that she had never once failed in her healing, she had quite a bit of leeway.

Naturally, if these people were to submit a formal job request for a mage hunter to tend to an illness, no one would ever accept it. Their only recourse would be to make a direct request to Pauline herself, but there was no guarantee that she'd accept it, either. So, it was not incomprehensible to Pauline that desperate folk might resort to such heavy-handed measures.

Kidnapping was a criminal act, of course, but that was no matter if it led to an illness being cured. Plus, there was nothing criminal about the gold. With this as her philosophy,

rather than growing angry at the kidnapping, Pauline cheerfully inquired about the patient:

"So then, where is the stricken party...?"

"*Uh*... Yeah, right this way..."

The kidnappers were slightly unsettled by Pauline's fearlessness, but knew it was far better than having her mess up her spell out of fear. Indeed, unlike combat magic, in which volume was more important than precision, healing magic was a delicate process. So they led her along without question.

What Pauline saw in the room she was brought to was...

a rotund young boy sitting in a chair, an eyepatch over his left eye, his left arm in a cast, and a copy of Miami Satodele's *Summoned into Another World: I'm the Friggin' Greatest! (The Novel)* in his hand.

"It's the eldest son, Lord Hieroman. The disease was called 'chuunibyou,' or something..."

"You expect me to cure *thaaaaaaaaaat??!!*"

And so, with a single gold piece as her consultation fee in hand, Pauline headed back home...

Afterword

Pleased to meet you. I'm Yuki Moritaka. Thank you so much for picking up *Everyday Misadventures*!

And congratulations on the anime, FUNA-sensei and Akata-sensei!

Thanks as always to my editors, the designer, and everyone else involved for your assistance!

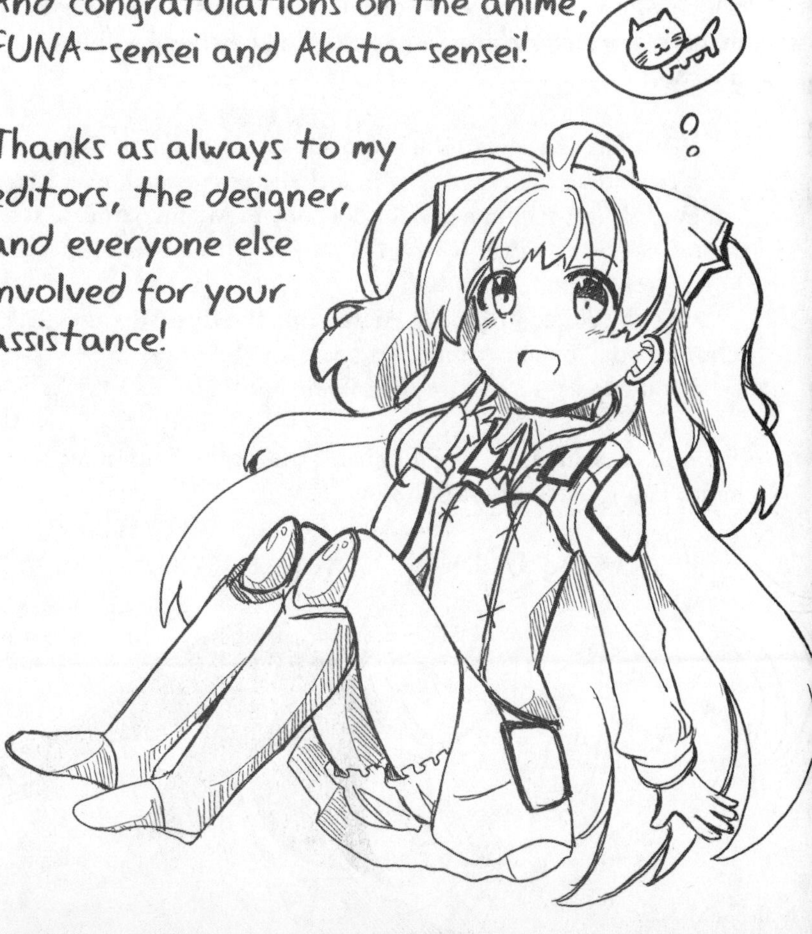

I always have so much fun getting to draw this!

Mile is so wild and free-spirited that I get super excited to draw her every time.

I always wonder if it's okay how many liberties I'm taking, but that's the way it goes! I'm going to draw lots more exciting everyday adventures for the Crimson Vow from here on out (for as long as they continue letting me draw it ˘˘)! I hope you'll keep on reading.

Thank you so much!

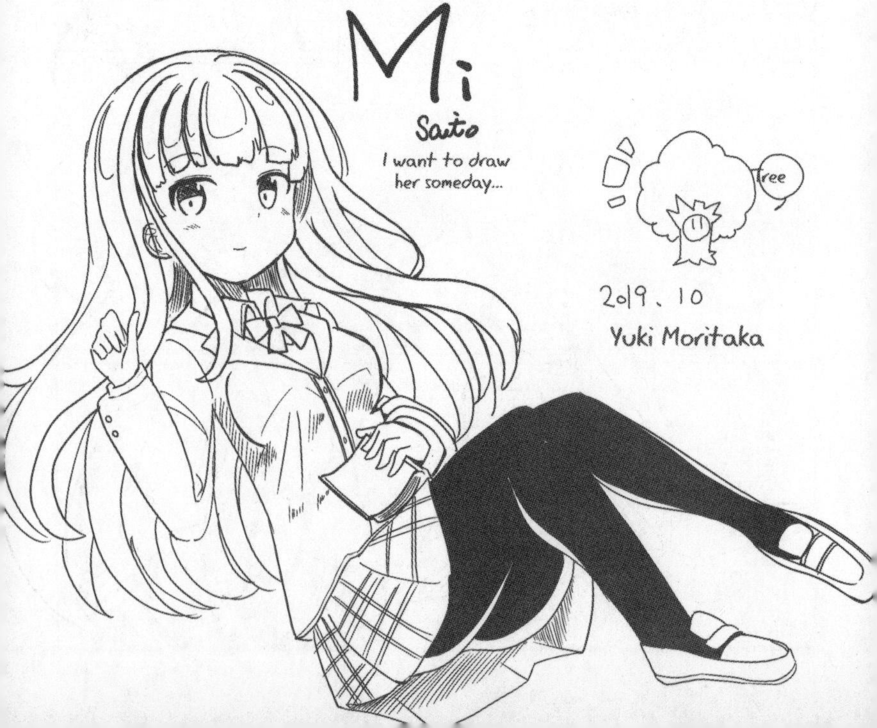
Mi
Saito
I want to draw her someday...
tree

2019.10
Yuki Moritaka

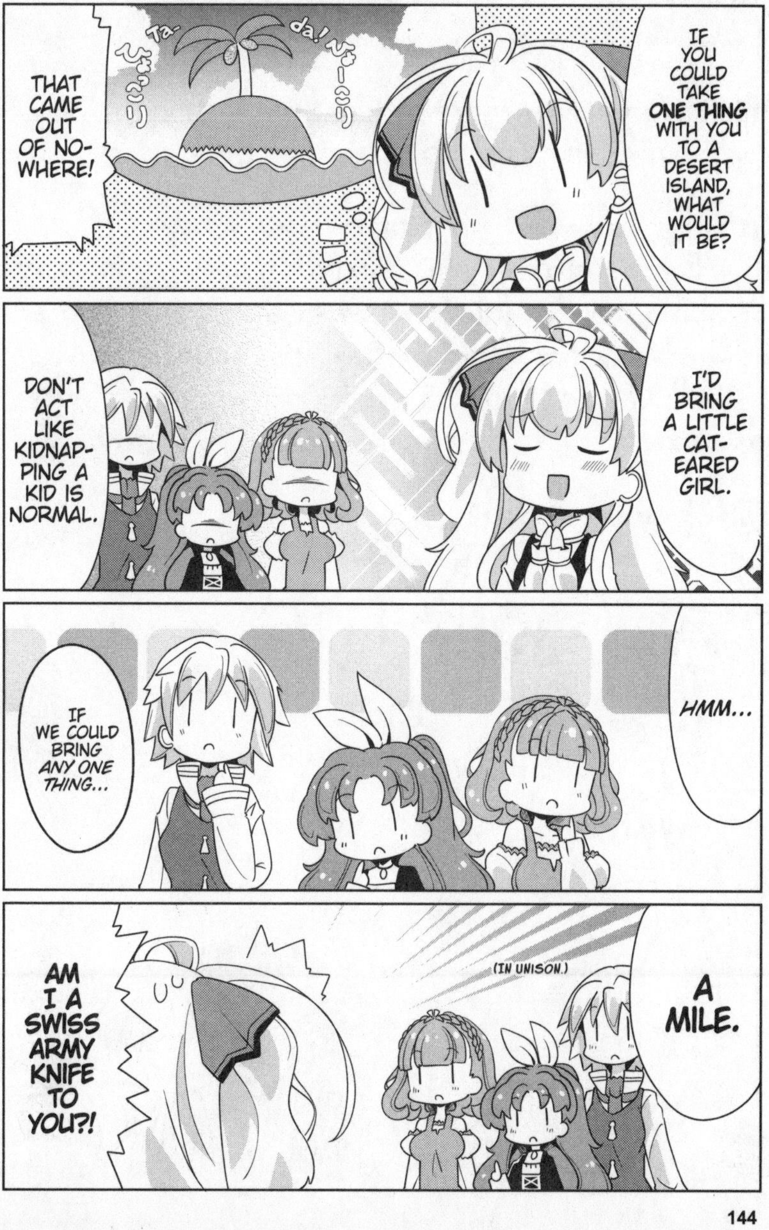

IF YOU COULD TAKE **ONE THING** WITH YOU TO A DESERT ISLAND, WHAT WOULD IT BE?
Ta-da!
THAT CAME OUT OF NO-WHERE!
I'D BRING A LITTLE CAT-EARED GIRL.
DON'T ACT LIKE KIDNAPPING A KID IS NORMAL.
HMM...
IF WE COULD BRING *ANY ONE THING*...
A MILE.
(IN UNISON.)
AM I A SWISS ARMY KNIFE TO YOU?!

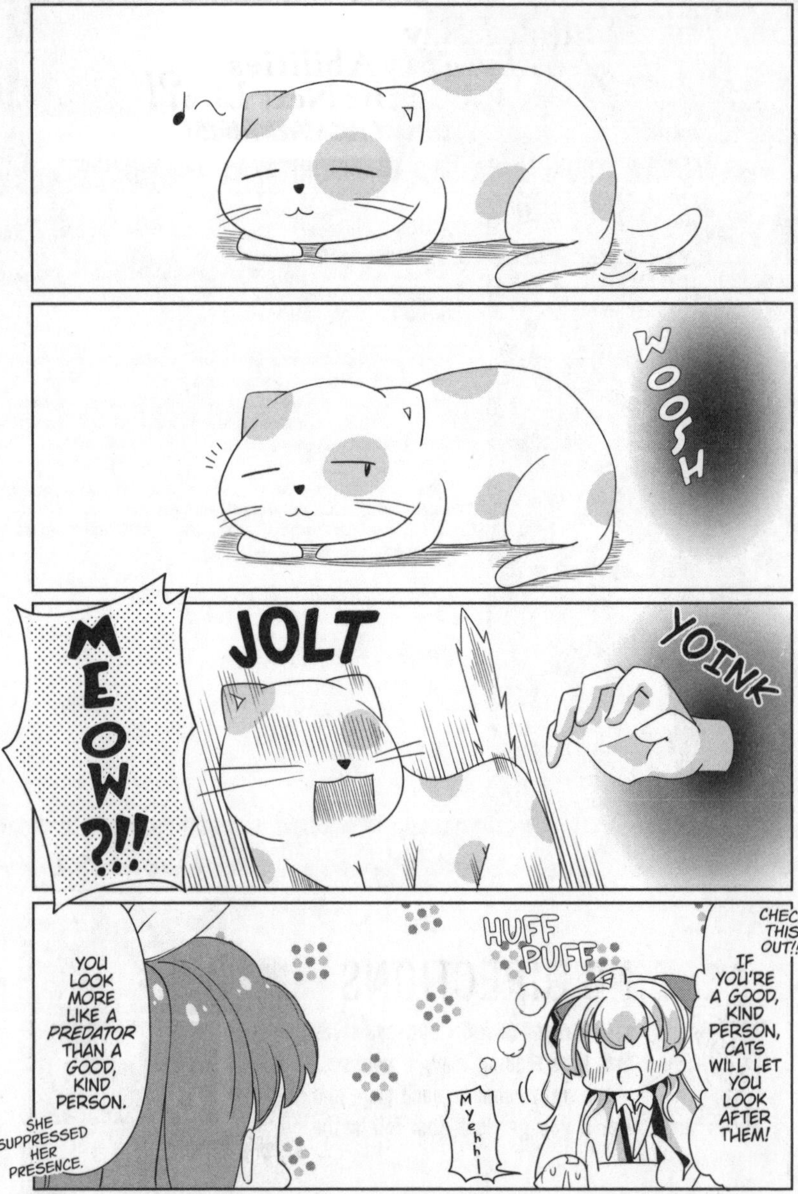
♪～
WOOSH
YOINK
JOLT
MEOW?!!
CHECK THIS OUT!!
IF YOU'RE A GOOD, KIND PERSON, CATS WILL LET YOU LOOK AFTER THEM!
HUFF PUFF
Myehh!
YOU LOOK MORE LIKE A *PREDATOR* THAN A GOOD, KIND PERSON.
SHE SUPPRESSED HER PRESENCE.

SEVEN SEAS ENTERTAINMENT PRESENTS

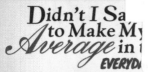

Didn't I Sa… to Make My… Average in t…

EVERYD…

story by FUNA & ITSUKI AKATA art by YUKI MORITAKA VOLUME 1

TRANSLATION
Diana Taylor

ADAPTATION
Julia Kinsman

LETTERING AND RETOUCH
Simone Harrison

COVER DESIGN
Nicky Lim

PROOFREADER
Stephanie Cohen
Dawn Davis

EDITOR
Shanti Whitesides

PREPRESS TECHNICIAN
Rhiannon Rasmussen-Silverstein

PRODUCTION MANAGER
Lissa Pattillo

MANAGING EDITOR
Julie Davis

ASSOCIATE PUBLISHER
Adam Arnold

PUBLISHER
Jason DeAngelis

WATASHI, NICHIJOU WA HEIKINCHI DETTE ITTAYONE! VOLUME 1

Originally published in Japan in 2019 by EARTH STAR Entertainment, Tokyo.
English translation rights arranged with EARTH STAR Entertainment, Tokyo, through TOHAN CORPORATION, Tokyo.

Seven Seas press and purchase enquiries can be sent to Marketing Manager Lianne Sentar at press@gomanga.com. Information regarding the distribution and purchase of digital editions is available from Digital Manager CK Russell at digital@gomanga.com.

ISBN: 978-1-64505-852-6

Printed in Canada

First Printing: December 2020

10 9 8 7 6 5 4 3 2 1

FOLLOW US ONLINE: www.sevenseasentertainment.com

READI…

This book reads…
If this is your…
reading from th…
take it from the…
numbered diagram here. It may seem backwards at first, but you'll get the hang of it! Have fun!!

3
1
2
5
4
8
7
9

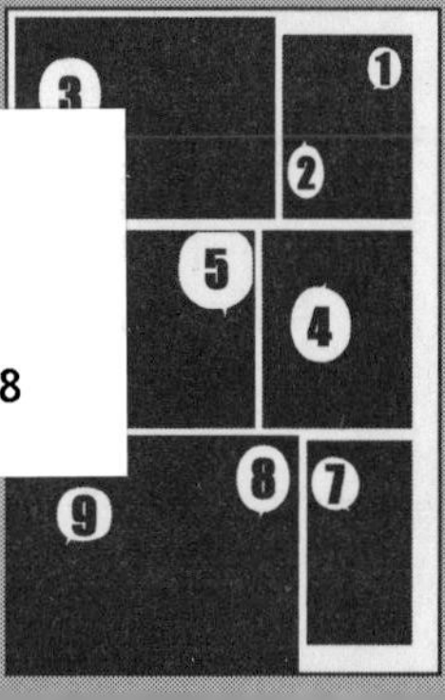